THE HEROES OF RAVENFORD

BOOK 2

Serpent Cult

F.P. SPIRIT

Revised Edition
Copyright @ 2016 F. P. Spirit
Cover Art by Jackson Tjota
Cover Design and Interior Formatting by S Professional Designs
Edited by Sandra Nguyen
ISBN-10: 0-9984715-1-8
ISBN-13: 978-0-9984715-1-8

Thanks to Tim for creating the world of Thac, and to Eric, Jeff, John, Mark and Matt for their roles in bringing the Heroes to life. Also, thanks to the rest of my friends and family who gave their time and support into the creation of this book.

ALSO BY F.P. SPIRIT

THE HEROES OF RAVENFORD

TABLE OF CONTENTS

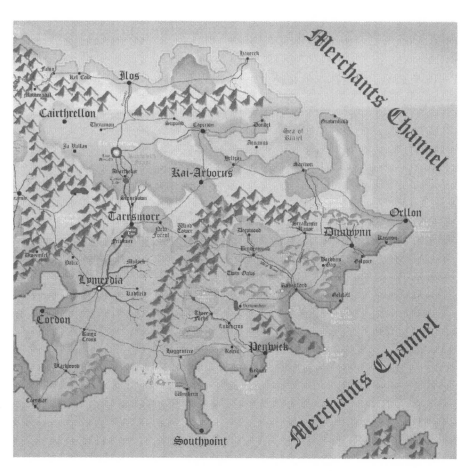

Eastern Thac as it exists today, circa the 7th millennium of the 4th age.
This current age, Laurentia, or the age of man, began over 7000 years ago at
the end of the Third Demon War. During the first age, Hai'Valan, the world
was primarily populated by ancient dragons of great power. The second age was
the age of the Titans, the lords of elemental forces. The third age, Kitharra, saw
the rise of the Fey races, including the elves. The end of each age was marked by
a great war with the adversaries of all races, the Demons.

- Lady Lara Stealle, High Wizard of Penwick

1
KNIGHTS AND DREAMS

I need to step up my game if I'm going to keep up with you

It started out like any other day in the little seaport town of
Ravenford. Farmers were up before dawn, tending to their fields.
Fishermen were out on the bay, pulling in the first catch of the
day. The smell of freshly-baked bread wafted on the breeze from the
town bakery. Local inns welcomed those who were up for a morning
meal or an early drink. The youngest children scurried about outside
the temple, waiting for the basic schooling taught by the local priests.
On the hill to the north, horns sounded as the guards of Ravenford
Keep changed for the morning shift.

The day marched onward, as usual, until sometime around noon.
The golden orb of the sun was now almost directly overhead. The
first wave of fishermen were returning in from the bay, and the farmers were coming in from their fields. The town's three inns prepared
for the onslaught of hungry villagers. Suddenly, shouts rang out from
the guardhouse at the southern edge of town.

"The heroes are back! The heroes are back!"

Lunches were left half-eaten, and boats poorly docked, while
those within earshot scrambled to be the first to arrive at the south
gate. The word spread like wildfire, and soon half of Ravenford was
pressed in on each other, striving to get a good view of the heroes.
The stories of their exploits had swept quickly across the little seaport town. They had first arrived in Ravenford a little over a month
ago, escorting a caravan they had saved from bandits. It had been the
first convoy from the west to reach the town in over three months.
Within a week of their arrival, the gifted teens proved themselves
again. Maltar, Ravenford's master wizard, had commissioned them

to clean out the old ruins southwest of town; the place had been crawling with monsters. The heroes dispatched the evil inhabitants, including a stone giant and a dark mage. Next, at the Baron's request, they returned west and routed the rest of the orcs who had been ambushing caravans. Immediately afterwards, they slew a giant that was terrorizing the farmlands to the north. After a brief respite, the group set out to take care of some unfinished business back at the old ruins. Rumor had it another stone giant still roamed around up there. The heroic youths had gone to finish it off, and were now returning from their latest mission.

These young heroes were a strange sight to behold. At the head of the returning group rode the elven wizard, Glolindir, an unusually tall blond elf in purple robes with a black raven perched comfortably on his shoulder. Glo, as his companions called him, was rather talented with magic—in fact, he had become Maltar's latest apprentice. Keeping pace with the elf was Aksel, the copper-haired young gnome cleric. He sat astride a riding dog next to his tall friend. Aksel's white robes were decorated with the symbols of his gnomish goddess, the Soldenar. Showing a wisdom beyond his years, Aksel was the unlikely yet implicit leader of the group.

Behind the duo rode Brundon and Titan, two well-known town mercenaries. They contrasted each other like night and day. Brundon was a dark-haired man dressed from head to toe in brown leather. Titan was a flaxen-haired woman encased in heavy plate armor with a keen silvery sheen. Despite the apparent disparity, these two were the best of friends and quite the capable duo. What came next both awed and unnerved the crowd. Cries of disbelief were mixed with nervous murmurs. "What is it? Is it alive? Did they capture it? Can it get loose?"

Behind the four riders trudged a stone giant. Easily nine feet high, its broad shoulders were almost half as wide as its height. A great stony head sat squarely on its torso, inset with two eerily glowing eyes. The massive shoulders supported thick, grey arms that hung to its knees, ending in hands the size of boulders. Large, flat feet thudded on the paved streets of the little seaport town, the ground trembling with each step. Had the stone giant not been passively following the procession through town, the crowd might have broken and fled. The townsfolk remained gathered along the roadside, buzzing with noise as they watched the bizarre sight.

The stone giant was immediately followed by a solid wooden wagon with varnished brown sides and a green painted roof driven by Elladan Narmolanya, the elven bard. He had joined the heroic group in routing the bandits from the Bendenwoods. Elladan was a flamboyant character. Garbed almost exclusively in white, only his cloak and boots were dark in color. Tightly combed black hair accentuated his handsome young face, electric blue eyes, and a strong chin. With a voice that could charm the wings off an angel, the young bard had been an immediate hit at the *Charging Minotaur*, the local inn where the heroes stayed. Seated in the wagon next to Elladan was a man also dressed in the brown leathers of a tracker. A thin mustache accented his rugged features, his face framed by long brown hair and a closely-cropped beard. More whispers sprang up amongst the crowd. "Who is that stranger? Where did they find him? Does he have anything to do with the stone giant? Is he a prisoner?"

The strange procession crossed over the wide stone bridge that spanned the Raven River and divided the town. More townsfolk joined the impromptu parade as they entered the busy market district. The same questions were murmured repeatedly. "How did they capture the stone giant? Who was the stranger with them? Where were the tall red warrior and the dark halfling?"

Once clear of the market district, the procession climbed the hill to Ravenford Keep. The whispering amongst the crowd was cut short when, a large red blur swooped out of the sky and strafed the riders. Cries of alarm sounded amongst the townsfolk. Shouts of "Red Dragon!" were heard here and there. Panic reigned until Elladan's voice rang out, "No cause for alarm folks! It's only Lloyd!"

The shouts and screams stopped, the townsfolk gazing uncertainly at each other. Before anyone could question the bard, the red object appeared overhead again. The crowd held its breath as the figure dove out of the sky toward them. This time it slowed and stopped, hovering a few feet above the riders. Clad in red leather armor, the flying figure was unmistakably Lloyd Stealle. A shock of tousled brown hair capped his handsome young face and two huge sword hilts peeked out from under his cloak.

Lloyd was quite well-known in Ravenford. The unassuming young noble had garnered the attention of Lady Andrella, the daughter of the baron and baroness of Ravenford and one of the most eligible bachelorettes in eastern Thac. According to the rumors around town, it was only a matter of time before the two would be married. Now the warrior had gained the power of flight. It seemed there was no end to what this young man could do. The modest noble scanned the crowd below. "Sorry, folks! Didn't mean to scare anyone!"

The crowd began to cheer in response. A chant of "Heroes" broke out as the parade made its way up the hillside. It came to a halt when they reached the gate to the keep. At that point, the last member of the heroes appeared. Seth, the dark halfling, nimbly launched himself out of the covered wagon and landed lightly on the ground next to the stone giant. Clad all in black, rumor had it that the halfling was some kind of assassin. He was certainly agile enough. He could also disappear at the drop of a hat, only to appear out of the blue and scare the unwary. The townsfolk watched with awe as Seth patted the stone giant on the leg.

The chanting resumed once again until the guards led the heroes into the keep. All that remained was the stone giant, standing completely still in front of the gate. The crowd eyed him uncomfortably now that their protectors had disappeared.

The companions waited in the main hall of Ravenford Keep while the guards informed the baron of their arrival. Their ranks had swelled this time—aside from Aksel, Glo, Seth, Lloyd and Elladan, there was now Brundon, Titan, and even the stranger, Martan, with them. Most of them were used to the vastness of the hall by now. Brundon's eyes swept the great room from top to bottom—the vaulted ceiling, large columns, balconies, plush red carpets, tapestries, and such. "Nice little place the Baron has here."

Meanwhile, Martan gazed around wide-eyed, his jaw hanging open the entire time. Titan, in contrast, neither gazed around nor commented. Instead, she casually strode over to the large mural on the wall. Lloyd decided to follow her. He stood beside the tall warrior, noting the trace of a smile on her lips.

"It is impressive," Lloyd said.

Titan nodded. "It is, isn't it? This was always one of my favorite things about the keep."

Lloyd raised an eyebrow. "You've been here before?"

Titan's smile briefly widened. "Once or twice."

Lloyd was now really curious, but before he could ask her about it, she changed the subject.

"See how well the artist depicts Ullarak?"

Lloyd nodded. It was actually a very good likeness of a black dragon—quite menacing, in fact.

"And note how regal the baron looks in armor—as if he was a full-fledged knight."

An armored figure sat astride a large warhorse on the opposite side of the mural. The figure brandished a large sword and shield.

"Yes, Baron Gryswold does look quite impressive."

Titan fell silent, her eyes locked on the mural. Lloyd wondered once again when she had been here before, especially when Brundon apparently had not been. She seemed so intent that he decided to leave her alone. He backed away and rejoined the others.

Elladan nudged his head toward the blonde warrior. "Titan seems mesmerized by that mural."

Lloyd merely nodded, peering at Brundon in hopes he could shed some light on the subject. The tracker wore a concerned expression, his eyes firmly fixed on Titan. "I'm not surprised."

"Really? Why's that?" Elladan asked.

Brundon appeared startled at first, but quickly recovered, his serious expression replaced with a thin smirk. "It's always been a dream of hers to be an actual knight someday. Personally, I think it's overrated—all that armor weighing you down."

A knowing expression crossed Elladan's face. "Everyone needs a dream. Without it, life would be too dull."

"What's yours, Brundon?" Seth asked with just a trace of sarcasm.

Brundon feigned humility. "Me? Oh, nothing too elaborate, just enough to keep me living comfortably through my old age, and maybe a good woman—or two." His smirk widened as he added those last words.

A half smile crossed Elladan's face. "Juggling more than one woman can be an interesting challenge"—his eyes fell on Titan—"depending on the women involved."

Brundon followed Elladan's gaze, the smirk fading from his lips. His expression grew concerned once more.

A faint smile crossed Lloyd's lips. He was no expert at love, but despite all Brundon's bluster, it was obvious he really only wanted one woman in his life.

Elladan turned to Lloyd. "What's your dream, my friend?"

"My dream?" The question took Lloyd by surprise. He had a tendency to live in the moment, especially with all that had gone on these last few weeks. When he had left Penwick all those weeks ago, it was with the idea of making a name for himself like his father before him. "I guess you could say I want to be a protector of the people like my father. I want to defend those who cannot defend themselves and serve justice to those who would harm others."

Elladan's expression grew serious. "That's a tall order there, my friend"—just as abruptly, a half smile crossed his lips—"but from what I've seen of your skill with those blades, I wouldn't want to bet against you, either."

The conversation might have continued, but the doors to the back hallway opened and Captain Gelpas strode through. Gelpas Ranblade was captain of the Ravenford guard, the town constable, and the baron's right hand man. Nearly as tall as Lloyd, and only slightly broader in the shoulders, Gelpas was quite shrewd. His usually-stern expression made him appear grim, but his fair-minded approach to things made him well liked by all.

"The baron is in a meeting right now," Gelpas informed them. "However, he has instructed me to meet with you all. There was something urgent you needed to discuss?"

Gelpas paused to look over the group. His keen eyes passed over Martan and Brundon, then came to rest on Titan. She returned his stare without flinching. Elladan introduced the newcomers.

"These are our comrades-in-arms, Brundon and Titan. They have been a great help to us on our missions thus far."

Gelpas eyed the tracker. "Brundon," he said with a slight nod. His eyes then returned to Titan.

"Delara," he said simply, his tone somewhat restrained.

"Father," Titan responded, her voice equally tense.

Lloyd's jaw nearly dropped. *Father? Gelpas was Titan's father?*

Gelpas remained stiff. "It has been awhile, daughter. It is nice to see you in such good health."

"It must be the company I keep," she responded, her tone laced with sarcasm.

You could cut the tension in the air with a knife. Lloyd stole a quick glance around the group. Glo had an eyebrow raised. Aksel's hand was on his chin, a concerned expression on his face. Brundon appeared pensive. Even Elladan, normally unflappable, seemed surprised. Only Seth appeared to find the situation amusing, a thin smirk on his face.

Aksel cleared his throat. "Captain Gelpas, concerning the reason we are here..."

Gelpas turned away from his daughter, though he stilled appeared tense. "Yes, sorry."

"This is Martan," Aksel said, pointing to their nearly forgotten guest. "We rescued him from a group that may have had ill intent toward Ravenford. In exchange, he has provided us with valuable information about said group."

"Is that so?" Gelpas eyed Martan intently.

Martan gazed back at the captain and responded in an even tone, "I think the good cleric here is being a bit too kind. I was hired out by the group in question to guide them here. Though never really a party to their plans, nonetheless, I was employed by them."

Gelpas regarded Martan for a few moments before answering. "Well, then, I appreciate your honesty." Gelpas faced Brundon and Titan once more. There was a distinct edge to his voice.

"I would like to thank both of you for your help in this matter, but I now need to question our guest. I'm sorry to say that my office is not big enough for everyone, so if you will excuse us."

"That's quite all right." Brundon responded smoothly. "Delara and I are merely happy that we could aid in protecting the town."

Gelpas eyed the tracker a moment. "Yes, that is one topic on which we all can agree."

His eyes fell on his daughter once again. Titan returned his stare, her arms folded across her chest. After a rather uncomfortable silence, Gelpas sighed. "Rest assured that the baron appreciates all you have done. To that end, please tell Telpin at the *Charging Minotaur* that your next meal is on the barony."

Titan's shoulders grew rigid. "That's rather generous of you, Father."

Lloyd couldn't help but wince at the ferocity behind those words. Even Gelpas seemed affected. His expression visibly softened, his eyes dropping to the floor. "It's—the least I can do."

"We'll just be going now." Brundon was obviously anxious to end this tense encounter.

Gelpas glanced back up at his daughter. "Very good." A brief smile crossed his lips then he turned around to leave the hall.

Before he could take a step, Titan spoke up again. "Father, one last thing."

Gelpas stopped in his tracks. He turned back around, his expression one of surprise. "Yes, Daughter?"

Titan hesitated for the briefest of moments, mixed emotions playing across her face. Her expression quickly hardened. "I have made my decision. I am going to apply for entry into the Knights of the Rose."

"Delara!" Gelpas and Brundon burst out simultaneously.

Lloyd was equally surprised. *The Knights of the Rose?* He knew of the order. They were a group of holy knights, dedicated to the protection of Thac. They had been around for centuries, even as far back as the Thrall Wars. He had little doubt that Titan would fit in that order, but he could not help wondering why now.

"Are you daft?" Brundon exclaimed.

"I have to agree!" Gelpas scowled. "Have you thought this through?"

"I have," Titan responded, her voice rising and her face reddening with anger, "and I'll thank you both not to question my decisions." She glared from her father to Brundon then took a deep breath. "All I am asking for is a good word from the baron."

The hall had grown so silent you could hear the creak of the guards' armor. Gelpas regarded his daughter quietly for a few moments, his face a mask of conflicting emotions.

"Very well, if that is what you wish, I will talk to the baron."

Titan nodded. "It is."

Gelpas appeared as if he was going to say more but abruptly stopped himself. He motioned to the others. "Gentlemen, shall we?" He then turned and left the chamber.

"Go ahead," Lloyd told his companions. "I'll be right with you."

As the others marched off, Lloyd spun back to Brundon and Titan. The duo had begun a heated conversation.

"What were you thinking?" Brundon was saying.

"It's my business. What do you care?"

"Your business is my business." Brundon scowled. "We're supposed to be a team, remember?"

"Maybe you'll remember that next time and not side with my father."

Brundon started to object, then stopped himself. He hung his head. "You're right. I should have had your back."

Titan glared down at him for a moment longer before her expression softened. She placed a hand on his shoulder, her voice soft. "You usually do."

Lloyd felt uncomfortable interrupting the two, but he was not sure when he would see them again. "Titan?"

She turned to face him. "Oh, Lloyd. I didn't realize you were still there."

"Yeah." Lloyd's hand went to the back of his neck. "Well, I just wanted to say I will miss fighting by your side, but I know you will make an excellent knight."

A smile spread across Titan's face. "Thank you, Lloyd. I will miss fighting by your side as well."

Lloyd grinned back, but then his expression grew serious. "If you don't mind me asking, what made you decide this now?"

Instead of answering, Titan strode up to him. She stood there for a moment staring directly into his eyes. Abruptly she leaned forward, brushed by his mouth and kissed him on the cheek. As she pulled away she said in a soft tone, "You did. I need to step up my game if I'm going to keep up with you."

Lloyd's cheeks began to turn pink until he was bright red. His eyes swept from her to Brundon. A brief pang of jealousy crossed the tracker's face, but it was gone in an instant.

"Yes, yes. This is touching and all," Brundon said, "but for now, how about we take your father up on that free meal?"

"Might as well." Titan took one last wistful look around the great hall.

Lloyd bid the pair farewell. He watched in silence as they crossed the large chamber until they reached the door to the foyer. The acoustics in the vaulted room were excellent, and he could easily hear their conversation.

"But afterwards I'm packing. I'm heading out the west road first thing in the morning," Titan declared.

"So you're planning on just going away without me?" Brundon asked sounding hurt.

"What am I supposed to do? It's not like you'll follow me."

"What would make you think that? I'm sure there's work out there for an enterprising man like myself."

"You could always join the knights."

Brundon laughed. "Me? A knight?"

Their voices faded as they disappeared into the foyer.

Lloyd grinned. He was quite sure Brundon would follow Titan just about anywhere. Suddenly it dawned on him that he was supposed to meet the others. His smile faded as he ran through the doorway to the back of the keep.

2
BLACK ADDERS

Dark magic users are not exactly a trusting lot

T he Black Adders, you say?" Captain Gelpas sat behind his desk, with his fingers pressed together in front of his lips. Martan sat in the seat opposite him while the companions leaned against the back wall and watched the interrogation. The archer shifted uncomfortably in his chair as he retold his story to the captain. Gelpas's burning gaze was not doing very much to put him at ease.

Martan let out a deep sigh. "Yes, as I said before, they are a sect of the Serpent Cult."

"And this Serpent Cult you speak of is what again, exactly?"

Gelpas stared intently at the archer as he repeated the question for the third time. It was a standard interrogation technique to ask the same questions repeatedly. If the person was telling the truth, the details would match each time. If they were lying, they would inevitably slip up—unless they were very skilled at it.

Martan took a deep breath and repeated his answer as if he had recited it a thousand times. "It's a group of mages who worship serpents. They are based out of Serpent's Hollow. They practice a dark magic that enables them to control serpents. Some of them can even change into snake form."

Gelpas's expression remained neutral. "And you were accompanying this dark wizard, Voltark, did you say?"

Martan merely nodded.

Gelpas eyed him for a moment. "Voltark, then. You were accompanying this Voltark to Ravenford. And what was his business here?"

Martan's tone grew weary. "I was never told. They weren't exactly the trusting types. They kept their business to themselves."

"And the whole time you were with them, you never overheard anything?" The captain's tone was laced with skepticism.

Martan shook his head. "Only the one thing I already told you. I was just hired to lead them to Ravenford. They were pretty closed-mouthed around me, so I don't know much about what they were planning."

"And what was that one thing you overheard?"

Martan let out another deep sigh. *Things are going as planned. We have them cut off on all sides.*

When Martan finished, he sat back and folded his arms in front of his chest. Gelpas continued to stare at him, drumming his fingers on the desk all the while. Abruptly, the door to the room burst open.

"Sorry I'm late!" Lloyd exclaimed.

"No, no, your timing is good." Gelpas rose from his desk. He motioned for all those standing to join him outside in the hallway. As they exited, he closed the door behind them.

A single guard stood outside in the hallway. Gelpas turned to him. "Keep an eye on our guest. We'll be right back."

The captain led them down the hall a short ways to another door. They entered a plain room which had been furnished with a long table and a bench on either side. A pitcher and some empty bowls were strewn across it.

"Guard room," the captain explained abruptly before anyone could ask. "Please sit down, gentlemen." The five companions all sat and turned their attention to Gelpas.

"What do you think of his story?" The captain asked.

Elladan was the first to respond. "What Martan told you about the elves of Kai-Arborous is true—they don't really trust humans. If they found Martan hunting near the city, he would have been thrown in jail."

Glo could definitely see that. His people were the same way. With all the spell wards and charms around Cairthrellon, it was highly un-likely that anyone could find their way into the city. If someone did manage to, though, especially a human, he would have been treated as a criminal.

Gelpas nodded in understanding, then turned to Glo. "What about these Black Adders and this Serpent Cult?"

Glo gazed around the group. "There are many dark magic practitioners in the world. Control of serpents and shape shifting into serpent form is indeed a real branch of the dark arts."

Elladan and Aksel both nodded their agreement. Lloyd listened intently. Seth, on the other hand, looked bored. He produced a knife and polished the blade. A thin smile spread across Glo's lips before he wrenched his eyes away from the disinterested halfling.

"However, these practitioners aren't the kind of folk to band together. Dark magic users are not exactly a trusting lot, even of each other. If there is a group of serpent-worshipping dark magicians out there, there is most likely a darker power leading them all."

The room fell silent. Gelpas appeared lost in thought. "That is even more disturbing."

Elladan spoke up once more. "Captain Gelpas, Serpent Cult or not, those Black Adders were definitely real. We brought back the body of the dark wizard that headed the group—and he had quite a crew with him. If we hadn't had the golem, we might not be sitting here right now."

"You're welcome," a familiar voice chimed in. Glo turned to see Seth still polishing his blade, a satisfied smirk on his face.

Aksel turned to the others and cleared his throat. "Ahem. I think what the captain is trying to get at is whether Martan was a willing participant or not. What I can tell you is that his motives are not evil. Whatever he may have gotten himself involved in, I do not believe he meant to harm anyone. However, if you can detain him until tomorrow, I can cast a spell which will detect whether he is telling the truth."

Gelpas had been pacing back and forth. He stopped as he considered Aksel's words. "I am inclined to agree with you, Cleric Aksel. I do not detect any ill intent in his story or behavior, but it would be nice to be certain." He gave a brief nod. "Very well, we will hold onto him until tomorrow, as you suggest. The baron will want to hear his story first-hand anyway." Gelpas paused once again, his expression clearly troubled. "What really worries me is that this dark wizard and his troop were headed to this town for the gods only know what reason. Not to mention that reference to having us *cut off on all sides.*"

Aksel's expression was sympathetic. "Yes, that was rather disconcerting, but that is why we brought his body back with us, Captain. If you can hold on to it until tomorrow as well, then I can use a spell to talk to Voltark's spirit. We'll see if we can find out what his purpose was in coming to Ravenford."

Gelpas's expression turned a bit more hopeful. "Very well, Cleric Aksel, we shall do as you suggest. We will keep the archer here at the keep overnight, as well as the dark wizard's body." The captain gazed around at the group in general. "Well then, gentlemen, I need to inform the baron regarding all that has transpired here. We will expect your return tomorrow morning, when we continue the investigation into this matter."

They all stood up and followed Gelpas back out into the hall. He gave them a curt nod, then quickly marched off down the corridor in the direction of the throne room.

The next morning, the companions gathered in front of the Charging Minotaur to say goodbye to Titan and Brundon. Titan packed the saddlebags on her quarter horse while Brundon tightened the cinch on his roan.

Elladan came up behind them and clasped them both on the shoulders. "So it's off to the Wind Tower for you two?"

Titan patted her saddlebags and grinned. "Got my letter from the baron right here."

"Glad to hear that worked out for you."

Seth spoke up next, a half smirk on his lips. "So, Brundon, what will you be doing out there while Titan learns to slay dragons?"

Brundon spun around, a smug look on his face. "Oh there's always work for a good tracker. I was thinking of hiring myself out as a guide through the mountains. I know the Korlokesels almost as well as I know the Bendenwoods."

"With all that's happened in those woods recently, that would be a good idea," Aksel agreed.

"Either way, good luck to you both," Glo added.

Lloyd wore a wide grin. "Titan won't need luck—not once those knights see what she can do."

Titan's face turned a slight shade of red. "Thank you, Lloyd. I'm sure you could teach them a thing or two as well."

The tall warrior stepped forward and hugged him and then each of the companions in turn. Even Seth allowed himself an embrace with her. Brundon shook hands with them all, until Lloyd got a hold of him and locked him in a bear hug. "Easy there big fellow—I'd like all my ribs intact."

Lloyd let go and grinned self-consciously. "Sorry."

The two riders then mounted and bid the companions farewell.

"Good luck on your next venture," Brundon said.

"Till we meet again," Titan told them.

"Till we meet again," they responded in unison.

Titan and Brundon spurred their horses and took off down the road. The companions watched until they were out of sight. Aksel was the first to break the silence. "Well then, best we head back up to the keep."

A short while later, the companions trudged up the hill to Ravenford Keep. A short way off the roadside, Glo noticed a number of wagons parked together. There were so many, in fact, it looked like a small village had cropped up just outside the castle overnight. There were tents interspersed in between the wagons, and a number of colorful characters milled around. "I wonder what's going on over there."

"Those are performers," Elladan declared.

"Are you certain?" Aksel asked.

A half-smile crossed Elladan's lips. "Uh huh. I recognize some of those wagons. Still, it's strange to see so many here in this little town. Something big must be going on."

"Maybe we'll find out up at the keep," Glo suggested.

Elladan shrugged. "Wouldn't hurt to ask."

When they reached the gate, the affable guard, Francis, was on duty. Francis had befriended the companions, helping them gain access to the town meeting where they first met the baron. Now the friendly guard appeared tired. He covered his mouth, trying to stifle a yawn as they approached.

Elladan gave him an understanding smile. "Guard duty again?"

"Yeah," Francis replied, his eyes drooping. "We are all pulling double shifts, with the party coming up and all."

"What party?" Aksel asked.

Francis's eyes snapped open. He suddenly appeared wide-awake. "You don't know? I thought everyone knew."

Seth snorted. "Yeah, about that. New to the area. Been out fighting monsters, dark wizards..."

Francis smiled sheepishly. "Oh, right. I should have realized. The Lady Andrella's eighteenth birthday is coming up in a few days, and the guests and entertainment are starting to arrive already." He nudged his head toward the gathering of wagons down the hillside. "It's a really big event. The Duke of Dunwynn himself is going to attend."

"The Duke of Dunwynn?" Glo repeated. "Isn't he the Lady Gracelynn's brother?"

"As a matter of fact, he is." Francis nodded. He stepped closer and spoke in a whisper, "Rumor has it, since his only niece is coming of age, he wants to bring her back to Dunwynn with him." The guard glanced briefly to his left and right. "The baron will never stand for it, though."

Glo remembered when they first arrived in Ravenford. Lloyd had told them all about the baron and his family, including their relationship to the duke. Further, since the duke had no children of his own, his niece, Andrella, was his one and only heir. "It would seem that the duke wants to start grooming her."

The guard gave a vigorous nod. "After all, if anything were to happen to him, she would become the next Duchess of Dunwynn."

Something about what Francis just said made Glo uneasy. "Is Dunwynn a large place?"

Francis seemed pleased to explain further. "It's the only Duchy in north eastern Thac. The city itself has over nine thousand subjects, but its influence extends over almost all of northeast Thac."

"You mean its control," Lloyd corrected him. There was a trace of anger in the young man's tone.

Francis glanced over his shoulder again then whispered, "Yes. Control is more accurate."

Glo noted that Lloyd was flushed. He obviously had little love for Dunwynn. From the sounds of it, the duchy held sway over most of northeastern Thac. Based on Lloyd's reaction, it was not a far stretch to think they were trying to extend their reach beyond that. Glo's previous thoughts rapidly crystallized into a very alarming possibility. The Lady Andrella's coming of age was not just a big deal for the town of Ravenford. In fact, it would affect the entire region. If the Black Adders had been headed here now, their purpose might have been directly related to the young lady's coming of age. They might have been planning to kidnap her, or worse. Thankfully, they had stopped them, but from what Martan had said, the Black Adders were part of a much larger organization—the Serpent Cult. If wind of their failure reached that group, they might just send someone else to do his job. The Lady Andrella could still be in serious danger.

Glo did his best to remain impassive. He would have to warn the others, but this was neither the time nor place. He would wait until later when they were alone with the Baron. Gryswold should be told of the possible danger to his daughter. Perhaps between the Ravenford forces and themselves, they could keep the young lady safe from any attempts to either take her or harm her.

While Glo mulled this over, the conversation had drifted back to the party. Elladan was speaking. "...so I take it with all these double shifts, the baron is concerned about security?"

Francis stifled another yawn. "Yeah, having the duke here is a big deal, and with all these strangers in town"—he nodded towards the wagons once again—"the baron doesn't want to take any chances."

"Hmmm," Elladan murmured, "I do know a lot of those folks. Maybe I can lend a hand."

Francis smiled at the bard. "That would be great. Maybe you can even get him to lighten up on these double shifts?"

Elladan gave the guard a half smile. "I'll do my best."

Glo nearly bit his tongue. Once he told the baron what he had surmised, the poor guards might actually be pulling triple shifts.

Captain Gelpas waited for them in the main hall. He led the companions down the back corridor through the throne room and into a side chamber. This was the very same room they had met the baron in after routing the bandits from the Bendenwoods. Gryswold, Gracelynn, and Andrella were already there.

Gryswold Avernos was a powerfully-built man. He appeared to be in his mid-forties, with piercing blue eyes, darkish brown hair, and a beard and mustache that same deep color. He wore simple finery of a military cut with a small herald of Ravenford emblazoned on the upper left corner. It had a background of red, white, and blue overlaid by a large black figure representing the dragon that he had slain to save the seaport town nearly twenty years ago. Gryswold stood as they entered, his expression grim. "Welcome, friends. It appears we have much to discuss since your return."

The Lady Gracelynn Avernos stood as well. She was a tall, slender woman with porcelain skin, long chestnut hair, and bright amber eyes. A small silver circlet adorned her brow. She wore a pale blue gown emblazoned with the symbol of the God of Light, Arenor—a golden circle with six rays spreading outward. Her regal carriage gave her the appearance of one from a much larger court than a mere barony. She waved her hand towards the long wooden table that practically filled the room. "Please be seated."

The table was surrounded by twelve chairs. All were currently unoccupied except for the one at the other end of the table. In that chair sat the Lady Andrella Avernos, a lovely young woman with strawberry blonde hair, cream-colored skin—her most prominent feature her electric blue eyes. While perhaps not quite as tall as the baroness, she carried herself with the same regal air. The young lady was garbed in an elegant green gown which set off her already dazzling eyes. Rising, she addressed them. "Welcome, good Heroes of Ravenford. Please do be seated."

She motioned to the empty chairs on either side of her. She smiled warmly at all of them, but her eyes ultimately came to rest on Lloyd. Elladan stood beside the tall warrior. There was a twinkle in his eye as he reached up and placed a hand on Lloyd's shoulders.

"You heard the lady."

Elladan guided Lloyd forward, making certain the young man took a seat next to the Lady Andrella. Lloyd appeared somewhat embarrassed as he sat down, his complexion turning a light shade of red. The Lady Andrella smiled demurely at him then seated herself as well. Elladan took the seat next to Lloyd. Once seated, his eyes sought out Glo and he winked. Glo could not help but smile.

Gryswold sent Gelpas to fetch Martan. In the meantime, they discussed the encounter with the Black Adders in the Dead Forest. When Martan finally arrived, Gryswold bade him to sit down next to him. The baron then addressed Aksel. "Cleric Aksel, I understand you have a proposal for speeding up this investigation."

Aksel rose from his seat. "I do, your Lordship. There's a spell I can cast which will cause all parties present to speak only the truth."

Gracelynn smiled with approval. "Oh, yes. I know of that spell. I should have thought of it myself. Very clever, Cleric Aksel."

"Thank you, Lady." Aksel nodded politely.

Gryswold gave him a curt smile. "Very well, please proceed."

Aksel's face took on an expression of deep concentration. His hands moved in a complex circular pattern in front of him. When he finally released the magic, a golden circle emanated outward, encompassing the entire room.

Glo had never seen this spell before. Interestingly, he did not feel any different. "How does the spell work?"

Aksel's tone was grim. "It stops you from speaking any intentional lies. Go ahead. Try it."

Glo tried to lie. "I am a hu... I am a hum..." His mouth froze each time he tried to tell the lie. *Interesting.*

"Well then, that seems to be working," Gryswold noted. He turned to face Martan. "Now then, Master Martan, tell us your story."

The archer proceeded to relate his tale once more. He repeated it exactly the way he had told the companions, and later Captain Gelpas. When he was done, there was no doubt of his sincerity. Gryswold addressed the archer, his tone apologetic. "Well then, Master Martan, you were obviously an unwilling participant in all this. You have also told us much we would not have otherwise known. You have the gratitude of Ravenford."

Martan stared at the baron and the baroness with clear disbelief. "That's it then? I'm free to go?"

The baron nodded. "Yes, Master Martan, you are free."

Elladan stood and strode across to where the archer sat, at the same time reaching into a pouch at his belt. He pulled out some coins and set them down on the table in front of Martan. "Here, as the baron said, you gave us a lot of information. This is for your time and trouble."

Martan eyed the proffered coins and then peered up at Elladan, mixed emotions playing across his face.

"Are you sure?"

The baron gazed at Elladan with clear respect. "Wish I had thought of that myself. Go ahead," he urged the archer, "You've earned them."

Martan's eyes glistened. His voice was choked with emotion. "That is... the first act of kindness... anyone has shown me in a long time." He picked up the coins, stood and gazed around the table. "Thank you. Thank all of you."

"Very good," Gryswold pronounced. "Gelpas, please have our friend Martan here escorted out of the castle—and have that body brought in as well."

Gelpas bid Martan to follow him and the two of them left the room. Once they were gone, Gryswold turned to face the others. The smile faded from his lips. "Well now, we know a lot, but there is still a lot we don't know. If you are up to it, Cleric Aksel, perhaps we can see what this dark wizard was up to."

Aksel rose from his seat once more. "I'll try my best, your Lordship."

3
SÉANCE

The disembodied head spun around the room, glaring at everyone there

A ksel spent the next few minutes in prayer. It wasn't long before Gelpas returned. He opened the door and let two guards in. They were carrying an object wrapped in cloth—the dead mage's body. They carefully placed it in the center of the table. As they stepped back, the Lady Andrella leaned over and whispered to Lloyd. Glo heard the entire conversation with his keen elven ears.

"This is a bit gruesome."

"Don't worry, my lady. I would never let anything happen to you."

Andrella gazed up at the tall young man, her expression softening. "Why, thank you."

The guards left the room. Gelpas closed the door behind them and rejoined the others. Aksel now stood quietly at the center of the table, facing the body. His eyes were closed, his brow furrowed in deep concentration as he prepared the spell that would allow him to speak to the dead.

Glo had spoken to Aksel about it the night before. It would appear as if Voltark's spirit had returned to speak with them. That would not be the case though. The spell would actually be tapping into the memories of the body. According to Aksel, the body retained an imprint of the soul, even after death. With this spell, one could gain access to those memories. The mechanics of the spell were quite complex, and thus it would take a number of minutes to cast.

Aksel was well into the process now. The entire room did their best to remain silent while the little cleric stood over the body. Glo, used to channeling magic, could feel the buildup of mana radiating from Aksel. The cleric drew in divine power bit by bit, creating a slow, massive buildup. After ten full minutes of preparation, Aksel was finally ready. He placed his hands over the corpse and let the divine magic flow out of his fingertips and into the body. He finished the spell with the words, *"Mortuus Loquere."*

The corpse glowed with a golden-white hue for a few moments, and then the effect faded. Aksel stood back and took a deep breath. As he did so, rays of golden white light began to radiate from the body. They intersected at a point about three feet above the corpse. A moment later, a black spot appeared in the air at that point. It slowly expanded outward until it was a hole about three feet in diameter. Waves of darkness emanated from the void, and an eerie, icy feeling crept across the room. Glo shuddered involuntarily.

A semi-transparent, light grey cloud appeared in the center of that empty space. The cloud coalesced and in a few moments formed into the image of a head. The visage floated there in the middle of the black hole three feet above the dark wizard's corpse. It had the features of the mage, Voltark. The disembodied head spun around the room, glaring at everyone there. Glo was impressed. This memory of Voltark was quite vivid, right down to the scowl on the mage's face. His eyes swept across the table to see the others' reactions.

The baron stared back at it grimly, looking as if he was ready to wrestle with the dark mage single-handedly. Gracelynn, in contrast, appeared cool and calm, merely fixing the image with an icy stare. Gelpas stood at the baron's side, his posture defensive, ready to protect his liege if need be. Lloyd had a look of fascination on his face. In contrast, poor Andrella seemed quite unnerved. When the head turned toward her, she grabbed Lloyd's arm and buried her face in his shoulder. A tender expression crossed the young man's face. He whispered to the young lady, "Don't let it frighten you. It isn't real."

Lloyd glared back at the visage. The disembodied face laughed noiselessly, then turned away. Elladan appeared completely unimpressed by the floating head. As the head spun toward Seth, a wicked smile crossed the halfling's face. He drew his dagger and raised it in front of him. He pointed to the dagger and then toward Voltark. He repeated the motion a couple of times until the face scowled at him. Abruptly it turned away.

The reaction elicited a number of grins from around the table. They soon faded as Aksel cleared his throat. He spoke to the visage in a commanding tone, "You who were known as Voltark in this life, we have called you here to answer our questions."

The head slowly turned toward Aksel. It floated there, regarding him disdainfully, but remained silent. Aksel tried again. "Why were you headed to Ravenford?"

Voltark's visage continued to glare at him. Aksel's expression remained stern, his brow still furrowed with concentration. He tried once more in that same commanding tone. "What was your mission here?"

The bodiless apparition refused to respond. It continued to glower at him. Aksel turned toward the baron, exasperation clearly written across his face. "I'm sorry, your Lordship. I can't seem to control him."

Gryswold's disappointment was also quite apparent. He let out a deep sigh. "Very well, end this."

Aksel waved his hands in front of the disembodied head and the image slowly dissolved. As it faded away, a few chilling words escaped its incorporeal lips. "You'll be sorry... they'll enthrall... you all..."

A chill ran up Glo's spine. *What did Voltark mean by that? And why specifically use the word enthrall?*

Glo gazed at Aksel, but the little cleric's eyes were firmly locked on to the image of the mage. Finally, the visage faded. The glow from the body dissipated and the corpse returned to normal. The oppressiveness in the room lifted, and Andrella noticeably relaxed. She suddenly realized that she was holding onto Lloyd's arm and let go, blushing.

"Are you alright, my lady?" Lloyd asked.

"I'm... fine. Thank you," she responded, though color continued to bloom over her face.

Voltark's departing words still haunted Glo. He tried to catch Elladan's attention, but the bard was too busy staring at Lloyd and Andrella. Glo sighed, deciding to keep his thoughts to himself. Voltark's visage had obviously unsettled Andrella, and he did not want to add to her discomfort. It was bad enough that she might be the Serpent

Cult's target.

Aksel apologized once again to the baron. "Sorry, your Lordship, he was an evil man, and thus difficult to control. If you want to hold the body, I can try again a week from now."

Gryswold opened his mouth to reply when Gracelynn interjected. "Although it would be good to try this again, we have Andrella's party coming up. With all the planned festivities, I think it would put a damper on things knowing this dark creature's vessel still resides in the keep."

The baron exchanged a brief glance with his wife then nodded his head in agreement. "You are very wise, my dear. Glolindir, as Maltar's apprentice, do you think you could take the body to him and ask if he could keep it under wraps until we are ready to try again?"

Glo needed to report to Maltar anyway. He had not seen him since he got back, and he owed the wizard a visit. "I most certainly can, your Lordship."

Gryswold's relief was quite plain. "Very good. Captain Gelpas, please have the body removed and prepared for transport."

"Yes, my lord." Gelpas went to the door and motioned the two guards who had brought the body back inside. They hauled the corpse out of the room. Gelpas addressed Glo. "If you wait by the front gate, I'll have the body brought to you." The captain then left to follow the guards.

Gryswold took his wife's hand, and they rose together. "Now that that's settled, we can concentrate on Andrella's birthday party. Thank you for coming, everyone."

The companions stood and shuffled toward the door. Glo tarried behind, waiting for the baron and baroness. He hoped to pull them aside to discuss his concerns about Voltark's mission and the safety of their daughter. Andrella was still seated at the other end of the table. Her eyes were fixed on Lloyd as the young man headed for the door.

Elladan halted at the doorway, Lloyd stopping just behind him. The bard turned toward the baron and baroness. "Your Lordship?"

"Yes, Elladan?"

"I understand there are some concerns about security with all these strangers in town."

The baron glanced at Gracelynn, and they both nodded. "Yes, that has been on our minds."

"I might be able to help with that. I am very familiar with the entertainers' community. I could keep an eye on them quite easily without them knowing the wiser."

Gryswold and Gracelynn held a brief whispered conversation. When they were done, the baron turned back to Elladan, a broad smile spreading across his face. "Thank you, Elladan. We accept your generous offer. In fact, we would like to put you in charge of the entertainment for our daughter's party."

"Would you be so kind as to emcee for us and handle the arrangement of performances?" Gracelynn added.

Elladan appeared genuinely touched. He replied with a bow and a flourish. "Why, I would be honored, your lord and Ladyship." He stood back up and gave them a half smile. "I'll head down and check out the performers' camp in a few minutes—but first, let's start with the guest of honor."

The bard turned around and grabbed Lloyd by the arm, dragging him back toward the Lady Andrella. Lloyd had a puzzled expression on his face, but let Elladan lead him. They stopped in front of Andrella. "Lady Andrella, my drummer and I would love to play all your favorite songs. I need to go down and check out the camp, but maybe you could sit here with him and make a list?"

Lloyd gazed at Elladan, wide-eyed. His skin flushed, but otherwise he remained silent. Andrella began to blush as well. Abruptly she realized that all eyes in the room were on her. The young lady composed herself and responded graciously, "Why, thank you, good bard. I would be happy to provide your drummer with such a list."

"Thank you," Elladan said. He pushed Lloyd down into the seat next to Andrella. The young man did not resist, although he was quite red in the face.

Elladan headed back toward the door, a mirthful glint in his eye. Meanwhile, Andrella began dictating her list. "Now, let's start with the classics..."

Glo was hard pressed not to laugh. Elladan had pulled that off flawlessly. Lloyd and Andrella's "romance" was moving at a snail's pace. Elladan had just given it a rather firm boost. Further, while they were busy, it would give Glo the much-needed chance to talk to the baron and baroness without their daughter. As Elladan passed by him, Glo whispered, "Gather the others in the throne room."

Elladan arched an eyebrow but said nothing, merely exiting the room. Glo waited at the door for the baron and baroness. They were slowly heading his way, watching the innocent young pair so engrossed in song selection. As they drew near, Glo whispered, "Your Lord and Ladyship, there is one more thing—but not here."

Glo gazed over at Andrella as he said the last. Gryswold followed his gaze and raised an eyebrow. He whispered back, "Outside, then."

Elladan waited in the throne room with Aksel and Seth. Glo quietly closed the door behind them, and the group drew close together in the otherwise empty chamber.

Gryswold's expression was grim. "What is this about?"

Glo felt horrible, but he had to voice his concerns. "Your Lord and Ladyship, I don't want to unnecessarily alarm you, and I may be wrong—but I can't ignore the possibility."

"Go on," Gracelynn encouraged him, although she also appeared quite apprehensive.

Glo drew in a deep breath. The group watched him curiously, but were otherwise silent. Glo realized there was no easy way to say this. He took in another deep breath and then explained his concerns, keeping his voice very low.

Gryswold grew more agitated as Glo spoke. When he was done, he responded loudly at first. "Are you saying..." The baron caught himself and lowered his voice. "Are you saying that Andrella was the target of this dark wizard?"

Glo grimaced. "I believe so."

Gracelynn was beside herself. "Oh, Gryswold." She grabbed onto her husband's arm, a look of horror on her normally composed face. "What if it's true?"

Gryswold grasped her hand and patted it reassuringly. "There, there, Grace, it's nothing we can't handle." As he peered up at the others, though, Glo saw something in the baron's eyes he had not seen up until now—fear.

Aksel spoke in a soft voice, his expression dreadfully serious. "I'm sorry to say, your graces, but what Glolindir is saying does make sense."

"Again, I may be wrong," Glo added, "but I could not in good conscience let this go unsaid."

Silence hung over the throne room. Gryswold was the first to break it. "No, no, Glolindir, you did the right thing. However, your thoughts shed a grim light on things."

Aksel spoke once again, his tone quite sympathetic. "Your Lordship, if I may make a suggestion?"

"By all means, go ahead," Gryswold said.

"Aside from the double shift of guards, perhaps you could begin screening anyone coming in and out of town, both at the guard-houses and the docks."

Gryswold's face brightened a bit. "That is an excellent idea! We will begin doing so at once."

Lady Gracelynn chose that moment to pull Gryswold aside. She whispered something into his ear. The two of them began a hushed conversation until they both nodded. The baron and baroness then turned to face the waiting companions.

Glo had heard the entire thing; he was stunned by the decision. He did his best, though, to pretend he had not overheard. He had discovered humans found it rude that elves could listen in to their private conversations.

Gryswold wore a thin smile now. "In the short time that you have been among us, you have proven to be a tremendous asset to this town. Once again, we must call upon your services, but this time specifically for the protection of our daughter. Therefore, we would ask you to attend our daughter's eighteenth birthday party, three days hence."

"You will be both our guests and there to keep a close eye on things for us." Gracelynn gave a warm smile.

Glo still could not believe it. Even with the need to protect Andrella, this was an auspicious occasion—attended by nobles like the Duke of Dunwynn and others of high rank. Coming from a noble elven family, he was keenly aware of the protocols that were being broken here by inviting them to this party.

Aksel executed a deep bow. "We would be deeply honored to attend the Lady Andrella's eighteenth birthday party, your lord and Ladyship. Be certain that we will keep a close watch over her."

"Excellent!" the baron declared. "Then it's all settled. We will have formal invitations drafted up for all of you this very day."

"Thank you again, your Lordship. Now if you will excuse us, we have much to do." Aksel bowed low once again, Glo, Elladan, and Seth following suit. The four of them then exited the throne room.

Elladan was the first to speak as they strode through the castle halls. "Well now we are all invited to Andrella's party."

"Just remember, despite all the finery, it's still a job," Aksel cautioned.

"I just hope the food's good," Seth replied.

Glo eyed the halfling as if he were crazy. "Really? We just get invited to the biggest event in northeastern Thac and all you can do is think about the food?"

Seth shrugged. "What can I say? I have my priorities."

Glo just shook his head. The foursome reached the entrance to the keep and climbed down the steps into the courtyard.

"Speaking of priorities," Seth continued, "while you wait around for the stiff, I'm going to head down into town and see if anyone's seen or heard anything out of the ordinary in the last few days."

"Good idea," Aksel agreed.

When they reached the gate, Seth continued on, leaving Glo, Aksel and Elladan to wait for Voltark's body. Elladan surveyed the wagons below. The sounds of voices and music reached their ears, making it sound like a party had already begun down there. Finally, Elladan could stand it no longer. "I really should head down there and scout around. You two wouldn't care to join me?"

Glo cast a glance at Aksel and shrugged. Voltark's body had still not arrived, and considering the potential threat to Andrella, it wouldn't hurt to add their eyes to Elladan's. Francis was still on duty at the guard station. Glo called out to their weary friend, "Francis? The captain is having a box delivered here for us to take. Do you think you could keep an eye on it when it comes?"

Francis walked over, doing his best to stifle a yawn. "Sure, I'm on guard duty for a few more hours anyway. Take your time."

"Thanks. We won't be too long." Glo turned back to Elladan and said, "Lead on.

4
THE LUCKY COIN
The angel rode up and commanded the sea monster to drop the sailor

Glo and Aksel followed a short way behind Elladan as he strode down the hillside and entered the camp. The elven bard zigged and zagged through the makeshift accommodations, stopping to talk with the various performers and stagehands. There were actors, jugglers, acrobats, clowns, stage magicians, and other bards. Elladan was definitely in his element—most of the other entertainers were either directly acquainted with him or knew him by reputation. He was also rather good at gathering information. His easygoing manner was quite disarming, allowing him to steer the conversation in the direction he wanted. It only took a few stops to gain a list of all the performers currently camped there and when they had arrived. Elladan seemed to know most of them. Only a few names appeared unfamiliar to him and would require checking out.

They continued through the camp until Elladan stopped short. A plaintive female voice could be heard singing a melancholy tune somewhere off to their right. Elladan turned and headed in that direction. They skirted a large tent and came across a good-sized crowd gathered around a makeshift stage. On that platform stood a tall, sultry woman with wavy brown hair that fell to her shoulders, tinged with golden blond highlights in the midday sun. She wore a frilly white tunic beneath a forest green vest, and tight fitted brown pants stuffed into knee-length brown leather boots. She deftly accompanied herself on the lute as her melodic voice crooned a heart-wrenching ballad.

Elladan stopped a few paces back from the crowd, Glo and Aksel halting just behind him. They stood there, captivated, until the lady bard finished her performance. When she was done, the crowd applauded in earnest, obviously moved by the heart-felt performance.

The three companions clapped as well, but held their ground a short way back from the gathering. The lady bard took a few bows, smiling as she scanned the crowd of fellow performers. Her eyes finally came to rest on Elladan, a single eyebrow raised as she stared at the elven bard. A brief smile crossed her lips and then she stepped down off the stage, disappearing into the crowd below. A few moments later, the onlookers parted and the songstress reappeared, slowly sauntering toward them.

Elladan continued to clap. "That was very nicely done."

"Thank you," she replied, a delightful smile spreading across her lips.

The lady bard was quite lovely. Her light brown hair framed a heart-shaped face with deep blue eyes, a tiny nose and high cheekbones. Glo felt the blood rush to his face as she stood there in front of him. The lady bard did not notice him, though. Her eyes were firmly fixed on Elladan, her expression quizzical. "You wouldn't be..."

"Elladan Narmolanya," he finished for her, bowing deeply. "At your service, Miss..."

"Shalla," she said in a soft voice, her eyes still locked on him. "Shalla Vesperanna."

"Shalla," Elladan repeated the name, "a lyrical name for a lyrical lady."

She smiled wryly, a soft laugh escaping her lips. "Well, Elladan, I can see your reputation is well-deserved. You are both handsome and a charmer."

He flashed her a sparkling smile. "Well thank you, Shalla, but the same could be said about you—both beautiful and charming all in one."

Shalla laughed once more, her face turning slightly red. "Touché, Elladan. If your singing is half as good as your charm, then I am in serious trouble."

"Why don't we see for ourselves?" Elladan unslung his lute and held out his other hand. Shalla slipped her hand into his and the duo walked together toward the makeshift stage. A crowd was still gathered, and slowly parted as the two bards approached. Murmurs could be heard amongst the throng.

"That's Elladan."

"Is he going to play?"

"Maybe they both will."

When they reached the platform, Shalla spun around and addressed Elladan, her tone mischievous. "You've already heard me play. I think it is your turn."

Without missing a beat, Elladan deftly leapt up onto the makeshift stage. He glanced back down at Shalla and said simply, "As you wish."

The elven bard walked around the platform while strumming his lute. He started with a few jokes and some minor melodies. Before long, the place was packed with everyone in the area. At that point, Elladan launched into a full-fledged song. Glo and Aksel had seen him perform at the Charging Minotaur, but it was nothing like this—this was electrifying. Elladan practically danced around the stage, not missing a beat, all the while belting out a melody in his superb contralto. When it was over, the crowd went wild, begging for more.

"Thank you. Thank you very much. I would be happy to do another song for you"—he gazed down at Shalla—"but only if the good Mistress Shalla here will join me."

The crowd began chanting, "Shalla. Shalla. Shalla."

Shalla gazed around at the gathering with an expression of amazement. She broke out into a broad smile then threw up her hands and called out over the din, "All right! All right! I'll do it."

The crowd cheered as she climbed back onto the stage. The two bards had a brief discussion, but there was so much noise that Glo could not hear what they were saying. Abruptly, they separated and moved to opposite sides of the stage. The crowd hushed as they spun around and began their duet. Elladan and Shalla strutted back to the center and pranced around each other as they took turns singing. The obvious chemistry between the two made it extremely entertaining to watch. When they reached the end of their performance, the applause was deafening.

Elladan pointed toward his partner and shouted above the noise,

"The incomparable Shalla Vesperanna!"

Shalla smiled graciously and took a short bow. She then held out her arm toward Elladan and cried, "The one and only Elladan Narmolanya!"

The applause went on for quite some time before finally dying down. Shalla addressed the crowd, "Thanks for stopping by, everyone, but that's it for now."

There were a few groans of disappointment, but then the crowd dispersed. Elladan exchanged a few words with Shalla, then jumped down off the stage and came over to rejoin the others.

"That was amazing," Glo said.

"Quite," Aksel agreed.

Elladan gave them an appreciative smile. "Thanks. Listen, Shalla and I decided on performing our duet at the Lady Andrella's party. It's still a bit rough around the edges though, so we need to spend a good amount of time together refining it the next few days. Between that, planning the show, and checking up on the performers, I'm going to be swamped."

"Go ahead," Aksel said. "We can handle carting Voltark's body over to Maltar's without you."

Elladan gave him his customary half smile. "Thanks! I'll keep you up to date if I find anything amiss with the performers." He left the duo and rejoined Shalla. The two of them clasped arms and strolled off together through the camp.

Glo couldn't help smiling after the duo. Once they disappeared, he turned to Aksel. "Guess we should be heading back up to the keep."

"Probably."

The two companions headed back the opposite way through the camp up towards the keep.

Maltar slammed the parchment down on the table. "I don't have time for this!"

Glo sat on the couch in his master's study, observing him. He was growing used to the mage's outbursts by now.

"How am I supposed to get anything done with these constant

interruptions? Now, Gryswold wants me to babysit the body of some half-baked wizard that got himself killed by a group of novices!"

The old wizard paused for a moment, suddenly realizing what he had said. "No offense, Glolindir."

Glo suppressed a smile. "None taken."

Maltar nodded briefly, then started to pace back and forth across the room while muttering obscenities. Abruptly he stopped in his tracks and faced Glo. "Who did you say this mage was in league with?"

"They're called the Serpent Cult." Glo had told him this when they first arrived, but Maltar had paid him little heed. "It's a group of mages who worship serpents. Shape shifters and the like. They are based up in Serpents' Hollow."

Maltar scoffed. "Shape shifters. Bah! More like children playing with magic beyond their comprehension." He started to pace again but suddenly stopped once more. "Serpents' Hollow did you say?" His tone was strangely pleasant.

Glo's eyes narrowed. "Umm... yes."

A smirk crossed the old wizard's face. "On second thought, maybe I was too hasty. I think I will keep the body of this... what was his name?"

"Voltark," Glo said.

"Voltark," Maltar repeated his tone still uncharacteristically pleasant. "Yes, I will look after the body. After all, Gryswold is an old friend. It wouldn't be right to turn down his request." The wizard's eyes became unfocused as if he was a million miles away.

Glo eyed Maltar with suspicion. There was no way he was doing this out of friendship or the goodness of his heart. He must have an ulterior motive for helping the baron. Glo had no clue what that motive might be, but if it helped their cause that was all that really mattered at the moment. "Very good, then—one more thing," he added, deciding to take advantage of the wizard's good mood. "If it is alright with you, I'd like to learn some new spells."

Maltar's eyes abruptly refocused. "Spells, you say? Yes of course. There is one other thing you can do for me, though."

Glo arched an eyebrow. "Yes?"

"A ship was supposed to arrive the other day with a shipment for me—a pendant specifically. If you could find out what has happened to the ship and track down the pendant, I will make it worth your while."

Another missing ship? This was starting to get serious. That made four now in the last month. "And the name of the ship?"

"The Lucky Coin."

"The Lucky Coin," Captain Gelpas said as he paced back and forth behind his desk. "It's the fourth ship now to disappear in the last month." He stopped and faced the companions. "The only difference is that this time, there were actually survivors."

"We know," Seth said. "I already talked with some of the sailors down at Falcon's tavern."

Gelpas folded his arms across his chest. "What did they say?"

"They were coming in at night when a storm hit. They spotted the beacon from Cape Marlin light to their north and adjusted course accordingly. Yet somehow they still hit the reef."

Gelpas's eyes narrowed.

Seth's face twisted into a half smirk. "And that's when the story gets weird."

Gelpas unfolded his arms and leaned over his desk. "Go on."

"It was dark except for occasional flashes of lightning. The ship was sinking—the rough sea rocking around the deck. That's when a large, scaly head rose out of the water. It snaked forward and grabbed one of them with its maw. It pulled him off the deck and dangled him over the raging sea."

Gelpas stood back up his hand going to his chin. "A sea monster? Really?"

Glo couldn't help smiling. Seth had told them the whole story before coming to the keep. "Oh wait, it gets better."

Gelpas's brow furrowed.

"Oh, it does." Seth rolled his eyes.

Gelpas peered at the duo uncertainly. "I'm afraid to ask."

A wicked smile crossed Seth's lips. "Right after the sailor was supposedly grabbed, that is when the angel appeared."

Gelpas appeared even more skeptical. "An angel?"

"Oh that's not the half of it. The angel had long blonde hair, shiny bronze skin, and rode a dolphin."

Gelpas's eyes went wide. "Rode a dolphin?"

Seth snorted. "Didn't I say it got weird?"

"You were not exaggerating, Master Seth," Gelpas agreed.

"Anyway, this angel rode up and commanded the sea monster to drop the sailor. The serpent immediately obeyed, dropped him into the surf, and then the creature disappeared. The angel fished the sailor out of the water and carried him to the shore. In fact, she carried all of them one by one to the beach until they were all safe. When she was done, she completely vanished. The sailors huddled on the rocks until the next morning. The skies had cleared and the seas were calm, but there was no sign of the Lucky Coin. Funny thing is, they saw the lighthouse to their south."

"To their south?" Gelpas repeated dubiously. "How can that be?"

"That's what we were wondering," Aksel said.

Glo mulled the story over in his mind. It was a well-known fact that angels and serpents existed. However, an angel shooing off a sea monster and then carrying the men to shore on a dolphin back seemed a bit far-fetched. More than likely, the sailors were drunk and made up the whole thing. Still, that did not explain how they made it safely to shore, nor how the lighthouse had mysteriously moved. There was far more going on here. It definitely warranted further investigation.

Captain Gelpas agreed. "That's an interesting story, but sea monsters or angels notwithstanding, whatever is sinking these ships has to be stopped. Some very important party guests are due to arrive via ship, but now no vessel will dare sail past Cape Marlin to Ravenford."

He paused and stared intently at the four of them. "We really need this taken care of now."

"Very well, Captain," Aksel said, "but how are we to get out there when no ships are willing to sail to the Cape?"

Gelpas shuffled through the papers on his desk. "There is one ship—the *Endurance*. The captain, Rochino, is one of the best sailors on the high seas. He doesn't scare easily."

Gelpas finally found the parchment he was looking for and handed it over to Aksel. "As before, this is interfering with trade. The town merchants are offering a substantial reward for stopping whatever is behind the disappearing ships. Five thousand gold pieces outright and a fifteen percent finder's fee on for any lost cargo recovered."

Seth stepped forward and peered over Aksel's shoulder. The two of them reviewed the parchment carefully. After a few moments, Aksel glanced up at the captain. "We were going to check this out anyway, but that is indeed an added benefit."

"You can say that again," Seth added, a familiar gleam in his eye.

Gelpas nodded. "Very good, I will notify Captain Rochino. The Endurance should be ready to sail first thing in the morning."

"We'll be ready as well," Aksel stated.

5
SAILING SHIPS AND GOLEMS
He can ride the anchor!

L loyd had been strangely silent during the meeting with Gelpas. Now that they had left the captain's office, he finally spoke up. "I really don't like leaving the town just now."

Glo exchanged glances with Aksel and Seth. Lloyd had been extremely upset when he found out the Lady Andrella might be the target of the Serpent Cult. Glo couldn't blame him for not wanting to leave Ravenford.

Aksel's expression was one of keen sympathy. "I agree with you, this trip does come at a rather bad time. However, in good conscience, we can't let whatever is going on off the coast continue."

Lloyd stared at Aksel, mixed emotions playing across his face.

Glo tried to console him. "Don't forget, the baron is aware of the danger, the castle guards are on double duty, and they are screening everyone coming in and out of town."

Lloyd sighed. "I know, I know. It's just..."

Seth mouth twisted into a thin smirk. "You want to be the one to protect her."

Lloyd grinned sheepishly, his hand going to the back of his neck. "Yeah, I guess."

They exited the double doors of the large keep and stopped on the steps to the courtyard beyond. There were castle guards everywhere—at least ten men in the yard itself, two at the gate, and another eight up on the walls.

"I think they've got it fairly well covered for now," Glo said.

Lloyd gazed around his eyes widening as he saw the number of guards on duty. A wan smile crossed his lips. "Sorry. You're right. We have a job to do and that comes first."

"We shouldn't be gone for more than a couple of days," Aksel assured him. "I've been puzzling this over in my mind, and I think I know a way to speed this investigation up."

Lloyd peered at him with keen interest. "How's that?"

"A large bonfire on the cliffs north of the cape could easily have been mistaken for a lighthouse signal. However, that means the actual lighthouse would have to also been put out of commission."

"So we need to investigate both—which can be done at the same time if we split up," Seth added.

Aksel grinned. "Exactly. You and Brundon can head up the coast while the rest of us check out the lighthouse. That will easily cut down on the time needed to investigate—"

"Umm, Aksel, you said Brundon," Lloyd interrupted him.

Aksel stopped and stared at Lloyd, sudden realization crossing his face. "I did, didn't I? Force of habit, I guess. Still, that leaves us without a tracker, unless..."

"Martan!" Glo and Seth exclaimed at the same time.

"He was good enough for the Black Adders," Elladan pointed out.

Lloyd appeared puzzled. "But didn't he also leave town?"

"Yes, but that's not a problem," Glo replied. He doffed his backpack and rifled through it. "Not when we have this." He stood up and held out a clear glass ball the size of a small melon.

Recognition dawned on Lloyd's face. "Is that..."

"...Voltark's crystal ball," Seth finished.

As it turned out, it didn't take long to find Martan. He was camped in the foothills just north of town. When they showed up and offered him a steady paying job, Martan jumped at the chance.

Early the next morning, Aksel, Lloyd, Seth, Glo, and Martan arrived at the docks. The Boulder trailed slowly behind them, its heavy footsteps shaking the ground and causing passing townsfolk to stop and stare. Although Lloyd warned him that the heavy creature would not make it up the gangplank, Aksel brought the golem along anyway.

The Endurance was easy to spot—it was the tallest ship of all the ships at the docks. They left the Boulder standing at the foot of the pier and trekked down the long dock. Lloyd gave them a detailed explanation of the parts of the ship, pointing out the various sections as they went.

"That's a galleon—see the three masts? The front two, the fore, and main are both square-rigged. You can tell by how the yard crosses the mast. But the mizzenmast, the one in the aft of the ship, is a bit shorter, and it's lateen-rigged. Look how the yards on that mast are angled. Also, you can see the long beakhead on the bow and the square galley at the stern—"

"Lloyd!" Seth shouted.

Lloyd stopped and stared at the halfling. "Yes?"

Seth folded his arms across his chest, his head cocked to one side. "You do realize that everything you just told us is pure gibberish."

Lloyd grinned sheepishly in response. "Oh. Sorry. It's been awhile since I was down at the docks. I guess I got a bit excited."

"Want to try that again in small, understandable words?" Seth chided.

Lloyd fixed the halfling with a long hard stare. When he responded, it was in a slow, flat tone. "Big ship... Go fast... Carry lots of cargo."

"Okay, now that makes sense," Seth responded rather cheerfully.

Glo shook his head. Seth was incorrigible—though not wrong. Glo hadn't understood a word Lloyd had said, either. *Guess it's to be expected—his father is Admiral of the Penwick Navy.* Unlike Lloyd, Glo had never sailed before. In fact, he had never even seen the sea. He had spent most of his life in the city of Cairthrellon, deep in the great forest of Ruanaiaith. Glo remembered his amazement the first time he'd gazed upon the vast expanse of Merchant Bay. It was so large that its sparkling waters stretched to the horizon. What intrigued him the most though was the waves—the rhythmic way they flowed toward the beach and back. There was something very serene about the sea—something that calmed the soul. Glo began to understand why sailors were drawn to it, never wanting to spend more than a few days on land. The companions resumed walking down the dock while Lloyd continued talking about his seafaring family.

"My brother, Pallas, is the real sea-dog. In fact, he's a Captain in the Penwick Navy."

"Is he much older than you?" Glo asked.

"He's twenty-six."

It was Seth's turn to be curious. "Isn't that a bit young to be a ship's captain?"

"Maybe, for some, but Pallas has been living on ships since he was about eight. He's probably logged more hours at sea than most of the sailors in the fleet. Not to mention, a few months ago he saved an entire town from pirates, without losing a single man. For him to be Captain of the *Avenger* is really not that much of a stretch."

A gruff voice called out from ahead of them. "Did I hear someone say the *Avenger*?"

They were approaching the gangplank, a number of folks already gathered there. In their midst stood a dark bearded man wearing a sailor's coat and a broad brimmed, three-cornered hat. Glo recognized the folks around the man. They were the same merchants they had met a few days ago, during the victory celebration over the orc bandits. One of the merchants in particularly had a sour look on his face. It was Haltan, owner of the "Shop of Wonders" in Ravenford.

Lloyd stopped in front of the dark bearded man and saluted smartly. "Captain Rochino."

Rochino responded with a hearty laugh. "Yeah, lad, but this is no military vessel. No need to salute me." The captain turned his gaze upon the rest of them. "And you must be the group they call the Heroes of Ravenford."

Aksel responded for them. "That's not how we refer to ourselves, but it seems to make the townsfolk happy."

Rochino laughed heartily once more. "Simple folk do need their heroes to look up to. Me? I'm a simple man. Just give me a ship and the open sea, and I'm content."

Lloyd gazed up at the Endurance with a wistful expression. "She is a beauty, captain."

Rochino followed Lloyd's gaze, his expression filled with pride. "Aye, that she is, but she's no warship like the Avenger."

Lloyd stared up and down the length of the vessel. "Maybe not, but judging by the lowered forecastle and the long hull, I'd say she's faster than most."

Rochino gazed upon Lloyd with an expression of approval. "You've got a good eye there, lad. She's the fastest ship in these northern waters. Tell me, how do you know so much about sailing?"

"His father is Kratos Stealle," Seth replied before Lloyd could answer.

Rochino's eyes widened. "Kratos Stealle? Admiral of the Penwick Navy?"

"That's my dad," Lloyd admitted.

Rochino appraised Lloyd anew. "Well then, lad, no wonder you know your ships! Come aboard, and I'll give you the grand tour." Rochino led Lloyd up the gangplank, the two in deep conversation. Glo's keen ears picked up some of it.

"So that would make Pallas your brother," Rochino was saying.

Lloyd sounded incredulous. "You know Pallas?"

"Aye, lad. Met him down the coast a few months ago. Helped him and his crew out of a nasty jam with some pirates."

A thin smile spread across Glo's lips. It was indeed a small world.

"Well if it isn't the Heroes of Ravenford," a familiar voice addressed them, the tone rather contemptuous. It was the merchant, Haltan. He strode up to the companions as he continued to speak. "Where's your bard friend? Isn't he joining you on this venture?"

Once again, Aksel responded for the group. "He's a bit busy right now coordinating the entertainment for the Lady Andrella's party."

Haltan's expression soured even more, if possible. "Ah, yes, that would make sense. He is really quite good with that lute of his. Some would say too good." Those last few words practically dripped with malice.

"Guess you would know that first hand," Seth responded with a wide smirk.

Haltan glared at the halfling disdainfully. "Yes, I guess I would."

Glo could barely suppress a smile. Haltan was a despicable individual. It was not the fact that he price-gouged that made him so. All merchants had the right to get the best deal they could. What made him contemptible was that he purposely withheld information about the hammer they had found just to improve his bargaining position. Elladan handled the situation shrewdly by putting Haltan under a spell, forcing him to reveal what he knew. Thus the merchant now had little love for the bard.

Aksel cleared his throat. "If you will excuse us, we have a ship to board."

Haltan glared at them a few moments longer, then reluctantly moved out of the way. The foursome passed the sour-faced merchant as they made their way to the foot of the gangplank. Before they could ascend it, though, Haltan spoke again. "I hope you are successful on this journey. After all, I would like to get my cargo back. I've lost a lot of shipments this last month."

Aksel did not bother to turn around. "We'll do our best to recover all the merchants' shipments."

Haltan snorted contemptuously. "As long as I get mine." With those parting words, Haltan marched off down the docks back toward town.

Seth stared after the merchant, his eyes like daggers. "I really don't like that man."

Glo had to agree. Any further conversation on the matter was interrupted by a cry from up ahead. "Guys!" Glo cast a glance upward and saw Lloyd at the head of the gangplank. "The Captain and I think we've figured a way we can take the Boulder with us."

Seth rolled his eyes to the heavens. "Now this I've got to hear."

When they finally boarded the Endurance, Glo did not know where to look first. He had never been on a sailing ship, and this one appeared vast. A long deck stretched out before them, the thick mast of a tall sail right in the center. There were ropes and pulleys up and down the rails, and crates and barrels here and there along the main deck. Toward the front of the vessel was a higher deck with two sets of stairs leading to it. A door stood between them that probably led to inside cabins and the lower decks. To the rear was another high deck with two more sets of steps leading up to it, and another doorway between. A large wheel was mounted on the rear deck—the main steering mechanism of the vessel.

Lloyd waited with Captain Rochino for them to board. The moment they all set foot on deck, Lloyd began to explain what he had discovered. "I was telling the captain about the stone golem—how heavy it is and all."

Rochino nodded. "Aye, the lad here is right. There's no way that thing will ever make it up the gangplank. Still, there might be a way we could take it with us."

Aksel appeared intrigued. "How's that?"

"He can ride the anchor!" Lloyd blurted out, unable to contain himself any longer.

Glo was not sure he had heard that right. He was about to ask Lloyd to repeat that again when Seth fell on the deck. The halfling began to laugh uncontrollably. "Ride... ride... ride the anchor!" he cried between fits of laughter.

Lloyd folded his arms and glared at Seth. "I'm serious."

"Oh... that's... good... ," Seth managed to say, still rolling around on the deck and chortling. "You're serious!"

Rochino cleared his throat. "It should work, lad."

Seth immediately stopped laughing though his eyes continued to dance with amusement. "Oh, you are serious then."

"Lad, when it comes to my ship, I don't kid." He spun around and motioned for them to follow. "This way." Rochino headed across the deck toward the front of the ship. The followed him up the stairs to the forward deck. On the way, Lloyd continued the discussion.

"Glo, you said the golem weighs about 2,000 pounds?"

Glo nodded. "Yes, that's about right."

"The captain said the anchors on the Endurance weigh about 1,200 pounds, but the chains can hold nearly triple that."

"Aye lad," Rochino agreed. "We had her fitted with a single heavy anchor at one point, but now she's got one on either side at half the weight."

"So they should be able to hold the anchor and the golem," Lloyd finished in a triumphant tone.

They had reached the bow of the ship. The captain showed them the winch and the thick chain that was attached to the anchor on this side of the vessel. Glo and Aksel exchanged glances. Aksel just shrugged. The math certainly made sense and the chain looked rather sturdy. Glo merely nodded. "If the captain thinks it will work, I guess it's worth a try."

Seth was not convinced. "Even if it does hold, that's a lot of extra weight. How do you plan on pulling that off the ocean floor?"

Rochino winked at the halfling. "We thought of that, too. All we really need is some extra muscle to turn the winch."

Lloyd stepped forward, proudly flexing his muscles. "And that's where I come in."

Seth eyed the pair as if they were crazy.

Rochino grinned. "Oh, don't get me wrong, lad. We'll have to compensate a bit for the extra weight when we steer the ship, but it ain't nothing my Endurance can't handle." He reached over and affectionately patted the ship's rail.

Seth shrugged. "Fine with me—as long as we don't have to pay for a broken anchor chain."

"Okay then," Aksel declared, "here goes nothing."

He walked to the railing and gazed back down the dock to where the golem waited. Sailors and townsfolk alike stood around the huge, still form, staring up at it. Aksel held out the hand wearing the golem's ring. He closed his eyes, an expression of deep concentration crossing his face. After a few moments, his eyes snapped back open. "That should do it."

Glo watched as the golem began to move. People scurried out of its way as it walked down past the docks to the water's edge. The creature slowly walked out into the water, submersing itself in the deep river. They all now peered over the railing, into the clear waters below. The water was quite deep, though, making it hard to see the bottom. After about five minutes, the ship began to sway. It rocked toward the dock, then away from it. It finally abated, the Endurance growing still once more.

"Looks like we're good to go," Lloyd declared.

"Now comes the real test." Rochino opened his mouth wide and boomed out a command to the crew. "Get ready to weigh anchor!"

"That's my cue," Lloyd said.

He joined about half a dozen sailors who gathered at the winch. On the Captain's mark, they began to heave. It was slow going, all of them straining with each rotation of the winch. Miraculously, the crank held, and in a few minutes, the anchor, along with the Boulder, had been hoisted up from the river bottom. Lloyd stepped back from the winch and wiped the sweat from his brow.

Aksel gazed over the side. The golem stood quite comfortably on the raised anchor. Aksel appeared amazed. "It actually worked."

"Of course it did!" Rochino cried with a broad grin. "You need to have a little more faith, lad."

Glo raised an eyebrow, and Seth snickered. Aksel's mouth hung open, caught off guard by the remark. It was not every day a cleric was told he needed more faith. Rochino did not wait for a response, though. Instead, the he spun around and strode across the deck, bellowing orders to get underway.

6
CAPE MARLIN

What kind of noble went barefoot at the beach, hiding among the
rocks?

T he Endurance followed the northern coast of Merchant's
Bay, never losing sight of land. The day was bright and sunny,
the crystal blue waters of the bay clear and calm. In this fair
weather, it was hard to imagine the raging storms that sank the Lucky
Coin a few nights ago. Lloyd stood at the prow of the Endurance,
staring out at the waters ahead. Aksel had gone below deck for a
nap. Martan went in the opposite direction, nestled high above in the
crow's nest. Seth, as usual, was nowhere to be seen.

Glo found himself fascinated by the large sailing ship. He took
the opportunity to roam around the deck and investigate every inch
of the vessel. The structure of the Endurance was purely function-
al—its wide frame designed for carrying large amounts of cargo,
yet its hull stretched out to compensate. The front deck also did not
rise as high as the rear. This was to decrease wind resistance. Three
thick masts stood at equal distances along the ship's length. The two
front masts carried the main sails. These ran across the ship and were
what pulled it forward. The aft mast stood shorter than the others.
Its sails were aligned with the ship and helped steer the vessel. The
ship's main steering mechanism was the large wheel firmly attached
to the rear deck. It connected to a rudder, a large wooden fin at the
back of the ship below the water line. Overall, it was actually quite
an ingenious design.

With the wind behind them, the ship's white sails were now completely unfurled. They bowed out in front of them like enormous
kites against a backdrop of the deep blue sky. It was a breathtaking
sight. There was a beauty to sailing beyond measure. Between that

and the allure of the sea itself, it was no wonder that sailors never stayed long on land. Glo had wandered the entire deck of the Endurance and now found himself at the prow. Lloyd stood there by himself staring out at the empty waters in front of them. Glo strode up beside him and leaned against the rail.

"I forgot how peaceful the sea is," Lloyd said, his tone wistful.

"There is a certain appeal to it."

"My father never seems to get enough of it. Sometimes I think the only thing that brings him back to shore is my mother—or the school."

"School?"

"The *Stealle Academy of the Sword*," Lloyd explained with a certain measure of pride in his voice. "My father formed it after the victory over the Pirate Warlord Eboneye some twenty years ago. He's been training Penwick soldiers and townsfolk there ever since."

Glo found that interesting—a school owned and run by Lloyd's father. It made sense, though. The entire city had been overrun by pirate hordes, and many lives were lost reclaiming it. Afterwards, they would have had to train a whole new generation of warriors. Who better to do so than Kratos Stealle, the best swordsman in all of Penwick?

"Is that where you studied to be a Spiritblade?"

"Mostly, although we do have a separate training area set up in one of the barns at the ranch."

A training area in a barn? It sounded like Kratos took sword work very seriously. It made Glo think of his own father, Amrod. Glo's father was a wizard by trade, one of the best in Cairthrellon. He also took his craft very seriously, so much so that Glo rarely saw him. However, that all changed when he became Amrod's apprentice. Unfortunately, they didn't see eye to eye on anything. From magic to politics, their viewpoints were completely opposite. It was the main reason Glo had left home. Now, nearly two months later, Glo actually found himself missing the old man. Experience had shown him that Amrod was not wrong about everything. Still, Glo was not ready to reconcile with his father just yet. "So you spent a lot of time with your dad?"

A frown formed across Lloyd's brow. "I guess—if you consider training with the sword spending time."

Glo felt a wave of compassion for his friend. It was another thing they had in common. Kratos seemed very much like Amrod in that respect. Both only had time for their sons when it came to teaching them their trade. Be it the sword or magic, it was still the same. Glo knew exactly how Lloyd felt. "My father was also that way. We only saw each other during my magic studies. Otherwise, he was holed up in his lab or at a council meeting."

Lloyd nodded slowly. "Between the Navy, the Penwick Council and the school, my father does not exactly have a lot of free time."

"Still, he was a proponent of you becoming a Spiritblade."

Lloyd appeared surprised, as if he had never even considered the alternative. "Yes, of course. Dad taught all of us: me, Pallas, and even Thea."

"Is Thea your sister?"

"Yes. Althea is my older sister by two years—but if you call her by that name you are likely to receive a punch in the arm." Lloyd finished with a wink.

Glo eyed Lloyd curiously. From what little he had told them, Glo had assumed Lloyd's sister was a cleric. Yet that description just now didn't sound very divine-natured. "I thought you said your sister was a healer?"

"She is. She's an Auric Priestess of Arenor," Lloyd said with obvious pride.

An Auric Priestess of Arenor—that was impressive. They were devoted servants of Arenor, the God of Sun and Light. A noble calling, it was also about as far away as you could get from being a warrior. Glo felt even more puzzled. "If she was studying to be a spiritblade, what made her join the clergy?"

"Well..." Lloyd's voice faltered. His skin paled and his eyes took on a faraway look. When he finally spoke, it was barely above a whisper. "She kind of died."

Glo's eyes went wide and he felt the blood drain from his face. Death was not something to be taken lightly, even with magic that could bring back the dead. First, "Resurrect Dead" spells were costly, and not everyone could afford them. Second, if the body was not intact or too decomposed, the spell would not work. Third, the spirit had to be willing to return from the dead. Sometimes a soul was finished with life and wanted to move on. In that case, either the spell would fail, or worse, a malevolent spirit would take its place. Finally, even if the spell worked, death changed people. They were never quite the same after such a traumatic experience. For these reasons, laws had been crafted to prevent someone who had died from holding any position of power. When Glo found his voice again, his tone was hushed. "Lloyd, I'm so sorry. How did it happen? That is, if you don't mind talking about it."

Lloyd took a deep breath. "No. It's okay. It was about seven years ago. Thea was far more adventurous back then. She had this weird obsession with pirates, particularly Eboneye." A slight smile crossed his lips at the thought.

Glo smiled sympathetically in turn. This was obviously a hard topic for the young man.

"There were rumors that he had a hidden treasure hoard somewhere in the city. Thea was determined to find it. She and her friends spent all their free time searching for clues to its whereabouts."

Lloyd let out a deep sigh. "Then they got the bright idea to check out the old abandoned fort on Thorn Isle. No one knows exactly what happened, but somehow, they were all killed..." Lloyd stopped talking altogether, his face taking on a pained expression.

Glo had no idea what to say. He stood beside his friend in silence until Lloyd resumed the story.

"That is where it gets strange. The priests claimed it was the work of Alaric—that the kids were rescued by a storm dragon. The dragon brought their bodies to the Temple along with enough treasure to pay for their resurrections and more."

Glo arched an eyebrow. *A storm dragon?* Alaric was the God of Storms. Storm dragons were his servants. Yet as far as he knew, no one had seen a storm dragon in over a hundred years. "Do storm dragons still exist?"

Lloyd shook his head. "Your guess is as good as mine. All we know is what the priests told us—but I do remember there being a bad storm that night. Strangely, Thea and her friends remember nothing of what happened to them. They claimed there was another girl with them, but they never found any sign of her." The young man paused and shrugged his shoulders. "Anyway, Thea was never the same after that. She stopped treasure hunting, as well as her spiritblade training. Instead, she enrolled in the priesthood. When asked, she would say, "*It is the will of Arenor.*"

Glo let out a soft whistle. "That's some story." He had read of this—life-changing events coupled with visitations from the gods. An incident like that left a mark on an individual. If Lloyd's sister had been touched by Arenor, then it is no wonder that she joined the priesthood.

Lloyd interrupted his musings. "What about you? Didn't your father want you to become a wizard?"

A wry smile crossed Glo's lips. "Want is not exactly the word I would use. More like require or demand."

"What do you mean?"

"I had to begin my studies with my father when I was eighty—"

Lloyd's eyes went wide, causing Glo to stop in mid-sentence. *Right. Lloyd probably didn't know about elven ages.* "Sorry, I forget myself sometimes. While elves are longed-lived, it also takes us longer to mature. So an elf at eighty would be the equivalent of a human at twelve."

Lloyd gulped but said nothing, so Glo just smiled and went on with his story. "For the last forty years or so, my father set both the curriculum and pace of my studies. Everything had to be repeated over and over until it was perfect. I was not allowed to move on to the next lesson until he was absolutely satisfied." Glo felt a tinge of frustration as he finished describing this to Lloyd. Maybe he didn't miss his old man that much after all.

Lloyd still appeared to be struggling with what Glo had just told him. The young man finally found his voice. "So how old are you now?"

"One hundred and twenty."

One hundred and twenty, Lloyd mouthed the words. He was still obviously wrestling with the concept. Glo decided not to interrupt him. When Lloyd finally spoke, his voice was quiet. "Does that make you an adult then?"

A broad smile crossed Glo's lips. "Yes, a young adult. Think of me as eighteen, if it helps."

Lloyd considered that for a few moments, until a grin broke out across his face. "Then we're basically the same age!"

Glo laughed aloud this time. "Yes, indeed. You could say that."

The two friends, still smiling, fell silent. They stood together and watched the ship plow through the waters ahead. After a short while, Lloyd spoke up again. "Sorry your father was so difficult."

That caught Glo by surprise. He gazed at Lloyd but the young man was still staring at the waters ahead. Lloyd never ceased to amaze him. It was a simple statement. Still that small phrase meant more to Glo than he could ever put into words. Swallowing hard, he responded in kind. "Sorry for what you went through with your sister."

"Thanks."

The duo stood silently after that, watching the sleek vessel knife through the tranquil blue waters ahead.

The Endurance made it to Cape Marlin in just over two hours. As they rounded the Cape, the lighthouse came into view. The tall, white cylindrical structure stood alone on a little isle a few hundred yards off shore. The shoreline itself appeared clear and pristine. A wide expanse of brilliant white sand glistened in the afternoon sun. The beach stretched maybe thirty yards from the water's edge before backing up against a high cliff face. The cliffs themselves rose at a steep angle, to a height of nearly two hundred feet. The top of the bluffs was covered with dense woods that ran as far north as the eye could see. Rochino had been here before. He used his spyglass to point out a trail up the cliff face to the forest above. Once the party made shore, Seth and Martan would climb the trail and head north in search of the "second lighthouse."

The ship weighed anchor a few hundred yards offshore. Once they were stopped, Aksel ordered the Boulder to head to the beach. The Endurance wobbled once again as the heavy creature let go of the anchor. When the ship settled, a rowboat was dropped and the companions climbed aboard. Lloyd and Martan manned the oars and began rowing them slowly to shore. They had only gone about a hundred yards when the Endurance unfurled her sails. With all the strange events in these waters, Rochino was not going to wait here overnight. He would return and pick them up in the morning. The companions watched as the Endurance's huge white sails billowed out with the wind. The tall ship leapt forward and quickly made the wide turn around the cape and headed south, back into the bay. She was soon out of sight.

Glo now turned his attention to the shoreline. He scanned it up and down until his gaze fell upon a rocky area to the north. A sudden movement caught his eye. *Is that a figure on the beach?* He nudged Seth. "What do you make of that?"

Seth stared intently in the direction he was pointing, his eyes squinting for a better look. "Looks like a small figure—I'd say about half a mile up the beach."

"That's what I thought."

"Didn't Rochino say there was no one out here?" Aksel called back to them. The little cleric was perched comfortably in the bow of the rowboat.

"The nearest town would be Gelcliff," Martan answered, grunting as he pulled on the oar. "That's about ten miles north of here."

"Whoever it is, they picked a good place to hide out," Seth added. "Those rocks provide excellent cover. We wouldn't have seen them at all if they hadn't stepped out in the open for a few moments."

Glo's eyes flickered back up the beach. The figure had in fact disappeared from view. "I'll send Raven to take a look."

His familiar had already gone ahead to shore. Her tiny black form spiraled over the trees directly west of them. Glo concentrated for a few moments until he made contact with her mind. He formed a mental picture of where he wanted her to go. It only took a few seconds for Raven to understand. Moments later, the tiny black speck banked and headed north, up the shore.

A little while later, the small company reached the beach. They disembarked into the surf, then Lloyd and Martan dragged the boat out of the surf and onto the beach. With his first step onto the sand,

Glo felt a warm sensation in the pit of his stomach. It slowly spread across his entire body. He halted mid-step, trying to determine the origin of the feeling. It abruptly dawned on him—the emotion had come from Raven. The bird was in a state of utter joy, as if she had met an old friend, but whom would she know out here? With the exception of Elladan, everyone they knew was here with Glo. *It couldn't be someone from Cairthrellon—could it?*

"What's the matter?" Aksel asked.

The little cleric stood beside Glo, his expression one of concern.

"I'm getting the strangest feeling from Raven."

"Strange bad?" Lloyd's voice rang out from the water's edge.

"No, strange good actually."

Seth cocked his head to the side. "Strange good? You sure all this sun and salt air hasn't gone to your head?"

Glo gave the halfling a dark look. "I'm fine, thank you." He turned back to Aksel. "It's almost as if Raven knows whoever it is."

Aksel's hand went to his chin. "How is that possible? Didn't you say your people don't travel around?"

"No, they don't," Glo affirmed. Internally, he was still struggling with the waves of happiness from his familiar coupled with his own bewilderment.

Seth peered up at the sky. "Why don't you three go check it out? Martan and I had better get going. We have a long walk ahead, and it's already midday."

Glo followed his gaze. The sun was now directly overhead.

"Right," Aksel agreed. "Good luck. We'll meet you back here by sundown."

"Come on, Martan." Seth motioned the archer to follow, then trotted down the beach. Martan nodded to the others, then quickly took off after him. From where they had landed, it was only a few hundred yards to the base of the trail up the cliff side.

Lloyd gazed up the beach. "Okay, I'm real curious to see who Raven found."

He began to march northward through the soft white sand. Aksel and Glo were right behind him.

A short while later, they reached their destination. Large boulders loomed ahead, blocking their view of the shoreline to the north. Glo felt the nearby presence of his familiar. "We are almost there."

They'd just reached the first outcropping when a small figure stepped out from behind it. Glo started, but immediately saw it was only a little girl. She appeared to be human, probably not more than eight years old. A cute little thing, she had long, golden blonde hair, bright blue eyes, and big dimples on either side of her mouth. The girl did not appear startled at all. She wore a wide grin and spoke rather nonchalantly. "Oh, there you are." Her voice sounded child-like, but there was something strangely melodic about it. The young girl stopped where she was and called back over her shoulder, "Ves, they're here!"

Aksel sounded puzzled. "You were expecting us?"

The girl fixed him with a stare, her hands going to her small hips. "Of course, silly. Raven said you would be coming to find us."

This time Glo was baffled. "Raven told you that?"

A frown crossed the young girl's face, but it was quickly replaced with a cute smile that accentuated her dimples. "Oh, that's right. I forget that other folks don't talk to animals like us. I can speak to her in her own tongue, though Ves says she speaks perfect elvish."

Glo did not know what to make of this strange little girl who apparently could talk to animals. He was about to ask who this Ves was when another figure appeared from behind the rocks. The question died on his lips. A young woman, perhaps in her late teens, strode into view. She had a well-tanned complexion, with long golden-blonde hair framing an oval-shaped face, a thin upturned nose and slim cheeks, but Glo was immediately draw to her vivid blue-green eyes. The woman was garbed in a shimmering bronze dress that clung to her shapely figure as she walked barefoot through the white sand. She came up and stopped just behind the young girl. Although only perhaps a foot taller than the girl, this woman had a magnetic presence about her that made her appear larger. Glo was further amazed to see Raven perched comfortably on the young woman's shoulder. That was not something she normally did with anyone but him.

The young woman addressed the little girl first. "Maya, where are your manners?" She gazed up then at the others, each in turn. "Children, what is one to do?" She said with a slight shake of her head. Aksel, Lloyd, and Glo all stood there speechless. When no one responded, a bemused smile crossed her lips. "I am Ves, and this is my sister, Maya. We were just having a picnic lunch on the beach. Would you care to join us?"

Her speech was casual, but she had a refined air about her. It was almost as if she were some sort of nobility. Still, what kind of noble went barefoot at the beach hiding among the rocks? Glo found himself quite intrigued by this Ves.

"I am rather hungry," Lloyd admitted.

"You're always hungry," Aksel said without missing a beat.

Glo tore his eyes away from Ves and shifted his gaze toward the gnome after that rather Seth-like response. The corners of Aksel's lips were slightly upturned—he was obviously joking. Perhaps Seth was indeed rubbing off on him. The hint of a smile disappeared off Aksel's face as he turned to Ves. He replied to her in a formal tone, "We would be honored to accept your gracious invitation."

Ves clasped her hands together. "Wonderful. Right this way." She spun around and strode back the way she came.

Aksel and Glo exchanged glances. The former merely shrugged and followed after the young lady. Lloyd was already moving as well—the offer of food obviously more than enough for him. Glo raised an eyebrow but trailed after the others, Maya falling in next to him.

As they followed Ves through a maze of tall boulders, Maya spoke to Glo in a very serious tone. "I really like your bird."

Glo could not help smiling at the delightful young girl, but he responded in an equally serious tone. "Thank you."

Maya grinned back at him. "What I like the most is that you actually named her Raven!" She ended her statement in a fit of giggles.

"Maya! Behave yourself," Ves called back over her shoulder.

"It's okay," Glo called forward. "I still find it amusing myself."

"Raven," Maya gasped, now giggling uncontrollably.

The maze of boulders gave way to a large, flat area ringed in on both sides by the large boulders. They ran from the shoreline all the way to the cliff face some thirty yards back. The area was thus effectively sheltered from view on three sides. In the very center sat a fire pit with a makeshift rack standing over it. Tongues of flame reached up from the pit, licking the fish that sizzled on the rack. The smell reached Glo's nose, instantly revealing that he was hungrier than he had thought.

Ves strode over toward the fire pit, calling back over her shoulder, "Lunch should be ready in a little bit. In the meantime, please make yourselves comfortable."

Glo, Lloyd and Aksel all exchanged glances. The three of them shrugged, then the elf and the tall warrior followed Ves over to the fire pit. Aksel, however, remained behind.

7
THE THREE SISTERS
You see, our family has some special—talents

While Lloyd and Glo followed Ves up toward the fire pit, Aksel stayed with Maya down by the water. The young girl picked up a rock and began skipping stones. She had managed to skim the water three times before the small stone finally sank beneath the surface.

"Nice one," Aksel complemented her.

Maya grinned back at him with that infectious smile. "Thanks."

She immediately bent down to search for another stone. Aksel did likewise. Searching the sand, he swiftly found his own small rock. Maya picked a small flat stone as well.

"Do you and your sister come out here often to the beach?"

She eyed him as if he was crazy. "Of course not. We don't live around here, silly. We are on a trip. We only just got here a day or two ago."

Interesting. That's about when the Lucky Coin sank, Aksel thought.

The two of them pulled back their arms and let go of their stones simultaneously. Maya's only skipped twice this time while Aksel's skimmed the water four times and landed quite far out.

The young girl looked at him admiringly. "Wow! You're really good at this."

Aksel responded with a wry smile. "I grew up by the sea. Trust me, there are folks far better than I am back home."

Maya bend down to search for another rock. "That's okay. *We are all best at something,*" she recited. "That's what Ves always says, anyway."

Aksel shook his head, and his smile widened. The young girl was positively delightful. He reached down to pick up another rock himself.

"So where are you headed?"

Maya kept her eyes on the stone she had just sent skimming across the waves. "Oh, we don't know exactly, just yet."

Aksel was amused by the girl's nonchalant attitude. "How will you find out then?"

"Oh, Ves will take care of it. She's good at that kind of thing."

Aksel found Maya's implicit faith in her older sister intriguing. Having no siblings of his own, he never had anyone to look up to or depend on. He was about to ask her another question when a strange feeling came over him. It was as if he were being watched. The little cleric peered around until his eyes fell on a black cat. The creature sat atop a large boulder a few yards away. Its bright green eyes appeared to glow as the creature watched him intently. Aksel found himself fascinated with the strange feline. *Where did you come from? Do you belong to the girls?*

He turned to ask Maya about the cat but found she was no longer standing next to him. He quickly spied her heading up the beach toward the others. Aksel shook his head. The girl was still rather young and her attention span probably not that great. He turned back toward the boulder with the mysterious cat, but the creature was no longer there. Aksel searched all around but saw no trace of the black feline.

"That's weird," he murmured.

He was just about to give up when a movement caught his eye. About half a dozen yards out in the water, a figure rose out of the sea! It was another girl! Now where had she come from? There had been no sign of a swimmer out in the surf moments ago. Aksel briefly scanned the horizon but saw no boats in the area either. He turned his attention back to the girl. She was blonde like Ves and Maya, but her hair was a few shades darker and also cut rather short. As she waded toward him, more of her appeared out of the water. She wore a black leather tunic, her outfit glistening from the beads of water that stuck to it as she exited the surf. Her eyes, an emerald green, were fixed on him with a strange intensity. Aksel felt mesmerized, as if she were trying to look into his soul. She finally turned her head and the feeling quickly passed.

Minor differences aside, this girl bore a striking resemblance to Ves and Maya. Aksel was not very good at guessing human ages, but he placed her somewhere between the two in years. The girl stopped briefly to shake herself off, then strode up the beach right past him without so much as a nod. She moved with feline grace as she stepped lithely through the white sands. Shrugging his shoulders, Aksel followed her. He briefly peered around, wondering if any more young blonde girls would be popping up to join them.

Up ahead, Ves stood next to the fire pit. She held a stick in one hand and used it to poke the fish as they sizzled over the open fire. When she spied him and the new girl, she placed the stick down, wiped off her hands and gave introductions all around. "Everyone, this is my sister, Ruka. Ruka, this is Lloyd, Glolindir, and Aksel. They are here to investigate the ships that disappeared."

Maya was dancing around the outskirts of the campfire. "You mean the sunken ones down by the reef? There are four of them, you know," she added, as if trying to impress everyone.

Glo eyed the young girl curiously. "That's right. Just how did you know that?"

Maya continued to dance around as she answered him. "Oh, we've seen them—while swimming with our dolphin friends. They told us where to find them."

"Maya!" Ruka growled. The girl had sat down on the sand somewhat apart from the others.

The little girl stopped dancing and whirled toward her sister. "What?"

Aksel watched both girls. Ruka glared at her younger sister. Maya's expression changed to a pouty one, her hands going to her small hips defiantly. He really felt Ruka was overreacting. After all, Maya probably just had a vivid imagination. Her statement about the four ships was most likely a lucky guess. Still, something about the exchange nagged at the back of his mind.

Ves interrupted the staring contest, her voice was calm and even. "It's fine, Ruka." The oldest sister now stood in front of the fire pit, her arms folded across her chest as she stared at her middle sister.

Ruka turned to glare at her older sister. "Sure, it's fine. Go ahead. Give away the family secrets. See how far it gets us."

Ruka stood up and stormed away down the beach, everyone there staring after her. Ves quickly tried to smooth things over. "You'll have to forgive her. Ruka is not very trusting of strangers. Give her time to get to know you. She'll come around."

Aksel gave her a strained smile but otherwise did not respond. *Just what did she mean by family secrets?* There was definitely something strange about these sisters. Still, he did not feel threatened by them. Instead he was intrigued. Aksel shifted his gaze to Glo. The corners of the elf 's mouth were slightly upturned, and his eyes danced with amusement. Glo nodded back almost imperceptibly. Aksel took that to mean that he agreed with his assessment. The situation was strange but not dangerous.

"We have a companion like that," Lloyd was telling Ves.

The young woman nodded, as she circled back around the fire. "Yes, Raven had said there were five of you." She picked the stick and poked the sizzling fish once more. "Where are the others?"

"They went looking for the signal fire, north of here."

A puzzled expression crossing Ves's face. "Signal fire?"

"It's a long story," Glo interjected.

Ves' eyes shifted to the elf, her expression still perplexed.

"We can get into it after lunch if you would like," he added.

"Very well," she agreed. Ves gazed back down and poked at the fish once more. A moment later, she glanced back up, her eyes sweeping around the small group. "Now then, lunch is ready."

Aksel, Lloyd and Glo seated themselves around the fire pit. Ves picked up a few short sticks she had stacked neatly on the ground and proceeded to skewer each fish. She gave them one at a time to Maya who walked around and handed them out. Aksel was somewhat hesitant but graciously accepted the skewered fish. He had grown up by the sea, but had never eaten fish this way before. Still, he did not want to offend their hosts. He slowly raised the stick to his mouth and carefully took a bite. It was delicious! The fish was cooked to perfection. Aksel quickly devoured the rest of it and found himself asking for seconds. Ruka came over and grabbed a skewer but then stalked away, back to her original spot.

When lunch was over, Ves dumped a collection of seashells in front of her youngest sister. The little girl now sat quietly playing with them. Ves sat down next to her and bade Glo to fulfill his promise. Glo obliged. He began with the story they had heard from the sailors of the Lucky Coin. Ves appeared quite interested through the entire narration. Ruka did not move from her spot. She stared at the surf, apparently disinterested in the story, but Aksel had the feeling that she was listening carefully.

When Glo reached the portion about the lighthouse, Ves interrupted him. "That's strange. We've been here a couple of nights, and the lighthouse has never been lit."

Aksel found that strange. "Hmmm, that confirms a theory we have been developing."

"What's that?" Ruka called from her solitary perch.

She was listening after all, Aksel noted wryly.

"That someone has been making a false lighthouse signal north of here," Lloyd said to her.

"Interesting idea," Ruka replied. She got up and slowly sauntered over toward them.

Meanwhile, Ves pondered the implications of what they had just told them. "If the ships saw the false signal, thinking it was the lighthouse..."

"...then it would draw them off course and into the reef," Aksel finished for her.

"Guess you aren't as dumb as you look," Ruka commented. She now stood right behind them, a slight smirk on her lips.

"Ruka!" Ves cried, her face turning red with embarrassment.

Aksel, Lloyd, and Glo all exchanged glances, then the three of them began to laugh.

Ruka stared at the trio curiously. "Was it something I said?"

Glo wore a bemused grin. "It's like Seth never left us."

Lloyd continued to chuckle. "They could be twins."

Ruka's smirk faded. She pursed her lips then murmured, "Hmmm.

I think I'll have to meet this Seth."

Glo resumed the story of the Lucky Coin. When he reached the part about the sea monster, Maya began coughing violently. Lloyd reached down and gently patted her on the back. "Easy there, little girl."

Maya glanced up from her shells and began to giggle. Ves fixed her sister with a hard stare. Maya clamped her hands over her mouth, but some giggles still managed to escape. Ves shook her head in exasperation. "Anyway, please continue, Glolindir."

A thin smile crossed Glo's lips, but he went on with the story. This time he finished without any interruptions. Aksel did notice one other peculiar thing during the course of it. When Glo described the angel, Maya cast a sidelong glance at Ves. The young woman ignored her sister, her eyes locked firmly on Glo. Still, Ves's face appeared slightly flushed.

Once Glo had finished, Ves cleared her throat. "That is a very interesting story, but we have been here on this beach for the last few nights and have not seen anything like that at all."

"But have you seen the sunken ships," Aksel asked.

Ves hesitated, mixed emotions playing across her face. Her eyes flickered toward Ruka, but the younger girl looked away, her expression indifferent. Ves sighed, her eyes shifting back toward Aksel. When she spoke, it was tentative at best. "Yes, we have seen the sunken ships. You see, our family has some special—talents. Our father is Rodric Greymantle."

Aksel eyed her curiously. *Rodric Greymantle? One of the greatest wizards of all time?*

Glo mirrored his thoughts. "Rodric Greymantle? The great wizard from the Thrall Wars?"

"That's our dad!" Maya cried exuberantly. She dropped her seashells, stood up, and began to dance around the seated group.

Ves nodded. "Yes, indeed, that is our father. We are on a—pilgrimage—to see where he grew up." She paused a moment, as if collecting her thoughts. "You see, after the war was over, Father moved back with Mother to her homeland—the Glittering Isles. Ruka, Maya, and I all grew up there. None of us has ever even been to Thac. We really wanted to see where Father was born and raised. So—here we are." She finished with a wan smile.

Silence hung over the group as Aksel pondered Ves's explanation. Rodric Greymantle was indeed one of the greatest wizards of all time. He had been a member of the Wizard's Council, the body that rules over the entire magical community of Thac. Still, that had been nearly a hundred and fifty years ago, during the time of the Thrall Wars. When the war was over, Rodric disappeared. It was assumed that he had been killed in the last great battle with the Thrall Masters, but his body was never found. Since then, sightings of the mage had been reported from time to time around Thac. Most people chalked it up to fanciful imaginations, but if what Ves had just told them were true, it would explain a lot.

Lloyd finally broke the silence. "If your father was around during the Thrall Wars, wouldn't that make him over a hundred years old?"

That was something Aksel had been wondering himself. There were a number of possible explanations, but he was curious what Ves's answer would be. She appeared very uncomfortable with the question, though, not answering immediately, instead gazing down at the ground in front of her. Surprisingly, Glo came to her rescue. "It is more than possible."

"How's that?" Lloyd asked.

"A great wizard would have access to spells of considerable power. That being the case, he might very well have made himself immortal."

Ves glanced back up, her expression one of clear relief. She smiled gratefully at Glo. "Yes. It is as you say. Not complete immortality, but both he and Mother will live a very long time."

Glo appeared impressed. "Interesting. I would love to know the particulars of the spell he used for that. Perhaps I could meet your father someday?"

"Perhaps," Ves responded. She was still smiling, but her tone was evasive.

Aksel felt they had heard enough. It was time to bring the conversation back on track. "So you girls all have special talents, such as talking to animals?"

Ves nodded. "Yes, we can talk to animals."

"And dolphins!" Maya added exuberantly. She stopped dancing around and put her hands together in front of her. She then began to bob her head up and down, mimicking the marine mammals.

"And dolphins," Ves said, smiling patiently at her younger sister.

Dolphins! Something clicked in Aksel's mind. Maya had said something about seeing the sunken ships—about her dolphin friends pointing them out to her. At first he thought it a fanciful tale, but what if it wasn't? "So you swim underwater with these dolphins?"

"Oh, yes!" Maya cried. "Ves and I are good, but Ruka is the best! You would think she was a dolphin if she wasn't—"

Ves cut her sister off harshly. "Maya! That is quite enough!"

Maya's mouth hung open as she turned to look at her older sister. Abruptly she closed her mouth, folded her arms in front of her, and sat straight down on the sand with a "Humph!"

Ves realized that everyone was staring at her and began to flush with embarrassment. She tried to cover it with a transparent effort to straighten her dress. Maya sat where she was, her head turned away from her oldest sister. Ruka, on the other hand, stared directly at Ves with a look on her face that screamed *I told you so.* Aksel glanced at Glo, but the elf merely shrugged in response. Lloyd appeared mortified at the sudden outburst.

Ves finally managed to regain her composure, although her face was still a bit flushed. When she spoke, her voice was soft. "Sorry for my outburst—but Maya can get a bit carried away sometimes."

Maya remained silent, still turned away from her older sister. Aksel was not quite sure how to respond to all this. Ves had been calm and collected since they'd met. Albeit, that was only an hour ago, but this sudden outburst seemed drastically out of character. She obviously didn't want anyone hearing what Maya was going to say. He could not help wondering what it had been.

Glo finally responded to her, his voice equally soft. "We are sorry if we have offended you. We are merely trying to find out who, or what, is responsible for the sinking of these ships."

A thin smile crossed Ves's lips. "You have not offended anyone. It is just—we are a very private family. We are not used to discussing personal matters with anyone else."

Glo's expression was sympathetic. "I understand. Please be assured, we do not wish to pry into your personal business. We merely need to recover any sunken cargo that we can. Because of your special talents, you three are far better suited for underwater salvage than any of us."

Maya had turned around and was watching Glo with clear interest. Ves also stared at him, but remained silent as mixed emotions played across her face. Ruka eyed the elf skeptically.

"Would it be possible, then, to enlist your aid?" Glo asked his tone tentative.

Ves's response was hesitant at best. "I'm not sure..."

"How much?" Ruka cut her off.

Glo appeared as surprised as Aksel at the girl's sudden interruption. They all spun to face her. "How much what?" Glo asked.

"How—much—are you willing to pay us for our services?" Ruka spelled it out for him.

Glo's eyes shifted to Aksel, clearly unsure how to respond. Aksel had to admit, this was an unexpected turn of events. Ruka had wanted nothing to do with them. Now, at the mention of payment, she was suddenly interested in their mission. Perhaps she was indeed just like Seth. Aksel shrugged his shoulders and addressed Ruka. "What would you say to 5% of the finder's fee?"

"How is that calculated?" She stared at Aksel intently, a strange light in her eyes.

"It's one twentieth of the fee for whatever we can salvage. The more cargo we recover, the more we get paid."

Ruka's expression remained passive, but the light in her eyes grew brighter. "That sounds interesting."

Ruka turned to Ves, the two exchanging glances. From the intensity in her eyes, it was obvious that Ruka wanted to do this. It was also equally obvious that Ves did not. In the end, Ruka won out in the silent exchange. She broke off their staring contest and turned to face them. "Alright, we'll do it on one condition."

"What is that?" Aksel asked.

"Since we would be doing most of the work, I think 50% is more in order."

Aksel raised an eyebrow. For a young girl, she sure knew how to bargain. She was not altogether wrong, though. The three sisters would indeed be doing most of the work.

Aksel shrugged. "You make a fair point. Tell you what—one third and we'll send Lloyd down with you."

"We will?" Lloyd asked, clearly surprised by the offer.

Aksel gazed at the young man. "Don't worry. I have a spell that will let you breathe underwater."

Lloyd's face lit up. "Cool."

Aksel turned back to Ruka. She seemed to be mulling it over in her mind. Finally, she nodded. "Alright. Deal."

"Excellent," Aksel said. He felt relieved that things had been settled so smoothly. "Still, before we can begin, we need to check out that lighthouse." His mind thought ahead to what they might find there. "It would be better if the Boulder were with us," he mused aloud.

"The Boulder?" Maya giggled, her previous anger seemingly forgotten.

"Yes," Aksel told her. "He is our stone golem."

"And you named him The Boulder?" Maya shrieked in a high-pitched voice. She abruptly fell backwards onto the sand and grasped her stomach. Snorts and giggles erupted from her mouth as she rolled around back and forth. "That's... funnier... than... Raven..." she managed in between breaths.

Aksel and the others watched the young girl with amusement— all except for Ves. She appeared quite displeased with her little sister's display. She remained silent, though, most likely not wanting to reprimand Maya again after her previous outburst. When Maya had finally laughed herself out, she sat back up. Between the occasional giggling she said, "The Boulder... he is almost to the shore. The dolphins told me just before lunch."

Aksel smiled down at her. "Thank you." It seemed these girls talents were coming in handy already. This might just work out after all. He got up from his sandy seat. "Then let's walk back down the beach."

A short while later, the companions and their newfound friends returned to where they had left their rowboat. They did not have to wait long until the Boulder appeared out of the water. The stone golem slowly trudged out of the surf and waded up onto the beach. Once there, the creature stopped, waiting for its master's next command. Maya ran down and circled the golem. She looked him up and down, holding her tiny hand to her chin. When she was done, she nodded her head approvingly. "Boulder. It suits you well."

Aksel could not help but smile. Maya was positively delightful. The smile quickly faded from his face, though. They had work to do. He also strode down to the Boulder. "Well then, let's get started." He commanded the creature to head to the isle of the lighthouse. The golem slowly turned and trudged back into the surf, this time in the direction of the tall building. "Well, that will take a while," Aksel noted with annoyance. "I should have just sent him directly to the lighthouse in the first place."

Glo gazed at him with a wry smile. "We can't all be perfect."

Aksel let out a short sigh. "I guess you're right. No use second-guessing myself." He turned to Lloyd. "Let's get the boat in the water and head over ourselves."

Glo offered to give Lloyd a hand. The duo walked over to the rowboat and grabbed it from either side. Together they lugged it out into the water. They held the boat steady, allowing Aksel and Ves to board. Ves turned out to be quite nimble, leaping into the rowboat without assistance. Meanwhile, Maya and Ruka waded into the surf. The two young girls insisted on swimming over themselves. Lloyd and Glo climbed on board and manned the oars. Ves seated herself next to Aksel in the aft of the boat.

Maya and Ruka pulled out far ahead. They swam like fish toward the lighthouse isle. As they fell behind, Ves turned to face Aksel. "Please forgive them. They are both a bit exuberant."

Aksel shrugged. "They are still rather young."

"Yes, they are," Ves said with a faint smile.

Aksel watched the two girls as they approached the lighthouse isle. His gaze then wandered toward the tall structure beyond. He silently wondered what they would find there. *Well, we will know soon enough.*

8
THE DESERTED LIGHTHOUSE
A stone the size of a human head headed straight for the little girl

The companions moored their boat at a small dock on the south side of the isle. The lighthouse appeared deserted. There was no sign of life, other than a few gulls flying overhead. Ruka and Maya were yet to arrive. The two girls treaded water a short distance offshore, surrounded by a group of dolphins. The aquatic mammals made clicking noises and Maya echoed them back.

Glo watched in amazement. "Guess she really can talk to dolphins."

Ves stared at him coolly. "Maya is quite conversant in their language. We all are."

She had become quite aloof since her outburst. It was a stark contrast to the friendly young woman they had met only hours ago. Glo was convinced it had to do with her family secrets. She had distanced herself to keep them from learning anything more about her and her sisters.

Lloyd watched the girls with keen interest, oblivious to Ves's unfriendly attitude. "What are they saying?"

Ves regarded Lloyd icily for a few moments before replying. When she spoke, her tone was still quite cold. "They are talking about the strange stone man at the bottom of the ocean. He is walking toward the island with the tall building on it."

A broad smile spread across Lloyd's face. "That is amazing. It must be so cool to speak with animals in their own language."

Glo could not help but smile. Lloyd was a veritable gem, always finding joy in the diversity of others. Even Ves appeared affected by him. Her expression softened, the beginnings of a smile crossing her lips. Perhaps with enough time she'd realize they meant her family no harm. Ruka and Maya finally bade their dolphin friends farewell and swam to shore, joining the others at the end of the dock.

A small dirt path wound its way up the small, rocky hill on which the lighthouse stood. Aksel led the way up the path, the others falling in behind. The tall structure rose high above them, framed by the deep blue sky. The top of the lighthouse was enclosed in glass and capped with a bright red roof, housing the great lantern that guided ships away from the reef. A red catwalk encircled the tower just below the lantern room, blocking the view through the large glass windows. Smaller windows were built into the sides of the lighthouse, appearing at regular intervals from the top to the base. These were all closed and dark. At the base of the building stood a single iron-bound wooden door. It was locked tight, and knocking produced no response.

Glo cast a wry smile at the others. "Where's a good lock-pick when you need one?"

Aksel's response was equally glib. "We don't need a lock-pick. We have a Lloyd." He held his hands out toward the door. "Lloyd, would you care to do the honors?"

Lloyd cast an uncertain glance at Aksel, but stepped forward nonetheless. He put his ear to the door and tapped on it in a few places. "Seems fairly solid—probably two inches thick." He paused for a moment as if considering his options, then finally stepped away from the door. "You might want to step back," he called over his shoulder.

Everyone took a few steps back. The young warrior fell into a fighting stance, but with his left foot forward. Further, he did not draw his blades. He stood completely still, drawing in slow, deep breaths. All of a sudden, he lashed out with his back foot. It was a swift motion, almost too fast to follow. His right foot slammed into the door with terrifying force. There was a loud *crack* and the thick wood splintered. The large door hung there for a moment, then the entire thing fell backward into the lighthouse. It landed with a resounding *thud*.

Maya clapped and giggled. "Ooh, he's pretty strong."

"Yeah, not too bad," Ruka said in a grudging tone.

Lloyd grinned sheepishly, his hand going to the back of his neck. "Hope that wasn't too much."

Ves actually smiled for the first time since her outburst on the beach. "I don't think so. I'd say that was just right."

Lloyd's face reddened at the praise.

The interior of the lighthouse, now visible through the open doorway, appeared rather dark at first. On closer inspection, dim light could be seen filtered down from above. Not a sound came from beyond the doorway. The lighthouse appeared to be deserted.

Lloyd stepped forward and drew his swords. "I'll go first."

The others followed, filing one by one through the open doorway. Glo went next, then Aksel, with the three sisters in the rear. They found themselves in a circular room with the base of a staircase directly across from them. On either side of the stairs was a door leading further back into the lighthouse. The staircase wound its way up the inside wall of the lighthouse, to the lantern room far above. The top of the stairs was hidden in shadows, barely visible to even the keenest of eyes.

Aksel spoke in a hushed voice. "Let's be care—"

Before he could finish, Maya danced past all of them out into the center of the room. "Oh this is big," she cried, twirling around with delight. Her voice echoed off the walls, sounding fainter and fainter as it traveled up the empty chamber.

The eerie sound drew Glo's attention to the dark shadows far above. *Did something just move up there?*

"Maya, get back here!" He heard Ves cry, but Glo's eyes were locked on the upper stairwell. Abruptly something appeared out of the darkness. It was whitish-grey and semi-circular—it was also getting bigger. Abruptly the realization hit him—it was a stone!

"Look out!" Glo yelled, pointing upward. To his horror, more stones fell into view.

Lloyd immediately spurred into action. The young warrior spun around and vaulted toward Maya but he was too late—the rain of stones had already reached them. A few hit the floor with loud *thuds*, but one in particular caused Glo's heart to jump into his throat. A stone the size of a human head headed straight for the little girl.

"Maya!" he cried instinctively reaching out for the girl.

Time appeared to slow. Maya spun around to face him, a quizzical expression on her face. Lloyd continued to plow forward, closing on the young girl. The stone sped toward its unsuspecting target. Just before Lloyd could reach her, the rock connected with the little girl's shoulder. Glo felt a sinking feeling in the pit of his stomach. He cringed, expecting to see Maya's shoulder shatter. Yet, instead of crushing her side, the large stone shattered into pieces.

Glo's eyes went wide. *What the...*

Before he could finish his thought, a small grey blur slammed into his outstretched arm. Pain lanced up his limb and into his shoulder. It felt as if he had been hit with a hammer. Glo dropped his arm, and grasped it with his other hand.

At that same moment, Lloyd reached Maya and scooped her up off the floor. He cradled the little girl in his arms and kept on going toward the back of the lighthouse. Glo watched through a haze of pain as the duo hurtled across the room. Stones continued to rain down on them, Lloyd shielding the little girl with his body. At that moment, Glo caught a glimpse of Maya peering over Lloyd's shoulder. She was giggling!

Glo's mouth fell open in astonishment. He stood there paying little heed as stones continued to fall around him. Abruptly, strong hands grabbed him from behind and pulled him against the lighthouse wall. The owner of those hands was pressed against the wall next to him, still grasping his good arm. It was Ves!

"Stick to the wall!" she hissed.

Glo's senses suddenly returned to him and he nodded his understanding. Ves let go of his arm and motioned for him to follow, then slid along the wall toward the back of the room. Glo trailed close behind.

Across the room, Lloyd had reached one of the doors at the back of the lighthouse. Still cradling Maya in his arms, he placed his shoulder against the door and pushed against it with his body. There was a cracking noise followed by the door swinging open. Lloyd and Maya then disappeared inside.

Glo suddenly remembered Aksel. A quick glance backward confirmed that his friend also hugged the wall. Aksel and Ruka slid along a few feet behind him. It didn't take long for all of them to reach the open door.

Glo paused as the others ducked through the doorway. The rocks had stopped falling and everything had gone quiet. Glo closed his eyes and reached out with his mind, swiftly making contact with Raven. She flew around the island, enjoying the company of a flock of gulls. Glo directed her to fly past the top of the lighthouse. Perhaps she could get a look at who, or what, was throwing rocks down on them from up there.

Glo opened his eyes and peered into the open doorway. It was dark beyond the entrance, the only light coming through the open door. He lifted his arm to light his staff. That was a mistake. Pain shot up his shoulder. Glo grimaced but continued on, finally managing to get the staff lit. He blinked briefly as his eyes adjusted to the bright light. They were in a small room, surrounded by boxes and crates piled up to the ceiling. Lloyd stood in the center of the room, still holding Maya in his arms. Ves and Ruka stood to one side with Aksel on the other.

When Maya saw Ves, she began to giggle hysterically. "Did you see it, Ves? He rescued me!"

Lloyd gently placed the young girl on her feet, a puzzled expression on his face. Maya proceeded to fall on the floor and have another fit of giggles and snorts.

"That was very gallant of you." Ves told Lloyd, ignoring her little sister. Her demeanor had visibly softened, once again appearing to be the friendly young woman they had met on the beach.

"Yeah, it actually was," Ruka added. From her tone, it was clear she had not expected such gallantry.

Lloyd turned a bright shade of scarlet. "It was nothing. Anyone would have done it."

Ruka's mouth twisted into a smirk. "Ha. Not from what I've seen. That was almost—heroic." She stared intently at Lloyd, as if reevaluating her opinion of him.

Through all of this, Maya still rolled on the floor giggling uncontrollably. Glo could not fathom her reaction—unless she knew she was never in any real danger. That large stone should have crushed her shoulder. Even Lloyd would have had a hard time shrugging that off. Glo was thankful that Maya had not been hurt, but there was far more going on here than met the eye. He watched intently as Ves knelt down beside her sister. She grabbed the little girl by the arm and said, "Maya, compose yourself."

Maya stopped rolling. She sat up and wiped the tears from her eyes. She tried, rather unsuccessfully, to suppress any further giggles.

"Now let me see your wound," Ves said emphasizing the last word. She proceeded to examine the little girl's shoulder. From what Glo could see it looked completely fine. He cast a glance at Aksel. The gnome almost imperceptibly shook his head. Glo arched an eyebrow. If Maya was fine, then what was Ves playing at here?

Ves held out her index finger over her sister's shoulder. A brilliant blue light appeared at her fingertip. It quickly grew and covered the little girl's shoulder. Glo's eyes flickered toward Aksel again. This time the little cleric nodded. Well aside from her other talents, Ves was also a healer. Was there anything these girls could not do?

After a few seconds, the blue light disappeared. Ves drew back her finger and spoke to her sister in an overly loud tone. "How is it now?"

"Oh, it's just fine," Maya replied overdramatically. The little girl tried unsuccessfully to hide a grin.

"Very good," Ves nodded. She stood up and fixed her gaze on Lloyd. She spoke to him in an authoritative tone, quite obviously used to ordering others around. "Now let me see your back. I counted at least two stones that hit you squarely."

Lloyd appeared uncertain. He glanced over at Aksel. The little cleric merely nodded his approval. Lloyd's face reddened, but he complied. He unbuckled his sword belts, then unfastened his leather armor, pulling it over his head. Lloyd finished by removing his shirt, standing there naked from the waist up and looking rather uncomfortable. Glo could not fathom why Lloyd seemed so self-conscious—he was in excellent shape. His upper body practically rippled with muscles. He stood there looking like some kind of godling.

"Now turn around so I can see your back," Ves directed him.

Lloyd slowly spun around. Sure enough, there were two large bruises on his back. They were already an ugly shade of black and blue. Ves stepped forward and reached out with her hand. As she touched his back, Lloyd involuntarily flinched.

"I don't bite, you know," she told him.

For some reason, Maya found that hysterical. The little girl began to giggle all over again. Ves gave her sister a sharp look. Maya placed both hands over her mouth and proceeded to snicker into them.

"Sorry," Lloyd said, quite obviously embarrassed.

Ves continued to examine each wound. Finally, she withdrew her hand and held out her index finger. That same blue light appeared at its tip and spread over Lloyd's back. She moved her finger over each bruise in turn, enveloping them both in the brilliant blue light. When she was done, the bruises were gone. Ves withdrew her finger and took a step backwards. Her voice was soft. "How's that?"

Lloyd glanced over his shoulder. He rotated his arms around, twisting his torso back and forth and flexing his broad muscles. He finally stopped and turned to face Ves. A shy smile crossed his lips. "It's just fine now. Thank you, Ves."

The young woman smiled warmly back at him. Abruptly, she spun around to face Glo. She stared at him gravely, her arms going to her hips. "And as for you..."

Glo was startled. *Did I do something wrong?*

The room grew silent as she glared at him. Suddenly her hands fell from her sides and her expression softened. "Thank you, as well, for warning us—but next time don't just stand there waiting to be hit." Her eyes danced with amusement as she watched the bewildered elf.

A wry smile spread across Glo's lips. "Sorry about that. Guess I caught up in the moment."

The corners of Ves's mouth upturned slightly. "It can happen to anyone. Now let me see that arm." The last was said in that authoritative tone once again. She stepped forward and peered up at him expectantly.

Glo somehow knew better than to argue. He merely rolled up

his sleeve, wincing in pain as the fabric passed his elbow. There was a huge lump where the stone had hit him just below the elbow joint. It was a nasty shade of black and blue. Ves reached out with both hands and grabbed him gently above and below the elbow. Her hands were surprisingly cool to the touch. She examined the bruise closely at first, then let go with her right hand. Still holding his forearm with her left, she lifted up her right index finger. The bright blue light appeared at the tip and quickly spread out to envelop his arm. It was a bit more intense this time, so bright that he could not stare at it directly. Thankfully, the pain in his arm began to abate. Ves held the blue light over his wound for quite a bit longer than she had for either Maya or Lloyd. Perhaps ten minutes went by. Finally, the intensity of the light faded and it disappeared altogether. When Glo examined his arm, the lump was completely gone along with any discoloration. It no longer hurt in the slightest.

Ves released her grip and stepped back. Her expression was apologetic. "Sorry that took so much longer. The bone had a slight fracture."

Glo flexed and unflexed his arm. It felt as good as new. He rolled down his sleeve and looked at Ves with gratitude. "Thank you, Ves. That was a remarkable job of healing."

"Yes, rather expert, I would say," Aksel added.

Ves turned toward Aksel and curtsied quite gracefully. "Why, thank you, good cleric. I spent a few years studying in Lanfor at the Temple of Arenor."

Aksel pursed his lips. "I must say that I am very impressed. You are quite skilled for someone who only spent a few years studying."

Ves reddened slightly. Her eyes fell as she adjusted her dress, avoiding eye contact. Any further conversation was interrupted as a small black form flew into the room. It hovered above them a moment then landed on Glo's shoulder.

"*Manina de eller?*" Glo asked. *What is up there?*

"*Otso goblins,*" Raven replied, "*Er ure.*"

"Seven goblins, one large," Ves translated.

Glo nodded. "Indeed."

Ves smiled demurely in response, all her former discomfort gone.

"One large," Aksel repeated. "I wonder what that could be." His hand went to his chin as he mulled over Raven's words.

Glo thought back to the many books of monsters and races in his father's library at home, but nothing immediately came to mind. "I'm not sure. I've never heard of a large goblin. I don't suppose you girls would know?"

Ves and Ruka exchanged glances. Once more, Glo got the impression of a silent conversation transpiring between them. It only lasted a few moments then Ves responded. "No. Not really."

Aksel rubbed his chin for a few moments. "I guess there is only one way to find out." He turned to Lloyd. "You up for some goblin carving?"

Lloyd's eyes lit up at the thought of battle. "Sure." He finished buckling his second sword belt in place. It neatly overlapped his first, making an "x" across his waist. Once he was done, he headed to the doorway and slipped out into the main room. The others followed close behind. Glo paused a moment in the doorway to extinguish his staff. There was no sense in giving the goblins a target to aim at. As he stood there, someone shoved past him. It was Ruka. She had pushed him aside without a word. Glo gazed silently after her retreating form.

What was that all about? Shaking his head, he followed behind her.

9
CRASH AND BURN
The angry red ball streaked toward its target at incredible speed

T he stairs were a short distance away along the wall. They all
gathered there at the base of the stairwell, well hidden from
anyone or anything at the top. Lloyd ascended the stairs with
Ruka right behind. Glo waited until they were a couple of steps up,
then climbed up as well. Ves followed two steps behind him. Aksel
and Maya brought up the rear.

About twenty steps up, Ruka hissed, "Stop!"

Everyone froze. Lloyd did not turn around. "What is it?" he
whispered.

Ruka kept her voice low. "There's a trip wire right in front of
you—on the next step."

Glo narrowed his eyes, squinting at the step above Lloyd. Sure
enough, there was a thin wire stretched across the stairwell about
three inches above the step. It was very hard to see in this dim light.
Ruka must have excellent eyesight to have spotted it.

"Couldn't I just step over it?" Lloyd whispered.

"Sure—right into the next trip wire on the step above it," Ruka
answered, her voice dripping with sarcasm.

Lloyd's voice was filled with frustration. "Now what?"

Glo's eyes moved from Ruka to Ves. "I don't suppose either of
you know how to disable traps?"

Ves shook her head. Ruka folded her arms across her chest.
"What do I look like? A thief?"

Glo shrugged his shoulders. Ruka was a lot like Seth in tempera-
ment, but that was apparently where the similarities ended.

"Might as well head back down," Aksel called up in a semi-hushed voice.

They regrouped at the bottom of the stairs. The only avenue they hadn't tried was the door on the other side of the stairs. Lloyd went to check it out. Ruka followed him once again. The duo returned a short while later. They had found the kitchen, nothing more.

Silence fell over the group. Aksel's hand went to his chin, his head tilting to the side. Lloyd grasped the handles of his swords, twisting his hands on them impatiently. Ruka leaned against the wall, folding her arms in front of her. Ves gave her middle sister a look that practically screamed, *"I told you so."* Maya was the only one who did not appear pensive. She stared up at Glo expectantly, dimples dotting each side of her mouth. The corners of Glo's lips turned up in response. Her apparent faith in him was startlingly justified. He had just learned a new spell that would help in this situation—two, in fact. It was not without some risk, but it might be their only alternative. Glo's eyes swept around the group, but everyone remained silent. Shrugging his shoulders, he spoke up.

"I believe I might have an idea."

All heads turned in his direction. Glo followed his statement with a single word. *"Labes."*

There was no immediate effect from his viewpoint, but everyone else tilted their heads or squinted at him. Lloyd was the first to speak.

"You look kind of—blurry."

Glo chuckled. "That's the general idea."

"It's a spell of distortion," Aksel explained. "It will make him harder to hit."

"Hopefully," Glo added. The spell would help but it was not foolproof. He would still be a target as soon as he stepped out into the open.

Aksel eyed him curiously. "So, what other new tricks do you have?"

All heads turned to him once more. Glo's eyes swept around the group, momentarily halting on a particular pair of blue-green eyes. He suddenly felt rather warm. He also experienced a rather strange desire to show off. "Oh, I believe I have the perfect spell."

Aksel raised an eyebrow but otherwise remained silent.

Without another word, Glo spun around and headed for the door. He was still wrestling with himself, uncertain as to why he was acting this way. Normally he would have explained himself to Aksel, but when he looked into Ves's eyes, his mind suddenly clouded over.

"Wait!"

That had been Ves. Glo halted in mid-stride. He turned around just in time to see the young woman walking toward him. Glo stood there as if transfixed. As she closed the distance between them, Ves searched his eyes with her own. There was a strange intensity behind them, almost as if she were trying to read his thoughts. When she drew within arms' reach, Ves stopped. Glo continued to stare at her, dumbfounded. The corners of her mouth upturned slightly, and then her arm came up and touched him lightly on the shoulder. From the point of contact, a shimmering white sheen spread out across his body. Her hand then fell away.

"Maybe that will help," Ves almost whispered. She gazed up at him, her eyes no longer intent, but now mirroring real concern. She stood there a moment longer, then stepped back.

Glo lifted his arms and stared at the bright opaque sheen that now surrounded them. He looked over his shoulder and confirmed that it extended all around his body. He gazed back at Ves questioningly. "What is this?"

"A shield of the faith," Aksel answered for her.

A shield of the faith? That was a divine spell. It created a magical shield around a person that deflected most solid objects. Glo was quite touched by the gesture. A smile spread across his lips. "Thank you, Ves."

"You're welcome," she responded in a quiet voice.

He stood there a moment longer as mixed emotions played through his mind. He was nervous about what he was about to do, but that was now tempered with warm feelings for the enigmatic Ves. Abruptly, Glo spun around again. He marched forward with the words, "Here goes nothing."

As he exited from under the stairs, stones began to hurtle down around him. Some came rather close, but somehow they all missed. When Glo reached the center of the room, he stopped, reached into a bag at his waist and pulled out a pinch of sulfur. His arms began to twirl around in a circular pattern. He made a wide arc with them then drew his hands together at his waist. Glo then peered up towards the top of the lighthouse. He was just in time to see a stone hurtling directly for him. With no time to dodge out of the way, Glo flinched. Mere inches from his face, the rock hit the shimmering field that surrounded his body. It appeared to hang there for a moment, then it neatly bounced off to the side.

Glo let out a heavy sigh. *Thank you, Ves!*

His momentary relief was swiftly replaced with anger. He glared up at the top of the tower, barely making out shapes moving at the top of the stairwell. Glo's resolve hardened. He pushed his hands out in front of him, palms facing outward, toward the top of the lighthouse, and spoke a single word. "*Augue.*"

A small bright red ball of light appeared between his palms. It hung there for a split second, pulsing as the light intensified, then shot away toward the top of the tower. The angry red ball streaked toward its target at incredible speed. In less than a second, it traversed the distance to the top of the stairwell. As it neared its target, the ball suddenly expanded—it was now ten times its original size. It hung there for a fraction of a second longer, and then exploded. Bright red light flooded the top of the tower, accompanied by the *whoosh* of the expanding flames. High-pitched screams cascaded down from above—they were punctuated by a dreadful roar. It was a low, guttural sound that echoed off the inside walls of the stone tower.

"What was that?"

Glo's eyes had been fixed on the scene above. Gazing around now, he saw that the others had joined him in the center of the tower. "I'm not sure..."

Boom! A loud explosion suddenly rocked the building, the ground trembling beneath them. Glo shook his head in bewilderment. His spell wasn't supposed to do that.

"Oh, my gods!"

That was Ves. She was staring upwards, her expression incredulous. Glo followed her gaze his own jaw dropping. The entire top of the lighthouse had disappeared. A large patch of blue sky was now visible where the floor of the lantern room had been moments ago. Daylight streamed in, clearly illuminating the inside of the structure. Large cracks developed in the walls, starting from where the top floor had been, and swiftly running down the sides of the lighthouse. Small chunks of rock began to break away and careen downward, and it wouldn't be long before the entire tower came crashing down upon them.

Abruptly, Aksel's voice rang out. "Everyone out the front door! Now!"

Lloyd reacted immediately, scooping up Maya and sprinting toward the entrance. At the same moment, Ruka grabbed Aksel, lifting him up as if he weighed almost nothing, and bolted after Lloyd.

"I have legs, you know," the little cleric protested.

It was a strangely comical sight despite their impending danger, but Glo had no time to smile. Ves was suddenly at his side. She tried to grab him like Ruka had Aksel, but before she could, he looped his arm around her waist. Her face flushed with anger. "What are you doing?"

"We go together or not at all!" he declared.

The sound of straining metal caused them both to look up. The stairs above were coming apart and large chunks of the wall had now separated and began to careen downward. Ves immediately looped an arm around Glo's waist. "Together then!"

She rushed forward, dragging Glo with her. She was surprisingly strong for such a small woman, and he was hard pressed to keep up. They swiftly covered the distance to the doorway. The others had already passed through and waited on the other side. Glo and Ves were only a few feet away from safety when time ran out.

Barooooooommmmmm! The ground trembled violently as something large smashed into the floor behind them. The stone beneath their feet buckled and shifted. The duo stopped in their tracks, struggling to maintain their balance. Glo nearly fell, but Ves somehow managed to regain her footing and held onto him. Yet they were far from safe. As Glo teetered over, he caught a glimpse of a huge boulder bearing down on them. If they did not get out of its way, they would be ground to dust! Ves must have seen the terror in his eyes, and reacted without hesitation. Her grip tightened around his waist and then she sprang forward, making a mighty leap toward the open door. They practically flew those last few feet and shot through the doorway, landing with a heavy thud on the ground just beyond.

Baroooooommmmmmm! The duo huddled together just outside the tower as the earth shook violently beneath them. Taking a quick breath, Glo pulled Ves closer, covering them both with his robes. Less than a second later, a large cloud of dust expelled through the doorway and blew out all around them. Glo and Ves lay there quietly until the tremors subsided and the dust dissipated. Finally, Glo opened his eyes. The cloud was mostly gone. He slowly pulled back his robes, uncovering Ves. The young woman coughed and sputtered for a few moments, then peered up at Glo.

The two of them lay there, still holding onto each other, their faces mere inches apart. Her body felt warm and soft next to his. He could smell the scent of her hair, like a fresh ocean breeze and the heat of her breath fell across his face. Her eyes gazed into his, a mixture of emotions passing through them. Glo felt the blood rush to his cheeks as he stared back into those deep blue-green eyes.

Abruptly, Ves pushed herself away. She quickly sat up, her face flushing furiously. Glo was still confused by the sudden rush of emotion. He sat up, as well, his eyes sweeping the area. Aksel and Ruka both sat on the ground off to their left. Lloyd was seated over to their right, still holding Maya in his arms. The young man let out a heavy sigh. "Phew, that was close."

Maya giggled. "Thanks for saving me again, but you can put me down now."

Lloyd smiled sheepishly, gently setting the little girl down on her feet. Glo gazed upward and saw a dark cloud of smoke rising from the top of the tower far into the blue sky above. The structure itself had a number of cracks running down the sides, and small pieces of rubble began to rain down to the ground around them. Aksel coughed out some dust before trying to speak. "I suggest—cough, cough—we put a little more space between us and the lighthouse."

"Good idea," Glo agreed.

The six of them retreated along the path up the hill their attention focused on the burning lighthouse behind them. No one spoke until they drew near the dock. Aksel was the first to break the silence.

"Well, there goes our ride."

Glo turned around and saw their rowboat completely submerged underwater with a large stone in its very center. He let out a heavy sigh. It was a long swim back to the shore. Not to mention they needed that boat for their salvage operation. Suddenly, another explosion rocked the island. Flames now shot skyward from the top of the tower. It now looked more like a giant torch than a lighthouse.

Aksel glanced up at Glo. "A bit of overkill there?"

Glo's eyes remained fixed on the spectacle before him. His spell was definitely not supposed to do that. "Not intentionally. Just exactly what were they storing up there anyway?"

"Um—oil," Aksel said as if the answer should have been obvious.

Glo's eyes went wide. "Are you serious?"

There was not a hint of mirth in the cleric's expression.

Glo was dumbfounded. "Why would anyone use oil? Why wouldn't you just use magic?"

Aksel's hand went to his forehead. "Remember, spell casters are not common here on the east coast. That's one of the reasons we came out here in the first place."

The realization hit Glo all at once. If spell casters were rare, then so was magic. Things he took for granted, like magical lights, would not be as commonplace out here. He suddenly felt quite stupid. "Oh..."

"Well, I think it looks pretty," Maya said clapping her hands together and jumping up and down.

"I kind of like it, too," Ruka agreed.

There was a short pause then Ves chimed in. "I also agree."

Glo arched an eyebrow. Ves did not appear to be the type to approve of wanton destruction. The young woman appeared somewhat startled as their eyes met. She quickly glanced away from him, her face reddening slightly as she continued to speak. "Not that it's pretty or nice, mind you. Still, I also don't think you should be blamed. After all, you were just trying to protect us."

Glo was at a loss for words. He was touched by the unexpected support from the three sisters. He finally managed a quiet reply. "Thank you."

Aksel's tone had lightened as well. "Oh, well, there's no helping it now. But you have to admit Glo, you do have a certain affinity for fire spells."

A thin smile crossed Glo's lips. Aksel did have a point. This was the second time he had blown up a tower with a spell involving fire. He was about to agree when Lloyd interrupted them.

"Look at that!"

Glo followed the young man's gaze. Something came flying out of the flaming tower and landed on the ground not a dozen yards in front of them. Whatever it was, it was huge.

10
DEMON

It was goblin-like, with hard yellow eyes, long pointed ears, and a mouth full of razor-sharp teeth

A dozen yards back down the trail lay a large smoldering ball of fur. It was still for a few moments, then slowly uncurled itself and rose up onto all fours. A pair of baleful eyes fixed on them, and a menacing growl escaped a rather impressive set of jaws. The creature had the appearance of a wolf, but nearly twice the size, yet it was the face that sent chills up Glo's spine. It was goblin-like, with hard, yellow eyes, long pointed ears, and a mouth full of razor-sharp teeth.

"What is that thing?" Aksel asked, his tone betraying a mixture of curiosity and fear.

Lloyd's response was grim. "I don't know, but I don't like the way it's staring at us." The young warrior moved forward, drawing his blades and positioning himself between the creature and the rest of the group.

"Barghest," Glo hissed. Now that he saw it face-to-face, he remembered reading about it. The pictures in his father's books did not do it justice.

"Barghest?" Aksel repeated. "A demon?"

Glo nodded. "A shape-shifting demon. They take on the form of goblins, or wolves, or even mix them." He paused and gulped, his mouth suddenly dry. "But make no mistake. It is neither. It is all demon. Hell-bent on killing and devouring innocents, body and soul."

The barghest remained still, growling ominously as it continued to stare at them. Its malevolent eyes shifted around intelligently, assessing the group. Deep down inside, Glo was petrified, yet he pushed down his fear and moved forward, taking up a position next to Lloyd.

He was not about to let this thing get anywhere near the sisters. The creature was staring at neither him nor Lloyd; instead, staring past them. Glo chanced a look over his shoulder. The demon was staring directly at Ves. Strangely, the young woman did not appear afraid. In fact, she stared back at the demon, her eyes burning with anger.

Glo did not know what to make of it. These three sisters were not easily frightened. Glo turned his gaze back toward the demon. The creature was now acting rather oddly, shifting uncertainly on its four legs. It gave one angry snort, then spun around and broke for the water. It loped across the isle and reached the water's edge before any of them could react. The creature then leapt into the air and dove into the sea. Lloyd led the way as they rushed to the water's edge. They had almost reached the spot where the demon entered the water when the creature resurfaced. It was fifty yards off shore, and took off west at a fast pace toward the mainland.

"We could be in for more trouble if it's going for reinforcements," Aksel noted.

"Don't worry. I'll find out what it's up to," Ruka responded. She pushed her way through them and ran to the edge of the isle. She paused a moment, turning toward them. "You better keep an eye on Maya while I'm gone. If anything happens to her, I will hold you responsible." Her eyes shifted from Lloyd to Aksel then Glo. She then spun around and launched herself into the water, disappearing beneath the surface.

They stared in silence after the blonde girl. About a half minute later, she resurfaced about one hundred yards west of the island. She swam at a pace to rival the barghest. These girls were fast swimmers indeed. They were nearly as fast as their dolphin friends.

Lloyd turned toward Ves. "Will she be alright?"

Ves appeared genuinely surprised by the question. "Ruka? Don't worry about her. She can handle herself."

Glo stared at Ves, his eyes narrowing. *Is she serious? A barghest is nothing to trifle with.* Yet Ves appeared completely unconcerned. A vision of the large stone breaking on Maya's shoulder flashed through his mind. He also remembered how easily Ves had dragged him around the lighthouse. In fact, she had practically flown him through the door with that last leap. Furthermore, the barghest ran from them without a fight. That was definitely not demon-like. The creature had appeared almost scared—right after it had locked eyes with Ves. Maybe it sensed something they did not about the three sisters. Yet if that were true, what was it about them that they could scare off a demon?

His thoughts were interrupted by a heavy stomping sound. The Boulder had finally reached the island. The stone golem stopped next to the rowboat and lifted it out of the water. Water drained through the boat's bottom as the golem held it aloft. The Boulder then carried the now-empty boat to shore. It trudged up with it onto the beach and gently laid the boat down on dry land. The golem then stood back and went still.

When they reached the boat, they saw a large hole in its very center. Aksel stepped into the boat, stood over the gap, and cast a spell to mend it. A magical aura appeared around the hole and the gap shrunk considerably, but was still too large to make the boat seaworthy. Ves stepped into the rowboat alongside Aksel, and cast a mending spell as well. The two of them continued until the hole was completely closed and had vanished. With the boat now repaired, they both disembarked.

"There," Ves said, admiring their handiwork. Without warning, she bent down and picked up the boat, easily lifting it into the air as if it weighed nothing. She walked with it out onto the dock, bent down, and placed it gently back in the water.

Glo was incredulous. He cast a glance at Aksel. Aksel stared back at him with an eyebrow raised. He shifted his gaze to Lloyd. The young man's mouth was agape. Glo peered back at Ves. She still stood there, a pleased expression on her face.

Glo slowly walked up to stand next to her. "Um, Ves?"

Ves peered up at him with a pleasant smile on her face. His expression must have betrayed his thoughts, though, for her eyes suddenly went wide. Her hand went to her mouth, and she began to blush furiously.

"Oh, my," she gasped.

Glo was completely bewildered. She looked like an ordinary

young woman, but there was no denying the feat of strength he had just witnessed. Not even Lloyd could have lifted that boat so easily.

He spoke to her in a soft voice. "Can we talk?"

"Okay," she answered, her voice filled with trepidation.

Glo ushered her to the end of the dock. Ves folded her arms across her chest and turned away from him. Her gaze was firmly fixed on the mainland as if she were unable to look him in the eye.

"Ves?"

She slowly turned around. "Yes?"

"I really don't mean to pry. After all, you are entitled to your privacy..."

Ves stared at him with those vivid blue-green eyes. Glo suddenly found it hard to concentrate. "...but we are in this together... and as you may have noticed, we do try to watch out for each other..."

She continued to stare at him a trace of a smile appearing on her lips. "I have noticed."

"Yes..." Glo cleared his throat. He had completely lost his train of thought. "Well, um..." *What was he was saying?* "It's just..." *Something about watching out for each other? Yes. That was it.* "...it's hard to look out for one another... if we don't know each other's strengths... and weaknesses..."

"Ah-ha." Ves nodded. Her smile widened just a bit as she continued to stare at him with an innocent expression.

Glo opened his mouth to speak again, but then stopped. *Why is this so hard?* He took a deep breath and cleared his mind, then reached out and gently grasped her shoulders. "Look, Ves, we are just trying to look out for you and your sisters. You agreed to help us, and we want to make sure you get through this safe and sound."

"I can see that," Ves replied. Mixed emotions played through her eyes, but then swiftly faded. She gently pushed his arms away. "But it is really unnecessary. My sisters and I can take care of ourselves."

Glo felt disappointed by her sudden coldness. "I am coming to realize that. Look, as I said before, you are entitled to your secrets, but I thought we'd proven you can trust us."

"If only it were that easy." She let out a deep sigh, then turned away again, folding her arms across her chest once more.

"It is," Glo insisted. "We are all different. I'm an elf. Aksel's a gnome. Lloyd's a human. You haven't met Seth yet, but he's a halfling. We all come from different races and backgrounds, but we have learned to trust and even depend on each other."

Ves spun around again, though her arms were still folded across her chest, and her expression remained impassive. Glo continued despite her apparent indifference.

"And that is because we all believe in the same things. Everyone deserves to be treated fairly no matter what his or her background. No one has the right to impose their will upon another, be it through force of arms or any other means. We have spent the last few weeks taking down monsters and people who believed otherwise. And we will continue to do so."

Glo had gotten a bit loud there at the end. His eyes briefly flickered toward the isle where he noted Lloyd and Aksel staring back at him, both wearing curious expressions. Glo merely shrugged and turned back to Ves. Her arms were still folded, but her expression had softened. He might have cracked the ice after all. Glo took a deep breath and tried one last time.

"One thing you can count on. No matter how different you are, we will be the first people to accept you."

Ves eyes began to glisten with moisture, her hands falling to her sides. After a moment of silence, she spoke. "You are indeed extraordinary people. Against my better judgment, I do find myself trusting you." She paused for a moment as if searching for the appropriate words. "It is obvious that my sisters and I are different, yet—somehow I do believe that you would understand if you knew the truth."

For a moment, it appeared as if she were going to say more, but then she stopped herself, her eyes falling toward the dock. "Alas, I cannot. My sisters and I are on a quest, and I made a promise. A promise that I would not divulge our true nature to anyone until that quest is over." She glanced back up at him, her internal struggle quite apparent on her face.

Glo felt suddenly torn at the thought of hurting her. "I am truly sorry. I did not mean to cause you any distress. Forget I even asked."

A smile spread across Ves' lips. She reached up and wiped the moisture from her eyes. "You are a true gentlemen, Glolindir. I will swear this to you. Once our quest is over, I will seek you out and reveal the truth to you. Perhaps then you can even come and meet my father, as you wanted."

Glo found himself smiling in response. "I look forward to it."

"For now, though, we will help you with your mission as we promised."

"That would be most appreciated."

"Now if you will excuse me."

She flashed him a bright smile, then hurried off back down the dock past Aksel. Maya had wandered off toward the burning lighthouse, and Lloyd was having a hard time catching her. Glo walked back down the pier, rejoining Aksel and relaying his conversation with Ves. They both watched as the older girl chased her little sister around the base of the lighthouse. Lloyd came back to join them, and Glo repeated what had been said.

When Glo finished, Aksel appeared pensive. "Well that told us a whole lot of nothing."

"At least they're on our side." Lloyd pointed out.

Aksel's response was somber. "Hopefully it'll stay that way. If Seth were here, I don't think he would be very trusting of them."

Glo snorted. "Seth isn't trusting of anyone. Speaking of Seth, shouldn't he be back by now?"

The trio peered over toward the mainland. There was no sign of their halfling companion nor the archer, Martan.

Aksel's expression grew even more concerned. "Yes, he has been gone for a long time."

"I'll send Raven up the coast to see if she can find them," Glo offered.

Aksel nodded. "Good idea."

11
ANGEL OF MERCY
The brilliant blue light lit up her face, revealing her intense concentration

Martan lay at the foot of the cliff in a heap. Seth knelt over the archer and examined him. He was still alive, but just barely. Luckily, the cliff here was not a sheer drop or the outcome would have been decidedly different. When the two of them had jumped off, they had slid down the steep slope. They would probably have been fine if that wolf hadn't caught up with them.

Seth had been focused on the cliff face below them. They were moving quite fast—there were outcroppings, cracks, and small bushes to navigate around. Thankfully, he and Martan were agile enough to circumvent those obstacles. In between sliding, twisting, and turning, Seth had managed to keep track of the archer's progress. They had made it halfway down the cliff side when a grey blur slammed into Martan. The archer was thrown completely off balance.

Seth watched in horror as Martan and the grey form went tumbling out of control the rest of the way down the cliff. When Seth finally arrived at the bottom, he found the archer in a heap on top of the wolf's body. The wolf was dead. It had inadvertently saved the man it just tried to kill.

Seth smiled briefly at the irony of the situation, but his mirth quickly faded. Martan was seriously hurt. Seth did not know how bad the archer was injured, but he had enough medical background to know it was not good. A rudimentary knowledge of medicine was a necessity when you grew up in a family of thieves and cutthroats. It would be a bit too obvious if you ran to the healers after every robbery or murder in the area. Not that it happened often, but hazards came with that kind of job. Since it was assumed he would one day join the family business, Seth had been taught the basics of healing. Still it was not something he readily shared, and it didn't seem to matter with Aksel around. Now, however, it might mean the difference between life and death for poor Martan.

Seth did not want to move the man, for fear of internal injuries. He took a blanket from his backpack and covered the hapless archer. He then put his hands over the man's body and began to scan for injuries. He had been taught to run his hands a few inches over the body and feel for changes in temperature or energy.

This probably comes as second nature to Aksel.

Seth, on the other hand, was having trouble finding anything. He finished one pass over Martan's body with no success. The archer appeared worse now, his skin paler and his breathing weaker. Seth took a deep breath and forced himself to remain calm. He started the process all over again, passing his hands slowly over Martan's body. As he reached his upper torso, he felt something. There was a drop in temperature around the archer's lungs.

I found it!

Now, of course, he had to heal it. Seth hoped to the gods that it was merely cracked ribs. He calmed his mind and called forth the energy to heal. Seth felt the warmth build in his abdomen and slowly spread up to his heart. Finally, it expanded into his hands. His palms glowed with a white-blue light, not nearly as intense as Aksel's, but bright nonetheless. The light filtered down from his hands and over Martan's chest. Seth held his hands as still as possible, letting the healing energy flow into the archer for a long while. Martan's breathing finally steadied and slowly became stronger.

Seth sat back and wiped his brow. His hand was full of sweat. *Healing's definitely hard work.* Aksel made it look easy, but it actually took a lot out of you. Seth reached into his backpack and pulled out a canteen. He took a long swig, cooling himself off. Martan was out of danger for now, but he was still not fully healed. Seth had merely stabilized him for now, but had used up all his energy doing so. All he could do now is keep the archer warm and hope that his friends would come looking for them soon.

It was late in the day, the sun hidden behind the tall cliffs that bordered the western edge of the beach. The sands were now completely blanketed in shadow. There was a slight chill in the air, signifying the impending fall of night. Lloyd and Glo sat in front of a glowing fire as Ves prepared dinner. Aksel was down by the water, helping Maya collect seashells. A little more than an hour had passed since they returned from the lighthouse isle. Lloyd, Glo, and Aksel set up camp in the rocky area where they had first met the three sisters. In the meantime, Ves and Maya went fishing. The girls reappeared a short while later with a fish in each hand. When asked, Ves explained, "Using a pole is unfair to the fish."

Normally, Glo would have questioned her response, but he was somewhat distracted. Seth and Martan had been gone for too long now, and the more time passed, the more anxious he became. Abruptly, Glo's anxiety turned into full-fledged fear. He shot up from his seat.

Lloyd stood up next to him. "What is it?"

Glo's eyes were fixed on the northern sky. "It's Raven. Something is definitely wrong."

He strode down to the water's edge with Lloyd and Ves behind him, dinner all but forgotten. They met up with Aksel and Maya.

"What's going on?" Aksel asked his expression one of deep concern.

"It's Raven," Ves responded, nodding northward.

The eastern horizon had turned dark—the blanket of night moving quickly across the heavens. Glo strained his eyes, but saw no sign of Raven as of yet.

Abruptly Maya cried out. "There she is!"

Glo followed the young girl's finger and barely made out a black speck in the darkening sky. *Wow, she has good eyesight. Better than an elf's, in fact.*

Less than a minute passed before Raven landed on Glo's arm. She squawked in her tiny voice, *"Perdaur for. No' sii."*

"Half a league north. On the beach," Ves translated.

"Martan neva gurtha."

Glo's eyes went wide. Ves let out a short gasp.

Lloyd stared at them both with clear apprehension. "What is it?"

Glo's eyes shifted from Lloyd to Aksel. "It's Martan. It's not good."

Ves' face darkened her expression grave. "What can we do to help?"

Glo's mind raced as he thought it through. It would take a half hour at best to get to them on foot, but Martan might not last that long. However, if Ves could swim as fast as Ruka, she could be there in half that time. "Can you to go to them? You may be their only hope."

Ves nodded. "I can, but you'll have to keep an eye on Maya."

"We will watch her," Aksel promised.

"Very well," Ves agreed. Without another word, she waded into the surf. Just before diving in, she called back over her shoulder, "Oh, and Maya?"

"Yes, Ves?" the young girl responded.

"Behave yourself."

Seth felt relieved when Raven showed up. He knew it was only a matter of time until help would arrive. What he was not prepared for was the manner of its arrival. Dusk had fallen. He sat quietly next to Martan, keeping close watch over the archer's condition. There was a chill in the air, and he wished he could make a fire. Unfortunately, that might also attract the wrong kind of attention.

Seth and Martan had run across a small party of goblins in the forest above. What's worse was they had wolves with them. They had taken care of the goblins, and eluded the wolves, or so Seth had thought. That one wolf, however, was Martan's undoing. At this point, there was no telling what still lurked in the forest above. Therefore, Seth remained in the dark with Martan, vigilantly watching the surrounding area. His hands instinctively went to his knives when he saw a form emerge from the water. He watched cautiously as the figure came out of the surf and up onto the shore.

Seth quickly identified the form as a young human female. She paused a moment, her head turning from side to side. Her gaze finally focused in their direction, and then strode up the beach directly towards them. As she drew closer, Seth got a better look at her. She had long pale hair, currently wet and matted to her scalp. From shoulder to mid-calf, she wore a tight-fitting dress with a strange metallic sheen. In the dusky light, Seth was not quite sure of the color, perhaps copper or bronze.

As the young woman approached, she called out softly, "Are you Seth?"

"I might be," he replied warily. "Who wants to know?"

She stopped a few feet away from them. "I'm Ves. Glolindir sent me."

"Then where is he?" Seth quickly scanned the surrounding area, making sure that no one else was creeping up on them.

"He's back at our camp a half a league down the beach. He is waiting there with Aksel, Lloyd, and my little sister. Raven told us where you were. She also said Martan was near death. I could get here the fastest, so they sent me."

That sounds reasonable. Still Seth was not sure how this girl made it nearly two miles up the beach in the mere minutes. His eyes fell on Martan. The archer was still out cold. He appeared very pale. If he didn't get more healing, he was not going to make it. Seth's gaze shifted back to Ves. She seemed harmless enough. She stood there with her hands folded in front of her, not moving a muscle.

Seth shrugged. "Very well. Martan took a nasty fall down the cliff. I was able to stabilize him, but he needs far more than I can do. He should not be moved. Can you go back and bring Aksel?"

"That won't be necessary," Ves replied evenly. "May I?" she asked politely, nodding her head toward the wounded archer.

Seth let out an exasperated sigh. "Fine." He stepped back and out of the way. She was not going to find out anything different than he had already told her, but if it meant getting Aksel here quicker, then he would not argue the point.

Ves knelt down next to the unconscious archer. Just as Seth had done earlier, she ran her hands a few inches over the top of his body. She stopped over his chest and concentrated on that area.

At least she found the right spot. "Like I said, he needs a lot more healing," Seth repeated impatiently.

"Then we shall give it to him," she responded. She lifted her right hand and pointed a finger at his rib cage. To Seth's surprise, a brilliant blue light appeared at her fingertip. It was far brighter than anything Seth could produce. It quickly spread out, enveloping Martan's upper torso. The light grew more intense, to the point where Seth had to shade his eyes. This strange young woman was putting out a tremendous amount of energy. In fact, she was quite possibly as strong a healer as Aksel.

Seth watched in fascination as Ves kept the energy flowing into the unconscious archer. The brilliant blue light lit up her face, revealing her intense concentration. She knelt there the entire time, intent on healing his wounds, never complaining or faltering once. As Seth watched on, he realized this was no ordinary woman. He was quite impressed with her strength of will. After a full twenty minutes, the intense blue light began to fade. When it finally went out, Ves sat back and took a deep breath.

"That should do for now," she pronounced.

It was now completely dark. Seth reached into his backpack and took out a small covered lamp. He chanced lighting it, holding it close to the archer. In the lamp light, he could clearly see that the color had returned to Martan's face. Then, much to his surprise, Martan began to stir. The archer opened his eyes and actually began to sit up!

"Hold on there," Ves cried. She leaned forward and grabbed his shoulders, stopping him from rising further. "You took a nasty fall and almost died," she continued.

"Who are you?" Martan asked groggily. His eyes finally focused on her, and he blinked a few times. His expression was one of disbelief. "Are you an angel?" he asked in a hushed voice.

"Hardly," Ves responded.

Something suddenly clicked in Seth's mind. The long blond hair, the bronze shimmering dress, and the angel reference—it sounded too much like those sailor's stories from the tavern. Seth spoke tentatively. "Excuse me, Ves."

"Yes?" She did not take her eyes off Martan.

"You didn't happen to travel up here on dolphin back by any

chance?" Hearing it out loud, he felt foolish for even saying it.

Ves peered at him with curiosity. "Yes. As a matter of fact I did. How did you know that?"

He was right! Seth did his best to remain nonchalant. "Oh, just a lucky guess." This young woman, Ves, definitely had something to do with the rescue of those sailors. He was certain of it.

"Angel," Martan repeated as he lay back down and closed his eyes. "Beautiful angel."

"That's good," Ves said in a soothing voice. She adjusted the blanket around him. "Rest for now."

Ves stood up and motioned for Seth to follow her. She led him a few yards away from the sleeping Martan. "That is the most I can do. His ribs are healed, as is the internal bleeding. What he really needs now is to eat and sleep. That would be best done back at camp."

Seth raised an eyebrow. "Dolphin ride?"

A thin smile graced Ves' lips. "Yes. We shall ride dolphins. Gather your things and meet me down by the water." With that, the young woman spun around and headed down toward the surf.

The moon had risen in the east. It was low in the night sky, its silvery light tracing a long line from the horizon to the shore. It lit up the waters, clearly outlining Ves as she walked down to the edge of the water. He heard some strange clicking and squealing noises come from the young woman. A short way off shore, another form reared up out of the surf. It practically danced across the surface.

That is most definitely a dolphin. The creature plunged back into the water and disappeared from sight. Seth smiled to himself as he went to gather his pack. This was going to be interesting. He checked briefly on Martan. The archer slept soundly, his color good and his breathing regular. Leaving him, he went down to the water's edge.

"How is he doing?" Ves asked.

"Sound asleep."

"Good." Ves pointed out into the water. "Our rides are here. I have talked with them, and you may ride on one's back. I will go fetch Martan."

"Do you need a hand with him?"

"No, that won't be necessary." Ves spun on her heels and headed up the beach toward the resting archer.

Seth watched her for a moment, then shrugged and entered the surf. Two dolphins waited out in the water, side by side. He waded out to them and easily climbed on one's back. Once mounted, Seth saw a figure walking down toward the beach, carrying a second figure. It was Ves, holding Martan as if he weighed no more than a child.

Note to self. Do not piss this woman off, Seth thought wryly. A sudden smirk crossed his lips. *Well, maybe not too much.*

12
DARK PLOTS BREWING
By the way—why is the lighthouse burning?

Aksel collected seashells with Maya while keeping an eye out for Ves. Glo stood by the fire, cooking dinner in the young woman's absence. Lloyd busily put up tents for their overnight stay. Nearly an hour had gone by since Ves left. Darkness had fallen, but the night was lit by the silvery glow of the rising moon.

Maya was the first to spot the returning companions. She jumped up and down, pointing out into the surf. "They're back!"

Aksel followed Maya's finger and saw movement a short distance off shore. He immediately recognized the dorsal fins of two dolphins traveling side by side. A small figure sat on the back of one of the marine mammals. Another figure was crouched over the other. A third figure was in the water, hanging onto the hunched figure.

Glo and Lloyd came down to join them. The four of them watched with fascination as the strange procession swam to within a few yards of the shore. When they finally stopped, the figure in the water stood up. The moonlight glimmered off its shiny outfit, confirming it was Ves.

The shorter figure jumped off its dolphin and cried out with excitement. "That was cool!"

Aksel smiled. That was most definitely Seth. Ves picked up the figure that could only be Martan off the other dolphin's back. She held him easily in her arms. The young woman exchanged some clicking noises and squeals with the dolphins. Almost immediately, the two aquatic mammals took off back out into the deeper water. Ves and Seth waded through the surf and onto shore. She briefly explained Martan's condition then proceeded with him up toward the camp. The others followed, Seth falling in beside Aksel.

As they walked up the beach, Seth leaned over and whispered softly to Aksel, "Does she do that often?"

"Do you mean ride dolphins, talk to them, or carry heavy objects like it was nothing?"

"Yes."

Aksel shook his head and chuckled. "It's good to have you back, Seth."

They reached the camp and Ves gently placed Martan down in one of the tents. Lloyd brought blankets for them to wrap themselves in while their clothes dried. Ves took the wet clothes and laid them out by the fire. Meanwhile, Glo passed out plates of cooked fish.

As Glo handed Seth his plate, the halfling asked in a casual voice, "By the way—why is the lighthouse burning?"

Glo dropped the plate in Seth's lap, spun around, and walked away without a word.

Aksel tried hard not to laugh. "Long story. We'll tell you later."

The reunited companions had dinner with the two Greymantle sisters. Ves sat next to Martan, hovering over him like a mother hen. Aksel noticed Glo eyeing the pair. When he caught Aksel staring at him, Glo gave him a wan smile and shrugged his shoulders. Seth related his and Martan's story while they ate. A couple of miles north, they ran into a small party of goblins. The goblins were riding wolf mounts.

Aksel truly disliked goblins. They were small, yellow-skinned creatures, about the same size as halflings. They were typically scrawny, except for their large heads, which were far too big for their bodies. Goblins were nasty, though. They traveled in packs and attacked anyone unlucky enough to cross their path. Worse, these filthy little creatures would eat whoever or whatever they caught.

Seth and Martan, both accustomed to the wild, managed to evade the goblins at first. As luck would have it, the wind shifted and the wolves caught their scent. The duo was forced to retreat up into the trees. Through a combination of Martan's archery, Seth's acrobatic/

knife wielding skills, and the clever use of some modified smoke bombs, the pair dispatched the goblins and a number of wolves. The rest of the pack chased them down to the cliff's edge. Having no other options, Seth and Martan jumped. Martan had been severely injured on the way down, but luckily, Seth was able to stabilize him.

Aksel was surprised that Seth had healing skills. They would have to talk more when they got a chance. When Seth was done with his tale, Aksel told the story of their encounter at the lighthouse.

When he was finished, Seth wore a wide smirk. "Don't worry, Glo. It's not like that's the first time you've blown something up. Admittedly, the top of the tower at Stone Hill only had a small cauldron of oil on it. This beats that by far!"

Glo refused to respond to Seth's taunting. Instead, he stood up, snatched the halfling's empty plate out of his hand, and stalked off toward the water with the dirty dishes.

Seth continued, undaunted by his friend's reaction. "So then, is anyone else seeing a pattern here? We find a scouting party of goblins to the north where the fake lighthouse signal would have been. Then you find the lighthouse occupied by another party of goblins and a goblin demon. I'm just saying, probably not a coincidence."

"You may just be on to something." Aksel's hand went absently to his chin. "Finding goblins at both sites could very well point to a conspiracy. That, in turn, might explain all the sunken ships off the coast."

Glo walked back up from the water. "Goblins are not bright enough to come up with that kind of scheme themselves. A barghest, on the other hand, just might be. However, sinking ships does not seem like a demon's style. They are more likely to be found in the center of wanton death and destruction."

Seth laid back on the sand and peered up at the night sky. His voice sounded distant, as if he were thinking aloud. "Agreed. Someone else is pulling the strings here—someone who is far more interested in disrupting trade and looting treasure." Abruptly he sprang up. "Is it me, or is this all starting to sound vaguely familiar?"

There was a moment of silence, and then Lloyd cried out. "You mean the orc raids on the caravans!"

"Exactly." Seth nodded approvingly at the young man.

Aksel continued to rub his chin. *This was all starting to make sense.* The attacks on the caravans and the sinking of the ships could be related. The means were similar, using orcs or goblins to do the dirty work.

Lloyd wore an expression of deep concentration. "Do you think the same dark mages that were funding the orcs could also have hired out these goblins?"

Aksel was impressed. Lloyd was thinking things through now, both on and off the battlefield. "I thought the same thing. The real question though is why? How does disrupting trade to Ravenford benefit these mages?"

Glo let out a gasp. All the color had drained out of the wizard's face.

Lloyd placed a hand on his friend's shoulder. "What is it, Glo?"

The tall elf turned toward Martan. When he spoke, his voice was hushed. "Do you remember what Voltark said that time you caught him talking to himself?"

Martan's face went blank. He appeared rather weary, but managed to recite the words. *"Things are going as planned. We have them cut off on all sides."*

A sudden chill went up Aksel's spine. That sounded far too much like what was happening here on the coast and along the west road. *This was bad.*

"Well, things certainly took a dark turn," Seth commented.

Lloyd's eyes swept around the circle. "Let me get this straight. Are you saying the dark mages and Voltark were all in league with each other?"

Aksel nodded. "That pretty much sums it up."

"So then the Serpent Cult is behind all of this—the attacks on the west road, the sunken ships, and the plot against Andrella?"

"It would appear so," Glo agreed.

It grew quiet as they all huddled around the crackling campfire. The night air had become decidedly chilly. The dark shadows outside the firelight appeared to lengthen, despite the silvery moon overhead.

Ves' voice broke the eerie silence. "What is this Serpent Cult?"

Martan, the expert on the matter, repeated the story he had told them back in the Dead Forest and again in Ravenford. He related everything he knew about the Black Adders and the Serpent Cult. The entire group listened in silence until the archer was done. When Martan finished, Ves stared at him intently.

"You're certain that these mages can shape shift into serpents?" she asked slowly.

"I never actually saw Voltark change, if that's what you're asking," Martan told her. "But those were the rumors that were flying around, even in Kai-Arborous."

Ves appeared thoughtful. "Interesting." Her voice sounded distant, her mind a million miles away.

Without warning, Maya jumped up from her seat by the fire.

"Did you hear that Ves? Shape-shifters. Ooh... scary." The little girl made a frightened face, her tone spooky as she waved her hands in the air as if afraid. After a moment or two, she fell over onto the sand giggling and snorting wildly.

Seth's eyes flickered to Aksel. "Does she do that often?"

Aksel nodded. "Seems like it."

"Maya, get a hold of yourself," Ves admonished.

Maya ignored her sister and continued to roll on the ground, snorting and laughing. The conversation halted at that point, everyone waiting for the little girl to finish her bout of snorts and giggles. Finally, Maya laughed herself out. Obviously bored, she got up and traipsed down to the water's edge.

Glo sat forward. "Just one more thing. Maltar asked me to check the cargo for a pendant he was expecting."

"A pendant?" Seth repeated. "Did he say there was anything special about it?"

Glo shook his head. "Not really. He just said he would make it worth our while if we found it."

Seth smirked. "How much you want to bet it's some kind of artifact?"

Aksel stroked his chin. "If Maltar wants it that badly, then you may be right. But we'll know for sure if we do find it."

It was late in the evening now, and the chill in the air became more pervasive. They all decided it was time to bed down for the night. Martan offered to take the first watch. Ves said she would only allow it if she could stand watch with him. Martan didn't argue the point.

Glo had been resting peacefully when he heard something outside the tent. His eyes snapped open. It was still dark—if he had to guess, about four in the morning. The flap of the tent pulled back, revealing the silhouette of a small figure. It was Seth. He motioned to Glo to step outside. Aksel still slept peacefully under his blankets, so Glo got up as silently as he could and exited the tent.

The moon hung just above the top of the cliff as it traveled west across the sky. Its pale light still illuminated the beach below, giving it a silver sheen. Soon the whitish orb would drop behind the cliff face. The beach would be totally shrouded in darkness until the sun rose a few hours from now. Seth led Glo down toward the water where another figure awaited them. It sat on a rock facing the sea. In the moonlight, Glo could clearly see short pale hair and a leather tunic. It was Ruka. She had finally returned.

"I see you two have met."

"Yes," Seth and Ruka replied simultaneously. The duo cast a sidelong glance at each other, not sounding very trustful. Glo found their behavior rather amusing. What he heard next, though, wiped any traces of a smile from his face. Ruka kept her eyes fixed on the sea as she related the details of her chase.

"I followed the demon to the shore. Once on land, it took off up the cliffs and into the forest. I tracked it for few miles north, where it turned inland. A couple of miles west, it entered a large clearing."

Ruka paused and spun around to face him. In the pale moonlight, he could see her serious expression.

"There must have been over a hundred goblins camped there. There were also wolves and wargs sleeping around the campsite. When the demon arrived, the entire camp came to life. The wolves began howling, and the smarmy little creatures came pouring out of their tents."

Ruka paused again. Glo estimated their chances against a small army of goblins and wolves. No matter how he figured it, they were sorely outmatched. Ruka continued with her story.

"The demon marched through the camp, with all the little toadies following it. As the thing got close to the center, five black-robed figures came out of a big tent. The creature and the black robes stood there for a minute or so. There was a lot of hand waving going on, but there was too much noise from the twerpy little goblins and their stupid howling wargs to hear what they were saying. After that the demon and the black robes went into the big tent."

Ruka jumped down off the rock and stretched her lithe form.

"I figured I had seen enough so I headed back. It wouldn't surprise me though, to find an entire army of goblins at our doorstep in a few hours."

Glo had to agree. That was indeed what they could expect. "Thank you, Ruka. I believe you are right. It won't be long before we're neck-deep in goblins. Without your timely warning, we'd be in for the fight of our lives. At least now we have some time to decide what to do."

"It also confirms what we already thought. The Serpent Cult is definitely behind all this," Seth pointed out.

Ruka stared at him curiously. "The what?"

Glo quickly repeated their discussion from last night. Ruka's reaction was a bit different from her sisters, though. Her eyes gleamed, and she rubbed her hands together. "Sounds like there might be something of real interest down in those ships."

"It's definitely worth a look," Seth agreed his voice ripe with anticipation.

"Um, you two do realize that we might have to fight off an entire army of goblins to get to whatever is down there?" Glo reminded them.

"And?" Ruka and Seth said in unison.

If things hadn't just gotten so dangerous, Glo might have laughed out loud.

Ruka eyed Seth speculatively. "I like your priorities."

"I could say the same," Seth replied.

Glo shook his head. "I hate to interrupt this mutual admiration society, but I think we should wake Aksel and tell him what's going on."

A short while later, Ruka finished repeating her tale to Aksel. All signs of sleepiness left the gnome's eyes once she was done. "It sounds like it won't be long before we're neck-deep in goblins."

"That's exactly what I said," Glo half laughed.

"We should probably start the salvage operation as early as possible," Aksel mused aloud. "But a party that size will take a while to mobilize. He paused, stifling a yawn. "There are still a couple more hours until dawn. Since we really can't do anything until it is light, I suggest we all get a bit more sleep."

"Probably a good idea," Glo nodded.

They all went to the tents and tried to fall back asleep, or in Glo's case, rest. All except for Seth, who remained on watch. Glo found it difficult to relax, especially knowing what would soon be on their doorstep. The elven wizard lay on his blanket, trying his best to meditate in preparation for what was sure to be an eventful day.

13
THE SUNKEN SHIPS

The sunken ship lay partially on its side, its tall masts jutting out at an angle away from the reef

Lloyd's eyes snapped open, immediately alert. He heard breathing to his left—Martan lay peacefully under his blankets. Lloyd silently rose and gathered his things. He carefully lifted the tent flap and exited, leaving Martan to his much-needed rest. The sun rose over the sea to the east. Still low on the horizon, the bright orb glowed with an orange hue, its light reflecting off the waters, making them appear as if aflame. The sky was clear, foretelling another beautiful day. Lloyd immediately spotted Seth sitting on a rock down by the water's edge. No one else appeared to be about. Lloyd strapped on his swords and strolled down to join him.

"Morning, Seth. Guess I'm the first one up?"

"Not by far. The sisters are already out fishing. It's interesting that they don't use poles or anything."

"Ves said it was unfair to the fish." Lloyd scanned the waters for any sign of the girls.

"Yeah," Seth scoffed, "like that's real important."

"It is to them. They have some kind of connection with the sea creatures."

Seth spun around to face him. "Yeah, about that—Aksel told me a bit about the sisters. What do you make of them?"

Lloyd paused to gather his thoughts. "They seem nice enough. I mean Ves is, and Maya is cute. Ruka is a little rough, but not any more than you are." He finished with a thin smile.

Seth nodded a slight smirk on his lips. "Point taken, but what about all these strange abilities they have? Doesn't that concern you at all?"

Lloyd stretched his body as he answered. "Honestly, I don't think they're all that strange."

"Really?"

"Well, yeah. Then again, I'm used to strange," Lloyd admitted. "After all, as a spiritblade I can do things that most people can't—and I haven't even scratched the surface yet. You should see some of the things my father can do."

"I would imagine they're quite impressive."

"Very—and look at Glo. Kid all you want, but that fireball took off the top of the lighthouse and incinerated a whole platoon of goblins. That demon looked pretty singed, too."

"I wish I had been there to see it." Seth chuckled softly, a wide grin spreading across his face.

"And look at yourself, Seth. Half the time, I don't even know where you are. How many wizards have you killed in the last few weeks? You're pretty darn deadly, if you ask me."

The grin faded from Seth's face, his expression turning grave. He spun around to face the sea, speaking softly over his shoulder. "Thank you, Lloyd."

The response took Lloyd by surprise. He was so used to Seth's sarcastic wit that he expected a smart comeback. Yet Seth appeared almost humbled by the compliment. *Just what kind of upbringing had Seth had?* Lloyd wondered. His own father was a tough taskmaster, but even he gave out encouragement now and then. Seth, on the other hand, acted as if he never heard a kind word in his life. Lloyd had no idea how to respond. He stood quietly looking out to sea until Seth broke the silence.

"So you don't find the sisters just a bit off?"

Lloyd shrugged. "Well they definitely have some kind of secret, but whatever it is, it's really their business. I'm sure they'll tell us eventually."

Seth spun around to stare at him. "Simple, naïve Lloyd..." A smirk briefly crossed his lips. "But don't let the world change you. It needs people like you to balance out people like me."

The word "naïve" irritated Lloyd. It was something his older brother accused him of constantly. When he heard the rest though, his anger swiftly dissipated and a grin broke out across his face. "I guess we do kind of keep each other in check."

A sudden splash disrupted their conversation. A lithe figure popped out of the surf. Short blonde hair and a dark leather tunic revealed it to be Ruka. The girl held a fish in her mouth and one in each hand.

As she waded her way toward the shore, Seth murmured under his breath. "Like I said, strange..."

The Greymantle sisters made breakfast. The smell of fresh fish cooking roused the rest of the party. Lloyd saw Martan exit their tent. Aksel and Glo followed close behind the archer. Martan looked like a brand new man—the only trace of yesterday's near fatal encounter was the large crack in his bow. While still intact, the bow could not be drawn hard enough to fire an arrow. Martan insisted though, that it could be repaired once they got back to Ravenford.

During breakfast, Ruka recounted the story of her demon chase. Lloyd was not surprised to hear about the goblin army. Where there was one goblin, there were usually a lot more. Nor had he been surprised to hear about the five men in black robes.

"So it's just as we thought," Lloyd commented in-between bites. "The Serpent Cult is behind this as well."

Aksel nodded. "All things considered, I think it best that we break camp immediately after breakfast and get an early start on the salvage operation. There's no telling how long before those goblins show up."

"You want me to wait for them?" Lloyd offered. To be honest, the challenge of facing an army of goblins intrigued him. "I could keep them busy for a bit. Maybe even kill a few here and there. Just signal me when you are done, and I'll jump into the surf."

Aksel raised an eyebrow. "Thanks, but getting away might not be quite that easy. We'll just leave The Boulder here on the shore. He can keep the goblins busy for a while."

Lloyd sighed. Aksel was probably right. The goblins were sure to have archers with them. There were also those black mages, and the demon.

Aksel smiled at him. "Cheer up, Lloyd. We're going to need you and Martan to help bring cargo up from the wrecks. I have a spell that will allow the two of you to breathe underwater."

A grin broke out across Lloyd's face, the goblin army now completely forgotten. "Really? That sounds cool."

"Oh it is!" Maya squealed with delight. "Wait until you see the reef. It's beautiful! All the colors and all the fish—you'll love it!"

Martan did not seem so enthusiastic. "Anything we need to be worried about down there? Like sharks, for instance?"

Lloyd eyed the archer curiously. He started to say something but then reconsidered. With everything Martan had been through, Lloyd couldn't blame him for being reluctant.

"The dolphins will keep them away," Ves reassured him. "We will ask them to set up a perimeter around the wrecks."

"Thanks," Martan replied, smiling sheepishly at her.

Aksel turned to Glo. "Can you man the boat while the rest of them dive?"

"Sure, but what are you and Seth going to be doing?"

"We want to take a little side trip," Seth interjected, "to the lighthouse, now that it's stopped burning, that is."

Glo glared at the halfling, but finally sighed. "Let me guess. You want to be dropped off on the way to the reef?"

Instead of answering Glo directly, Seth turned toward Ves. "I was hoping maybe we could borrow a pair of dolphins?"

"I suppose that could be arranged." There was a trace of a smile on her lips.

"Yes!" Seth cried, pumping his fist. "Dolphin ride."

Aksel gave Seth a sidelong glance. He seemed far less enthusiastic. Aksel turned toward Ves. "Thank you. Please don't go to any trouble on our accounts."

"It's really no trouble at all. The dolphins seem to like you anyway."

"They do! They do!" Maya agreed. The little girl had gotten up and spun around in circles on the sand, trying her best to make herself dizzy.

"Okay," Aksel agreed, still sounding uncertain. "Then let's break camp."

The sea was calm out by the reef. The jagged ridge of rock, coral, and sand was visible ten feet below the water line. Lloyd sat in the rowboat with Martan and Glo. The Greymantles had guided them here. The sisters were now underwater, searching for the sunken ships. Once they found them, Lloyd and Martan would help recover any cargo they found. The rowboat sat about 200 yards off shore. Directly south stood what was left of the Cape Marlin Lighthouse. Aksel and Seth were currently on that island, searching through the wreckage.

Glo broke the silence. "The Endurance should be here soon. With any luck, we'll be done with the salvage operation before those goblins show up."

Martan scanned the shoreline. "The cliff still looks clear."

Lloyd followed his gaze. He could just make out The Boulder's large form standing on the beach. There was no sign of movement on the cliff above. A sudden splash made him turn around. A small head popped up out of the water by the side of the boat. It was Maya.

"I found one! I found one!" the young girl cried with excitement.

"Which one is it?" Glo called.

"The Zep-hyr," Maya shouted back not realizing the "ph" made an "f " sound.

"The Zephyr," Glo corrected her. "That's definitely one of them. Good job, Maya."

The young girl beamed and spun around in the water. A few moments later, another of the sisters popped up next to her. It was Ves.

"I found two ship wrecks, fairly close together. By the looks of them, they must have sunk recently."

"Could you see the names?" Lloyd asked curiously.

"One was the Gale Runner, and the other was the Sydion."

Glo nodded. "Yep, that's two of the others. Now all we need is to find the Lucky Coin."

"Done!" A voice cried from the other side of the boat. All three of them turned around to see Ruka floating effortlessly on the water.

"A bit up the reef from here, but I found it."

"That's all four!" Lloyd shouted with excitement. "Let's get to it."

Lloyd and Martan stripped down to their trunks. At the same moment, a group of dolphins swam up and circled the boat. Ves spoke with them. When she was done, the dolphins shot away in different directions. "I sent them out to patrol the area, so we should not be disturbed."

"Thank you." Martan half smiled, clearly embarrassed.

Ves smiled gently in return. "Ready whenever you are, gentlemen."

"Let's go, Martan." Lloyd launched himself off the boat and executed a perfect swan dive out into the water. He cut the surface like a knife and went straight down to the reef below. The sun shone down from above, lighting up the vibrant colors of the ridge. It was breathtaking. Abruptly, he realized he was breathing underwater. Aksel's spell had worked. Lloyd quickly surfaced to rejoin the others.

"Sorry about that," he apologized. "I got sidetracked down there. It is beautiful."

"Told you so!" Maya still spun gaily in the water.

"How do we want to do this?" Ves asked.

Lloyd thought it over. "Let's start with the two wrecks you found together. That might be easier. Then we can split up and hit the last two in separate teams."

"Sounds good," Ves agreed. "I'll lead. Follow me." With that, the young woman dove beneath the surface.

"See you in a bit." Lloyd waved to Glo and then dove in after Ves.

Glo sat alone in the rowboat. He gazed over at shore, but there were still no signs of the goblin army. He turned toward the lighthouse isle—the remains of the structure had stopped smoldering. Glo felt a momentary twinge at how he had destroyed the building. He let out a heavy sigh. When they got back, he would have to tell the Baron what he had done.

Something bright caught his eye beyond the burnt-out tower. It was the tall white sails of a ship. *It's the Endurance.* The vessel was rounding Cape Marlin Point. Glo watched the vessel sail around the lighthouse and head north. Fifteen minutes later, it dropped anchor about two hundred yards farther out from him, a nice safe distance from the reef. A rowboat dropped from the side of the ship and quickly filled with crew. Rochino was sending help to cart cargo back to the ship. Now they just needed to find it.

Lloyd followed Ves down the side of the reef. He had a hard time keeping up. *She can really move underwater!* Two figures suddenly shot by him—Maya and Ruka. Lloyd felt extremely slow all of a sudden. The girls stopped every once in a while, and waited for him and Martan to catch up.

The area around the reef teemed with life. There were all sorts of strange-looking plants of many different colors. Vibrant reds, deep greens, and electric blues—it was like an underwater rainbow. Even the fish were colorful. Lloyd saw one that was yellow, blue, and purple. A school of green and blue fish swam by, dispersing as the swimmers passed. He even caught sight of a dolphin at one point. It came up to the girls, nuzzled Maya, and then swam on. The divers continued downward until they were just above the sea bottom. The yellow sand of the sea floor stretched out below them, away from the reef.

Lloyd glanced up and caught his breath. The rays of the sun shone down from above, fanning out like a shower of light in all directions. The sight had him mesmerized. A sudden tap on his shoulder broke him out of his reverie. Maya floated in front of him, a wide grin across her diminutive face. She hung there a moment, then motioned for him to follow.

The girls headed north along the reef. They swam for quite a while, passing by myriads of multicolored plants and sea life. Finally, Lloyd caught sight of the sunken ship. It appeared as a dark, fuzzy mass at first, nearby the reef in the distance. As they drew closer, the mass grew in size and was easier to see. It was a galleon, just like the Endurance. The sunken ship lay partially on its side, its tall masts jutting out at an angle away from the reef. One of the masts had broken off and lay on the sea floor.

As they drew closer, Lloyd saw a huge gash in the front of the hull. The ship must have slammed straight into the reef, causing the entire bow to split open. Just behind the tear, he could clearly see the ship's name written on the hull. It read the *Gale Runner*.

The vessel was surrounded by sea life, many swimming in and out of the sunken ship. As soon as the divers approached, the fish swam out of the way. The girls slipped through the hole in the ship's hull. Lloyd and Martan followed. It was dark inside, but the area suddenly lit up. A group of bright spherical glowing lights had appeared out of nowhere.

Lloyd immediately recognized them as a spell. His mother used it all the time. One of the girls must have cast it. These sisters were full of surprises. Lloyd's eyes swept around the area. They were in a large open area—the ship's cargo hold. There were boxes strewn all over, many smashed open. They must have been knocked around when the ship hit the reef.

The divers split up and checked the crates for anything marked "Ravenford". A few minutes later, he felt a tap on his shoulder. Spinning around, he saw Maya floating there. The little girl had an uncharacteristically serious look on her face. She waved for him to follow. Lloyd swam behind her, over to where Ruka waited. The two girls stood there over a number of smashed crates. Ves and Martan soon joined them.

Ruka lifted up a piece of crate and pointed to it. There was writing on it. It read R-a-v. Maya had picked up another piece. She held it up next to Ruka's. The letters on it spelled f-o-r-d.

Ravenford! They had found the lost cargo. Lloyd bent down and rummaged around. There was nothing inside the broken crate. There should have been at least some sign of what had been stored inside. The divers exchanged hand signals and then all fanned out. After a brief search, the remains of four more Ravenford crates were found. However, there was still no sign of cargo—no food, materials, or anything.

What could have happened to it all? Lloyd was completely baffled. Unless...a chilling thought came to him. *What if the Serpent Cult had already been here?* It certainly made sense. It would explain why they could find no trace of any cargo, but if that were the case, were they just wasting their time down here?

Lloyd immediately dismissed the thought. They were here to do a job, and they would do it. They would check every wreck on the chance there was still salvageable cargo. Lloyd signaled the others to move on. Ves and Ruka nodded their agreement.

The girls led the way out through the tear in the hull. When they were all outside, Ves motioned for them to stop. After another flurry of hand signals, Ruka and Maya swam off away from the reef. Ves motioned for Martan and Lloyd to follow her. She took off in the direction they had originally come.

As they swam, Lloyd peered in the direction the other girls were headed. Off in the distance, he could just make out the outline of a second wreck. So Ves had sent Ruka and Maya off to check out the nearby *Sydion*. Meanwhile, the rest of them would move on to the next wreck. Lloyd turned his attention back toward Ves and continued to follow her through the deep. Silently, he hoped they would find some cargo still untouched.

14
FLYING BLIND
Without warning the main mast burst into flames

O ver on the island, Seth and Aksel poked through the ruins of the lighthouse. The remains of the tower were still hot, even though it had stopped burning early in the morning. What remained was mostly junk, but they had found a ruby ring and a silver scimitar. As the duo made one more pass, Seth nudged Aksel.

"What?" Aksel cried, sounding a bit more annoyed than he intended. Seth merely smirked as he pointed toward the shore. Aksel glanced in that direction and arched an eyebrow. The cliff top was covered with dozens of tiny dots. The goblin army had finally arrived.

"Guess we should ask The Boulder to go greet our friends," Aksel stated calmly.

He reached inside his robe and gingerly pulled out the golem's ring. Aksel put the ring on and concentrated. He thought in his mind repeatedly, *Climb the cliff. Defend yourself. Climb the cliff. Defend yourself.* He figured those commands were simple enough. You couldn't be too complicated with golems. They weren't very bright. Finally, he felt a tingling sensation from the ring. That meant the golem was taking action.

"There," he said with a deep sigh.

"Did it work?" Seth asked curiously.

Aksel nodded toward the shore. "Look for yourself."

Over on the beach, a large grey figure lumbered across the sand. It reached the cliff and started winding its way up the trail that led to the top.

"This is going to be epic!"

"Yes," Aksel agreed, trying to sound equally enthusiastic. Secretly, he worried about The Boulder. The stony creature was tough, and it was immune to magic, but there were a hundred goblins up there on that cliff, not to mention that demon. "Anyway, I think we're done here. We should probably go join the others."

"Sounds good," Seth agreed. "Any excuse to ride a dolphin."

Aksel smiled wanly. Although it was nice to see Seth so happy, riding dolphin back was just not his cup of tea. He had to admit, it did come in handy. Oh, well, no use looking a gift horse, or dolphin, in the mouth. Putting away the golem ring, Aksel followed Seth down to the dock and their aquatic mounts.

Glo nearly fell out of his seat. The rowboat had begun moving on its own, and he caught himself just in time. Otherwise, he would have tumbled over and into the water. He spun around and saw two fins sticking out of the water. A pair of dolphins was pushing him along. Glo raised an eyebrow then spun back around. They were headed due north, paralleling the reef. They traveled about a mile before the dolphins finally veered off.

Glo grabbed the oars and slowed the boat to a stop. He peered over his shoulder and saw the other rowboat far in the distance. It was still headed in this direction, but had been left far behind.

It's no match for dolphin power.

Abruptly, three divers surfaced around him. It was Ves, Lloyd, and Martan. Strangely, they were empty handed.

"Where's the cargo?" Glo called out.

"Gone!" Lloyd cried.

"Gone? What do you mean gone?"

Lloyd, Ves, and Martan all swam closer. They quickly explained what they had found or, more accurately, had not found, in the shipwreck down the coast.

Glo frowned. "That's not a good sign. Hopefully we'll have better luck in the other wrecks."

His musings were interrupted by Martan. "Glolindir, I think that's your bird."

Glo tilted his head up and saw Raven circling above them. The black bird glided her way down and finally landed on his arm.

"*Nir' goblins no' cabed*," Raven squawked.

"What's going on?" Lloyd asked.

"Looks like the goblins have arrived," Ves answered for him, nodding toward the shore. Indeed, dozens of tiny dots moved around at the top of the cliff.

"Good thing we're out of bow range," Martan noted, sounding awed at the sight of so many goblins.

Glo had to agree, their sheer numbers were daunting.

"We really should get back down there," Ves reminded everyone. "Ruka and Maya are already headed to the last wreck," she added. With that, the young woman dove back underwater, disappearing from sight.

"Be back soon!" Lloyd cried. He dove in after Ves.

Martan nodded and then disappeared below the waves as well, leaving Glo alone once more.

Aksel hung on to the dolphin's fin for dear life as they plowed through the water. The sea sprayed up all around him, drenching his clothes. Chancing a quick look over his shoulder, he saw Seth hanging on to his dolphin with one hand. The halfling pumped his other hand into the air and screamed, "Yahoo!"

Despite his own discomfort, Aksel could not help smiling. Suddenly, he felt his hand slip! Aksel whirled his head forward and grasped the dorsal fin as tight as he could.

"Phew," he sighed. He resolved to keep his eyes fixed solidly ahead of him for the rest of the ride. The large hull of the Endurance went whizzing by them, then a rowboat full of sailors. A short while later, a second rowboat came into view. In it sat a solitary figure with long flaxen hair and garbed in purple robes.

"Yo, Glo!" Seth cried as they drew within shouting distance.

"It's about time!" the elf cried back. "What took you so long?"

"We were having too much fun riding dolphins!" Seth yelled.

Yeah, some fun, Aksel thought. The entire ride had him feeling sick to his stomach. Thankfully, the dolphins had slowed down. The duo pulled up next to the rowboat and climbed aboard. Seth leapt over easily, while Aksel gratefully accepted Glo's outstretched arm. Once he was safely seated onboard, Aksel began to feel better. He faced Glo. "What are we doing all the way out here?"

"We moved the boat over the shipwrecks to speed up the salvage process," Glo explained. "They've already been to the first two ships. The third one is right below us now."

Aksel's eyes swept across the empty boat. "Um, Glo? Where's the cargo?"

"Gone."

Aksel arched an eyebrow. "Gone? What do you mean gone?"

Glo quickly told them about the destroyed Ravenford containers and the missing contents.

"Yeah, why am I not surprised?" Seth smirked.

Glo smiled wanly in response. "Anyway, Ves, Martan, and Lloyd are down below at the *Zephyr*. Ruka and Maya headed out to the last ship, the *Lucky Coin*. Hopefully they have not been scavenged yet."

"I wouldn't hold my breath on the *Zephyr*," Aksel mused, "but maybe the Lucky Coin. After all, it only went down two days ago,"

"How about you two? Find anything of interest?" Glo changed the subject.

"Just a couple of trinkets," Seth replied nonchalantly. "We'll show them to you later."

Abruptly, the boat nudged forward.

"Hold on!" Glo cried. "It looks like we're going on another ride."

Oh, no, not again! Aksel braced himself. The boat turned around in a wide arc and began to head south again. Luckily, it was a lot smoother than riding dolphin back.

As the boat sped up, Seth stood up in the bow. He spread his arms wide and cried, "Wahoo! Not bad! Not bad at all!"

"Looks like you were right about the *Zephyr*," Glo observed.

Aksel nodded. Ves wouldn't be having them moved if there was any cargo to load on board. He glanced over toward the shore. "Anyway, things should be getting interesting up on the cliff."

"He sent The Boulder up to greet the goblins," Seth added over his shoulder. "Something tells me they aren't going to like the welcoming committee."

Glo chuckled softly in response. "Somehow, I don't really feel sorry for them."

A short while later, the dolphins veered off and the boat came to a stop. Glo estimated they were about a half-mile south of where they had previously been. The Endurance was moored about a half-mile further south. The second rowboat was now only about a hundred yards away, and closing fast. They had not been stopped more than a minute when two figures broke surface. It was Ruka and Maya, and they both were holding onto cargo crates.

"There's a few more down there," Ruka cried as she swam over towards them.

They were not small containers, Glo observed. He estimated them to each be 3 feet by 3 feet by 4 feet. He also saw writing on the side. On closer inspection, he clearly saw the word Ravenford.

"Looks like you were right again," he told Aksel. "Two days was not enough time for the cult to scavenge the wreck."

They managed to load the crates onboard without tipping the rowboat over. This was mostly due to an incredible display of strength on Ruka's part. The two girls then dove under once more. They both resurfaced a few minutes later, each with another crate, just as the second rowboat pulled up to them. With the help of the sailors, the two crates were easily loaded onto the rowboat. Then both girls dove under again. They resurfaced a few minutes later with just one more crate. Glo noted with surprise that the crate had Maltar's seal on it. *That must contain his pendant!* They had found it. Maltar would be pleased. *Well, about as pleased as he ever could be,* Glo amended wryly.

The last crate was loaded onto the sailors' rowboat. Once done, they manned the oars, turned the boat around, and began rowing back toward the Endurance. Lloyd, Martan, and Ves surfaced just as Maya and Ruka rejoined them.

"Nothing on the other boat?" Ruka called over to her sister.

"Just smashed crates again," Ves confirmed. "Looks like you had some luck, though."

"Third time's a charm!" Ruka grinned back at her sister.

Technically, it was the fourth time, Glo noted, but he wasn't going to quibble over it.

Lloyd and Martan climbed aboard and wrapped themselves in waiting towels. The girls, however, remained in the water. Three dolphin fins appeared behind them. Each girl grabbed hold of a fin and hitched a ride as the aquatic mammals pushed the boat back down the coast.

Aksel perched atop one of the crates. "I was starting to think those girls were part fish."

Lloyd grinned. "They may not be as fast as a dolphin, but they could easily out-swim any of us."

Aksel watched with keen interest as the sisters practically flew over the sea. *Their mastery of water is impressive. Add to that their unnatural strength and near invulnerability*—his eyebrow suddenly shot up. *That's it!* Aksel believed he knew the sisters' secret, and if he was right, it was huge. *No wonder they don't want anyone else to know.* Aksel cast a glance at Glo. The elven wizard eyed the sisters with a shrewd look. Perhaps he had reached the same conclusion. Still, Aksel decided to remain silent about it. The sisters had chosen not to share their secret and he had resolved to honor their choice.

The little cleric spun back around on the crate, turning his gaze toward the shore. The top of the cliff, previously filled with tiny goblin dots, was now empty. There was no sign of the goblin army, nor The Boulder. "I wish I knew what was going on up there."

They quickly came up on the Endurance. Thanks to dolphin power, they had caught up to the other rowboat and now ran beside it. The tall ship towered above them, its main mast reaching high up into the sky. They were about thirty yards off her starboard bow when, without warning, the main mast burst into flames.

"Would you look at that!" one of the sailors cried.

A moment later, a bolt of lightning hit the deck. It was accompanied by a loud thunderclap.

"But there's not a cloud in the sky!" another sailor yelled.

Glo knew better. That was not cloud lightning—that was a spell. Glo scanned the skies, quickly spotting three black-robed figures circling above the burning mast.

"Up there!" Glo shouted, pointing at the black forms. The three figures circled the large mast twice more, then abruptly flew off in the direction of the shore.

Lloyd shot up out of his seat. "Oh, no, you don't!" He grabbed his cape and cried, "Fugere." The warrior abruptly rocketed into the air after the receding figures.

"Look, Ves!" Maya cried, "Lloyd can fly! You would think he's one of..."

"Hush!" Ruka hissed, cutting off her little sister.

Lloyd moved swiftly across the sky on an intercept course with the three figures. His blades were drawn, poised to strike. Abruptly, one of the mages flipped over and pointed an arm at him. A strange black light encircled the warrior's head. It only lasted for a moment, but afterwards Lloyd slowed down and flew erratically.

"They've blinded him!" Aksel cried in dismay.

Glo also recognized the spell. Lloyd had no chance of catching the black mages now. Worse, he had no way of getting back to them safely.

"I'll get him!" Acting on impulse, Glo reached into his bag and pulled out a feather. He made a quick motion, then spoke the same word Lloyd had used moments ago. "Fugere."

Glo felt his body lift up out of the boat. It was awkward at first, and he almost lost his balance. *Maybe this wasn't such a good idea.* The first time he attempted to fly was only two days ago. That hadn't gone so well. He had barely gotten off the ground when he started to wobble. Glo panicked and flipped completely upside down. At that point, he had dove for the ground, swearing never to fly again. Yet now he had no choice. Lloyd was in trouble, and Glo was the only one who could help him.

Pushing down his nerves, Glo thrust his arms out away from his body. It worked, stabilizing him as he rose into the air. Now, of course, he had to reach Lloyd. The warrior hovered in midair, completely disoriented, swinging his blades wildly. Glo hardened his resolve. He leaned forward, aiming his body toward his frantic friend. He wobbled again, but this time did not panic. Instead, he mimicked

Lloyd, pushing both hands straight out in front of him. It definitely helped. Glo steadied himself and moved faster, quickly closing the gap between himself and the sightless warrior. When he was about a dozen feet away, he stopped and shouted, "Lloyd! It's me! Glo."

"Glo?" Lloyd cried nervously. "I can't see!"

"I know," Glo yelled back. "Put your blades away, and I'll help you down."

"Okay." Lloyd gulped and sheathed his weapons. He hovered quietly until Glo finally reached him.

Glo took Lloyd's arm, trying to sound as reassuring as possible. "It's okay. I'm leading us back to the ship." Too bad he didn't feel as confident as he sounded. It must have worked, though. Lloyd visibly calmed as Glo guided him toward the Endurance.

Halfway there, Lloyd's normally curious nature kicked in. "Glo, when did you learn how to fly?"

Glo chuckled. "No, Lloyd. What you do is fly. Me, I flail around through the air like a beached whale."

A smile spread across Lloyd's lips. "You just need practice—but either way, thanks for coming to get me."

"Anytime, my friend. Anytime."

15
DIVERSION
If I have to chase down another crate, someone is going to be very sorry

Lloyd and Glo landed rather awkwardly on the mid-deck of the Endurance. The young elf sprawled across the surface like a fish out of water. Not Lloyd, though. Despite being blinded, the young warrior managed to roll through the landing and end up on his feet. Glo slowly got up onto his hands and knees and swept the deck with his eyes. Luckily, no one seemed to notice their less-than-graceful arrival. The crew was busy with a water brigade, passing bucket after bucket from the sea to the flaming mast. Captain Rochino oversaw the line and urged his men on. "Faster! Faster, unless you want to limp all the way home!" Thankfully, the fire was almost out. The crackle of flames died down, replaced by the hiss of smoke. The mast looked blackened in spots, but appeared otherwise intact.

"Sorry about that landing," Glo cried over the commotion.

Lloyd grinned. "Hey, I'm just happy to be on a solid surface!"

Glo could not help but smile at his friend. Leave it to Lloyd to make the best out of any situation. He got up and helped Lloyd over to a pile of crates, sitting him down on one of the larger ones. He then watched the brigade finish its work. A short while later, the fire was completely out. Some of the sailors remained behind to clean up, but Rochino dispersed the rest of them back to their stations.

"Lloyd! Glo!"

Glo spun around and saw Aksel rushing across the deck toward them. He was followed by Seth, Martan, and even Ves.

"Lloyd!" Aksel stopped in front of them and took a deep breath. "What were you thinking?"

Seth snickered as he walked up behind them. "Heh. You said

Lloyd and thinking in the same sentence."

Lloyd's face turned red. His hand went to the back of his neck. "Guess I really wasn't."

Aksel sighed. "Well, what's done is done."

Glo noticed that Ruka and Maya were not with them. He turned to Ves. "Where are your sisters?"

"Ruka decided to stay with the crates till they are loaded on board. I'm sure they'll join us soon."

"I can go check on them," Martan offered.

Ves smiled demurely at the archer. "That would be nice."

Martan nodded, his face reddening. "Be right back." He took off at a run back the way they came.

A soft laugh escaped Glo's lips. Martan was quite obviously smitten with Ves. Frankly, he couldn't blame him. She was beautiful, intelligent, and classy, a hard combination for any man, or elf, to resist. Further, she had saved the archer's life. Her attention to Martan had bothered Glo at first, but it was probably just as well. His thoughts were interrupted by a gruff voice. "That was one heck of a landing!" Glo spun around to see Rochino striding toward them.

"I didn't think anyone noticed," Glo admitted, still embarrassed at his inept arrival.

The Captain stopped in front of them and let out a hearty laugh. "Trust me, lad, any landing you can walk away from is a good one!" The laugh abruptly died on his lips. Rochino bent in front of Lloyd and waved his hand in front of the young man's eyes. "By the Gods man, what have they done to you?"

"Blindness spell. It's only temporary," Glo explained.

Rochino stood up and cleared his throat. "Well then, I'm sure we'll have you fixed up in no time—especially with your cleric friend over here." He nodded at Aksel.

Aksel, however, wore a pained expression. He turned to Ves. "You don't have a cure for the blindness spell handy, by any chance?"

Ves' face fell. "No, unfortunately not."

Aksel grimaced. "I'm really sorry, Lloyd. I'm afraid you'll have to put up with it until the morning." Lloyd sighed, a look of resignation crossing his face. Aksel's expression grew more pained. "I swear, it will be the first thing I do."

"Don't worry, lad," Rochino said cheerfully, "the day's already half over anyway." Lloyd managed a lackluster smile in response.

Just then Martan rejoined them. "Crates are all loaded and your sisters are on their way up."

"Sisters? You mean there are more of these charming young ladies floating about?" Rochino stared openly at Ves.

Aksel's eyes shifted between the two. "Oh, where are my manners? This is..."

"Ves!"

The cry came from over the side. It sounded like Ruka. Ves whirled around and ran for the deck rail. Martan and Seth were right behind her.

Glo turned to Rochino. "Captain, can you keep an eye on Lloyd?"

Rochino nodded. "Sure, lad. You two go ahead."

"Thanks!" Glo and Aksel both said as they rushed after Ves.

"Ves!" the cry came again. She leaned over the wooden railing and yelled down. "What is it?"

Glo and Aksel reached the rail and peered over the side. Ruka treaded water next to the ship's hull below. Maya floated beside her.

"Someone threw one of the containers overboard! We're going to get it now," she cried up to them. Before Ves could respond, both girls dove under and disappeared.

Ves wore a puzzled expression. Her eyes flickered over the group around her. "Why would someone throw one of the crates overboard?"

Why indeed? Glo mused. *Who on board would have any reason to throw a crate over the side? Unless...* Glo raised an eyebrow as the answer dawned on him. He motioned everyone closer. As they all drew in, he spoke in a hushed voice. "Well, we know the Serpent Cult has already scavenged the other three ships..."

He was interrupted by a familiar gruff voice. "What's going on?"

Glo spun around and saw Rochino leading Lloyd over to them. He motioned them in close, then brought them up to speed. "The Lucky Coin would have been next if we hadn't gotten there first. So, what if the attack on this ship was a diversion?"

Aksel stroked his chin. "A diversion? If so, to what end?"

"To get a spy on board," Seth hissed.

"A spy?" Rochino repeated perhaps a bit too loud. His eyes went wide, his hand going to his mouth. He glanced over his shoulder but any nearby sailors appeared to be minding their own business. Satisfied, he turned back to the group and whispered, "Not on my boat!"

"Trust me, Captain, it's easier than you think," Seth said, keeping his own voice down. "A good spy is a master of disguise. He would take on the guise of someone else on board."

Rochino fixed him with a stare. "Look, lad, I make it my business to know every man in my crew. If there was an imposter on board, I would know it!"

"Even with all the commotion going on?" Seth smirked, folding his arms across his chest. Rochino scowled at the halfling, but Seth continued, unperturbed. "Think about it. Have you had a chance to look over everyone in your crew since the attack? What if someone snuck on board and waylaid one of them while everyone else was busy?"

Rochino appeared pensive as he considered the possibilities. Seth was right. Still, the halfling's familiarity with the subject gave Glo pause. Seth seemed to be as knowledgeable about spies as he was about thieves and cutthroats. However, this was neither the time nor the place to delve into Seth's sordid past. "It all makes sense, otherwise why the attack by those mages? There was little real damage to the ship, and they flew off before we even gave chase."

Aksel nodded. "So then it was all a mere distraction, designed to allow someone to get at those crates we just salvaged."

"And all this just for that pendant you mentioned?" Ves asked.

"Maltar's pendant," Aksel corrected her.

"Maltar? He's involved in all this?" Rochino's face turned dark at the mention of the wizard's name.

"Yes." Glo regarded Rochino with curiosity. Maltar was irritable at best, but that did not warrant the grim look on the Captain's face. *What does he know about Maltar that we don't?* He explained to Rochino about the pendant that had been shipped on the Lucky Coin, and the crate they had found with Maltar's seal on it.

Rochino mulled it over, his expression turning grim. "Well now, if Maltar is involved, then I am beginning to understand all these dark goings-on."

Glo raised an eyebrow. He was about to ask Rochino what he meant by that, but just then, a sudden cry reached them from the waters below. Peering over the rail, they saw Maya and Ruka had re-surfaced, the latter holding onto a crate.

"We found it! We found it!" Maya cried with delight. The little girl grinned up at them as she spun around in the water, making pirouettes.

"Bring it aboard!" Ves called down.

They all headed toward the rear of the vessel, except for Seth and Martan. The halfling had a suspicion about the crate that had been thrown overboard, so the duo veered off to see what was missing among the crates they had salvaged. When they reached the cargo winch, Ruka was already waiting below. The Captain commandeered Lloyd to help man the crank, then dropped the line and had Ruka tie it around the crate. They had just finished hauling it up when Seth and Martan rejoined them.

Seth's eyes swept the area, and then he spoke in a hushed tone. "Just as we suspected, it's gone."

Aksel let out a deep sigh. "Looks like you were right."

Rochino shook his head in resignation. "Aye lads, and that means we have a spy on board. On my ship!"

Sure enough, the crate that had been tossed overboard was the container with Maltar's seal on it. Yet the seal on the crate was still intact. Glo felt relieved. "Thank the gods they didn't get what was inside."

Seth was not so easily convinced. "Maybe, but that crate didn't just throw itself overboard. I still think we should search the ship."

"Sounds like a good idea," came a voice from behind them. Glo glanced over his shoulder and saw Ruka striding across the deck, still dripping wet. Maya pranced gleefully behind her, grinning at the sail-ors as they went by. "Because if I have to chase down another crate, someone is going to be very sorry."

Rochino broke out into a broad grin. "I like your style, lass." That was no idle threat. Ruka and her sisters were not anyone you wanted to anger. "In the meantime, I suggest you keep a good eye on this container of yours."

The suggestion sparked an idea for Glo. He grabbed Lloyd by the arm. "I have an important job for you."

"What is it?" Lloyd sounded rather uncertain, given his present condition.

Glo led Lloyd over to the crate with Maltar's seal on it. "We need you to sit on Maltar's crate and guard it. If anyone comes near other than us or the Captain, you have my permission to swing first and ask questions later."

Lloyd broke out into a broad smile for the first time since he had been blinded. "With pleasure!" He drew his swords and sat down on the crate, listening intently around him. Ruka watched him for a few moments, then nodded to Glo in approval. At the same moment, someone grabbed him by the arm. It was Ves.

"That was very thoughtful of you, Glolindir, and prudent as well."

Her close proximity and the sparkle in her eyes made him suddenly rather uncomfortable. He could feel the warmth rush up into his cheeks. Luckily, Seth saved him from having to reply.

"Yeah, yeah, if you want to be prudent, have your sisters surround the boat with those dolphin friends of yours. That way we'll know if anything else ends up overboard."

Ves regarded the halfling for a moment, and then nodded with approval. "Excellent idea, Master Seth." She waved her sisters to follow, leading them to the nearest railing. The entire crew stopped what they were doing as the three sisters gathered there. They all watched as the three of them dove overboard.

Rochino wore a wry smile beneath his black beard. "That's quite an interesting diving crew you've got yourselves there."

"You don't know the half of it." Seth rolled his eyes heavenward.

16
IMPOSTER
The large vessel rocked from the force of the explosion

While the three sisters set up a perimeter, Seth, Aksel, Martin, and Glo began a thorough search of the ship. The foursome went room by room, but discovered nothing until they made it to the ship's vault. Unhindered by any lock, Seth had the vault open in a matter of seconds. Inside, they were horrified to find the dead bodies of two men. Neither corpse was clothed. They quickly headed top-side to inform the Captain. When they reached the main deck, they found Rochino surrounded by a crowd of sailors. Everyone was excited, talking all at once. There was so much noise that Glo only heard bits and pieces of what they were saying. He caught the words "dead body" and "strange girls."

Abruptly, Rochino's loud voice rang out over the others. "Alright! Alright! That's enough! Back to your stations!"

The sailors slowly dispersed, grumbling as they went. As the crowd thinned, Glo caught sight of the Greymantle sisters on either side of the Captain. He motioned for the others to follow, then pushed forward through the slow-moving throng. When they reached the center, they halted abruptly. The Captain and the sisters stood over yet another dead body. The torso of the corpse was half-naked, a sheet of canvas draped over the lower half. Rochino wore a pained expression on his face. "He was one of my officers."

Ves' face was filled with sorrow. "We found him tossed over the side."

Seth cast a quick glance around then whispered, "We also found two more bodies in your vault."

"In the vau..." Rochino slapped his hand over his mouth silencing himself. He, too, glanced around then spoke in a hushed tone. "Two more of my crew? Dead?" Seth merely nodded. The Captain's face went pale. He took a few moments to collect himself before speaking again. "Any idea who they were?"

Aksel shook his head. "I'm sorry. Their uniforms were gone as well."

Rochino's expression slowly changed from one of shock to anger. "You fellows were right, we have an imposter on board—and when we catch him, I'm going to personally gut him and hang him from the yard arm." When he finished, his eyes fell on the sisters. "No offense, ladies."

Ruka did not miss a beat. "None taken, Captain. In fact, I just might help you gut him."

Rochino's mouth dropped open, but then he grinned. "Lass, you'd make a fine sailor."

Before she could reply, a familiar voice called out from across the deck. "Glo!"

It was Lloyd. He still sat on Maltar's crate, his swords drawn. Nothing appeared amiss around him, but looks could be deceiving. Glo turned back to the others. "I'll see what he needs."

Rochino gave a curt nod. "You go ahead. I'll get things taken care of here, and then I'll check out the bodies below."

"You go ahead, Captain. I'll stay here," Aksel offered.

"As will I," Ves chimed in.

"That would be... most appreciated." Rochino bowed his head for a moment, but Glo noted a hint of moisture well up in his eyes. He then spun around and took off across the deck.

"Glo!" Lloyd called again.

"Coming!"

Seth's eyes narrowed. "I think I'll join you. I'm curious as to what's got him so stirred up."

"So will I." Ruka fell in beside them.

Maya took a step after her sister, but Ves reached out and placed a hand on the young girl's shoulder. "We will stay right here."

Maya folded her arms across her chest and pouted. "Aww, what fun is that?"

Martan knelt down next to the little girl and unslung his bow. "Would you like to see how this works? It's a bit damaged, but if you're careful, you can draw the string."

Maya's face lit up as she reached for it, but then stopped herself and looked up at Ves. "Oooo, can I?"

Ves nodded, casting a grateful look at the archer. "Go ahead."

"Martan one, Glo zero," Seth said under his breath.

Glo glared at the halfling. "What was that?"

"Oh, nothing."

Seth sauntered away across the deck toward the waiting Lloyd. Ruka's eyes fell on Glo, a short, closed-mouth laugh escaping her lips, then she took off after Seth. Glo shook his head and followed. When he caught up with them, Seth was already interrogating Lloyd.

"Shhhh." Lloyd moved his head from side to side, glancing around with unseeing eyes.

Glo scanned the nearby area, but there was no one else around. "It's okay, Lloyd, we're alone."

The young man nodded then spoke in a hushed tone. "While I was sitting here, I overheard a couple of the sailors talking. They were complaining about another sailor not knowing what he was doing."

"Interesting," Glo mused. "Did they indicate where this fellow might be?"

Lloyd nodded. "Matter of fact, they did." He leaned forward. "He was fumbling around with the port rigging over by the mizzen mast."

"And that would be exactly where?" Seth asked pointedly.

"The left side of the rear-most mast," Ruka answered smugly before Lloyd could speak.

Seth gave the girl an acid look, but declined to comment.

Glo had to stop himself from chuckling. "Thank you, Lloyd—that is a great help." Lloyd beamed with pride in response to the compliment. "Now stay put while we look into this."

"I'm going to go scope out that part of the ship," Seth said.

"So am I," Ruka added.

Seth gave her a scathing look. "Whatever."

"Okay, but don't do anything until we get there," Glo told the pair. "I'm going to get Rochino. I don't want us grabbing the wrong guy and then have the real spy get away."

"Can't promise anything," Seth responded. Before Glo could say another word, he strode off with Ruka close behind. She had a bemused look on her face as she followed the disgruntled halfling.

Glo scanned the deck, but Rochino was nowhere to be seen. *He must have gone below to the vault.* Glo headed below deck, quickly catching up with the Captain. He swiftly relayed what Lloyd had uncovered. Eager to flush out the imposter/killer, Rochino led the way back on deck and up toward the rear of the ship. On the way, they passed Aksel, Ves, Maya and Martan. The officer's body had been blessed and wrapped, and two crewmen were carrying it away to be stored below for the duration of the ride home. Glo quickly repeated what Lloyd had overheard, and what Seth and Ruka were now up to. Ves, obviously concerned for her sister, immediately joined them, as did the others. Rochino led the way across the deck to the stern of the ship and up the stairs to the rear deck where the mizzenmast resided. He pretended to give the group a tour, all the while subtly scanning the crew. At one point, he stopped and casually nodded at a sailor.

Glo repositioned himself so he could see the man out of the corner of his eye. His back was to them, but from what he observed, the man appeared rather ordinary. He was of average height and build, dressed in a sailor's uniform which seemed to fit him well. He fiddled with one of the large ropes that ran from the railing up to the large mast above. As far as Glo could tell, it all seemed perfectly normal, but Rochino obviously knew better. A quick scan of the deck confirmed the locations of Seth and Ruka. The pair cautiously moved from behind a stack of crates and barrels off to one side of where the man in question stood. It was then that Glo realized Martan was gone. After another sweep of the deck, he caught sight of the archer on the opposite side of the man in question from Seth and Ruka. Martan was also closing in on him.

The companions held their breath as the stealthy trio moved in on their target. They had almost reached him when the man suddenly whirled around. Something gleamed in his hand as he lunged at the nearby Martan. A sharp gasp escaped the archer's lips as the man stabbed him in the gut! Before anyone could move, the imposter whipped Martan around and pulled him back toward the railing, using him as a human shield. The two of them teetered there, looking as if they would fall over the rail at any moment.

Without warning, Seth launched himself across the deck. Before the imposter could react, Seth tackled Martan out of the man's grasp! They landed in a heap on the deck a few yards away. The imposter hesitated a moment, surprise registering on his face at having his hostage stolen from him so neatly. Then, without so much as a word, the man spun around and leapt over the side of the vessel.

"Oh, no you don't!" Ruka cried. She reached the railing a second later and launched herself after the murderous imposter.

The rest of them rushed forward. Martan lay in Seth's arms, the halfling holding his hands down on the archer's abdomen. Seth glanced up at them. "It's pretty deep."

"Thank you, Seth. I'll handle it from here," Ves responded, immediately kneeling down next to the fallen archer. As Seth let go his grip, she grabbed his tunic and ripped it open. The wound looked like a clean cut from what Glo could see, but it was bleeding profusely.

Martan smiled wanly at the young woman, his voice racked with pain. "Sorry. This just hasn't... been my week..."

"Quiet," she shushed him. "Lie still. And no talking until I am done."

"Yes... ma'am..." He tried to smile, but it was a meager effort at best.

Yet again Ves held out her finger and brought that blue-white light to bear over the archer's exposed abdomen. The healing energy fanned out and covered the wound so intensely that it could not be looked at directly.

"Gods, she is powerful," Glo whispered to Aksel. The little cleric nodded in agreement.

At that moment, a loud *boom* sounded off the side of the ship. Glo saw a large column of water rise into the air a few dozen yards out. The large vessel rocked from the force of the explosion. Everyone but Ves, Seth, and Martan flew to the rail. They watched in amazement as water flowed into a temporary hole that had been blown into the sea. A few seconds later, Ruka popped out of the water. With one arm, she held onto a limp body. Even from this distance, the figure appeared a bit charred. *Ves was not kidding when she said that Ruka could handle herself.*

Ruka dragged the imposter's body through the water and then up the ship's ladder. Once on board, she unceremoniously dumped the body on deck in the midst of a gathering crowd. The body was indeed charred—there was a wide black circle radiating out from the center of the imposter's torso, the center of which displayed an ugly burn. Ruka stood back and leaned nonchalantly against the rail. "Sorry, Captain. Don't think there's much left to gut."

The crew stood gaping at the young girl's handiwork. Seth sauntered over and leaned against the railing next to her. "Got what he deserved, if you ask me."

Ruka cast a sidelong glance at the halfling, the corner of her lips upturning slightly. At the same time, Aksel bent down to examined the charred body. "He's still alive, though barely." The little cleric held out his hands and white light began to pour down from his palms over his critical patient. As Aksel tried to stabilize him, a voice sounded from behind the group.

"Thank you. Thank you." Martan now sat up, Ves still kneeling beside him. He grabbed her hands and kissed them, still thanking her profusely. "You are like my own personal angel." Ves blushed, but did not push his hands away.

An ironic smile spread across Glo's face. There was obviously a connection between these two. The only problem he foresaw was that Ves and her sisters had a secret. It was a mystery that Glo still hadn't unraveled, though he had his suspicions. Whatever it was, it was not small. He suddenly felt quite sorry for Martan. The poor archer had no idea what he was getting himself into.

Aksel still poured energy into the imposter. The man's wounds began to look better, the charred skin already healing. Rochino stepped in front of them and addressed his men. "Alright, alright, enough lollygagging about. Back to work, the lot of you."

There were a few grumbles, but the men knew better than to question their captain. As the sailors dispersed, Martan and Ves rejoined them, the latter holding Martan up under one shoulder. Aksel continued to work feverishly on the imposter. Minutes flew by as they watched his heroic efforts. Finally, the burn marks completely disappeared. The white light faded, and Aksel sat back drawing in a deep breath. He slowly stood up and turned to Seth, weariness quite evident on his face. "He's all yours."

"Finally," Seth exclaimed with a melodramatic sigh. He strode past the drained cleric with a wink. He reached into his backpack, pulled out a length of rope, and proceeded to tie up the imposter. Once satisfied with his handiwork, Seth performed a thorough search of the man. "Well, what do we have here?" he exclaimed. A knife suddenly appeared in his hand, and he cut into a section of the man's tunic. Reaching inside, Seth pulled out a shiny, round, golden object. As he held it aloft, it dropped down, suspended from his hand on a long chain.

Glo did a double take. He shifted his gaze toward the crate Lloyd was sitting on, then back at the pendant in Seth's hand. "May I see that?"

Seth held the object out to Glo, a wide smirk on his face. "Looks like that crate wasn't so secure after all."

Glo ignored the jibe and took the pendent from Seth's hand. He examined it closely. It was indeed an amulet. It had a golden outer ring, that was inscribed with strange runes. Glo knew a number of languages, but these were unfamiliar to him. The center of the amulet was jet black. As he stared at it, it seemed as if something moved in that darkness. Glo shook his head. His eyes must be playing tricks on him. He cast the spell of identification, but no matter how hard he concentrated, nothing came to him. After a few minutes, he gave up. *That cinches it. This is definitely not an ordinary amulet. This is an object of power, an artifact.* It had to be the one Maltar was expecting. Glo was not quite sure how the imposter had removed it from the box. The crate was still sealed tight. Obviously, the man was quite good at his craft. Glo took the amulet and slipped it into one of the secure pockets inside his robes.

Seth had finished his search of the spy. The only other item he found was the dagger that had been used on Martan. Seth pocketed the knife and rubbed his hands together. "That's that."

Rochino stepped forward, standing over the spy, his expression grim. He drew his cutlass and poked the tied up man with the pointy end. "It's a shame you went to all that trouble healing him, lad. Now I just have to gut him again."

Aksel stood at the railing, staring intently at the empty shoreline. He acted as if he hadn't heard a word the Captain said. "I really wish I knew what was going on over there."

Glo looked from one to the other and placed a hand on the Captain's shoulder. Rochino's eyes shifted toward him. "Perhaps we can save the gutting for a later time?" He nodded toward the distraught cleric.

Rochino let out a heavy sigh. "Lad, you sure know how to ruin a sailor's fun." He paused a moment, then called over two of his men. "Throw this brigand in a cell and stand guard over him. If he escapes, he won't be the only one keel-hauled."

"Aye, Captain!" both sailors exclaimed. They grabbed either end of the tied-up spy and carried him down below.

Meanwhile, Ves gently extricated herself from Martan and joined Aksel at the rail. The little cleric still silently stared off at the shore. "There might be a way to find out what is going on over there."

Aksel glanced up at her, a pleading look in his eyes. "If there is, I would be most interested."

Ves gave him a slow nod. "Very well, but we will need some privacy."

"Captain?" Aksel called.

Rochino strode over to the rail. "What is it, Master Aksel?"

"We need a section of the deck cleared. We are going to try something to find out what is happening on the shore. We need somewhere out of sight to do so."

Rochino stroked his chin, glancing around the deck as he pondered the request. His gaze fell on a high stack of crates at the rear of the vessel. "I believe I have just the spot."

A thin smile crossed Aksel's lips. "That would be perfect."

Rochino smiled in turn then spun around and bellowed to his crew. "All hands to the main deck!"

The sailors on the rear deck all turned toward him. Some of them wore curious expressions on their faces, but nonetheless, they all filed off the rear deck down the two sets of stairs to the main deck. Rochino nodded curtly to the others, then followed his men. The companions also followed, stopping to pick up Lloyd on the way.

"Did you find him?" Lloyd asked excitedly. "I thought I heard an explosion or something."

Glo grinned at the young man's enthusiasm. "We'll tell you on the way," He grabbed Lloyd's arm and led him down to the main deck, all the while explaining to him about the spy, Martan's mishap, Ruka's chase, and the strange amulet. As he finished the story, Glo heard a loud flapping noise coming from up on the rear deck. Gazing upward, he watched in amazement as a giant eagle winged its way off the ship. On its back sat Aksel! They all gawked at the magnificent creature as it rose high above the Endurance. It quickly flew off, its huge wings propelling it quickly toward the shore.

"Would you look at that!" one of the sailors whistled. "Where did it come from?" another sailor cried.

Glo turned to Seth and winked. That pretty much confirmed it. Aside from their other considerable talents, the sisters were also shape shifters. Well Ves was, at the very least.

"What's going on?" Lloyd asked, his head swiveling from side to side.

Seth smirked. "Oh, nothing out of the ordinary—just Aksel riding a giant eagle."

Lloyd's expression was incredulous. "A giant eagle? Where did he find one of those?"

Glo tried rather unsuccessfully to repress a smile. "Let's just say that Ves found it for him."

Lloyd let out a low whistle. "Ves? I knew the girls could talk to sea creatures, but now giant eagles?" The young man shook his head, a look of wonder on his face.

Seth's eyes shifted from Glo to Lloyd. "Like I said before, strange..."

17

A Copper Dragon

Glo felt as if he hung there forever, suspended between the dragon and the ship

Aksel had flown before, but that was only kites, back in his home town of Caprizon. Those were nothing compared to this. The eagle was incredibly fast, and the wind felt exhilarating against his face. He held tight onto her back as they shot through the air. This must be what it felt like to ride one of Glo's missiles. The water flew by below them in a blur. Before he knew it, they had reached the shoreline.

Seth would love this! It was even faster than riding dolphin back. Strangely enough, Aksel was not nervous at all. Despite the great speed, the ride was extremely smooth. He suspected the eagle was purposely trying to keep it that way for her small passenger, and for that he was deeply grateful.

Aksel admitted he had been taken aback at first. His eyes had gone wide when Ves shifted forms. The creature that stood before him was close to ten feet tall, with golden-brown feathers, a long hooked beak, and deadly-looking talons. The wings probably spanned twenty feet. The eyes, however, were what threw him the most—they were bluish-green. Those eyes stared at him curiously as he slowly approached the large creature. Aksel had to remind himself that this was still Ves before finally climbing onto the eagle's back. Once he was comfortably situated, the eagle unfolded its vast wings and, with two great beats, lifted off the rear deck of the Endurance. As soon as they cleared the railing, the eagle shot away from the ship at an incredible rate. They quickly gained altitude, and minutes later were flying high over land. The lush greenery of the forest spread out for miles below them in every direction save the sea. From this height, it was hard to see much down below, but Aksel was certain that there was nothing moving between the cliff and the forest.

"Can we get any lower?" he cried over the wind.

The huge eagle let out a screech and then spiraled downward in a slow arc. Aksel peered in all directions, trying to find some trace of The Boulder or the goblin army. As they descended, Aksel could make out more details in the landscape. The forest had appeared solid from above, but was in fact broken up by patches and long lines that were most likely clearing and trails. There was one wide line in particular, about a mile west of them. It cut through the forest from the sea as far north as the eye could see. That had to be the main road from Cape Marlin to the cliff-side village of Gelcliff.

As they continued their descent, Aksel spotted a wide clearing about a half mile back from the cliff. A tall grey figure stood alone in its center. Aksel pointed toward it and cried, "Over there!" Ves turned her great head to see where he was pointing, then banked and turned in that direction. As they passed overhead, Aksel cried out in triumph. "That's it! We found him!"

The figure below was indeed The Boulder. The clearing around the golem was littered with the bodies of small yellow creatures. The remains of the goblins were bloodied and broken from their encounter with the unstoppable stone creature. Aksel decided it best not to land. There was no telling how many more goblins still lurked in those woods, not to mention the barghest and those dark-robed mages. Instead, he grasped the golem's ring with his hand and concentrated.

Go back to the big boat, he thought repeatedly. After a few times, he felt the now-familiar tingling. Below, The Boulder began to move. It turned around and headed back toward the cliff.

"That should do it!" he cried aloud. The eagle screeched in reply and then banked around toward the sea. The great wings beat hard against the air, and they soared back up into the sky.

A short while later, Aksel again stood on the deck of the Endurance. Ves dropped him off and then winged away, not wanting anyone to see her change back from eagle form. Aksel rejoined the others, and described the scene they had found in the forest.

Lloyd sighed, a trace of envy in his tone. "That must have been one heck of a fight."

Glo placed a hand on his shoulder. "Trust me, with the Serpent Cult skulking around, there's bound to be plenty more fighting before we're through."

Lloyd visibly perked up. "And next time I'll be ready for them."

A little while later, Ves, Ruka, and Maya climbed aboard. The latter two had dove over the side just after the eagle took off with Aksel. Their excuse was they were checking out the shoreline, but Glo suspected it had more to do with covering the disappearance of Ves. The sailors gawked as the sisters strode up to join the companions. Ves appeared oblivious to the fuss around them, while Ruka cast dark looks at the crew. Maya danced along, happily waving to everyone around them.

When they were finally in earshot, Ruka called out to the companions. "I think your golem was in one heck of a fight. It's got two large gashes in its body, one in the front and another in back."

Seth fixed Aksel with an accusatory stare. "Well, that's not good."

Aksel let out a deep sigh. "No, it isn't. It looks like we are going to need more scrolls from Maltar to repair him."

"Maybe he'll give us the scrolls for his pendant," Glo said. "He promised us a reward anyway."

Aksel visibly brightened at the idea.

An hour later, the ship tilted and then gently rocked. The Boulder had reached the anchor and climbed aboard. With that, Captain Rochino gave the order to weigh anchor, and start the journey back to Ravenford. The companions gathered on the rear deck, near the port railing, amongst the crates labeled Ravenford. Lloyd, still blinded, sat quietly listening to the conversation. The Endurance rounded Cape Marlin point, the rubble of what was once the lighthouse still smoldering in the center of the isle. Rochino came over to join them.

"I never got a chance to ask you what happened over there. It looks as if a bomb went off or something."

"Or something," Seth snickered.

Glo cast a dark look at the halfling, but refused to retort.

"It was an unfortunate side effect of our run-in with the goblins," Aksel explained.

Rochino responded with a gruff laugh. "Well, that must have been one strong side effect, lad."

"Explosive, one might say," Seth needled, a wide smirk spreading across his face.

Glo threw his hands up in exasperation. "Fine, Seth! I blew up the lighthouse! Are you happy now?"

Rochino stared the wizard up and down, his eyes widening. He then leaned toward Seth and spoke in a soft voice. "Piece of advice there, laddie. I'd think twice about pissing off anyone who could blow up a building like that."

Seth glanced up at the Captain, his expression unchanging. "What can I say? I like living dangerously."

Glo smiled in spite of himself. Seth was incorrigible. He shrugged his shoulders and excused himself, strolling over to the port railing. Glo leaned over the rail and watched the clear waters roll by below. He stood there a few minutes, the waves making him feel peaceful. He quickly realized he was no longer alone. Seth and Aksel stood on either side of him. Glo arched an eyebrow.

"Yes?"

"Can you identify some things we found?" Seth asked politely. He wore that all-too-familiar innocent expression on his face.

Glo sighed. No matter how hard he tried, he couldn't say no to the halfling.

"Of course," he said, putting his hand out. Seth handed him the dagger he had found on the imposter. Glo cast the spell of identification and concentrated until an image coalesced in his head. "It is a magical dagger with a better-than-average chance of puncturing its target, no matter how tough the hide."

"Sweet!" Seth declared.

Glo handed Seth the dagger. The halfling gingerly stuffed it in his belt.

Next, Aksel held out a ruby ring. "We found this at the lighthouse."

Glo took the ring and held it until images formed in his mind. "It is a ring that will enhance your overall health to a minor degree." Glo handed the ring back to his friend. As Seth pulled out another object, Martan strode over to them.

"There's something I think you should see." The archer turned toward the stern of the ship and pointed to the sky.

Glo peered in the direction the archer pointed. Off in the distance, there was a barely-visible speck. Glo was amazed that Martan had seen it at all. Glo narrowed his eyes, trying to get a better look at the object. It appeared reddish-brown in color. It was also getting larger. "I can't quite make it out, but whatever it is, it's headed this way."

"I know what that is. It's a copper dragon," Seth declared.

A copper dragon? What would a copper dragon be doing out here over the sea? Copper dragons normally dwelled in the hills or mountains. They were earth dragons, and not typically fond of water. Either way, this was an amazing opportunity. Glo had never seen a real live dragon before, and coppers were notoriously friendly. Based on his studies, he knew that all metallic dragons were friendly. They were noble creatures and meant no harm to the other races. Non-metallic dragons, on the other hand, were a different matter. Black, red, green, blue, and white dragons were inherently evil. The dragon Ullarak, the one that had terrorized Ravenford, and that Gryswold had slain, was a black dragon.

Glo's musings were interrupted by a tug at his arm. Ves stood at his side, her expression worried. She grabbed his arm and gently pulled him away from the others. Glo was a bit surprised but said nothing, instead allowing her to lead him farther down the railing. Ruka and Maya stood waiting there. Glo surveyed the three sisters. Ruka appeared concerned as well. Even Maya, normally unflappable, was subdued.

Glo whispered to Ves, "What's the matter?"

She responded in a quiet voice, her tone anxious. "My sisters and I cannot be spotted by that dragon. Please do not tell it that you have seen us."

Glo was surprised by the strange request. *Could the sisters be afraid of the dragon?* His eyes swept across all three of them, but he saw no evidence of fear. *If they're not scared, then why don't they want the dragon to see them?* He was dying to know the reasoning behind all this. He suspected it had something to do with the girls' true nature. However, he also knew if he asked them, he wouldn't get a straight answer. He responded with a slow nod. "Okay, but where will you go?"

"We will hide underwater until he is gone," Ves replied, with just a trace of a smile at the corners of her mouth.

A thin smile spread across Glo's own lips. "Very well, I will tell the others to keep silent about meeting you."

Thank you, Ves mouthed. She flashed him a smile and then all three sisters jumped overboard. Glo peered over the rail after them, but they were already gone from sight, having disappeared beneath the waters of the bay. He soon rejoined his companions, informing them of the sisters' odd request. They all agreed to keep their secret, although Seth couldn't help commenting.

"Like I said... strange..."

The dragon now loomed larger in the sky, quite visible to the ordinary eye. Panic began to spread among the crew. The companions reacted swiftly to head it off, explaining to the Captain that this type of dragon meant them no harm. Rochino responded immediately, ordering his men to calm down.

A short while later, the copper dragon drew up to the ship. It was a striking sight. The creature flew with a majestic grace, effortlessly gliding on its massive bat-like wings, only occasionally beating them to propel itself forward. Glo could see the large horned head quite clearly now. It sat astride a long, thick, armored neck, connected at the other end to a strong, muscular body. Four powerful legs were tucked tight against the dragon's torso, each ending in large clawed feet. The long, sinuous tail extended straight out behind the creature, all the way to its very tip. The dragon's body, was covered from head to tail with warm reddish-brown scales, speckled here and there with small spots of blue. The large wings spread out far from the body connecting in a V-like shape all the way down, almost to the tip of the creature's tail. The head was crowned with two broad, flat horns which pointed backwards toward the creature's body. A multi-pointed frill extended from either side of the dragon's jaw. It was a breathtaking sight. Glo found himself caught in the splendor of this noble being—then something struck him. *The creature looks awful small for a dragon.*

Nearly even with the Endurance now, Glo was able to estimate its size. It appeared to be about thirty feet long, its wingspan maybe one and a half times that. It was not small by any means, but somehow he thought that a dragon should be larger. Then Glo remembered—in his father's *Book of Dragons*, it noted that copper dragons were smaller than their brethren. A red dragon, for instance, would be nearly twice the size of this one. So this was indeed a full-sized, adult copper dragon.

The dragon now flew parallel to the Endurance. It slowed down to stay even with the craft. Without warning, Seth climbed up on top of the recovered crates, waved toward the dragon, and yelled out to the creature. To Glo's surprise, he greeted it in its own language, Draconic!

"*Hail, winged traveler,*" he cried in the dragon's tongue.

Glo was rather impressed. He had no idea the halfling spoke Draconic. Glo himself knew it because his father had insisted he learn it—that and about a dozen other languages. Still, he had to wonder at how and why Seth had picked up the dragon's language.

"*Hail in return, good person,*" the dragon responded, its voice a deep rumble. "*You honor me greatly by speaking in my own tongue.*"

"*The honor is ours, noble one,*" Seth replied eloquently. He followed the response with a low bow.

Glo arched an eyebrow. It appeared that Seth could be quite refined when he wanted. Glo's eyes flickered around the deck. Everyone stared at either the halfling or the dragon. They appeared mesmerized by the curious exchange, though he doubted that any of them understood the conversation.

"*How may we be of service?*" Seth continued.

"*I am looking for three... girls,*" the dragon rumbled its reply. "*They are in my care, but I have... lost them.*"

Seth responded without batting an eye. "*Can you describe them?*"

"*They would be... blonde... and young. They are sisters.*"

Seth put his hand to his chin, making a great show of contemplating the matter. *"Hmmm... three young, blonde sisters, you say?"*

"Yes," the copper creature rumbled, its massive head turning to regard the small being.

Seth cocked his head and tapped his foot on the top of the crate. Finally, he shook his head. *"I don't believe so. Let me ask my friends."*

Seth spun on his heel, knelt down, and whispered to Lloyd. The young warrior sat on the crate next to him, his expression one of deep concentration. Seth spoke so softly that Glo only caught two of the words, "sisters" and "truth". Glo did his best to keep his expression impassive. He was not certain if the dragon would be familiar with the facial expressions of other races, but he decided not to take the chance. Finally, Seth sat back. Lloyd, still blinded, lifted his head and peered in the direction of the dragon. He cried out in the common tongue, "I am sorry, but I have not seen the girls you are asking about."

Glo nearly choked. *That was brilliant!* Lloyd currently could not see anything, so of course, he was telling the truth. The dragon was quiet for a long moment. Glo began to wonder if it understood common, when it finally responded in that tongue.

"I thank you then for you time. I must be off now and continue my search."

With a great flap of its large wings, the copper dragon propelled itself forward. It shot ahead of the Endurance like a missile. A few hundred yards out, it shifted its huge frame and gracefully banked away. Abruptly something went wrong—the maneuver must have somehow thrown the dragon off balance. The dragon flapped its great wings wildly, only making things worse. Glo watched in horror as the great creature spiraled out of control. It plummeted downward and crashed into the bay, sending a tall spray of water in all directions!

"What just happened?" Lloyd cried in dismay.

"The dragon just dovetailed into the bay!" Seth responded incredulously.

Glo barely heard them, already on the move. He rushed across the deck toward the opposite rail. On reaching it, he leaned far over the side. What he saw made him sigh with relief. The dragon had resurfaced about a hundred yards ahead of them.

"It's oka..." Glo started to say then halted. He had spoken too soon. The dragon was floundering in the water. It couldn't swim! Glo reacted instinctively, reaching into his pouch and pulling out a small strip of leather. Moving his arms in concentric circles, he brought them together above his head. As his hands touched, he incanted a single word. "*Subvolo.*"

In the waters ahead, the dragon stopped thrashing about. Its large form lifted partially out of the bay. It sputtered water out of its huge mouth and took in a deep breath, yet its wings were still submerged.

It's not enough, Glo realized. Without another thought, the elf vaulted for the nearest ladder.

"Glo! Where are you going?" he heard Aksel's cry behind him.

"For a swim!" he yelled over his shoulder without stopping. The Endurance was at full sail and would quickly pass the drowning creature. Glo needed to hurry. He swiftly reached the top of the ladder, vaulted over the side and grabbed the rungs, half climbing, half skidding down. The entire time Glo kept an eye on the dragon. They were nearly on top of it now. He cried out to the creature in its own language, "*Please stay still!*"

The dragon swiveled its large head around and looked directly at him. "*Did you make me float?*"

"*Yes! And if you hold still, I may be able to get you out!*"

"*I will try,*" the dragon rumbled back. It turned its large head forward and did its best not to move.

Glo was only halfway down the ladder, but if he waited any longer, they would pass the creature by. He realized he had no choice—he had to risk a jump. Before he could talk himself out of it, Glo launched himself off the ladder. He went flying through the air toward the dragon's back. Time slowed and Glo felt as if he hung there forever, suspended between the dragon and the ship. Glo's stomach tied into knots. *Seth makes this look so easy.*

Time suddenly sped up again, and he plummeted onto the dragon's back. Glo landed hard, the impact nearly knocking the wind out of him.

Gods, its scales are tough! He felt as if he had slammed into a stone wall. His body ached, but somehow he managed to grasp the scales and hold on. Glo took a few moments to catch his breath then tried to sit up. The Endurance had passed them, and they were being buffeted by its wake. Up on deck, he could see Aksel, Seth, Martan, and Rochino. They were all staring down at him.

"Are you alright?" Aksel cried.

"I think so!" Glo yelled. He turned his attention back to the dragon. It remained stationary, but the waves rocked the creature mercilessly. "*Hang on, friend,*" he said in Draconic.

"*You do the same,*" the creature rumbled in response.

Glo waited until the rocking died down then carefully sat up. He gingerly reached behind his back and into his pack. Rummaging around, he grasped the end of a length of rope. *Thank you, Elladan,* he thought silently. The elven bard had insisted they all have ropes, lanterns, and the like whenever they set off to travel. At the time, Glo thought the other elf silly, but right now, he could kiss him. Glo laid out the rope on the dragon's back and began casting another spell. His arms ached as he moved them around, but he forced himself to finish the motion. He ended the spell with the words, "*Funem Dolum.*"

The effect was instantaneous. The rope in front of Glo snaked straight up as if it were alive. When it was done, it hung there suspended in mid-air, reaching a good fifty feet above them. His arms were sore, but Glo could not stop now. He needed to get out of the way so that the dragon would be free to use the rope. He grasped on and slowly pulled himself until he could also clamp his feet onto the cord—then Glo began to climb. Hand over hand he shimmied upward. It was slow going, and his arms still ached, but Glo continued to climb. Finally, after what seemed an eternity, he reached the end of the rope. At the top, Glo saw what appeared to be a fluffy cloud. There was an empty space inside, large enough for a number of people. Glo reached forward and touched the cloud. It felt solid. Intrinsically, he knew it was supposed to be—it was part of the spell, but part of him just wanted to be sure. Glo pulled himself up and into the cloud. He then spun around and peered down. The dragon still floated in the water some fifty feet below. Its head and back were above the water line, but its wings were still mostly submerged.

"*Grab the rope!*" he yelled to the large creature.

"*Are you certain?*" the dragon responded.

If Glo did not know any better, he would think the creature sounded nervous. "*Trust me! Grab the rope!*"

"*Very well,*" the dragon rumbled. "*I hope this works.*"

Glo raised an eyebrow. The dragon indeed sounded nervous. He watched in fascination as the copper dragon attempted to lift its front legs over its head. It tried to grasp the rope, but could not quite reach it. It tried twice more with the same result. On the last attempt, the dragon apparently overstretched itself. It suddenly wobbled and then flipped completely over. The creature submerged itself, sending spray splashing all the way up to Glo!

Glo wiped the spray from his face with the sleeve of his robe. When he looked once more, the great head was above the water again. The dragon forcefully sputtered water from its snout. When it was done, it focused on the rope once more. Two large legs reached up out of the water and firmly grasped hold of the rope. The copper dragon then slowly, but surely, pulled itself up out of the water. Miraculously, the thin rope held the heavy dragon's weight. It wouldn't have normally, but luckily that was also part of the spell. Finally, the dragon was out of the water; only the end of its long tail was still submerged. The creature unfolded its great wings as it continued to grasp the rope and beat them back and forth, shaking the water off of them. The dragon hung there until its wings were dry, then peered up at the waiting wizard.

"*Thank you,*" it said simply.

"*You are most welcome, noble one,*" Glo replied.

"*I owe you my life,*" the dragon said gravely. "*It is not a debt I take lightly. How may I repay you?*"

Glo was not certain how to respond. He hesitated before replying. "*We are headed to* Ravenford. *Meet us there tomorrow.*"

He was not sure what kind of favor to ask from a dragon, however, he was extremely curious about the creature. He wanted to see it again under better circumstances. He had not forgotten the sisters, either. If the dragon returned tomorrow, that would give them ample time to hide if they wanted.

"*Very well*," the copper dragon responded, its tone solemn. The creature then launched itself off the rope, and with a great beat of its wings, shot off over the water and out of sight.

Glo stuck his head out of the cloud and saw the dragon wing its way high up into the sky. It made a wide circle and then headed off swiftly to the north.

18
RUNAWAYS
You see, I haven't exactly been honest with you

Ashort while later the Endurance returned to pick him up. The large vessel drew up directly beneath him, the main deck only twenty feet below his cloudy perch.

"Nice going, lad!" a gruff voice called out. Rochino stood by the ship's wheel, smiling broadly up at him.

Glo gave him a short wave then shimmied down the rope. He was back on the main deck a minute or so later. Aksel waited there for him there.

"That was quite a stunt you pulled."

A wan smile spread across Glo's lips, his elbows and knees still aching. "Trust me, it's decidedly less impressive when you realize that I almost missed."

"We can fix that." Aksel motioned for him to follow. He led them back to the Ravenford cargo, where Lloyd, Seth, and Martan waited.

Seth shook his head at Glo. "You're such an amateur."

"Looked pretty good to me," Lloyd said genially.

Glo cocked his head to one side. "Ummm, Lloyd, aren't you still blind?"

Seth smirked. "Exactly."

Aksel let out a heavy sigh. "Glo, do us all a favor, never do something like that again."

Glo grinned sheepishly. "Trust me. I'll leave the heroics to Lloyd and Seth from now on."

The sounds of footfalls on the deck caused them to spin around. Ves and Maya ran across the deck toward them, with Ruka trailing slowly behind. The two sisters reached Glo first and threw their arms around him. Ves stood up on her toes, pulled him down, and kissed him on the cheek. Glo was taken completely off-guard. It was the second time Ves had been this close to him. This time there were no dust clouds, though, and he could smell the scent of her hair. It was like a fresh ocean breeze. Glo felt the blood rush to his cheeks as she hung on to him. He was going to ask her what that was for, but he lost his train of thought as he gazed into her sparkling blue-green eyes.

"Thank you for saving Cal," she said in a soft voice.

Glo opened his mouth to reply, but no words came out. Then he felt his waist being squeezed. Gazing, down he saw Maya's sweet face grinning up at him.

"Yes, thank you for saving Cal!" she cried.

He managed to smile back at her, but still felt confused. He shifted his gaze from Maya to Ves and finally managed to speak. "Who's Cal?"

Ves pulled back a bit, a look of surprise across her face. Yet her arms remained draped around his neck. "Why our dragon friend, of course," she replied as if it were obvious. "That was very brave of you to come to his rescue."

"Personally, I thought you were going to totally miss and fall into the ocean," Ruka said from behind her sister.

Seth snickered. Lloyd and Aksel chuckled.

"I almost did," Glo admitted. "I'm not exactly an acrobat."

"Either way, you saved our friend's life, and we are *all* grateful." Ves gave him another peck on the cheek and then pulled away. Maya followed her sister's lead and let go of him.

Glo was still bemused by the sudden display of affection. He gazed around and saw Aksel trying to suppress a smile. Seth still smirked at him. Lloyd, though he could not see, had an amused expression. Only Martan seemed unhappy. The archer stood on the other side of Lloyd, glaring at Glo, but turned away when he saw the elf staring back at him. That brought Glo to his senses. He understood how Martan felt. He, too, had experienced a touch of jealousy when he had first seen Martan with Ves. There was nothing he could do about it right now—there were more important matters to discuss. Glo pulled himself together. It was time to have a serious talk with the sisters. He spoke to them as politely as possible. "Ves, Ruka, Maya, may I please have a word with you—alone?"

Without waiting for a response, he headed toward the rear deck. A glance over his shoulder showed that Ves and Maya followed him, with Ruka trailing not far behind. Glo led them up the stairs and over to a stack of crates and barrels. It was the same spot where Ves had changed into a giant eagle earlier that day. Glo stopped and faced the trio. Ves looked like a young girl who had been called to the school-master's office. Ruka stood there with her arms folded, staring at him suspiciously. Maya just smiled sweetly as she twirled around on deck.

Glo admitted he had mixed feelings concerning them. Ves, although distant at times, was a selfless healer, Ruka, despite her gruff-ness, was a formidable ally, and Maya was an absolute joy. Still, their helpfulness had to be weighed against the risks they brought with them. The encounter with the dragon had been dangerous, although not in a usual way. The danger had been to the ship itself. If the dragon had crashed into the vessel, it would have snapped the masts like twigs, or worse, punched a hole in the side.

Glo paused, searching for the right words. When he finally spoke, he tried to be polite. "I am glad that I was able to save your friend. However, you ladies must realize that your actions put this ship at risk."

Ves's eyes dropped down toward the deck. "We're sorry. We didn't mean to cause any harm."

Glo felt a momentary pang of guilt. He hated to treat the young woman this way. Still, things had gotten too far out of hand. He steeled his resolve, trying to sound firm. "That's all well and fine, but if you are to continue to associate with us, then you need to explain a bit more about yourselves."

Ruka opened her mouth to speak, but Glo cut her off. "I am not asking you to reveal your true nature. That is your business. I just want to avoid any further surprises."

Ves sighed, her eyes misting as she glanced back up at him. "You're right. I guess that is only fair." She took a deep breath. "The dragon you just saved is named Calipherous. He is a friend of our father's. He has been watching out for us while he is away." Ves hesitated, shifting from one foot to the other. "You see, I haven't exactly been honest with you."

Glo arched an eyebrow. Something about this young woman tugged at his heartstrings. Still, he managed to maintain a firm expression.

Ves attempted a wan smile, still shifting around uncomfortably. "When I told you we were on a pilgrimage, that was a lie. We actually snuck away from home without anyone knowing. That is why Calipherous is looking for us now."

Glo's expression softened, his curiosity getting the better of him. "Why did you run away?"

Ves must have noticed his change in demeanor—her face brightened a bit. "Well you already know our father is Rodric Greymantle, and that he was once a member of the Wizard's council. I also told you that he married our mother, and the two of them moved to the Glittering Isles."

She glanced at Ruka, the young girl staring back intently. Glo could swear a silent exchange took place between them again. Ruka finally nodded. Ves turned to Glo and moved closer, dropping her voice even more.

"However, several months ago, Father was approached by some members of the council. They told him that several of their order had recently disappeared. They asked for his help in finding them. Dad agreed. He's been gone for some three months without as much as a single message. Her voice cracked as she finished her explanation.

Glo suddenly felt horrible. He had berated these girls when all they were doing was trying to find their lost father. "So you and your sisters decided to go looking for him yourselves."

"Yes," Ves nodded, her expression lightening further, a thin smile spreading across her lips.

Glo smiled in return. Everything was finally starting to make sense. If members of the Wizard's Council were disappearing, it would follow that the other members might seek out help, and who better to turn to than the legendary Rodric Greymantle? The only thing that didn't quite fit in all this was the copper dragon. "This Calipherous is a friend of your father's?"

Ves nodded, glancing down at the deck once more. She did not appear very comfortable with the question.

Glo's eyes narrowed. "Does your father have a lot of dragon friends?"

Ves exchanged glances with Ruka yet again. The younger girl shook her head slightly. Ves turned back to Glo. "Many dragons... make their home on the Glittering Isles. It is sort of a...haven for them... away from the prying eyes of other races."

Glo nodded. He could understand that. His people had done the same thing, holing themselves up in the deep forest of the Ruana-iaith. It was obvious that Ves wasn't telling him everything, but the rest was not important right now. She'd been honest enough. He smiled in earnest. "Thank you for your sharing with me as much as you could. I understand your plight. I am somewhat of a runaway myself. The only difference is that my parents knew that I left; they just didn't approve of it."

Ves's eyes filled with sympathy. "That must have been difficult."

An image of his mother resurfacing in Glo's mind. He could still see the sorrow on her face as the two of them bid goodbye at the edge of Cairthrellon. It had nearly made him change his mind about leaving home. A small sigh escaped his lips. "It was. However, now that I know your story, I think we may be able to help you."

"Really?" Maya squealed stopping in mid-twirl. "You can help us find Daddy?"

Glo knelt down and looked her in the eye. "Perhaps, little one."

She ran over and threw her arms around him. "I knew I liked you!"

Glo smiled at the young girl, then gently extracted himself from Maya's embrace. "First I must talk this over with the others. They have a right to know what is going on, too."

Ves nodded. "That is most understandable. We will wait here for your decision."

"I'll be back soon," Glo promised.

As he walked away, he could hear the three sisters talking softly amongst themselves. He could make out none of it, but Ruka sounded angry. Glo rejoined the others on the main deck. He swiftly recounted Ves's story. When he was done, they were all silent. Aksel was the first to speak.

"You know, I find it strange that this is happening at the same time the Serpent Cult has surfaced."

"You think the Serpent Cult has something to do with the disappearing council members?" Lloyd asked.

Aksel's expression was pensive as he gingerly stroked his chin. "Maybe, then again, maybe not. I just think the timing is interesting."

"Either way, I still don't completely trust these sisters," Seth stated flatly.

Glo glared at the halfling. "Is there anyone you do trust?"

"No. Not really," Seth admitted.

"Well, I think we should help them find their father," Lloyd declared.

"As do I," Glo agreed, thankful that someone else was willing to do the right thing.

Aksel turned toward Martan. "What do you think?"

Martan stared back at the cleric, his expression incredulous. "Me? You want my opinion?"

"As a matter of fact, I do," Aksel told him.

Martan's expression turning thoughtful. "Well then, the sisters are different... there's no denying that... but I believe they mean well." A wry smile abruptly crossed the archer's face. "Heck, I owe Ves my life... twice now in the last two days. In all honesty, I think we should help them."

Aksel spun to face Seth. "Well?"

Seth eyed him for a moment, then threw up his hands. "Oh, why the heck not. It might even be interesting."

Aksel's eyes swept around the group. "Then it's unanimous. We will help them. The question, then, is what do we do first?"

"Maltar might know more about this," Glo offered. "We could take the girls to see him."

Aksel cocked his head to one side as he thought it over. "Maybe—at the very least he might know more about the disappearing council members."

"Then it's settled. I'll go tell the girls," Glo said. He strode back to the rear deck, but when he reached the top of the stairs, he saw Ves standing alone by the ship's railing. Ruka was still by the stack of crates, sitting with her arms folded in front of her. Maya danced around her middle sister, oblivious to the tension in the air.

Glo joined Ves by the rail. "Is everything alright?"

"Yes, just fine." Her smile was forced though, her eyes contradicting her words.

Glo decided it best not to pry further. "Everyone is in agreement that we should help you in your search. When we arrive back in Ravenford, we can talk to Maltar. He most likely has connections with the council. He might even have more current news."

A thin smile spread across Ves's lips. "Thank you, that is very kind of you."

Glo smiled in turn. "It is the least we can do—after all, what are friends for?"

She glanced up at him, and a real smile crossed her face, her features softening markedly. "Friends," she repeated. "Yes, indeed. Let's go tell my sisters, then." She took his arm in hers and led him over to Maya and Ruka. Ves repeated what Glo had told her.

Ruka unfolded her arms and nodded. "Fine with me." Glo was surprised. He had expected her to object. "After all, we still need to collect our reward for finding the cargo." That was more like it, Glo thought wryly. "Though we still need to be careful, especially with Cal floating around. We don't want him finding us and spoiling all the fun."

Maya, still dancing around, glanced up at her older sister. "Ves, he couldn't make you come back even if he tried."

Glo's eyes flickered from Maya to Ves. *The dragon couldn't make her come back?*

Ves turned a bright shade of red. She wagged a finger at Maya. "Hush, dear. That's no way to talk." Her eyes shifted toward Glo, her face still a bright shade of scarlet. "Kids. They say the darndest things."

Glo merely smiled back at her, but his mind raced. Ves was super strong, a shape-shifter, and an expert cleric. Further, that Barghest demon had been afraid of her. Perhaps it was not so odd to believe she could stand up to a copper dragon.

Ves was still speaking. "However, I think it best if we do not arrive in town together. We would like to keep our comings and goings a secret."

Glo arched an eyebrow. If the sisters wanted to keep a low profile, it did make sense. Still he found himself strangely disappointed. "Very well then, where shall we meet?"

"Outside this Wizard Maltar's home. We will be in the forms of a peregrine falcon, a cat, and a flying squirrel."

Well, that answered one of his questions. They were indeed all shape-shifters. "Agreed, then."

Ves reached up and kissed him once more on the cheek. Maya gave him a brief hug, and then the three sisters marched over to the railing. All three spun back toward him. Ves and Maya smiled and waved. Ruka nodded. Then the three sisters dove overboard and were gone.

Half an hour later, the Endurance entered the mouth of the Raven River. The little town spread out around them on either bank. Folks stopped and stared as they headed up stream toward the docks. Rochino expertly guided the tall ship to the main Ravenford docks on the western bank. They pulled in next to the longest pier, and lines were thrown to waiting folks below. The large vessel was moored in place and the anchors were dropped. A gangplank was run from the main deck down to the dock below. A small crowd had already gathered there, composed of town merchants, including the insufferable Haltan.

Glo and Aksel decided to go ahead to Maltar's house and meet with the sisters. Seth would stay behind to oversee the unloading of the cargo and collect their fee from the merchants. Martan would stay as well, and keep an eye on Lloyd. Before they disembarked, Aksel gave Seth the golem ring. It would take a while for The Boulder to reach shore, and they would need bring the golem with them when they finally finished here. With all this decided, Glo, Aksel and Seth climbed down the gangplank together. Seth went first and headed off the eager merchants, allowing the others to make their "escape." As the duo hurried away, Glo could hear Haltan's voice ring out behind them.

"Well, I hope you found *my* cargo. And I hope it is *undamaged...*"

Glo shook his head. The man was insufferable.

The duo quickly reached the end of the dock. There they turned northwest and headed up the west bank of the wide river. As they strode along, Glo's mind raced. He wondered about the Serpent Cult and its plot against Ravenford. He thought about the disappearance of the Wizard Council members, including Rodric Greymantle. He was also bothered by Captain Rochino's reaction to Maltar. He recalled what Aksel had said earlier in the day, and decided to confide in him. "Do you really think the Serpent Cult has something to do with the disappearing wizards?"

Aksel had also been lost in thought. He appeared caught off-guard by the sudden question. "I was merely speculating out loud."

"I realize that, but I can't help shaking this feeling that they are somehow connected."

Aksel pursed his lips together. "That's all well and fine, but we really have no proof. Let's wait and see what Maltar can tell us."

Their conversation came to a halt as they reached a small square. Five roadways came together here. One continued northwest along the river bank. Another led up the tall hill to the town temple. A third headed south out of town. The fourth was the way they had come. The fifth led northeast over the main bridge that spanned the Raven River. The duo turned and headed that way. As they strode across the bridge, Glo's mind traveled back to Rochino's strange reaction to Maltar. "I just hope we are doing the right thing."

Aksel eyed him curiously. "What do you mean?"

"Did you notice the way Captain Rochino reacted when we mentioned Maltar's name?"

Aksel paused a moment as if trying to recall that moment. He slowly nodded. "Yes. Now that you mention it, he did seem to show a rather strong dislike for him."

"I thought so, too, at first, but did you catch that comment about

'Maltar being involved' and 'understanding these dark goings on'"?

Aksel's brow furrowed, then he nodded again. "He did say that, didn't he?" The duo reached the other end of the bridge. The road veered east at that point, past the Charging Minotaur and on toward Maltar's house. "I don't think we have much choice though. Maltar is really the only one around here who might have knowledge of the council members' disappearances."

Glo let out a sigh. "I suppose you're right. Still, I can't shake this funny feeling. Maybe we should listen to Seth and Elladan. Maybe we shouldn't tell Maltar everything we know."

Aksel's hand went to his chin as he mulled it over. Finally he nodded. "Agreed."

The duo continued in silence as they headed toward their meeting with the Greymantle sisters and the questionable Wizard Maltar.

19
ASSASSINS

The whirlwind whipped the elf around like a rag doll, spinning him mercilessly

Maltar lived in a large cottage, two stories high, with a dark wood exterior and paned windows, framed with green shutters. A partial third floor with a pair of dormers jutted out from the angled roof. The lot the cottage stood on was surrounded by a white picket fence. On either side of the house stood a tall thicket of trees, the opposite side of the street lined with woodlands. The nearest neighbors were the Charging Minotaur one street over to the west, and Haltan's shop a good hundred yards to the east around a bend in the road. There was no other house in sight. Aksel and Glo waited patiently out in front of Maltar's home. Nearly an hour had passed and there was still no sign of the Greymantle sisters.

Aksel finally spoke. "I don't think they're coming."

Glo let out a long sigh. "So it would appear."

It was a shame. Glo really believed they could have helped the sisters find their father. He thought they believed so as well. A familiar voice interrupted his musings.

"Hey, Aksel! Glo!"

Glo glanced up the road and saw Seth striding toward them. Martan and Lloyd followed close behind, the former leading the latter. Trailing the threesome lumbered The Boulder, the stone golem towering over even the tall Lloyd.

As they neared, Martan's eyes swept the area. "Is Ves here yet?"

Glo shook his head. "No. They never showed up."

"Oh," the archer said, his face dropping despondently.

Seth's mouth twisted into a half smirk. "Can't say I'm surprised. Ruka stopped by the docks for their share of the finder's fee. She wasn't exactly friendly—just took her money and left without a word."

Glo raised an eyebrow. That didn't sound friendly at all. He thought the sisters had come to trust them. Apparently, something had changed their minds.

"Well, at least we know they're in town." Martan sounded hopeful.

"Anyway, the rest of us are all here. We might as well go in and give Maltar his amulet," Aksel said.

They left The Boulder standing in front of the house. Glo opened the gate and led the way up the short stone path to the brown stone cottage. Seth and Aksel followed. Martan led Lloyd by the arm. Glo stepped up to the front door and knocked gingerly. He waited, but heard neither voices nor sounds of movement from inside the house. A full minute went by with no response.

"That's strange," Glo muttered. He stepped forward and knocked again. Another minute or so passed, but still no one came to the door. Glo began to worry. By now, at least one of the apprentices should have answered the door. There was always one in the house at all times. That begged the question, where was everyone? Abruptly he realized Seth stood next to him.

"May I?" the halfling said, looking up at him expectantly.

"By all means," Glo replied, ushering him forward.

Seth stooped in front of the door and closely examined the lock. A few seconds later, he stood up, grabbed the handle, and pushed on the door. It slowly swung inwards. Seth smirked and shrugged his shoulders. "The door was open."

Glo was about to retort, but the comment died on his lips. The entryway beyond was now visible. There on the floor lay a man in grey robes, blood pooling all around him. Seth and Martan immediately drew their weapons. Lloyd, hearing the sound of steel, crouched down, his hands going to his sword hilts. "What's going on?"

"Shhh," Seth hissed from the doorway as he scanned the room beyond.

Martan leaned over and whispered to Lloyd. "There's a dead body in the hallway."

A look of surprise registered on Lloyd's face. Nonetheless, he remained silent. Seth gingerly stepped through the door and into the house. Glo and Aksel followed close behind. The foyer of the cottage turned out to be empty, other than the body on the floor. On the other side of the room stood a set of double doors. They were cracked open a hair. Seth skirted the body and peeked carefully through the crack. He signaled the others to wait, then slipped through the doors. Meanwhile, Aksel knelt beside the body. Glo knelt down beside him. Aksel examined the figure, running his hands over the top of the corpse. There was no sign of any wounds.

"Help me roll him over," Aksel whispered. They turned the body and a trail of blood became visible down the back of the grey robe. Aksel examined the body further, then spoke softly to Glo. "Stab wound. Looks like he's been dead for a couple of hours. Did you know him?"

Glo nodded. "Abracus, one of Maltar's other apprentices."

"How many are there altogether?" Aksel asked.

"There are two more besides me, Flibin and Gristla."

At that moment, Seth slipped back into the room. "I checked the main hall and the rooms immediately off of it. The house is quiet, and there's no one in sight." The halfling went over to the front door, this time examining it from the inside. "The lock is undamaged. Whoever did this was either already in the house or someone let them in."

Glo arched an eyebrow. He had a brief vision of the first time he came to Maltar's house unannounced. Flibin had told him to "go away" and slammed the door on him. That started a battle. Glo had not known at the time that an invisible Seth had followed him. The halfling joined the fray and Flibin ended up dead. Strangely, Maltar found the whole incident funny and had even recruited Glo as one of his apprentices, on the condition that he pay for Flibin's revival. "As we both know too well, Maltar's apprentices don't just let anyone into this house."

Seth glared at him. The halfling had not intended to kill Flibin. The apprentice's death had struck a nerve with the normally cynical Seth.

Aksel interrupted their staring contest. "Looks like Abracus here was stabbed in the back."

Seth shifted his eyes to the body. "Let me see." He strode over and carefully examined the stab wound. After a few moments, he sat back, his expression grim. "This was done by a professional." Seth traced the wound with his finger. "One clean stroke with the angle of entry directly between two ribs and up into the heart."

Glo felt a chill go up his spine. "We're dealing with another assassin?"

Seth nodded glancing around the foyer. "Probably more than one, I would think, to hit a house this size."

Martan still stood in the doorway next to Lloyd. "If this is going to get ugly, I'm not going to be much use with just a sword."

Aksel stood up and reached behind his belt. He pulled out a small purse, stuck his hand in, and withdrew some coins. He held out the money to the archer. "Here, this should cover the cost of a new bow."

Martan's eyes widened as he gazed at the proffered coins. "That's way too much!"

"Well, it should be more than enough for a new bow and a spell to cure blindness from the temple," Aksel told him.

"Oh, I hadn't thought of that." Martan took the coins from Aksel's hand, then grabbed Lloyd by the arm. "Come on, Lloyd. Let's get you healed up."

An eager smile crossed Lloyd's face. "Right." The smile quickly faded, he unseeing eyes glancing around the room. "You all be careful while we're gone."

"I'm always careful," Seth retorted.

Glo nearly choked.

Seth glared at the wizard. "When it counts."

"Okay then," Aksel interjected before anything else was said. He motioned with his hand toward Martan and Lloyd. "Hurry back, you two." The duo nodded, then exited the house. Aksel spun back toward Seth. "Can I have the golem ring?"

"Sure." Seth reached into a small pocket in his vest and handed the ring over to Aksel.

Aksel put the ring on and faced the door again. A look of fierce concentration crossed his face. A few seconds later, he relaxed. Through the open doorway, Glo saw The Boulder move. The creature stepped over the short fence and slowly marched up the path to the front of the house. Its heavy footsteps resounded on the flagstone walkway. When it reached the open doorway, it bent down and inserted its huge frame through it. Once inside, the golem slowly turned around. When it stopped moving, it stood facing out toward the open door. "That'll stop anyone from sneaking up on us."

Seth nodded approvingly. "Not a bad idea."

Aksel ushered Seth before him. "Well then, let's start searching the rest of the house."

Seth smirked as he strode forward and slipped past Aksel. Glo followed the other two into the main hall. The house was silent as a tomb. A long hallway ran down its center. It was sparsely furnished, a red carpet stretched along its entire length, a small table against one wall. Lamps sat on sconces at regular intervals along the hallway, with a few paintings hung in between. The hall ended at a pair of glass double doors covered with opaque material that let the light in from the outside. On their immediate left and right were two closed doors. The one on the left led to the parlor where they had previously met with Maltar.

"The parlor's empty," Seth whispered over his shoulder.

Aksel pointed to the right door. "Where does this go?"

Glo called up a mental image of the house. "That leads down to the basement."

"I took a peek down there. It's pretty dark," Seth told them.

Aksel stroked his chin for a moment before speaking. "We'll come back to that later. Let's work our way up first."

The trio continued down the hall. A few feet farther up on their left was a finely varnished wooden staircase. An ornately carved banister rose along its side. At the top they could see a landing with more stairs visible through the dark wooden railing.

"What else is on the first floor?" Aksel whispered.

Glo pointed down the hall. There was a second hallway ahead, a few feet off to the right. "That leads to the apprentices' apartments."

"I checked those, too. All empty," Seth whispered.

At the end of the hall were two more doorways, one on either side. "And those?" Aksel pointed.

Seth ticked off on his fingers. "Dining room, and closet, and small porch behind the glass doors. All empty. There's also a back door off the porch. It was closed but unlocked. There was no sign of anyone out back."

Glo marked off the rooms Seth had mentioned in his mind. "That just leaves the kitchen. It's off the dining room."

"I peeked in there, too. Didn't see anyone," Seth acknowledged.

Aksel gazed up at Glo, his expression pensive. "Anything off the kitchen?"

Glo tried to picture the kitchen. He recalled two doors in that room. One led to the dining room. The other was lined with shelves of food. "Just a pantry."

Aksel peered past them down the hall, his hand still on his chin and his brow furrowed as he decided what to do next. "Let's take a quick look anyway."

Seth led the way. The kitchen indeed appeared empty. The inside walls were lined with dark grey stone counters and mahogany-colored cabinets. In the center of the room was a small island, topped with the same dark grey stone as the counters. A slab of beef, some utensils, and a few jars lay out on it. It appeared as if someone had been preparing a meal. Inset into the outside wall was a decently-sized hearth. A medium-size cauldron hung in it. It appeared as if the hearth had been lit, but the fire had long since died. Only orange embers remained now, scattered across the floor of the fireplace.

Seth entered the kitchen ahead of them. He crept around the island and suddenly froze in place. He gazed over his shoulder at them and silently raised a finger to his lips. He then pointed behind the island. Aksel and Glo quietly stepped forward and peered over his shoulder. There on the floor, between the island and the hearth, was a small pool of blood.

Glo closed his eyes and shook his head. *This doesn't look good.* Something brushed his arm. Glo nearly jumped out of his skin! He spun around and saw Seth behind him. The halfling pointed toward the pantry door. There was a faint red stain at the base. Seth crept to the door and carefully pushed on it. Glo felt himself tense as it swung inward. On the floor in the middle of the tiny room lay the cook! Aksel quickly pushed past them and knelt down beside the body. After a brief examination he gazed up at the others, his expression grave.

"Stabbed, just like Abracus."

Glo hung his head. He had only met the cook briefly. He had seemed like a nice enough fellow. He certainly did not deserve to die like this.

Aksel stood up. His face had gone ashen, but his voice sounded hard. "Let's move on upstairs."

The trio returned to the main hall, Seth leading the way once again. When they reached the base of the stairs, the halfling held out his hand.

"You two wait here," he whispered.

Glo and Aksel merely nodded. They watched in silence as Seth climbed the stairs and disappeared above.

Seth stealthily ascended the staircase. He could clearly see the upper flight through the wooden banister. It appeared empty. Seth crept across the bare floor of the landing and continued his upward climb. There was a hallway above and another flight of stairs visible through the banister. Seth stopped just before the last step. From this vantage point, he could see all the way down the hall to the right. This hallway was similar to the one on the first floor. A long carpet ran down the center, just like below. The walls also had lamps at regular intervals, but were otherwise bare. The hallway ended at a window. Seth leaned forward and peered around the corner to his left. This hallway ran the length of the house as well, ending in another window. *The silence up here is eerie.*

Seth carefully stepped out into the hall and gauged his surroundings. There were three doors to his left and three more to his right. The stairs upward were identical to the ones he had just climbed, made of finely varnished wood. The ornate banister continued upwards, but stopped a few stairs beyond the second landing. The rest of the flight was hidden behind a solid wall.

Something caught his eye on the staircase. There was a substance dripping down from the landing above. It was dark and red. Seth's eyes narrowed, his hand instinctively unsheathing a dagger from his belt. He slowly ascended the stairwell, his back to the wall as he went. The top of the landing finally came into view. It was covered with blood!

Seth peered through the banister at the upper stairwell. Just where the wall began, he caught a glimpse of something black. He stood perfectly still and listened sharply, but all remained silent. There was no hint of movement from above. Seth began his ascent once more. A black shape became visible on the upper stairs. It was a body—a body in a black robe. He reached the landing and skirted carefully around the pool of blood. He could now see all the way up the next flight. There lay not one, but two black-robed figures in a heap about halfway up the steps. Neither figure moved.

Well, I found the assassins. Or what's left of them, Seth amended.

Their faces were still shrouded in hoods, but the robes were sliced in a number of places. Cut flesh could be seen in those tears, blood dripping from the wounds, down to the landing below. The rest of the stairs appeared clear, but Seth knew better. Something had ripped these two to shreds. *Blade trap most likely. The trigger must be hidden under one of these stairs.*

Seth carefully climbed to the step just below the bodies. He knelt down and examined the corpses. One of the figures' lower arm lay bare, a tattoo of a serpent clearly visible on it. *Well, that answers that. Not just assassins, but Serpent Cult as well. Pretty bold move to attack Maltar's house... or desperate.*

Seth shifted his search to the stairs underneath the bodies. The second step up moved a bit under his hand. *Pressure plate. Nice little trap.*

He checked the next stair beyond and found a second pressure plate. Seth's mouth twisted into a half smirk. *Maltar doesn't trust anyone.*

The next step beyond was clear. Seth cautiously maneuvered his way over the two steps to that one, then climbed toward the top of the stairwell, checking each stair as he went. He also examined the walls. Somewhere, there had to be a mechanism to disarm the blades. Seth made it all the way to the top. The stairwell ended here, at a door to the third floor. He found the trap control mechanism right next to it. Seth shook his head. Maltar probably came upstairs, armed the device, and then went about his business. If anyone was foolish enough to follow him up here, it was just too bad for them.

The mechanism itself was fairly simple, a gear-and-pinion type device. Seth had it disarmed in less than a minute. Once the trap was disabled, he went back to the two bodies. He searched them thoroughly. Aside from a pair of nasty-looking knives, one of the men was carrying a huge diamond. The sparkling jewel must have been an inch in diameter. He just caught himself from letting out a low whistle. *This has to be worth a small fortune. Payment for the job of hitting Maltar's home, more than likely.*

That would explain why these assassins were so brazen. Greed made people do almost anything. Seth knew that only too well. *Oh, well, no use letting this go to waste.*

Seth pocketed the shiny stone, stood up and returned to the top of the stairs. He examined the door closely, but could find no trace of any wires. There was nothing to suggest another trap. The door was locked, of course. *Well, not for long.*

He got out his pick and began to work the lock. He almost had it when his pick scraped something next to the tumblers. *Dragon dung!*

Seth yanked out his pick, but it was too late. He felt a gust of wind suddenly pick up around him. Seth immediately spun around and bolted down the stairs. He leapt over the assassins' bodies, grabbed the railing, and vaulted himself over the landing. Seth's feet hit the flight below, not stopping as he ran down toward the second floor. He had almost reached the bottom when he vaulted over the banister again and landed on the next flight. Seth charged down those steps and yet again flung himself over the banister, this time yelling a single word ahead of him.

"Run!"

Aksel immediately heeded him, turning and sprinting down the hallway toward the front door. Unfortunately, Glo hesitated, a bewildered look upon his face.

"I said run!" Seth scrambled down the last steps, skirted passed the waiting wizard, and bolted down the hall beyond. Behind him, Glo began to move, but it was too little too late.

A quick glance over his shoulder confirmed what he expected to see. A whirling vortex came sweeping down the steps. Paintings flew off the wall, the small table in the hall upended, and lamps were blown off their sconces. It caught up to Glo and swept him off his feet, then stopped there at the bottom of the steps. The whirlwind whipped the elf around like a rag doll, spinning him mercilessly.

Seth screeched to a halt, whipping back around to face the creature that had his friend. The whirlwind was large. It spanned the width of the hallway and reached all the way to the ceiling. *Dragon dung! This Maltar doesn't fool around.*

It was a Great Air Elemental. The winds from the creature would soon tear Glo apart! *We need to get him out of there fast.*

Seth drew his knives and ran forward. He was not sure what his small blades would do against a creature made of air, but he had to try something. Suddenly the hallway around him began to shake. *What now?*

Seth halted and glanced over his shoulder. He was just in time to see the doors to the foyer fly off their hinges. They sailed out into the hallway, slamming into the walls on either side. A large figure marched through the entryway and lumbered straight for him. It was The Boulder. Seth jumped back and flattened himself against the wall, just in time. The stone golem stomped by him and marched toward the stairs, halting in front of the whirling elemental. The Boulder was tall, but the air creature towered over him. Glo was still caught inside the vortex. Seth could hear his cries as he was whipped around.

"Woahhh! Woahhh!"

The Boulder raised its huge arms. Seth flinched. If the golem started flailing away at the creature, Glo would be pulped! Yet, instead of swinging at the elemental, The Boulder took a step forward. It stretched its long arms out into the whirlwind.

It's trying to catch Glo! Smart, Aksel, very smart.

The little cleric had drawn up next to him. Seth nodded curtly to him, but Aksel's eyes lay fixed on the scene before them. The duo stood there, side by side, grim-faced as The Boulder attempted to grasp the spinning elf. The sudden sound of heavy footfalls caused Seth to whirl around and crouch into a defensive stance. A tall form rushed down the hallway toward them. Seth immediately recognized the figure. *Lloyd!*

Lloyd rushed passed them, drawing his twin blades, both coming alight as he did. Seth, daggers in hand, followed close behind. The Boulder's arms were now completely immersed in the elemental, its great weight preventing it from being buffeted by the fierce winds. Glo was now at the top of the whirlwind, the elemental trying to keep its captive out of the golem's reach.

Lloyd and Seth got as close as possible without being swept up themselves. Man and halfling swung and stabbed at the creature. They must have hit something in all that wind because the monster visibly shuddered from each swipe. Without warning, there was a blinding flash and a resounding boom.

Krrraaaacckkkk!

Seth and Lloyd jumped back instinctively as the elemental lit up from the inside. *That's lightning!*

Seth blinked his eyes until his vision cleared. Up above, Glo still swirled around at the top of the whirlwind. Seth was impressed. Somehow, Glo had managed to fire off that spell. In spite of the high winds, Glo's arms began to move again. Seth immediately recognized those motions. *He's trying to cast another spell.*

The elemental must have realized it as well. Without warning, it ejected Glo from its body. Seth's eyes went wide as Glo flew overhead. He arced through the air, landing far down the hallway. The hapless elf tumbled end over end until he finally stopped by the broken doors where he lay in a heap. Aksel was already on the move, reaching Glo's side in seconds and kneeling over the still form. Seth fought down the urge to run after them as well. Glo was in good hands, and they still had an elemental to take care of.

After a momentary pause, Lloyd weighed back in. He swung furiously at the elemental, both his blades burning bright. Seth darted in and out once more, stabbing at the creature with both daggers. The elemental continued to shudder, but neither man nor halfling slowed down or backed away. The Boulder then joined the fray. Overhead, two huge grey arms swung at the giant whirlwind. The creature visibly flinched from each blow. After a few more swings, the elemental tried to withdraw. Suddenly a red-hot beam arced overhead. It lanced past the golem and caught the elemental full on. Seth glanced over his shoulder. At the end of the hall, Glo was up again. He knelt on one knee, his right hand pointing down the hall while Aksel supported him under the other arm. A grim smile crossed Seth's lips. As he spun back around, he noticed something strange. *Is it my imagination or are the winds dying down?*

Inside the dervish, he could vaguely see the outline of a transparent figure. Its back was arched, and it appeared to be silently screaming. The winds died down a bit more, and then the form abruptly vanished! The whirlwind slowly sputtered to a stop and then completely disappeared.

Seth breathed a sigh of relief. *It's over.*

Lloyd was flushed from exertion. "That was some battle!"

Seth peered at the tall young man and for once genuinely smiled. "You can say that again."

Down the hall, Aksel held onto Glo, the latter with a look of keen satisfaction on his face. Seth sheathed his daggers and strode toward the duo. A number of smart remarks came to mind, but before he could utter a single word, Glo closed his eyes and slumped down. Aksel struggled but managed to keep him from falling. Seth and Lloyd reached them as Aksel eased Glo onto the floor.

Lloyd's voice was laced with concern. "Is he alright?"

"He'll be fine," Aksel assured them. "I told him you guys could handle it, but he insisted on shooting the thing."

Seth shook his head and let out a short laugh. "If he'd just listened when I said run..."

He was interrupted by a voice from the foyer. "Did I miss anything?"

Martan stood in the entryway, newly-fixed bow in hand. The archer's eyes were wide as he took in the smashed doors, the thrown furniture, and the general destruction up and down the hallway. "This place looks like it was hit by a hurricane!"

Seth, Aksel, and Lloyd all laughed.

"More or less," Seth quipped.

Martan eyes came to rest on Glo. His face went pale. "What happened to Glolindir?"

A wide smirk crossed Seth's lips. "I guess you could say he spun out of control."

20
DARK MAGIC
Here was clear evidence that he was dabbling in dark magic

Glolindir opened his eyes. He quickly shut them as brilliant light flooded his vision. He slowly reopened them. The light itself emanated from two small glowing hands that hovered over his body. Glo blinked a few more times until he was finally able to focus. The serene face of Aksel floated a couple of feet above those hands.

I'm being healed, but why?

Glo tried to move, but his entire body ached.

"Lay still," Aksel admonished him.

"What... happened?" Glo's throat felt dry. He barely managed to form the words.

"You mean aside from the fact you were tossed around like a rag doll?" a familiar voice responded.

Glo slowly turned his head. Lloyd and Seth stood a few feet away. Lloyd appeared worried, but Seth wore his usual smirk.

Glo's mind felt surrounded by fog. "Rag doll..."

Abruptly a whole slew of images flashed before his eyes: Seth rushing past him, a huge tornado flying down the stairs, being lifted off the ground, the entire room spinning around him, his friends and The Boulder below him, the flash of his own lightning bolt, flying down the hall and hitting the floor rather hard.

Now I remember! I was swept up by an air elemental. A rather large air elemental, he amended.

"Next time I tell you to run, maybe you'll listen," Seth chided.

Glo ignored the halfling's jibe. "Where did that thing come from?"

Seth shrugged his shoulders. "Oh, it was just a little present Maltar left for the unwary."

Maltar... of course. "Let me guess. There was a magical trap on the stairs."

"The door to the top floor actually. The stairs had a blade trap on it."

A blade trap, too? Maltar really doesn't trust anyone. Just what is he hiding up on that third floor?

Seth's lips parted, his mouth forming into a wicked grin. "It did a number on those assassins though."

Glo was startled. "You found them?"

"What was left of them." While Aksel finished healing Glo, Seth described the bodies he had found.

At the mention of the tattoos, Lloyd's normally genial face darkened. "The Serpent Cult again. They are getting far too bold. I am sick of them showing up every place we go."

Glo felt a wave of sympathy for the young man. He knew his main concern was for the Lady Andrella. "I think we all are, Lloyd."

The white light faded and Aksel stepped back. "You're all done."

"Thank you." Glo smiled at Aksel and slowly sat up. The hallway around them was in shambles. The little table had been smashed, broken lamps lay strewn about, and the doors to the foyer hung off their hinges. Martan stood in that doorway. He gave Glo a curt nod. Glo nodded back then stood. "Lloyd's right. The Serpent Cult has grown rather bold. No one in their right mind would attack Maltar's house."

Seth folded his arms across his chest. "Maybe, then again maybe they had no choice."

Lloyd stared curiously at the halfling. "What do you mean?"

"Maybe there was something in this house they desperately needed."

"Voltark!" Aksel declared.

They all turned to face him. Even Martan took a few steps closer. "If they recovered the body, they could still resurrect him. It's only been a few days since he died, after all."

Glo turned toward Martan. "Did Voltark ever mention his standing in the cult? Was he really that important?"

The archer was silent for a few moments, his brow furrowed. "I don't quite know for sure. I mean, he never mentioned a rank or anything. Still, he was the head of the Black Adders. I did get the impression they were some kind of elite group within the cult."

"That cinches it, then," Aksel said.

Lloyd still appeared agitated, his face slightly flushed. "I still think this was a bold move. Maltar would be a pretty dangerous opponent."

"Not if he wasn't home."

Everyone turned to face Seth.

"Remember, the front door was unlocked. What if they had an inside man? Someone who could let them know when Maltar was gone and even let them in?"

Glo was taken aback. *Someone on the inside?* That didn't seem likely. All of Maltar's apprentices were afraid of the irritant mage. Abracus, Gristla, and even...

"Flibin!" The name escaped Glo's lips the moment it dawned on him. Aksel, Seth, Lloyd, and Martan all turned to stare at the shocked wizard. "Flibin, the apprentice we killed. He was not very happy once he was resurrected. He would barely talk to anyone. Not even Abracus or Gristla."

Seth nodded. "Seems like our best suspect."

Aksel glanced around the hallway. "Well with all the ruckus we caused, I think it's safe to assume no one else is here."

"More than likely." Seth smirked.

Aksel gave the halfling a sideways glance. "Still, I would like to confirm whether Voltark's body is gone, so let's finish searching the house." Seth nodded and started toward the stairs. "Except this time, we'll stick together," Aksel called after him.

Seth stopped in his tracks and shrugged. "Suit yourself."

They sent The Boulder back to guard the front door then began to search of the rest of the house. Seth led the way, followed by Martan, Glo and Aksel. Lloyd brought up the rear. A quick examination of the second floor produced nothing. It was mainly composed of empty bedrooms. The only other room was the apprentice's workshop. That turned out to be empty as well.

Seth led the way up to the third floor with, Martan trailing close behind. The rest of them followed but stopped on the landing. When Seth reached the top, he knelt down in front of the door. He fiddled with the lock while Martan gazed over his shoulder. Glo, Lloyd, and Aksel did their best to avoid the crimson pool that had congealed in front of them while they waited. It was a rather gruesome sight, but not as grisly as the slashed figures on the stairs above. Finally, they heard a click from above, followed by a satisfied, "Child's play."

Seth stood up and opened the door a crack. He stuck his head through first, then his entire body disappeared. A few minutes went by with no sign of him. Glo started to worry. Abruptly, Seth's head popped through the partially open doorway.

"All clear," he called down.

Glo and the others ascended the stairs, carefully stepping around the black-robed corpses. When they reached the top, they found themselves in a short hallway. There were four doors here besides the one to the stairs. All of them had been locked, but Seth had already picked them.

Seth waved his hand in a wide arc around the hallway passed each door. "Okay, pick your poison."

Aksel turned to Glo. "Any thoughts on where to start?"

Glo shook his head. "I have no idea. Maltar never let anyone up here except for Abracus." Glo's eyes flickered around the hallway. There was one door on every wall, in all the cardinal directions. "I know his bedroom is up here, and his lab. Probably his library as well. Other than that, you've got me."

No one moved or said a word. Finally, Seth strode towards a door and placed a hand on the knob, his mouth twisting into a half smirk. "North it is, then."

"Lead on." Aksel shrugged, giving in to the halfling's whim.

Seth slowly opened the door and peered inside. "Lab," he called back over his shoulder. He pushed the door the rest of the way open and stood aside, allowing the others to file in after him.

Glo carefully scanned the lab. It was a long, L-shaped room with multiple tables along the walls, the tabletops covered with vials and beakers of various-colored liquids. Numerous stacks of thick bound books and parchments were scatter all around. Glo examined a parchment spread across the nearest table. It was a detailed map of the Island of Lanfor, a small island kingdom directly east of Thac. Lanfor itself was thousands of years old. The Queen of Lanfor, a powerful human sorceress, had ruled that nation for nearly three hundred years. Some said the Queen was immortal. Glo thought it more likely that she used magic to extend her life.

The capital city, Palt, was clearly marked on the western end of the isle. Palt was famous for many things, but no more so than the Greystone Halls. The Halls were a great institution of learning. Nearly every subject imaginable was taught between those walls. People came from all over the world to study there. It was also the home of one of the most extensive libraries in the world. Something on the map caught Glo's eye. There was an "X" hand-scrawled next to Palt. He scanned the rest of the map. There was another one on the north end of the island. *Did Maltar make these marks? If so, what could they mean?*

"Guys, you're going to want to see this," a voice called out.

Glo glanced up and saw it was Seth. He stood in a doorway at the other end of the room, wearing the strangest expression. Glo walked over to the open door, his jaw dropping as he peered through it. The next room was as large as the lab, except that it was square. There were two entrances here—one were they stood and another that had to lead to the hallway. The room was otherwise empty, with one glaring exception. There was a large diagram in the center of the wood floor. The diagram was composed of an outer circle paralleled by an inner circle. Within the inner circle was a pentagram. Around the five points of the pentagram, between the two circles, were various symbols.

Lloyd gaped at the drawing. "Isn't that the same as the one we saw in the orc caves?"

Aksel's eyebrows were raised as he, too, eyed the familiar diagram. "Yes, that is most definitely a summoning circle."

"Didn't you say these things were used to summon demons?"

"Demons or other interdimensional monsters. You know—your run-of-the-mill evil creature," Seth said.

Once over his initial shock, Glo pushed past the others into the room. He knelt down next to the circle and examined it closely. The first thing he noted was its size. It was probably ten feet in diameter. Further, the diagram was not hand drawn—it was painted. Glo slowly stood up. "This is a permanent circle."

Aksel eyed him curiously, but said nothing. Seth's expression grew dark. Lloyd and Martan both appeared puzzled.

"A circle like this can hold a creature almost indefinitely. There's no worry about it breaking, or the demon getting free. That way the summoner can take as much time as he or she needs learning to control the demon."

Lloyd's expression turned grim, as did Martan, but Seth now glared at Glo with an *I told you so* look in his eyes. Glo gave a deep sigh. Seth was not wrong. He had been far too trusting of Maltar. Glo gazed at the circle once more. *What was Maltar playing at?* He had thought the mage merely difficult. Yet here was clear evidence that he was dabbling in dark magic. The words of Captain Rochino replayed through Glo's mind. *Well now, if Maltar is involved, then I am beginning to understand all these dark goings on.*

Abruptly, Glo felt a presence at his side. Lloyd stood next to him, staring intently at the circle. The young man's tone was dark. "I may not know much about magic, but this does not look like something a good wizard would do."

Glo nodded his head slowly. "No, indeed it does not."

"I think we've seen enough for now." Aksel stood at the other doorway. "Let's try another room."

Glo took one last look at the summoning circle, then followed the others out of the room. They gathered in the hallway deciding where to head next. They had entered the north door and exited the west door. This time they chose to go south. The room beyond was Maltar's library, a long, L-shaped room, identical in size to the mage's lab. The room was lined with tall bookshelves reaching all the way up to the ceiling. Glo estimated there to be a few thousand books in here. It was the most comprehensive collection he had seen since leaving Cairthrellon. Still, it was only a fifth of the size of his family's library. That collection had been amassed by his ancestors over the course of many centuries, and most of those books dated back to before the Galinthral elves had secluded themselves away from the world.

"This is a rather impressive collection," Aksel said, mirroring Glo's thoughts.

There was a single table in the center of the room with a few piles of books stacked on it. One text lay in the center. It was entitled *Draconic Chronicles of the Great War.* Glo was familiar with the book. It gave an account of the first Demon war—the war between the great dragons of old and the demons from the Abyss. It was a titanic struggle, one that, thankfully, the ancient dragons won. However, it decimated their ranks and brought an end to *Hai'Valan*, the first age of the world. He wondered why Maltar had this particular book out.

Glo felt a presence next to him. Aksel stood there also staring at the ancient text. He gazed at Glo, his eyebrow raised. Glo merely shook his head. Aksel shrugged then called out to the others. "Let's move on."

There was another door at the north end of the room. It led to a small, rectangular room with a large ornate desk in the center and a single high-backed chair behind it. An open book lay on the desk. Both Aksel and Glo stepped around the desk to examine the book. The pages were handwritten, but the lettering was cryptic. Glo's brow furrowed as he attempted to decipher the text. "It looks like some kind of journal, but I don't recognize the language."

Aksel shook his head. "Neither do I."

Glo felt uncomfortable looking at what was probably the mage's journal. He thought of it as an invasion of privacy. Still, from what they had just seen, Maltar's practices were far darker than Glo had originally thought. The matter warranted further investigation and the journal might be their best source of information about the mage's activities. Glo closed the book and lifted it off the table. "Given all that has happened, I think we should take this with us."

Aksel nodded. "I concur—if there is any chance we are wrong about Maltar, we can always return it to him when we next see him."

A loud snort sounded from behind them. "I doubt it."

Aksel and Glo both spun around. Seth stood in the doorway behind them, pointing a thumb over his shoulder. "Maltar's bedroom—

the bed's made and looks like it hasn't been slept in for days.'

Glo raised an eyebrow. *So Maltar has been gone for a while, and from all appearances he left in a hurry. I wonder why.*

Aksel interrupted his musings. "Well then, that just leaves the basement."

The basement was pitch black. Only the first few stairs were visible, the rest swallowed by inky blackness. Glo lit his staff and held it aloft. The light fanned out down the stairwell, revealing a landing down below. Seth led the way down, followed by Martan, Glo, and Aksel. Lloyd brought up the rear. When they reached the landing, the light from Glo's staff revealed another flight leading the rest of the way down to the basement.

The cellar turned out to be one large room that ran the length of the house. Stone walls were visible in all four directions, but the floor was composed of soft dirt. Storage boxes, cabinets, and some old pieces of furniture lined the basement walls. At the base of the stairs, Martan held up a hand. Everyone stopped and waited while he stooped down and examined the ground. Martan nudged his head toward the dirt floor. "Look at this."

Glo stepped closer and peered over his shoulder. There were two sets of tracks in the dirt with two uninterrupted lines between them. "It looks like someone was dragged up to the stairs."

Martan followed the trail all the way across the basement to a bare spot against the opposite wall. The tracks abruptly ended there.

Seth's lips twisted into a half smirk. "Can you say secret door?" He stepped up to the wall and ran his fingers over the stone. After a brief search, he came to a sudden halt. "There's a false section here."

He pushed on a stone and a small hole appeared in the wall. Seth reached inside, a good portion of his arm disappearing. There was a loud click, followed by the grating sound of stone on stone. A section of the wall slid back, revealing a small room behind it. In its center sat a plain rectangular wooden box, about the size of a coffin, atop a wooden pallet.

"Looks just like the container we brought Voltark here in," Aksel said.

Glo stepped forward for a closer look. There were actually two boxes on the pallet, a second one behind the first. Both boxes were lidless and empty. "I wonder who, or what, was in the second box." The companions stood in silence, no one offering any suggestions. Glo finally shrugged. "Either way, you were right, Aksel. They were indeed after Voltark's body."

Aksel grimaced. "It is not a finding I take pleasure in, I can assure you. Anyway, I think we're done here. We should probably report to the Baron."

The companions filed out of the room and strode back across the basement. "We should also check to see if anyone knows Maltar's whereabouts," Glo told the others. "And probably Gristla, too, although I think we can forget about Flibin. If Seth is right..."

"I am," Seth insisted.

"...then Flibin would be long gone by now."

The companions reached the stairs and climbed upward. "Unfortunately, I don't think the same can be said about Voltark," Aksel said, his brow furrowed into a deep frown. "I think we can expect to see him again, sooner rather than later."

Seth, farther up the stairs, peered back down at them. He wore a wicked grin on his face. "Good. I haven't killed any mages in at least a couple of days now."

Glo glared at the halfling. "Really?"

Seth's face took on an innocent expression. "What? Evil mages. I meant evil mages."

184

21
STAND IN
Perhaps if I came clean about the lighthouse...

T his is an outrage!" Gryswold fumed. "An attack like this right in the middle of Ravenford?" He paced back and forth in front of his throne, the large chamber empty this late in the day except for Aksel, Glo, the Baron and the Baroness. Captain Gelpas had also been with them, but left upon hearing their story to dispatch a detachment of guards to Maltar's home.

"And who in their right mind would attack Maltar's house?" Gryswold cried. He stopped his pacing and swung around to face them. Mixed emotions played across the Baron's face.

Glo gave him a sympathetic smile. "I said the same thing."

Aksel, unflappable as ever, responded in a calm voice. "We're fairly certain Maltar was not there. There was no sign of him, and I highly doubt he would have been taken by force."

Gryswold stared at the cleric, his anger slowly abating, but his face remained riddled with doubt. Glo could see how torn the Baron was and tried to assure him further. "If such a struggle had taken place, we would certainly have seen evidence of it. The only real damage to the house resulted from our encounter with the air elemental."

Gryswold's gaze shifted back and forth between Glo and Aksel until the uncertainty faded from his eyes. Finally, he let out a deep sigh. "Yes, yes, you are quite right. Maltar would not have gone down without a fight."

"Poor Abracus," Gracelynn murmured. "He was a gentle soul. He did not deserve to die in such a foul manner." The lady wore a forlorn expression.

Gryswold turned to his wife, his face filled with compassion.

"No, most certainly not." He strode over and took her hand in his own. "Do not fear. We will see to his family—and the poor cook's as well."

A thin smile spread across her face—she looked lovingly into his eyes. "Thank you my dear."

Gryswold patted her hand, then turned back to the duo. "So you have no idea where Maltar might have gone?"

"The others are out combing the town," Aksel told him. "Hopefully someone will have seen Maltar or one his missing apprentices."

The Baron began to pace once more. "If Flibin is responsible, as you surmise, then he may be long gone by now."

"That still leaves Gristla," Glo reminded him.

"Indeed." Gryswold stopped and swung around to face them. "Let us know the moment you hear anything."

"We will, your Lordship," Aksel said.

A brief smile crossed the Baron's lips, then his expression grew serious. "That still leaves me with one problem. I was counting on Maltar attending Andrella's party tomorrow."

The Lady Gracelynn placed a hand on her husband's arm. "Gryswold?"

The Baron, lost in thought, turned to gaze at her. "Yes, dear?"

"What about Glolindir?"

"Glolindir?" His eyes opened wide. "Glolindir," he repeated, his face suddenly brightening. "Why, yes, of course! Why didn't I think of that?"

Both monarchs turned toward him. Glo gazed from Gryswold to Gracelynn. *Did I hear correctly? Are they suggesting I stand in for Maltar?*

Gryswold's expression grew solemn. "Glolindir, in the event that Maltar cannot be found, I would like you to stand in for him at Andrella's party."

Glo felt his knees momentarily buckle. *They were serious! They wanted him to stand in for Maltar—to take his place at the Baron's side.* Glo felt a wave of guilt wash over him. He was not sure he deserved such an honor. *Perhaps if I came clean about the lighthouse...*

Glo opened his mouth to speak, then stopped himself. These two already had too much to deal with. Between the threat of the Serpent

Cult, the assassin attack, and Maltar's disappearance, the last thing they needed to hear about was more destruction. He vowed instead to tell them when this was all over. He replied in a gracious tone. "Why, it would be an honor, your Lordship."

"Excellent!" Gryswold's expression softened, relief flooding his face. The Lady Gracelynn mirrored his response. A familiar young voice spoke out from behind them.

"I assure you, good wizard, the honor is ours." Glo spun around and saw the Lady Andrella entering the throne room. She walked up the center aisle toward them. "With all you have done for our town, it is the least we can do in return."

Glo felt the heat rise in his cheeks, not used to such praise. He bowed low in response. "It is our pleasure, your Ladyship."

Andrella's lips parted as she flashed him a dazzling smile. At the base of the stairs, she stopped, her eyes sweeping the chamber. "Where are your other companions?"

Glo suppressed a smile, quite aware of who the young lady was looking for.

"They had some errands to do around town," Aksel said.

"Well that's a shame." Andrella's face clouded over with disappointment, but she immediately caught herself and braved a tiny smile. "It's always... pleasant when the Heroes of Ravenford come for a visit."

"Thank you, good Lady," Aksel replied.

Andrella curtseyed quite courteously in return. She then whirled toward the Baroness. "Mother, may I speak with you in private?"

"Certainly, dear." Lady Gracelynn stepped down and took her daughter's arm. The two of them strode slowly away, arm in arm across the large chamber. Glo caught some of their conversation.

"Mother, I need a new dress..."

"But Andrella, we already had a new dress made for you!"

"But *Mother*, this dress needs to be *extra* special!"

The corners of Glo's mouth upturned. He was sure he knew why her dress needed to be "extra special." It had to do with a certain handsome young Penwick noble. Any further eavesdropping was interrupted by the Baron.

"Gentlemen."

Glo spun around and saw Gryswold motioned them to follow him. He strode toward the opposite side of the chamber from the two ladies. Glo cast a glance at Aksel, who merely shrugged in response. On the other side of the chamber, Gryswold addressed them in a hushed tone.

"This whole Serpent Cult thing has me more and more worried. It's bad enough that they sent this Voltark and his crew here, and that they may be targeting Andrella." He paused and glanced over at his wife and daughter. From what Glo could hear, they were still immersed in their discussion about dresses. "But this attack on Maltar's home makes them far more dangerous. There's no telling what they'll try next." His expression was grim. His eyes, however, told another story. There was clearly fear in them—not fear for himself, but for his family.

Glo felt a momentary pang of homesickness. He briefly wondered how his mother, Aerandir, was doing. When he left, he remembered seeing a similar look in her eyes. It was a fear born out of concern for him as he set out into the world on his own. Seeing that level of concern in Gryswold's eyes touched something deep inside the young elf. A warmth rose in him for this man and his family. Glo resolved that he would do anything to protect them.

In the meantime, Aksel did his best to reassure the Baron. "Do not worry, your Lordship. We already surmised they might try something at the party. We have a plan to deal with them."

"Truly?" Gryswold gazed intently at Aksel and Glo.

Glo gave the Baron a reassuring nod. He and Aksel had indeed discussed the topic on the way over from Maltar's house. They had fleshed out a basic plan, but the details still needed to be ironed out.

The Baron's expression grew hard. "What will you need?"

Aksel continued his explanation. "Primarily, we will need to position ourselves close to you and your family. If you can work out the seating arrangements..."

"Done!" Gryswold declared. The fear in his eyes had disappeared, replaced with the fire of conviction. Gryswold was a man of action, and now that he had a clear path to take, his doubts subsided.

"What else?"

"The perimeter of the keep will need to be watched as well. There-fore, some of us will need to forgo your gracious invitation. Instead, we will place ourselves at strategic locations around the grounds."

Glo suppressed a smile. Aksel and Seth had reservations about sitting with the nobles at the party, so this plan worked out well for the both of them.

Gryswold nodded. "Your sacrifice is duly appreciated."

Aksel smiled wanly at the Baron, a trace of guilt on his normally serene face. Glo took up the discussion from there.

"Finally, we will set up a method of signaling each other. That way, those on the perimeter can warn the others of any impending danger. So if the Serpent Cult makes a move, we will be ready for them."

Gryswold paused and stroked his beard as he mulled it over. Fi-nally, he shook his head, his expression one of approval. "A sound plan, my friends, a sound plan. Between yourselves and the castle guards, we should be able to handle any contingency—even dark mages that can turn into serpents."

That last was said somewhat in jest, but Glo knew that might be exactly what they would face. It was also not lost on him just how much faith the Baron was placing in them. Glo responded with a sincerity he felt to his very core. "Thank you, your Lordship, for giv-ing us this opportunity to protect you and your loved ones. We will *not* fail you."

Gryswold regarded him silently, then reached out and placed a hand on Glo's shoulder. "Thank you, Glolindir." His arm dropped back to his side and the Baron of Ravenford took a step back. "Thank you both. Your loyalty to my family, and our town, is very much ap-preciated."

The Baron then reached up with both hands and rubbed them across his face. He suddenly appeared quite tired. It struck Glo that he had probably not slept very much with all the added strain over these last few days. Gryswold's hands fell to his sides. "Very well, we will continue with our preparations for the party. Keep us apprised of any new developments in your search for Maltar and his apprentices."

"Will do, your Lordship." Aksel assured the weary monarch.

The two companions bowed then turned to leave. Glo noted that Lady Gracelynn and Andrella were still in the middle of their discussion. They had not gone more than a few steps when the Baron had called out after them.

"Oh, and one more thing."

The duo stopped and spun back around.

"There will be a tournament the morning after the party. I've taken the liberty of placing an entry in for Lloyd."

Glo arched an eyebrow. He exchanged glances with Aksel, who appeared as surprised as he.

Gryswold strode forward and continued to speak loudly. "I would think a young Penwick noble like himself would make a fine addition to the tourney."

Glo heard Andrella squeal from the opposite side of the room. "Ooh, Mother! Now I will *absolutely* need that dress!"

"Andrella..." Gracelynn began.

Glo never caught her response. Gryswold leaned in close and whispered conspiratorially. "Maybe he can show up some of these Dunwynn fops who keep fawning over my Andrella."

A stifled laugh escaped Glo's closed mouth. His gaze shifted from Gryswold to Aksel. Somehow, the little cleric managed to keep a straight face. He stared at the Baron and replied in an even tone. "That was very thoughtful of you, your Lordship. We will be sure to tell Lloyd."

22
ÅNGEL TEÅRS
Unfortunately, she's also been poisoned

W hen Aksel and Glo arrived back at the Charging Minotaur, they found Seth waiting for them. "There's no sign of Maltar nor Flibin anywhere in town. However, I did manage to find Gristla."

Glo raised an eyebrow. "Where is she?"

Seth's voice dropped down to a whisper. "Actually, she's right here. She's in a back room with Kailay."

That's right. Kailay is Gristla's sister.

Seth led them to a door off the common room. He stopped and turned, his eyes scanning behind them. Glo glanced back over his shoulder as well. There were a few guests, but no one seemed to be paying attention to them. Seemingly satisfied, Seth quietly opened the door and ushered them inside.

The room they entered was similar to the guest rooms upstairs. There were two beds, a pair of dressers, a wardrobe, and a mirror. On the south wall were two windows, side by side. The shades were drawn, making the light in the room rather dim. On the bed to their left lay a thin woman with angular features and long jet black hair. Her skin appeared extremely pale and sweaty, and her dark hair was matted under her head.

"Gristla," Glo whispered in shock. The wizard's apprentice looked far from well.

A buxom form with long, wavy strawberry blonde hair stood next to the bed. The figure spun around at the sound of Glo's voice. It was Kailay. The young barmaid appeared startled at first, but her expression quickly changed to one of recognition and relief.

"Oh, thank the gods!" she cried. Gristla moaned on the bed but otherwise did not move. Kailay stepped back to join them. "She's been stabbed," she whispered. "She's lost a lot of blood."

Stabbed! Glo thought. *No wonder she looks so pale.* He noticed a basin on the chair next to the bed. In it lay a blood-soaked rag. Gristla must have run into the assassins. It was a wonder that she had gotten away at all.

"Why haven't you taken her to the temple?" Aksel whispered.

Kailay let out a soft moan. "She wouldn't let me. She kept going on about men in black robes. She was afraid if I sent for a cleric they would follow them here." The young woman's frustration was obvious. Tears welled in her eyes—she appeared as if she was going to cry any moment. "She was scared out of her wits. Please, Cleric Aksel… can you help her?"

Aksel let out a deep sigh. "I'll see what I can do." He walked to the bed and bent over the injured woman, then held his hands out over the ailing wizard's apprentice. He ran them up and down her entire body.

Kailay stood there all the while, quietly ringing her hands together. Glo's heart went out to the poor girl. He reached over and placed a reassuring arm across her shoulder. Kailay peered up at the tall elf. Tears streamed openly down her face. She smiled briefly at his kind gesture, moving closer. She slipped a slender arm around his waist and rested there against his side. He could feel her body convulsing as she silently continued to cry. Over by the bed, Aksel finished his examination. He stepped back and rejoined them.

"It's not just a stab wound," he said softly. "That I can heal. Unfortunately, she's also been poisoned."

Kailay wailed in despair. "Oh, no! Is there anything you can do for her?"

A look of extreme sorrow spread across Aksel's features. He shook his head slowly, his reply barely audible. "I'm sorry. I haven't learned to heal poisons as of yet."

Kailay let out a sharp gasp then buried her head into Glo's robes. She sobbed uncontrollably, her entire body shaking. Glo placed his other arm around her shoulders. He gently patted her on the back, trying to comfort her.

"Oh, please," she managed between sobs, "there must be something you can do. Don't let her die!" Her voice broke on that last word.

"She's too weak to move," Aksel said, his expression still pained. "We should send for another cleric from the temple. She doesn't have much time."

Aksel's eyes shifted toward Glo, and he shook his head. Glo sighed. It appeared that poor Gristla had no time left at all. Kailay continued to sob into his chest, the wetness of her tears seeping through his shirt.

Tears? The word sparked something in Glo's memory. He grabbed Kailay by the shoulders and gently pushed her back. "Wait! I think I have something that will help."

Kailay's crying stopped and she gazed at him with a confused expression. Glo let go of her, unslung his backpack, and placed it on the floor in front of him. He reached inside and rummaged through it. Seth peered over his shoulder. "What are you looking for?"

"This!" Glo cried in triumph. He pulled his hand out of the pack and in it held a small vial filled with a white glowing liquid. Glo stood up and handed it over to Aksel. "Here, give this to her."

Aksel held up the glowing vial raising an eyebrow. "Where did you get *this*?" His voice was filled with wonder.

"It was in Telvar's stash at Stone Hill," Glo said. "I've been keeping it in case of an emergency."

Kailay stared at the vial as if mesmerized. "What is it?"

"It's Angel Tears," Aksel said as he hurried back to the bed. "It will cure her poison."

"Angel Tears?" Kailay repeated staring after him, her eyes wide.

"They're extremely rare." Seth sounded wistful as he too stared after Aksel.

Aksel called over to Kailay, waving her to join him. "Kailay, I need you to prop up her head."

"Of course." Kailay stirred into action rushing over to the bed. She gently slid her hand behind her sister's neck, pushing it up and forward.

Aksel carefully put the vial of Angel Tears to Gristla's lips, slowly pouring the contents into the poisoned woman's mouth. He held it there and waited until every drop had passed through her lips. When the vial was empty, he stood back and took a deep breath. "That should do it."

Kailay gently placed her sister's head back down on the pillow. Aksel placed his hands over Gristla's body and ran them up and down her frame. When he was done, he let out a huge sigh.

Kailay eyed him anxiously. "Did it work?"

A smile spread across Aksel's lips. "Yes, the poison has begun to recede. She is still injured, though, and needs healing."

"Of course." Kailay nodded, giving the little cleric a curt smile. She stepped back, rejoining Seth and Glo.

Aksel brought his hands together, his brow furrowed with deep concentration. After a few seconds, he held his hands out over the injured woman and white light filtered down from them, slowly spreading over Gristla's body. It enveloped her entire abdomen as if it were wrapped in a cocoon. The onlookers watched in silence as Aksel applied those miraculous healing energies. After a short while, Gristla's skin color began to change—it no longer had the sickly green pallor as before. As the minutes passed, the injured woman's breathing grew less labored. Eventually her complexion returned to normal. The white light slowly receded and then finally faded altogether. Aksel's hands stopped glowing. He stood back and breathed a long sigh, then turned to face Kailay. His expression was one of relief.

"The poison is gone now, and her wounds are healed. She needs rest, but she's going to be fine."

Kailay's face lit up. She rushed forward, bent down, and grabbed the gnome, hugging him tightly. "Oh, thank you! Thank you, Cleric Aksel! Thank you!" Tears once again streamed down her face, but these were tears of joy.

"That's... quite... alright..." Aksel managed to squeak out as she embraced him.

Kailay held onto him a few moments longer, then let go and stood up. She spun around and peered at Glo strangely. Before he could say anything, she strode up to him and threw her arms around his neck. Standing on her toes, she brought her face up to his and kissed him full on the lips. Glo's head swam as the ardent young woman hung onto him tightly. She smelled like fresh flowers, and her soft lips were wet against his. He felt his face grow warm as she continued to press up against him. Glo lost track of time, not sure whether it was moments or minutes that passed. Finally, Kailay pulled back. She looked up at him, a warm smile spread across her tear streaked face.

"Thank you, Glolindir," she said in a soft tone. "Those Angel Tears must have been awfully expensive."

"You have no idea," Seth murmured quietly off to one side.

They heard a moan from behind Aksel—it was Gristla. The wizard's apprentice was beginning to stir. Kailay let go of Glo and rushed to her sister's side. She knelt down next to her on the bed, grasping her hand. Glo still felt a bit flushed from Kailay's display of gratitude. He turned to see Seth smirking at him. The halfling's eyes danced as he stared back at Glo. Surprisingly there was no smart remark accompanying it. Glo smiled wanly, then strode to the edge of the bed.

Gristla's eyes were open as Kailay helped her to sit up. Kailay then sat back and grabbed her sister's hands. She sat there contently, a smile across her tear streaked face. Gristla appeared somewhat bewildered. She shifted her gaze around the room, momentarily startled to see them all standing there.

"It's okay," Kailay said, her tone reassuring. "You were hurt, remember? These folks healed you."

Gristla's expression changed from one of confusion to fear. She pulled back and cowered in the corner of the bed, a moan escaping her lips.

"Shhhh, shhhh," Kailay said, sitting up on the bed. She reached out and took her frightened sister into her arms. "It's okay. Everything's going to be okay now," she cooed, stroking her sister's hair gently.

Glo felt horrible. He did not blame Gristla for being afraid, considering all she had been through. He forced himself to smile and spoke in as reassuring a tone as he could muster. "You have nothing more to fear. The assassins are all dead."

"Dead?" Gristla peered up at him uncertainly from her sister's arms.

"Yes. They were caught in the master's trap." Glo continued to smile, despite the fact that he was lying. Some of the assassins had survived and made away with Voltark's body. However, he did not have the heart to tell that to the frightened woman. His words definitely had the right effect. The fear slowly drained from Gristla's face. She sat up a bit more, though she still held on tightly to Kailay. Now that she appeared calmer, Glo decided to question her. He would have liked to wait until she was fully recovered, but if there were still assassins out there, he couldn't chance it. He sat down on the edge of the bed and spoke to her in a soft voice. "Gristla... can you tell us what happened?"

A trace of fear momentarily rekindled in Gristla's eyes, but it quickly disappeared. She spoke slowly at first. "It was terrible. The Master had just left."

Glo's eyes moved from Aksel and Seth. That confirmed their suspicions. Maltar had not been there when the assassins attacked. As Gristla continued with her story, the words tumbled out quickly, her voice rising as her excitement grew.

"I was up in my room when I heard a commotion downstairs. Then I heard a scream! I rushed down the steps to see what had happened. When I got to the bottom, I saw these strange figures in black robes. Two stood just inside the hallway, and the other two knelt on the floor in the foyer. She paused a moment and flinched, her eyes growing wide. She began again in a hushed voice.

"There was something on the floor between them in the foyer... something grey. I suddenly realized... it was Abracus!" Her voice faltered on the apprentice's name. Tears welled in her eyes and streamed down her cheeks.

Kailay sat forward and drew her sister closer. Glo bowed his head as he thought of Abracus. Once again he saw him lying there in the foyer, surrounded by a pool of his own blood. He felt his anger rise. These Serpent Cultists and their blatant disregard for life infuriated him. Glo caught himself—getting angry wouldn't help now. He took a deep breath and gazed at Gristla. Kailay had managed to calm her down, and she began to speak once more. Her speech was halted, her voice thick with emotion.

"The two men... in the hall... must have spotted me. Without a word... they rushed down the hall... toward the stairs." Gristla's eyes widened and unfocused as she continued. It was as if she were seeing the events unfold before her again. "Without thinking... I turned and ran back up the stairs. When I reached the second floor... they were right behind me! At that point, I panicked. I forgot the Master had left. I ran up the next flight and yelled for him."

Her voice grew quiet. "They caught me on the landing. They grabbed my arms and held me. Then I felt this sharp pain in my stomach. I looked down and realized... I had been stabbed..."

Kailay gasped. She pulled her sister closer and hugged tight. Gristla gently pushed Kailay back. She smiled at her wanly. "It's okay, Sis. I need to tell them the rest."

Gristla's eyes fell on Glo. He forced himself to smile back. *Gods, she's brave.*

"I figured my only chance was to play dead. I let my body go limp. It must have worked because they dropped me to the floor." Gristla paused, shifting herself around on the bed. She appeared very tired. "As I lay there, I heard footsteps going up the next flight. There was a loud click and then all these swooshing sounds and screams."

A thin smile spread across her lips. "I knew they had walked into the Master's trap. Abracus had warned me about it. He said if I ever had to fetch the Master, to avoid the third and fourth steps on the last flight."

Glo's eyes flickered toward Seth. A thin smirk crossed the halfling lips.

"The screams finally stopped, and I heard two thumps on the stairs above. Then there was dead silence." A look of satisfaction crossed Gristla's face. "I silently counted to ten, then opened my eyes. The assassins lay on the stairs above me, sliced into pieces."

She took a deep breath. Kailay opened her mouth to speak, but Gristla held up her hand. "I'm almost done. My stomach felt as if it were on fire, but I managed to lift myself up. That's when I heard another scream from downstairs."

She paused once more and closed her eyes. She was tiring fast. Her eyes snapped back open, and she began to speak once more. "I carefully made my way down the steps and peered into the main hall. I was just in time to see the other two men in black enter the basement. I slipped out the front door and came straight here to the Inn."

Gristla sat back against the headboard. She looked exhausted. Glo found himself admiring this woman. Her courage and wit in such a dire situation was remarkable. He wanted to let her rest, but there was still one more question he needed to ask. He smiled at her with compassion. "You wouldn't happen to know what happened to Maltar or Flibin?"

She shook her head slowly. Her expression was puzzled. "No. I don't know where the Master went. Flibin was in the house with the rest of us, though. I thought maybe it was him I heard scream."

Glo shook his head. "That was the cook. We found his body in the pantry."

Gristla bowed her head, a pained expression on her face.

"However, there was no sign of Flibin. We searched the entire house."

Gristla gazed back up at him. "That is odd. I am sure I heard him downstairs before the whole thing started." She suddenly sat up, her eyes going wide. "You don't think he had anything to do with this? Do you?"

Glo shook his head again. "Sadly, it kind of looks that way."

Gristla's face took on a faraway look. "Now that you mention it, he had been acting kind of funny lately. He seemed very jumpy. Almost... nervous."

Glo let out a long sigh. His eyes shifted from Aksel to Seth. The latter had an *I told you so* look on his face. Deep down, Glo had known as well, but it was his nature to give everyone the benefit of the doubt. *Well, that confirmed it. Flibin had turned on them.* Glo put aside his thoughts and smiled warmly at Gristla. "Thank you. You've been a tremendous help. Rest now."

Still smiling, he stood up and backed away from the bed. Gristla smiled back, then her eyes closed. "You're... welcome..." She wearily slumped down into her bed.

Aksel stepped forward and ran his hands over Gristla's body. When he was done he whispered, "She's fine, just fast asleep."

"Rest now, Sis," Kailay said softly, gently rubbing her sister's forehead. She looked over her shoulder and mouthed the words, "Thank you." Glo smiled and nodded, then he, Aksel, and Seth left the room, closing the door to the servant's quarters quietly behind them.

23
MALTAR'S JOURNAL
It is described as a giant fireball with the power to level an entire city

B ack in the common room, Lloyd waited with Martan for the others to return. Both had scoured the town for Maltar and his apprentices, but failed to find anyone who had seen them. They had been sitting in their usual booth for a short while when Martan nodded behind them. "There's the others."

Lloyd saw Aksel, Seth, and Glo coming out of a door next to the kitchen. He stood and waved in their direction. The trio saw him and came over. As they slid into the booth, Lloyd noted how tired they all looked. He nodded toward the door they come through. "What room is that?"

"It's the servant's quarters," Aksel said. "Seth found Gristla in there."

"Really?" Now he was even more curious. "What's she doing here?"

"She's Kailay's sister," Glo said.

Lloyd nodded. Kailay's sister. The thought of the young barmaid made him momentarily flinch. Although they had worked out their differences at the party, Lloyd still felt guilty about hurting the barmaid's feelings. Although he still wasn't sure exactly what he had done to offend her. Lloyd's thoughts were interrupted by his rumbling stomach. The others laughed. Lloyd grinned sheepishly. "What? I haven't eaten since we made it back to Ravenford."

It had been a long day, and none of them had eaten in quite a while. It was dinnertime now, and they ordered a meal. While they waited, Glo recounted Gristla's tale. Lloyd listened intently. He was angry when he heard how she had been stabbed. He slammed his fist on the table. "I wish I had been there."

"I wish you had been there, too," a female voice agreed.

Lloyd spun around and saw Kailay standing next to their table. She held a large circular tray with their dinner on it. The young woman smiled warmly at him.

"I'm really sorry about what happened to your sister," Lloyd told her.

"Thank you, Lloyd," she smiled again. Kailay placed the huge tray on their table then stood back. Her eyes flickered around the table, her expression rather fond. "She's sleeping soundly now, thanks to all of you."

Lloyd was surprised by what happened next. Kailay bent in front of Glo. "And as for you... you let me know if you need anything *special.*"

Glo turned a bright shade of red. "Umm... th—thanks..."

Kailay laughed and stood up, then slowly sauntered back toward the kitchen. She glanced back over her shoulder and flashed Glo a devastating smile.

Seth smirked at Lloyd. "I think you've been displaced."

"I guess..." Lloyd trailed off. He was completely mystified by what had just happened.

Glo's face was flushed. "She's just... very friendly."

Aksel finished Gristla's story while they ate, then proceeded to tell them about their meeting with the Baron. Lloyd got excited when he heard about the tournament. When he found out that Gryswold had entered him, he was both surprised and touched. He vowed he would do his best to make Gryswold proud. When dinner was over, they all sat back. It was the first break they had gotten all day. Glo, silent all this time, finally spoke up.

"We should probably let Elladan know what's going on."

"Good idea." Aksel turned toward Martan. "Would you mind looking for him?"

"Will do," Martan promised. He slid out of the booth and stood up.

"Thanks. When you find him, tell him everything that happened, both out on the coast, and here since we got back."

Martan began to walk away.

Aksel called after him. "Oh, and one more thing."

Martan spun back around.

"Ask him to meet us here first thing in the morning. We should all be involved in the planning for tomorrow's party."

Martan nodded, then strode away to look for Elladan. Lloyd watched him exit the tavern. Once he was gone, Lloyd turned back toward the others. "I guess we should go report to the Baron."

Glo held up a finger. "Actually, since no one seems to know where Maltar is, I think we should look at his journal first."

Aksel agreed. "Good idea. There may be clues in it as to his current whereabouts."

"That makes sense," Lloyd said.

They all got up, left Kailay a good tip, and headed upstairs to their rooms.

The four of them reconvened a short while later up in Lloyd and Glo's room. Glo sat on his bed, took out Maltar's journal, and laid it out in front of him. The rest sat on Lloyd's bed facing the wizard. The sun had just set outside, the darkness of the night descending over the inn. Glo reached for the table lamp next to his bed. He drew it closer and adjusted the knob. The lamp flame sprung to life. Its flickering form cast dancing shadows against the walls of the room. Glo watched the shadows for a moment, an eerie feeling washing over him. He cast a sidelong glance at the others. Aksel and Lloyd were somber. Even Seth was abnormally subdued. Glo shook his head, then glanced back down at the journal. He opened it and began skimming through it, looking for entries of relevance. Lloyd, Seth, and Aksel continued to watch him in silence. Even the town outside had grown quiet. The only sounds that could be heard were the flipping of the journal pages in front of him. A few more minutes went by when Glo suddenly stopped. He had found a reference in the journal to the mage Telvar—the one they had crossed swords with up at Stone Hill. The entry was from about ten days prior.

Glo cleared his throat. "I think I've found something." Aksel, Seth, and Lloyd all sat forward.

"What is it?" Aksel asked.

"It's about Telvar," Glo said. He placed his finger on that section of the page and traced along as he read aloud.

"Iunius the 8th, 1047. It was only through luck that I heard about Telvar's find. Obviously bad luck for him since he now lies dead in my cold cellar. So intent on my preparation to face the council exam, I had scarcely credited the story, only bothering to send the usual crew of bumbling adventurers to recover the scroll, and expecting only a pile of charred ash for my small trouble.

But lo, what I now hold in my shaken hands is not what Telvar thought was a mere lost Magi spell but is instead a legendary incantation of supreme power and incalculable danger. It seems likely from what the crew of adventurers I hired say that somehow Telvar came across a stash of the Golem Master, Larketh.

The Golems that Telvar employed are of a type created from manuals that Larketh mass produced from the true Tome of Rarknothar during the Thrall War. They are mostly lesser creations compared to Larketh's main works but still far beyond Telvar's meager power. It is possible that the scroll was from a time before Larketh turned to undeath, perhaps a spoil from the ill-fated Invasion of Shadeanon, although the chronicles are unclear..."

Seth's eyes flickered around the room, a smug expression on his face. "I was right! That was no mere scroll."

"Maltar obviously didn't think so," Glo agreed. Maltar's description of a legendary incantation of supreme power and incalculable danger had him quite worried.

"And now we know what happened to Telvar's body," Seth added.

Aksel stroked his chin. "Indeed. Maltar must have retrieved it and kept it in the basement. That's what that second casket contained."

Seth wore a wide smirk. "Well, Glo, that Master of yours is looking darker and darker by the moment."

Glo hung his head. "Thanks, but I don't think I will be calling him Master again anytime soon."

Lloyd's face was a mask of uncertainty. "Does this mean that The

Boulder is actually one of the Golem Master's creations?"

Glo smiled. "Yes, Lloyd, I believe it does."

"And this *Tome of Rarknothar* was Larketh's?" Lloyd asked.

Aksel answered this time. "Indeed. It was Larketh's primary manual of golem creation."

Lloyd sat back on the bed looking quite impressed. While Aksel and Lloyd talked, Glo continued flipping through the journal. The next few entries caused him to raise an eyebrow.

Aksel peered at him curiously. "What now?"

"You're going to want to hear this," Glo responded. He recited the next group of entries.

"Iunius the 9th, 1047. I transcribed the spell and made a few brief test cants before I realized the dark power contained therein. Now I fear my shield not strong enough to hide what I in hasty folly have trifled with.

Indeed, for, if as I suspect, the source of this spell's power is one which shakes the very foundation of the world and gains notice from the hosts of both Infernal and Abysmal Darkness. If all is, as I fear it may be... perhaps, cold, dead Telvar is the lucky one after all..."

"Infernal and Abysmal Darkness..." Seth repeated, emphasizing each word individually. "Well, if there was ever any doubt then that pretty much clinches it. Maltar has joined the dark side."

The halfling wore a wicked smirk across his face. Glo refrained from comment. Seth was right. They could never trust Maltar again. *What a waste.* Well, there was no hope for it. Maltar was headed down a path there was no returning from. Glo glanced back down at the journal. "There's still more."

"Iunius the 10th, 1047. Blast Gryswold with his inane interruptions! I care not for his concerns of plots and Baronial succession. As if anyone would care if this mud-hole slipped into the sea. I only chose Ravenford as a quiet place to study, because it is inconsequential. I cannot spare time for nonsense.

I begin to feel watching eyes upon me, and I fear leaving my sanctuary at night. As always, I trust my instincts. It is time to move my research...

If I could just master this one spell, I could easily destroy my foes and secure my position on the Council with the Color of my choice. But I must wait for the Cruex Crystal to focus my casting and help shield me from the dark powers that will be released."

"That jerk!" Lloyd declared. "How dare he call the Baron inane and Ravenford inconsequential!"

Aksel placed a hand on Lloyd's shoulder. "Easy, Lloyd." Lloyd turned toward the little cleric, outrage still plain on his face. "Don't get me wrong. Maltar is definitely a jerk, but there's no use getting mad about that now."

Glo also spoke up. "Agreed. It's rather obvious that he cares little for anyone but himself. His only concern seems to be gaining a seat on the Wizard's Council."

"Any idea what a Cruex Crystal is?" Seth interjected.

Glo shook his head. He drew a blank on that one. It was the first time he had ever heard the term. Aksel shrugged his shoulders as well. Glo scoured the next entry for more references to the strange crystal. What he read made him go pale.

"What now?" Aksel's tone betrayed his growing irritation.

Glo's eyes flickered over his three friends, his own anger apparent in his voice. "Maltar is a fool. A dangerous fool."

Seth leaned in closer, his expression dark. "What does it say?"

Glo reluctantly picked up the journal and read from the next entry.

"Iunius the 11th, 1047. How the temptress got into my chambers I do not know. Were I not so prepared, and inured against her carnal charms, she would have had me. She appeared, of course, in the guise of an angel, with bright feathered wings and pure features. She spoke Celestial, and I pretended to believe her while I readied my Spiritwrack.

My temporary ruse bore some useful information, and perhaps I was a little hasty with my painful expulsion of her. She was bent (quite alluringly) over my notes and cheerfully pointing out mistakes in some of my translations."

The spell is indeed (as I suspected) a derivative of the ancient Til-

towait and comparable to the lost Armageddon spell. In the runes of Kara-Tur it is..."

Glo paused. "He lists the runes here."

"...which translates roughly to "Dragon-Rend-Kill", but she pointed out that it is certainly the same spell mentioned in the Draconic chronicles of the Great War as Doragun Sureibu."

Seth let out a low whistle. *"Doragun Sureibu,"* he repeated. Lloyd and Aksel eyed him curiously. "Dragon Slayer," he translated for them.

Aksel raised an eyebrow, but Lloyd still appeared puzzled.

Glo explained further. "It is described as a giant fireball with the power to level an entire city."

It was Lloyd's turn to let out a low whistle. "An entire city..." he trailed off, his eyes wide.

Glo nodded to the young man. "Yes. Maltar is playing with forces well beyond him."

Seth's mouth twisted into a half smirk. "We're lucky Ravenford is still standing."

Lloyd shook his head. "What I still don't get is why an Angel? I thought Maltar was worried about dark forces finding him?"

"He didn't seem to believe it was an Angel," Seth said.

Aksel stroked his chin furiously. "If Maltar was messing around with dark magics, it could very well have caught the attention of angelic forces. They might be on the lookout for that sort of thing."

"There's a little more to this entry," Glo told them. He read the rest of it aloud.

"I almost felt sorry for her; she looked actually shocked and sur-prised as the Spiritwrack enclosed on her. Quite a little actress! And powerful, too, she maintained her beautiful golden winged form even under the Spiritwrack. How she managed her escape spell while choking on so much blood, I can't fathom. Not that I gave it much thought, as I spent the rest of the night finding the holes in my wards. At least she helped me

a little with the translation and a lot with my security."

Glo looked up when he finished. Lloyd wore a dark expression on his face. "If it was an Angel, then it doesn't sound like he treated her very well," he said angrily. "Just what is a Spiritwrack anyway?"

"It's a nasty spell," Glo said, revulsion flowing through him as he described it. "It is used to catch creatures from another plane, typically demons or devils. Once caught, the device is used to torture them for information." Glo felt sick to his stomach. Maltar had tortured an angel.

Lloyd, however, was livid. "If we ever see this Maltar again, he is going to have to answer for his actions."

Aksel placed a small hand on the young man's shoulder again. "I couldn't agree more."

Lloyd glanced down at the little cleric then took a deep breath. He turned toward Glo and simply said, "Sorry."

Glo smiled back at the young man. "No need to apologize."

He gazed back down at the journal finding the next entry. It was the last one, only from two days ago. That was the last time Glo had seen his former 'Master'.

"Iunius the 12th, 1047. The ancient runes are difficult to decipher. It is down to ten possible readings, but to pick the wrong one would surely destroy this town and quite likely rend my soul beyond repair. But I may need the power of this spell against that which I fear comes to claim it. I have hidden the original scroll within Alaba and will work from my notes and the transcriptions below."

"There are more runes here, followed by a translation in what appears to be an ancient script. I am not familiar with it..." Glo trailed off. He puzzled over the transcription for a good half minute. Finally, he shook his head. "There is one last line here."

"I am running out of time. To pick the wrong translation, especially without the Crystal focus would be annihilation."

"The journal ends there," Glo said. He closed the book and placed it down on the bed in front of him.

The companions sat there in silence for a while. The flickering light of the table lamp continued to cast dancing shadows on the walls.

It was Aksel who finally broke the eerie silence. "It doesn't sound like Maltar got to finish his work."

Seth snorted. "Probably a good thing, or right now we'd be standing in a hole where Ravenford used to be.

Aksel ignored the halfling's comment. "I still find it interesting that he picked up and left in the middle of it. He seemed to feel he was being watched. Perhaps he knew the house was about to be attacked."

Lloyd spoke through gritted teeth. "So he just got up and left, leaving all his apprentices behind to fend for themselves. I am really starting to hate this guy."

Seth wore a wicked grin. "I wouldn't worry about him too much. I lay odds he'll blow himself up before we see him again."

"Hopefully, there is no one else around when he does so," Aksel said. The little cleric placed his hand on his chin once more, his brow furrowed, and a look of deep concentration on his face. He stood up and paced around the room.

Everything they had just read swirled around in Glo's mind. Angels, dark forces, and the Armageddon spell—a spell that could destroy an entire city. This was all far beyond him. It was far beyond anyone he knew, in fact, except for maybe his own father, or perhaps Lloyd's mother. She was High Wizard of Penwick, after all. What were they going to do about this?

Aksel cleared his throat—the little cleric had stopped pacing. He now stood in front of the windows facing them all. "I think it best that we sit on this information for now. With everything else that is going on, this is the last thing the Baron needs to hear."

Glo breathed a sigh of relief. He did not relish the thought of telling Gryswold this news. He had far too much on his mind right now, and this just might send him over the edge. "Agreed, unless, of course, Maltar returns. Then we have to warn him."

Seth snorted. "I doubt he's coming back. He was too worried that someone was after him. He's taken his scroll and whatever this Cruex crystal is, and is long gone."

Aksel nodded. "You're probably right. Anyway, there's nothing else we can do about Maltar tonight. We should go and tell the Baron that we found Gristla and what she told us. Then I want to come back here and rest up. It's been a long, strange day, and tomorrow looks like it will be just as interesting."

Lloyd's expression was incredulous. "Really? More interesting than the three sisters, a demon, a goblin army, an assassin, a dragon, four more assassins, and that whirling dervish?"

Seth chuckled at Lloyd's synopsis of the last couple of days. "That will be hard to top."

Glo found himself smiling despite himself. He peered over at Aksel, who also seemed somewhat amused. Still smiling, Glo forced himself off the comfortable bed. Just one more task and then he could rest. "Very well, let's go see the Baron."

24
PLANS FOR BREAKFAST
I made sure he worked hard these last few days

E lladan Narmolanya was a bit late getting down to the common room the next morning. He had been up early enough, a lot of things playing on his mind. Martan had found him at the performer's camp yesterday. The archer filled him in on all that had happened at both Cape Marlin and here in town. Elladan felt overwhelmed. A dragon, a demon, a goblin army, and assassins. The strange and unpredictable three sisters. The missing bodies of two dead mages. It was a lot to take in at once. He had to admit he was not surprised about Maltar. He hadn't trusted the mage from the moment Glo first mentioned him.

His last two days had been busy, but nothing quite so dangerous. Shalla had been a pleasure to work with. She was vivacious, feisty, and just a bit naughty—all things he liked in a woman. Judging by their practice sessions, their act was going to be spectacular. Elladan had also fulfilled his duties arranging the show schedule and investigating the entertainers as he had promised. To date, he had not found out anything that pointed to plots against Ravenford. Many of the performers had unsavory pasts, but nothing that even hinted at assassination or even kidnapping.

Elladan awoke rather tense this morning. Shalla distracted him from his troubles, and they quickly lost track of time. Now both bards hurried down the steps to the first floor of the inn. They rushed down the back hallway and burst out into the common room. There the two of them stopped short. The large room bustled with people. Many were performers, already dressed in flamboyant costumes. Others appeared to be just regular townsfolk. A few folk scattered here and there were garbed in finer attire. Those were most definitely nobles. Elladan peered through the busy crowd and caught sight of the companions. They sat at their regular booth near the fireplace. He and Shalla wove their way through the busy throng, greeting the other entertainers as they went. Finally, the duo reached their companions' booth. Elladan noted that breakfast had already been served—everyone's plate was full. Lloyd in particular dug into a large pile of hotcakes. The young man looked up from his towering breakfast.

"Elladan!" Lloyd cried with delight.

Seth eyed the young man with clear amusement. "Nice of you to finally join us. If you had waited any longer, Lloyd would have finished every last pancake in the house."

Lloyd swallowed another large forkful. "What can I say? I'm still growing."

A broad grin crossed Elladan's face. "That's alright, Lloyd. I, for one, prefer you well fed and ready for battle."

"Just don't eat too much," Seth countered, "or we'll have to roll you out onto the battlefield."

"You know, if you want to quit your day job, I hear they're looking for a stand-up comic for tonight's performance," Elladan shot back. "Oh, wait. No one would be able to tell if you were standing or sitting."

Seth gave the bard a withering look.

"Elladan!" Shalla smacked him on the arm.

Seth folded his arms across his chest. "Really? We're resorting to short jokes?"

"Okay, everyone," Aksel interrupted, "we've got a long day ahead of us. Let's all at least act like we get along?"

Elladan smiled jovially. "Of course we all get along! Isn't that right, Seth?"

Seth shrugged his shoulders. "Whatever."

"Good then," Aksel said. He bade everyone to make room for the two bards.

The companions shifted over, and Elladan and Shalla slid in on either side. Elladan sat next to Lloyd and Martan. Shalla sat next to

Glo, Seth, and Aksel.

"Well then, it sounds like you guys were quite busy these last couple of days," Elladan said.

"We could say the same about you," Glo responded.

Elladan gazed curiously at Glo. The blond elf sounded serious, but Elladan caught the thin smile on his lips and the way his eyes danced with amusement. Elladan's mouth twisted into a half smile.

Without missing a beat, Shalla said, "Oh, trust me, I made sure he worked hard these last few days."

Elladan glanced at her and noted the twinkle in her eye. Lloyd and Martan stopped eating. Aksel and Glo stared curiously at the bardess. Seth wore a thin smirk. Elladan arched an eyebrow. Shalla stared around the table, seeming quite satisfied with the response she elicited. When her gaze fell on Elladan, she winked and blew him a kiss. Kailay chose that moment to appear at their table. She carried a huge tray piled high with more hotcakes. She leaned forward and set the tray down in front of them. "Did you all lose your appetites this morning?"

Elladan flashed her a smile. "I don't think so. They're all just distracted at the moment."

Kailay stood back up and appraised the table. "I see." Her eyes flickered around with clear amusement. "Can I get anyone anything else?"

"Some juice for us, please," Elladan responded, pointing to himself and Shalla.

Kailay smiled sweetly. "Sure thing." Her eyes drifted toward Glo. "Glo? Anything you need? Anything at all?"

Elladan's gaze shifted from the barmaid to his fellow elf. Glo turned all shades of red as he stammered his response. "No... no thank you, Kailay."

A genuine smile crossed Kailay's lips. "Well, if you do, you know where to find me." She sauntered away, disappearing into the throng of guests.

Elladan watched her go then turned back toward his uncomfortable friend. "It looks like I missed more than I was told."

Glo was still a bit red faced. "She was just being... friendly."

"Ah ha," Elladan responded, although he knew better. "So when did all this come about?"

Glo appeared even more uncomfortable than before. Aksel spoke up for the silent elf. "Her sister was poisoned and nearly died. Glo saved her with Angel Tears."

Elladan let out a low whistle. "Angel Tears? Those are worth a small fortune." Glo, still red-faced, refused to comment. A half-smile crossed Elladan's face. "Well that explains her sudden interest in you, my friend."

Shalla swiveled toward Glo, slid her arm through his, and grasped onto him affectionately. "I think what you did was sweet," she said, smiling warmly at the blond elf.

"Thank you, Shalla," Glo finally spoke. He still seemed somewhat subdued.

Elladan sat back and regarded Glo. He was extremely bright, perhaps one of the smartest elves he had ever met. Yet he was also incredibly naïve, especially when it came to women. Elladan would need to have a talk with him about that at some point, but this was neither the time nor the place. "Not the change the subject, but I was wondering if you could do some special effects for our show tonight."

Glo's expression brightened at the change of topic. "What did you have in mind?"

"Oh, nothing too fancy." Elladan waved his hand around in the air for effect. "Perhaps some fog, maybe a few dancing lights, or even some pyrotechnics?"

"Oh, that's a lovely idea!" Shalla declared. "Could you, Glo?" She was still holding onto his arm and flashed him one of her devastating smiles. Poor Glo didn't stand a chance. When Shalla wanted her way, he dared any man, or elf, to say no to her.

A wide smile spread across Glo's lips. "I think that can be arranged."

"Thanks, Glo," Elladan said. Those extra touches would make tonight's performance spectacular.

"Ahem." Aksel drew everyone's attention to him. "Now that that is out of the way, we need to discuss the non-scheduled portion of tonight's events." His eyes briefly swept around the room. The place was still packed. "But perhaps this is not the best place to do so. Let's finish breakfast and reconvene upstairs."

Elladan agreed. There were too many folks around. Best to talk about this Serpent Cult business away from prying ears. After breakfast, the entire group adjourned to Glo and Lloyd's room. They spent about an hour discussing the plan for that evening.

Foremost, they needed to guard the Baron and his family. At the same time, the perimeter of the castle grounds had to be watched. Elladan and Aksel, both with keen minds for this sort of thing, helped devise a strategy that would allow them to do both. Seth, with his knowledge of all things shady, added a few fine points. When they were done, they had a solid plan to protect the Baron's family and maintain watch on the keep. Lloyd and Glo would stay close to the Baron, Baroness, and Lady Andrella. Seth would scour the rooftop of the keep. From there he would be able to see all around the outside of the castle. Martan would position himself atop Maltar's old tower. He would get a bird's-eye view of the front of the keep from there. Aksel would keep watch down at the gate. Elladan would be on stage with Shalla. Together they would watch the courtyard and the other performers for anything out of place. Finally, Glo would send Raven aloft to fly around the perimeter of the keep.

Once they were done, Aksel addressed everyone. "Now then, we all know our assignments. We have the rest of the morning free to prepare. Let's meet back here around noon time and then head on up to the castle together."

The companions said their goodbyes and parted for the morning. Elladan left the room with Shalla on his arm. The meeting had gone well. Individually, these folks were quite talented, but with a solid strategy behind them, they were nearly unstoppable. With his battle knowledge, they had easily taken down Voltark's minions. The mage himself had been a bit more difficult, though. Elladan wondered if tonight would be a repeat performance of that battle.

"What's on your mind?" Shalla asked, breaking his train of thought.

"Nothing really." Elladan smiled and took her hand in his. "I was just thinking how interesting this evening might turn out to be."

Shalla smiled in return. She put her head on his shoulder as the two of them walked down the hall.

25
OLD FRIENDS

I'm just a poor iterant artist trying to make an honest living...

A little while later, Elladan strode through the downtown section of Ravenford toward the clothier's shop. He had ordered a special outfit for tonight's show, cut from white fringed leather and studded with gold sequins across the chest and back. The merchants' quarters were packed with people hustling about here and there. He recognized many of them as other performers and exchanged greetings. Elladan finally reached his destination, but had to step aside when he opened the door. A trio of wealthy-looking patrons exited the shop, carrying bags that had to contain dress clothes for tonight's party. Elladan held the door open for them and nodded politely, then strode inside. The door closed, shutting out the noise from the busy street outside.

The inside of the clothier's was now empty except for one slight fellow. He leaned over the counter, flirting outrageously with the pretty female tailor. The fellow was fair-skinned with short, sandy blonde hair. He wore a brown leather vest over a white puffy shirt, his lower half was clad in brown—brown pants and knee-high brown leather boots. A slender scabbard hung at his side, capped by an ornate hilt. What drew Elladan's attention, though, were the pointed ears that jutted out from under his short-cropped hair. There was something strangely familiar about this elf. Elladan could swear he had met him before, but where? The blond elf was still flirting.

"Arwel is such a beautiful name... almost lyrical; a beautiful name for a beautiful woman."

The tailor was indeed an attractive woman. Glo had said she was Kailay's mother. Elladan noted the resemblance the first time he saw her. Arwel blushed profusely as the blond elf continued his amorous banter.

"Tell me... have you ever considered having your portrait done?"

Portrait?

Elladan suddenly remembered where he had seen this fellow before. It was a year ago, in the City of Lukescros, south of here down the coast, during the annual Lukescros Fair. A bardic competition was typically part of the festivities, and Elladan had planned to participate. He had been passing through one of the more opulent sections of the city, when he'd heard some shouts.

"Stop that elf!" came a loud voice from inside a nearby inn.

Elladan remembered gazing up and seeing a figure crash through a second story window. The form tumbled onto the canvas awning below and then somersaulted to the ground inside a wide courtyard.

Nice move, he remembered thinking.

The yard itself had been surrounded by a tall, black wrought-iron fence. Elaborate white stone columns split the fence into a number of sections. Elladan could clearly see the figure in the courtyard beyond—the same blond elf who stood before him now.

A moment later, the upper body of a pudgy man had poked out a window. It was the same window the elf had launched himself out of seconds ago. The man was dressed in finery, his face beet red. He cursed at the elf below and hurled things down at him. The blond elf easily dodged the flying objects, while straightening his disheveled clothing. He continued evading them as he bent to retrieve the belongings he had dropped in his tumble to the ground. A beautiful woman appeared at an adjacent window wrapped only in a sheet.

"Stop!" she yelled at the pudgy man. "It was only a portrait!"

The elf smiled up at the woman with a roguish grin. The woman glanced down at him and blushed. He bowed to her elaborately. "Thank you, milady! Perhaps another time?"

The elf then turned to walk away. He'd only gone a few steps when three young men came charging out of the inn. They were all large and muscular.

"There won't be a next time!" the opulently dressed man shouted from above. "Get him, boys!"

The elf whirled around as the three men drew their swords, approaching him menacingly. He backed away raising his hands in front of him. "Guys, there's been some misunderstanding here. I'm just a poor iterant artist trying to make an honest living..."

A sneer crossed one of the men's face. "The misunderstanding here is when you messed with our step-mother. Now you're going to pay."

He and his companions pressed forward until the elf was almost backed against the fence. The elf glanced behind him then stopped. He quickly reached over his shoulder and pulled out a long pole from his pack. He held it out in front of him threateningly.

Another of the men taunted him. "You think that puny stick is going save you?"

The elf shook the stick in his hand. Abruptly it split into three separate staffs attached to each other at the butt. "Aha!" he cried.

The men laughed as the elf continued to threaten them with his easel. One of them jeered. "Oooh, we're so frightened!"

Abruptly, the three men launched themselves at him. Elladan's eyes went wide at the spectacle he witnessed. The elf used the legs of his easel as a shield, parrying one opponent's blade while keeping the others at bay. He continued to caper around merrily between the lumbering young men. Occasionally he would whack one of his opponents with a leg of his easel, then dodge out of the way.

A crowd had gathered in the street, cheering on the plucky artist. The three young men quickly became enraged. One of them charged in, bringing his weapon down in a great sweeping motion toward the elf's head. Elladan half expected to see the elf's head split in two, but at the last moment, the wiry fellow brought up the butt-end of the easel and parried it. Unfortunately, the force of the blow split the legs of the easel apart.

The elf backed away, his merry expression disappearing as his face turned red. "You dastards broke my easel!"

The young men froze in place, surprised by their opponent's sudden change in attitude. The elf began to spin the remaining two legs in his hands. In a quick sweeping motion, he took out the legs of one of them while backhanding another, catching him in the back of the

head and knocking him out cold. The elf rose from the sweep directly behind the last one. He struck him hard across the back with both
sticks. That young man also fell to the ground, out for the count.
The first one tried to get up, but the elf knocked his blade from his
hand. A pole jabbed down sharply at the man's Adam's apple. His
eyes went wide as he saw it descend, but the elf stopped it a whisper's
length away from his neck.

"If you know what's good for you, you'll stay down." All traces
of humor were gone from his voice.

The young man's face went deathly pale. He quickly nodded his
surrender. The crowd went wild, cheers breaking out amongst them.
The blond elf turned and bowed elaborately.

"Get up!" the pudgy man cried from above. "Get up, you useless
muscle-bound oafs!"

The elf spun around and glared at the man. He then bowed to
the woman in the other window. "Some other time, milady."

She blushed, obvious adoration in her eyes as she gazed down at
him. The elf spun around once again and headed for the courtyard
gate. He never reached it. A number of town guards pushed through
the crowd, effectively blocking the courtyard entrance.

"Arrest that elf!" cried the pudgy man. "He accosted my wife!"

The crowd booed as the town guards entered the courtyard. The
artist backed away as he was confronted by the four of them. Unlike
the three young men he had just dispatched, these were experienced
fighters. The elf tried to reason with the guards.

"Aww, come on, guys, are we really going to do this? I'll just take
my things and leave. I'll promise never to come back, and we'll call it
even, okay? I really don't want to embarrass you..."

The town guards weren't impressed. They stood their ground,
swords drawn and ready. One of them spoke in a commanding tone.
"Now, come along quietly."

The blond elf sighed and shook his head. "Okay, guys, don't say
I didn't warn you."

In one swift motion, he cast aside all but one of the broken easel legs, pointed it at the guards, and charged. Elladan watched in
disbelief. The daring artist made his suicide run, but just before he

reached them, dropped the tip of the pole into the ground. The elf then vaulted up and over the surprised guards, somersaulting in mid-air and landing on top of one of the white columns in the fence. The crowd held its breath as he teetered there for a moment. The elf finally regained his balance and the crowd erupted into applause. He spun around and peered down at the astonished guards.

"Sorry, boys, got to run." He then jumped down and tumbled into the crowd below. Elladan pushed his way over to him and grabbed his arm.

"Quickly, this way," he whispered.

The blond elf flashed a quick grin then followed him around the corner of the inn. They could already hear shouts behind them. Pursuit would not be far behind. Elladan rushed down the busy street and around the next corner. Once out of sight of the inn, he stopped and reached into his bag, pulling out a cloak.

"Here, put this on."

The blond elf quickly threw the cloak over his shoulders and pulled the hood over his head. Elladan thrust a lute into his hands and whispered, "Now walk next to me and let me do the talking."

They fell into step and walked side by side down the busy street. A few seconds later, they heard footsteps running up behind them.

"Stop!" a voice yelled.

Elladan whirled around and saw the town guards standing there, swords in hand. He replied as cheerfully as possible. "Gentlemen, whatsoever seems to be the problem?"

The guards looked him up and down. Their expressions softened as they realized he was not the elf they were looking for. Their eyes fell on his companion, but he had his head bowed and plucked at the strings of the lute he held.

Not half bad, Elladan thought.

"Did you see a blond elf come running by here?" one of the guards barked.

Elladan shook his head and replied in a calm voice. "A blond elf? No, sir, just me and my lady friend headed up to the Bardic College." He paused a moment then said, "We're entering the competition."

The guards exchanged glances but in general seemed to buy it.

The one guard responded in an officious tone, waving them off. "Very well then, continue about your business."

The two elves turned and slowly walked away. They strode in silence until they were a few blocks away. The blond elf then stopped and threw back his hood. "Thanks for the assist back there, but it's not like I haven't eluded a few town guards before."

Elladan broke into a half smile. "I wouldn't be surprised at all. So, does this kind of thing happen to you a lot?"

"More often than I would like," the blond elf answered. He handed Elladan back his lute and doffed the cloak he had given him. "It seems the world is full of art critics."

Elladan took the lute and made it magically disappear. He could recall it whenever necessary. He then stored the cloak it in his pack. "Maybe it's not the art itself they don't like?"

The elf eyed him thoughtfully for a moment then a mischievous grin spread across his face. "I believe you hit the nail on the head, friend. It is the subject matter that they seem to object to the most. Who knew so many fathers and husbands hated art." His expression was innocent.

Elladan laughed. He was beginning to like this fellow.

"May haps I could buy you a drink. After all, you did just lend me a hand," the elf offered.

"I think I know a place," Elladan replied.

The duo proceeded down the street to the less opulent side of town. They stopped at a tavern, found a table, ordered some drinks, and exchanged stories. The blonde elf 's name was Donatello. He was an artist by trade, but as they continued to share ales and tales, Elladan discovered that he had quite a checkered past. If his stories were to be believed, he was a bit of an adventurer, and a pirate to boot. From the sound of it, he was also quite the ladies' man. That soon proved to be true. The two of them soon found themselves in the company of two lovely women. Shortly thereafter, they parted ways, each with a young lovely on his arm.

Donatello saluted his newfound friend. "Until we meet again!"

"Until we meet again," Elladan echoed.

Now, almost a year later, Donatello had turned up again, in

Ravenford of all places. A thin smile spread across Elladan's face. He just couldn't resist himself.

"Stop that elf!" he yelled from the doorway.

Donatello spun around and fell into a crouch, his hand immediately going to his sword hilt. He immediately spied Elladan standing in the doorway. The blond elf eyed him warily for a few moments. Abruptly, his expression changed to one of recognition.

"Elladan?"

"Who were you expecting, the town guards?" the bard replied with a half-smile.

"Elladan!" Donatello cried. He strode towards him, arms open wide.

Elladan met him halfway, and the two embraced, patting each other soundly on the back.

"You know each other?" Arwel called from behind the counter. The duo turned as one to face the winsome tailor.

"Oh, Donnie and I go back a ways," Elladan said.

"Lukescros, wasn't it?" Donnie added.

The duo strode over to the winsome tailor.

"Indeed," Elladan said. "A certain affluent gentlemen and his lovely young wife..."

Donnie nodded. "Ah, yes—the courtyard and the town guards..."

"...and a daring escape," Elladan added.

"And the bar afterwards..." Both elves smiled.

"Sounds like you two had quite the time." Arwel watched them with a wry look on her face. Elladan noted how she gazed back and forth between them, her cheeks slightly flushed.

"We did indeed, my lovely." Donnie leaned over the counter once more. "But we are here now in Ravenford, which is made all the more fair by your very presence."

Arwel blushed a bit more. "Flatterer—keep that up, and I just might let you paint my portrait..."

Donnie's face lit up. He leaned over the counter farther. "Well now, there are some details I would love to iron out."

Elladan cleared his throat. "Maybe you can hold that thought until I get my outfit?"

Arwel's expression changed to one of embarrassment. "Oh, why yes, of course. It's done, and if I must say so myself, it looks gorgeous! I'll go get it."

Arwel spun around and stepped through the curtain behind her. Donnie turned to Elladan. "Outfit? That wouldn't be for the party tonight by any chance?"

"I'm kind of the emcee."

A knowing smile spread across Donnie's lips. "I should have guessed." His voice dropped to a whisper. "Tell me, is there any way you can sneak me in?"

Elladan chuckled. "Let me guess, you want to offer to paint portraits for the guests."

Donnie made an expansive gesture with his hand. "Of course— life is a canvas, and I must paint its beauty!"

Elladan laughed. "Donnie, you are incorrigible."

Donnie grinned in response. "As are you, if I recall correctly."

Arwel reappeared through the curtain, holding up a bright white leather outfit on a hanger. Gold sequins sparkled brightly across the chest, and fringes hung down from the arms. She handed it across the counter to Elladan. "Here it is!"

Elladan inspected the outfit, carefully spinning it around and looking it up and down. He gave Arwel an appreciative smile. "This is a work of art."

"If you care to come in back, you can try it on," Arwel said in a soft voice.

"Thanks. I believe I will." He turned to Donnie. "Care to join us? I think I might have an idea on how to get you into the party."

Donnie made a lavish gesture with his hand. "By all means, lead the way."

The two elves followed the lovely tailor into the back room.

26
NEW ENEMIES
To a real knight, these backwater confrontations would be a mere trifle

About an hour later, the two elves exited the shop. Elladan was telling Donnie about some of the Heroes' exploits. "...then Lloyd slammed into the giant's back, and it went flying into the ground!"

Donnie wore an appreciative smile. "Sounds like my kind of fellow."

The duo began to head down the street, then halted. There was a crowd gathered at the corner, not ten yards in front of them. From the center of the throng, they heard a voice ring out.

"Non-humans are not to be trusted." Whoever it was talked with a pronounced lisp. "And Elves are the worst of them all," the voice continued. "They act all superior, like they are better than the rest of us. But in reality, they just keep to themselves because they are scared."

Elladan's eyes shifted to Donnie. Donnie returned his stare, a single eyebrow raised.

"I resent your attitude, *friend*," a deep voice resonated. "My companion here is an elf, and he has stood by me through more dangerous encounters than you'll ever see in your lifetime."

That's Lloyd! Elladan motioned for Donnie to follow him. The duo rushed forward and entered the crowd.

"I'm sure that whatever *encounters* you've had were challenging for one of your station," the first voice responded. "However, to a *real* knight, these backwater confrontations would be a mere trifle."

Elladan politely pushed his way through the throng. Donnie followed close behind.

"Some folks throw the term *knight* around loosely," Lloyd countered. There was more than a trace of anger in the young man's tone. "Where I come from, that isn't just some title given to every noble's son. It has to be *earned.*"

Elladan finally broke through the crowd. Lloyd stood in the center of the circle with his back to them, Glo beside him. Opposite them stood a man with shoulder-length brown hair, sporting a mustache and a goatee. He wore a blue doublet with lieutenant bars on the arms and an insignia on his chest that Elladan found unfamiliar. On either side of his waist hung a sword and an axe.

Donnie whispered, "That's a Dunwynn insignia."

Dunwynn! Just wonderful. He had heard rumors of that Duchy. They were Xenophobes, distrustful of all the non-human races.

"And just where do you come from?" the man in the blue doublet asked. He stood with his hands on his hips, a disdainful look on his sour face.

"The City of Penwick," Lloyd replied proudly, his arms folded across his chest.

"Ahhh, Penwick," the Lieutenant sneered. He slowly spun around gazing at the surrounding crowd. "That explains much." He continued to turn until he faced Lloyd again.

The sound of scornful laughter drew Elladan's attention to the other side of the throng. Three men stood there dressed in the same blue uniforms as the arrogant man, Dunwynn insignias on their chest.

This could get ugly fast.

Elladan turned to warn Donnie, but the blond elf was no longer next to him. He scanned the crowd and caught sight of the elusive elf working his way around the edge of the throng. Elladan groaned. Things just kept getting worse. Donnie, great as he was in a fight, was a bit of a loose cannon. If he decided to put in his two cents, it might add fuel to the fire.

The Lieutenant addressed Lloyd again. "It's a quaint little town, with charming customs to be sure, but it is a mere village when compared with the grandeur of Dunwynn." He stood there, gazing at Lloyd disdainfully, as if daring the young man to contradict him.

"Bigger doesn't necessarily imply better, *friend,*" Lloyd said, his anger now thinly veiled. He shifted his stance, unfolding his arms and dropping his hands to firmly rest on his sword hilts. It appeared as if he was seconds from drawing his blades. Elladan started forward, thinking he might still salvage the situation, but halted when Glo began to speak.

"Lloyd, pay no attention to this *gentleman*." His tone was thoroughly dismissive. "We have important matters to attend to. Let us not waste more of our time."

Ouch. Elladan had always been told that Galinthral elves were arrogant, but he had never heard Glo speak like that. If anyone deserved it, though, it was this self-important Dunwynner to be sure. The Lieutenant's face momentarily clouded over. He glared at Glo with clear hatred. The moment quickly passed, and the haughty man began to chuckle. He spun around toward his men.

"Oh ho, so the elf speaks," he mocked. His toadies all snickered. The Dunwynn officer whirled around once more and waved his hand dismissively. "Do run away, man of Penwick and little elf, before you start something you cannot finish."

Lloyd's shoulders stiffened. He began to draw his blades from their scabbards. Glo reached up and placed a hand on the young man's shoulder. Lloyd glanced at Glo, the elf almost imperceptibly shaking his head. Reluctantly, Lloyd re-sheathed his swords. Glo addressed the conceited Dunwynner once more. His tone was scathing.

"You, sir, have no clue what you are up against. I have personally seen my friend here mow down giants and trolls. I suggest you turn away now while you still can."

The Lieutenant's face twisted into a contemptuous sneer. "Oh. *Now* you want to stay and fight." He glared at Glo for a moment longer, then addressed Lloyd. "The likes of you and your elf-loving friend here do not scare me. We are made of sterner cloth in Dunwynn. We do not frighten so easily."

Glo dropped his hand from Lloyd's shoulder. When he spoke, his tone dripped with acid. "Then you are stupider than you look."

The Lieutenant's face grew red with anger. His hands strayed to his weapon hilts, his tone grim. "Those are fighting words. I am surprised an elf would show that much courage, but then, you do have this human to do your dirty work for you."

Glo's tone was cold as ice. "Oh, I can assure you, he will not fight alone." The wizard's hand strayed his belt, in obvious preparation for a spell.

This is getting way out of hand.

Elladan quickly stepped out of the crowd, hoping to still salvage the situation. He strode briskly toward the center of the circle, holding up his hands as he went. "Now hold on, friends. What's all this talk about fighting?"

All eyes turned on him. The anger faded from the Lieutenant's face, replaced with a look of surprise. Lloyd and Glo wore startled expressions. Glo gave him a questioning stare. Elladan merely nodded to his fellow elf, then returned his gaze to the Dunwynn officer. He gave him a half-smile. The Lieutenant's surprise quickly faded, replaced with a scornful sneer. Elladan did not stop, though. He strode on until he was in the very center of the circle, directly between his companions and the Dunwynners.

The Lieutenant finally spoke, his tone mocking. "And what have we here? Another elf. Why am I not surprised?" He spun around once more to face his entourage. The Dunwynn trio burst into laughter.

Elladan took advantage of the moment, whispering over his shoulder to Lloyd and Glo. "Steady, guys. Andrella wouldn't be happy with you fighting on her birthday." He didn't wait for a response. He shifted his gaze back toward the Lieutenant.

The officer had spun back around to glare at him once more. Elladan took a deep breath and spoke as calmingly as possible. "Listen friend, Dunwynn's reputation for upholding the law is widely known. Do you really want to ruin that with a street fight—especially on the Lady Andrella's birthday?"

The Lieutenant eyed Elladan up and down. When he finally replied, his attitude had not changed, but his disdainful expression had softened a bit. "Dunwynn's reputation is no concern to the likes of you, but you do bring up a salient point. The Lady Andrella's wishes are more important than a minor skirmish with some street urchins."

Elladan gave an inward sigh. *We might just get out of this without any blood being spilled.* Before he could respond, though, a familiar voice rang out from the crowd.

"That's a pretty speech there, *friend*, but I think that you would find this encounter anything but minor."

Elladan groaned. He knew that voice. He turned to see Donatello saunter out of the crowd toward them. Elladan sighed for real this time. He had been so close to ending this. The artist casually strolled up and stopped next to Elladan. He faced the Dunwynn Lieutenant, his hands on his hips.

"Yet another elf!" the man cried with clear exasperation. "The town is practically crawling with them!" He threw up his hands in apparent disgust.

"Who is that?" Glo whispered from behind Elladan.

"A friend," he replied over his shoulder.

Donnie continued in nonchalant manner. "I think I find your tone offensive, but I am in a good mood this morning and am inclined to let that slide. "However," he paused dramatically, "I am not really your problem here. I may be fair with a sword, but from what I've heard, these folks can easily handle themselves—be it against monsters or buffoons in uniform."

Elladan shook his head. He knew Donnie meant well, but this was not helping to diffuse things.

When the Lieutenant responded, his tone was insufferable. "Yes, yes, once again I'm sure that common riffraff like yourselves can handle the average creature or ruffian, but against trained troops from Dunwynn, let me assure you, you wouldn't stand a chance."

Those last words dripped with malice. Elladan recognized that tone. The Lieutenant was done talking. He had reached his breaking point. If the situation wasn't diffused right now, someone could end up badly hurt, or even dead.

Elladan tried to recapture the man's attention. "Excuse me, Lieutenant..."

The Lieutenant's gaze fell on him once again. The man practically sneered his response. "That is Sir—Sir Fafnar Strakentir."

Good, I have his attention. "Well Sir Fafnar, are you entered in tomorrow's tourney?"

Sir Fafnar glared at him as if he was a dolt. "Of *course* I am. I am of the noble Dunwynn house of Strakentir. Close personal friend to the Duke himself. My spot in the tournament was reserved well before my arrival here."

Elladan nodded. "Very impressive." He took a step back and placed a hand on Lloyd's shoulder. "However, you are looking at Lloyd Stealle, of the noble Penwick house of Stealle. His spot in the tournament has been reserved by Baron Gryswold himself."

Sir Fafnar's face dropped, and his eyes going wide. His gaze shifted from Lloyd to Elladan and back again, his expression one of disbelief. "You... you can't be serious." He quickly regained his composure, his astonishment replaced with a smirk. He spun around again toward his men. "Looks like they'll let anyone into these backwater tournaments."

The Dunwynn group snickered at his mean-spirited attempt at humor.

"Steady," Elladan whispered, grasping tighter onto Lloyd's shoulder. He could practically feel the warrior's hands twitching on his sword hilts. Elladan addressed Fafnar again. "Listen, friend, this entire group here are personal guests of the Baron tonight. So I suggest that if you have any grievance with us, you take it up on the tournament field instead of the streets."

At that moment, a soft cheer of *"Heroes. Heroes."* sprang up from the surrounding crowd. A strange expression crossed Sir Fafnar's face. He scanned the chanting onlookers. "It cannot be! You are the mighty Heroes of Ravenford we've been hearing so much about?" A satisfied smirk crossed the noble's face. "Just as I suspected—nothing but upstarts and hooligans. The town would be better off without you." He gazed around the crowd and raised his voice above the chanting. "What these people really need are some good Dunwynn knights protecting them."

A few boos and hisses escaped from the gathered masses. Someone yelled, "Dunwynn go home!"

Fafnar appeared unperturbed, instead glaring at the surrounding throng. "Of course, these backwards people would not know the first thing about real law and order."

The boos and hisses immediately died down, as did the chanting.

Elladan took advantage of the silence to draw the Dunwynn noble's attention back to him. "Well Sir Fafnar, being that you are so sure of yourself, would you like to make a little wager on tomorrow's tournament?"

Sir Fafnar stared at him with obvious scorn. "What do you have in mind?"

"If you can beat Lloyd here in combat, then we will pack up and leave Ravenford, never to return." Fafnar squinted at him, distrust written across his face. "But if Lloyd here bests you, then you have to publicly declare us protectors of this town."

Fafnar glared at Lloyd. "It will be no contest."

Lloyd stared back at the noble, unflinching, his tone as cold as ice. "You've got that right."

Elladan drove the point home. "Well then, are you going to take the bet?"

The crowd grew very still. Fafnar did not take his eyes off Lloyd. Their eyes were riveted together, the very air between them seeming to boil with anger. Sir Fafnar finally broke the silence.

"Fine!" he almost spat the word. "But bet or not, you can be certain that I will be keeping my eye on you until you are banished in tomorrow's tourney."

A half smile crossed Elladan's lips. "That remains to be seen."

Another chant of *"Heroes! Heroes!"* erupted from the crowd, louder this time.

"Bah!" Fafnar cried in disgust. He spun around on his heels and stormed off in the direction of his men. "Let's get out of here!" he commanded them as he pushed through his entourage. His men appeared uncertain but swiftly followed him. The crowd parted, allowing the Dunwynn group to pass through. All the while, they chanted *"Heroes! Heroes!"*

The companions watched in silence as the Dunwynners strode across the street. They stopped at a pack of tethered horses and mounted up. Sir Fafnar spun around on his horse to face them once more. "Enjoy your last day in Ravenford!" He then whirled his mount around and galloped up the road toward the keep. His men followed suit.

27
STALKER

If he's half as good with his sword as his is with his tongue, then he might just turn out to be useful

Elladan let out a sigh of relief. Donnie spun around to face the others. "What a pompous ass."

Glo cast a glance at Elladan, nodding toward the slight blond elf. "Are you going to introduce us to your friend?"

Elladan laughed. "With all the excitement, I never got the chance. This is Donatello, an old friend of mine."

Donnie doffed his hat and bowed. "At your service."

"Donnie, this is Lloyd and Glo," Elladan said, pointing to each of them in turn.

"*Saesa omentien lle,*" Glo said, his tone solemn.

Lloyd stepped forward, extending his hand. "I appreciate the kind words, friend."

Donnie reached forward to take the warrior's hand. Elladan suppressed a smile. He remembered his own hand throbbing for quite a while after his first meeting with Lloyd. "It was my... pleasure," Donnie managed, doing his best to endure Lloyd's vise-like grip. The young artist was saved further punishment when a small voice spoke up from behind him.

"That idiot from Dunwynn should be thanking you." Elladan whirled around as Seth appeared out of nowhere. "He was this close," the halfling held his fingers about an inch apart, "to singing soprano for the rest of his life."

They burst into laughter. Even Lloyd managed a chuckle.

"You're assuming that there was something there to cut off in the first place," Glo said with a half-smirk.

"Ohhhh!" Donnie groaned. "Low blow."

They all laughed in earnest that time.

"Well, I'm glad it didn't come to that," another familiar voice spoke up from behind them. Elladan swung around to see Aksel standing there. He gave the bard an approving nod. "Nice job diffusing the situation, Elladan."

Elladan responded with a half-smile. "I do what I can."

Donnie was introduced to Aksel and Seth. The crowd around them had dissipated, although the corner was still rather busy. Townsfolk and out-of-towners continued to bustle about in preparation for the evening's festivities.

Aksel rubbed his hands together gingerly. "Well then, if everyone is done with their errands, we should head back to the inn. We need to get ready for the party." He nodded to Donnie. "Nice meeting you." Aksel then spun around and strode in the direction of the Charging Minotaur. The others bade goodbye to Donnie as well, and fell in behind Aksel.

Elladan waved for Donnie to follow then rushed forward after them. The two of them quickly caught up and drew alongside Aksel. Elladan addressed the leader of the group. "I was thinking that Donnie here could join us at the party tonight. He's actually quite handy with that pig-sticker at his waist." Aksel halted and gazed at Donnie, his hand going to his chin.

"It's alright by me," Lloyd chimed in. "Anyone who can stand up to that fool from Dunwynn is okay in my book."

"Not to mention, the more elves in one place, the more we can annoy him," Glo said.

Aksel's brow furrowed, his hand going to his chin as he mulled it over. "We do have a lot of ground to cover this evening, and if you vouch for him, Elladan, then I'm okay with it." His eyes shifted to Seth. "I assume you have your usual objections?"

Seth shrugged, giving Elladan a sidelong glance. "Like that has ever stopped you before."

A closed-mouth laugh escaped Aksel's lips. "No, not really."

"If it's a problem," Donnie interjected, "I'm sure I can find my own way into the party."

Aksel eyed the elf speculatively. "You do realize it's invitation only?"

Donnie shifted his weight to one foot, appearing rather non-chalant. "Perhaps, but you'd be surprised how many doors my easel opens up for me."

Elladan couldn't resist throwing a jibe in at his old friend. "Isn't that usually bedroom doors?"

Donnie grinned in response. "Hmmm, you do have a point, but the same might be said of that lute of yours."

"Touché!"

Seth snorted. "If he's half as good with his sword as his is with his tongue, then he might just turn out to be useful."

Aksel let out a short laugh. "That's a first. A unanimous decision—Donatello, you're in."

The artist doffed his hat. "Thank you, gentlemen. I will do my best to help you in whatever your mission is at tonight's party."

The companions were now outside the merchant's district. The crowds had thinned somewhat here, but the road was still bustling with people going about their business. Over to their right lay the main bridge that crossed the Raven River. Down toward their left, through the trees, the rooftop of the Charging Minotaur was just visible.

Aksel gazed at Elladan. "How much have you told him so far?"

"Not much," Elladan admitted. "Just that we have earned the Baron's trust and that we were asked to keep an eye out for trouble."

"You need not tell me more," Donnie said humbly.

Aksel's hand went to his chin again. When he finally spoke, it was apparent he took Donnie at his word. "That pretty much sums up what our mission is. Protect the Baron, the Baroness, and their daughter. A number of us will be seated with or near the family, so that part is easy. The tricky part will be keeping an eye out for anything unusual."

"Unusual?" Donnie repeated, his one eyebrow arching upwards. "Are we looking for anything in particular?"

"Snakes," Seth hissed.

Donnie turned toward Seth. "Snakes?" he replied rather loudly, caught off guard by the halfling's response.

Seth gave him a dark look. "Shhh, you want the whole town to hear?"

Elladan briefly swept the area with his eyes. There were a few folks passing who were within earshot. None of them appeared to show any interest in their conversation.

Donnie dropped his own voice to a near whisper. "Sorry. What kind of snakes?"

"*Big* snakes," Seth responded with an evil grin.

Donnie's face went pale, and there was a trace of nervousness in his voice. "Just how big are we talking?"

"You'll see," Seth replied mysteriously. He was quite obviously enjoying making the artist uncomfortable. "Oh, and by the way, don't look now, but we're being followed."

Everyone except for Elladan disregarded the halfling's warning, looking this way and that. Seth berated them all, a look of exasperation on his face. "What part of 'don't look now' don't you understand?" He was right. Subtlety was not one of their strong suits.

"Where is this stalker, then?" Glo asked irritably.

"About a dozen yards down the way we came. Through the crowd, you can just make out a man in one of those Dunwynn uniforms."

Elladan peered out of the corner of his eye, down the street. A few yards back, he could just barely see a form in a powder-blue colored outfit. The figure held his ground as folks passed by him on either side.

"He stopped when we stopped, and has been just staring at us for the last few minutes," Seth said.

"So he's been back there the entire time?" Aksel asked, keeping his eyes glued on Seth.

"Pretty much since we left the market place," Donnie responded before Seth could answer.

Elladan's mouth hung open as he eyed the artist. Donnie stared back at his friend and threw up his hands defensively. "What? I thought you knew."

Seth folded his arms across his chest. "I did. I just didn't want him to know we knew. I figured if I said anything, one of you would give us away."

Elladan shook his head. He didn't know which one was worse, Donnie for being oblivious, or Seth for being so closed-mouthed.

Aksel appeared pensive. He rubbed his chin and tapped his foot anxiously. "We are almost to the Charging Minotaur, and it doesn't take a genius to figure out where we are staying. What really concerns me is what this man's orders are. If it is going to interfere with our mission, it would be best to know ahead of time."

"We could always ask him," Donnie said glibly.

Elladan was just about to remark on what a bad idea that was when Aksel caught him by surprise. "I believe I will!" The little cleric spun around and strode down the street toward the solitary Dunwynn soldier.

"Wait..." Elladan trailed off after him, but the gnome was already moving at a brisk pace. "Nice going, Donnie," he said to his friend, then took off after Aksel.

Elladan tried to walk as fast as he could without running. The gnome had a good head start, though, and his diminutive size made it easier for him to slip between the people in the street. The rest of the companions were now at Elladan's side. They all hurried to catch up with the gnome, and unfortunately got in each other's way—all except for Seth. The halfling used his own small size and agility to weave through the crowd and catch up to his cleric friend. Up ahead, the Dunwynn soldier stood his ground. He glared their way as they approached. Seth was whispering to Aksel. He was most likely trying to reason with the cleric before he did anything foolish. Elladan found the entire situation confusing. Aksel was the most level-headed and reasonable of the group. He wasn't sure what had caused this sudden reckless behavior. Aksel ignored Seth and continued to plunge forward. He finally pulled up short in front of the Dunwynner. Aksel stood there with his hands on his hips and gazed up at the soldier.

"Excuse me, sir, but why are you following us?"

The man did not answer. In fact, he would not even look at the little gnome. Instead, he stared straight ahead as if he had not heard a word. Elladan and the others stopped a few feet back. They watched on incredulously as the Dunwynn soldier ignored the gnome and the halfling in front of him.

Aksel tried again, his voice rising with his frustration. "I said, why are you following us?"

A few passersby paused to gaze at the strange site of the little gnome yelling at the soldier in blue. They did not stop, though, instead hurrying about their business. The Dunwynn soldier continued to overlook Aksel. Aksel grew livid—his face turned red and he openly fumed at being ignored. Elladan had never seen Aksel like this before. *Why was he letting this man rattle him so?*

Donnie strode forward to join Aksel and Seth. He placed himself directly in front of the Dunwynn soldier. The artist then spoke in a reproving tone to the man. "I believe my friend here asked you a question."

Instead of answering him, the soldier turned his head away. He gazed out into the street and refused to make eye contact with the elf. Donnie glanced over his shoulder toward the others. He raised an eyebrow and quipped. "I think this fellow's deaf and dumb!"

Elladan watched in astonishment as the Dunwynn soldier disregarded the threesome. Some folks actually stopped now to watch the strange spectacle. Lloyd marched forward to join the others. He wore a grim expression, his jaw was firmly set as he advanced on the rude Dunwynner. "You!"

The soldier momentarily blanched as he saw the tall warrior stride up to him. Donnie, Aksel, and Seth quietly moved out of the way. Lloyd stopped in front of the ill-mannered Dunwynner, folded his arms, and glared down at the blue-clad man. The Dunwynn soldier stared up at the towering youth. He did his best to appear indifferent, but Elladan noted that he involuntarily flinched. Lloyd silently sized up the rude soldier. When he finally spoke, his anger thinly veiled. "My friends here asked you if you were following us. Now answer their question."

"Of course, I'm following you," the soldier replied haughtily. He had that same self-righteous tone as Sir Fafnar. The man tried his best to act tough, nonetheless he inched back from the tall warrior.

"Why?" Aksel asked, his tone betraying his aggravation.

Once again, the man refused to answer. He did not even look at

Aksel. Lloyd, losing what little patience he had left, took a step closer to the Dunwynn soldier causing the man to shrink down and away from him. He glared angrily and yelled, "My friend asked you why!"

The man flinched even more this time. His voice lost all its indignance as he stammered his reply. "Sir Fafnar... ordered me... to keep an eye... on the lot of you."

"Fafnar," Lloyd spat the name as if it was a curse.

"*Sir* Fafnar..." the man began, a shade of haughtiness returning to his tone. He trailed off, however, as Lloyd glared menacingly at him.

This guy's an idiot, Elladan realized. Lloyd was about two seconds away from pummeling him into the ground. Elladan tried to lighten the mood. "He did say he would be watching us." More folks had stopped to watch the confrontation. Elladan sighed. *This is the last thing we need.* He strode up to the onlookers, his hands outstretched in front of him, and politely said, "Sorry, folks. Official town business. Please move on."

The spectators stared at him for a moment, recognition crossing their faces. There were a few whispers, and then the crowd slowly dispersed. Elladan wiped his forehead. One disaster diverted, now for the next. He spun back around to the ongoing interrogation.

Aksel was talking. "Why don't you just go back to Sir Fafnar. Tell him you failed your mission. It'll do you no good to spy on us, now that we know you are there."

True to form, the Dunwynn soldier ignored him once again. Elladan buried his face in his palms. He heard a squeal, then looked up to see Lloyd holding the rude Dunwynner aloft by his collar. The man flailed around wildly, his feet dangling a good foot off the ground. He hung onto Lloyd's fists, trying to keep himself from choking. Lloyd spoke between clenched teeth.

"Now, why won't you answer my friends?"

"They... they..." the man gasped, obviously having a hard time speaking.

Elladan strode forward and spoke in a calm voice. "Put him down, Lloyd. He can't answer you while you're choking his windpipe."

"Fine." Lloyd reluctantly released his grip on the man's collar.

The ill-mannered Dunwynner fell to the ground like a sack of potatoes. Lloyd stood over him, his anger barely reined in as he spoke. "One last time. Why won't you answer my friends?"

"They're..." the guard began but was interrupted by a coughing fit. He sat on the ground choking and sputtering, trying to clear his throat. Lloyd waited, unmoving, for a response. Elladan silently prayed that the Dunwynner had sense enough to answer this time. Finally, the man cleared his throat. He peered up at Lloyd and tried to respond, stammering and coughing the entire time. "They're not... they're not... human. Dunwynn... does not... associate with... non-humans."

Elladan hung his head and shook it slowly—he would never understand attitudes like this. The bard had traveled far and wide, meeting folks from all different races, yet despite their apparent differences, he found people to be more alike than not. He lifted his head, his eyes sweeping across the group. Glo seemed taken aback, his brow knit and lips curled in an expression of disgust. Aksel's reaction was similar to Glo's. Seth's response was a bit less emotional, his nose merely lifted as he glared at the Dunwynner with disdain. Donnie appeared the most surprised, his mouth hanging partially open in disbelief. Lloyd, however, was livid, his eyes narrowed and face a bright shade of red.

"That's dragon-dung!" the young man declared vehemently as he bent down and reached for the racist Dunwynner. The soldier, in turn, tried to crawl backwards, away from the tall warrior, a look of utter terror on his face. Elladan knew he had to act quickly, before Lloyd did something he'd regret. He stepped forward and placed a hand on the young man's shoulder. Lloyd halted before he could throttle the frightened soldier, turned his head and glared at Elladan, his face a mask of rage.

Elladan spoke to him as calmly as possible. "Lloyd, let me handle this."

Lloyd stared at him, conflicting emotions playing across his face. Finally, his good nature won out. He stood up, took a deep breath, and stepped back a few paces. "Okay."

The bigoted soldier sat frozen on the ground. He was pale as a ghost—as if he had seen his life pass before him. Elladan chuckled. *He mostly likely had.* Elladan reached back and unslung his lute. He knelt down in front of the frightened man and gently began strumming notes. "Friend, let me sing you a little tune."

The Dunwynn soldier went wild-eyed until the music finally caught his ear. Abruptly his eyes went blank and a stupid grin crept across his face. In another minute, he was staring off into space, seemingly without a care in the world. Elladan stood up and put his lute away. "There, see how easy that was? He won't be bothering us again for a while."

Lloyd nodded, a tight smile across his lips. "Thanks, Elladan, I almost did something there that I would have regretted."

Seth's lips were twisted into a half-smirk. "I wouldn't have regretted it."

They left the Dunwynn soldier in his magically-induced stupor, lying on the grass next to the road. Aksel led the way back to the Charging Minotaur. The companions remained uncharacteristically quiet, their usually jovial mood darkened by their recent run-ins with the soldiers from Dunwynn. When they finally reached the inn, they all went straight to their rooms. Elladan hoped that the rest of the day would turn out better.

28

ROADBLOCK

About halfway up the hillside, sat eight men on horseback, blocking the road

A little over an hour later, the company left the Charging Minotaur. The companions were still somber after their confrontation with the soldier from Dunwynn. Martan, who had missed the encounters, heard all about it from the others. Aksel, however, refused to comment. He sat high up on The Boulder, towering above even Lloyd. He remained silent as the group trudged through town, this morning's events plaguing his mind.

That last clash with the Dunwynn soldier had really rattled him. He usual kept a level head about such things. Allowing your emotions to get the best of you could be anywhere from embarrassing to disastrous. Aksel prided himself on the fact that he could remain detached, even in the worst of situations. For some reason though, this confrontation had been different. Aksel had never been ignored like that. The Dunwynn soldier had treated him as if he didn't even exist. True, it had not been directed solely at him—Donatello and Seth had received the same treatment. Still, something about it unnerved him. Perhaps it had something to do with his family. They had all disappeared when he was rather young.

Aksel's family was composed of adventurers and historians, ever in search of historical sites and artifacts. One by one, they had all vanished on such journeys, until only his mom, dad, and one uncle were left. When his uncle went missing, his parents had set out in search of him. They had left Aksel with the priests at the Temple of Caprizon. It was supposed to have been for no more than two weeks. Two weeks stretched into three, then four. An entire month passed with no word from them. Two months became three then four, then five. The church sent out search parties after his parents, but to no avail. No sign of them was ever found. Aksel remembered being devastated at first. Many a night he had cried himself to sleep. He had felt totally alone in the world. After six months, the priests had offered him permanent residence at the church. He had gotten used to living there by that time; he'd even shown some aptitude with divine magic, so Aksel had gratefully accepted the invitation. Still, it was never quite the same.

Aksel shook himself. *That's ancient history.* He had another family now: Seth, Lloyd, Glo, and even Elladan. He was not alone, and no one was going to ignore him. He was not going to disappear like the rest of his family. *Just let them try to overlook me now,* he thought from his perch atop The Boulder.

The group continued their march through Ravenford. The streets were still busy, but the townsfolk made way for them, waving and cheering. The companions' moods began to lighten. That abruptly changed when they reached the base of the hill. About halfway up the hillside, sat eight men on horseback, blocking the road. They wore powder blue uniforms.

Seth snorted. "Great. More idiots from Dunwynn."

Aksel's insides began to churn once more, but he forced those feelings down. "Not a problem. If we have to, we'll just march right over them."

Before anyone could say another word, Aksel spurred The Boulder forward. The stone golem slowly trudged up the hill toward the impromptu blockade. The others spread out around him. Aksel could see anxiety on the riders' faces as they drew closer. Their horses acted skittish as well, shuffling their hooves about uneasily.

"Hold your positions!" cried the middle rider, a dark-haired man, with a thin moustache and goatee. His expression was smug as he regarded the approaching group.

At first Aksel though it was Sir Fafnar, but as they got closer he realized it was not. *A Fafnar want-to-be then.* Very well, he would aim The Boulder at him. When they were within twenty paces, the lead rider held up his hand and cried, "Halt!"

Aksel actually admired the man's tenacity. He decided to stop the golem's advance—after all, he had the clear advantage here. He would give these Dunwynn folks a chance to be reasonable.

"In whose name?" Lloyd cried. The warrior stood beside him, his hands resting on his sword hilts.

"In the name of Sir Fafnar, right-hand man to the Duke of Dunwynn himself," the man responded. His sour face betrayed a hint of pleasure at the utterance of those words.

Aksel cleared his throat. "We do not recognize Sir Fafnar's right to give orders in the town of Ravenford. We have our own orders from the Baron himself that require our presence at this party. Now kindly move out of our way or we will be forced to move you."

The Dunwynn riders began to talk among themselves, casting nervous glances at the golem. The lead man replied in that now all too familiar haughty tone. "Those are big words from such a little fellow. I see that you ride a stone man. Are you a golem master or a great wizard perhaps?"

"Why, yes. In fact, I am a great wizard," Aksel said, keeping his expression neutral. He leaned forward and stared intently at the rider. "Perhaps you have heard of me. My name is *Maltar.*"

The leader of the Dunwynn troop was visibly startled, his face blanching at the mention of the wizard's name. The corners of Aksel mouth upturned slightly. This was going to be fun. He cast a quick glance at his companions. Elladan and Donnie stood straight-faced, the latter resting his hand nonchalantly on his sword hilt. Lloyd glared unflinchingly at the Dunwynn riders, his arms now folded across his chest. Glo wore a serious expression, though one eyebrow was raised. Seth wore a wicked grin. Only Martan seemed uneasy. The archer gazed up at him as if he were crazed. Aksel turn his eyes back to the blockade. The lead rider had regained his composure, yet he did not sound quite so self-assured this time.

"If you are the Wizard Maltar, as you claim to be, then show us some magic."

"Very well. If you insist." The little cleric made a grand gesture of rolling up his sleeves. He weaved his hands in a circular pattern. As both his hands came together in front of him he spoke the words, "*Cras Placerat*".

The Dunwynn riders were suddenly surrounded by four brightly glowing spheres of light. The lights hung over their heads for a few moments, then began to spin around them faster and faster. The riders watched the spinning globes uncomfortably, shading their eyes with their hands. Some of them even visibly flinched. They were obviously not very familiar with magic.

Seth let out a wicked laugh. "They're not very bright."

Aksel felt quite satisfied with the riders' reactions. He called out, "Is that good enough for you?"

The lead rider did not appear spooked like the rest of his men. Yet his haughty attitude had disappeared. "You may be a conjurer at that, but we still have our orders. You may not pass."

"Enough of these idiots," Seth said in exasperation. "We're wasting time. Let's go. If they're too stupid to move out of the way, then it's their own fault."

Aksel had to agree. This was getting them nowhere. He called out to the lead rider, "Very well, you leave us no choice." He concentrated briefly, and The Boulder moved forward.

"Anyone want to bet on how long it takes them to move out of the way?" he heard Donnie say.

"I give them until The Boulder is within ten feet," Elladan answered.

Seth wore a wicked smirk. "Personally, I don't care if they move or not."

Aksel watched the Dunwynn riders as they closed in on them. They appeared quite nervous. The horses began to whinny and buck. "Hold, I said!" the lead soldier cried out. He whirled around in his saddle to chastise his men. His attempts were in vain. As The Boulder drew closer, the riders and their mounts became more and more frightened. The lead rider had turned back around. He was so intent on the stone golem that he no longer noticed his men. When The Boulder was nearly on top of them, he cried out one last time. "Wait! You can't!" Yet it was to no avail. The stone golem continued to trudge forward. Aksel sat astride the tall creature, doing his best to keep a straight face. He was nearly on top of the blockade. Below him, the riders and their mounts grew frantic. The blockade broke ranks just before The Boulder waded into them. Spurring their already-frightened horses, the riders quickly moved to either side of the road.

"Guess they're braver than I thought," he heard Elladan say.

Donnie and Seth laughed. Aksel had to admit that this minor victory against the pompous Dunwynners felt good. A smile crept across his face. The little company moved forward at a steady pace up the road. The blue-clad soldiers made no further attempts to stop them. Instead, they fell in behind and followed them up the hill. The company had almost reached the gates of the keep when another rider trotted through the entrance. The familiar figure, garbed in a powder-blue doublet, rode down to meet them.

"What goes on here?" Sir Fafnar cried. "I thought I told you to keep these varlets away from the castle. Especially with that *thing*," he finished, staring disdainfully at The Boulder.

Aksel halted the golem once more. He was curious as to how this would play out. They were now in front of Ravenford keep. It wouldn't be long until someone noticed the gathering outside the gate, then let Sir Fafnar explain his actions.

"I'm sorry, Sir, but they would not stop," a voice called from behind them. Aksel spun around and saw the lead rider spur his horse forward. He rode around them and up to the Dunwynn noble.

"Well then, you should have forced them to," Fafnar responded peevishly. He fixed the man with an unrelenting glare. "These are mere ruffians. You are trained Dunwynn troops. You cannot tell me you are afraid of these upstarts?"

The lead rider's face went pale. "N-no, Sir! It's just..."

"It's just that they had no stomach to face us," Donnie finished for him.

"I guess your troops are not as brave as you think," Glo added with obvious pleasure.

Fafnar spun toward them. "I was not talking to you non-humans," he spat contemptuously. "You may have frightened my soldiers, but you will not get through me so easily." He sat tall in his saddle and glared at them, as if daring them to make a move to get past him.

Aksel was tempted to spur The Boulder onward. He was curious to see what the arrogant noble would do, but then Lloyd stepped out in front of the party and spoke. "We'll just see about that." There was a dangerous edge to his voice.

Fafnar recognized it as well. He began to dismount his horse when a familiar voice rang out from behind him.

"What goes on here?"

Aksel peered toward the gate. A Ravenford guard strode out of the keep. He recognized the guard immediately. It was Francis! Fafnar spun around and spied the guard approaching. He addressed him in that all-too-familiar arrogant tone. "These ruffians were headed up to the keep. I explained that the likes of them would not be welcome here."

Francis gazed past the man, at the companions. A look of recognition crossed his face and his expression quickly changed to one of confusion. He turned back to Sir Fafnar. "Why there must be some mistake. These are the Heroes of Ravenford. They are honored guests at tonight's proceedings."

"Indeed, there must be," Fafnar replied, his tone practically icy. He was obviously displeased at being questioned by the Ravenford guard. "We ran into these hooligans in the town a little while ago. I cannot believe that the likes of them are invited to tonight's festivities."

Francis opened his mouth to speak again, then stopped. He gazed at Aksel, still looking quite perplexed. Aksel merely shrugged. The last thing he wanted was to cause the kind guard any trouble. Amazingly, the group followed his cue and remained silent. Not even Seth had a smart remark. "There must be some mistake here," Francis finally managed. "I will fetch the Captain. He'll be able to straighten this out." With that, Francis spun around and hurried back up toward the gate.

"Uh, oh," Donnie taunted, "now you're in trouble now."

There were a few snickers from amongst the companions. Fafnar declined to respond. He sat silently on his horse, a sour expression on his face. Aksel and the others waited patiently for the proverbial axe to fall. It didn't take long. Barely two minutes went by when Captain Gelpas came storming through the gate and down the path toward them. He did not appear happy.

"What the blazes goes on here? The party is tonight, and there is still much to do."

"These morons won't let us into the castle," Seth said before anyone else could speak. It was times like these that Aksel loved the halfling's bluntness. He could not help but smile at his concise description of the problem.

Fafnar spun in his saddle to face the Captain. When he spoke, his tone was haughty. "I'm certain that these elves and whatnot are not on the guest list."

"Of course they are!" Gelpas cried, staring at Fafnar as if he was daft. "They're honored guests of the Baron and Baroness. In fact, their presence is essential at tonight's proceedings."

Sir Fafnar gazed down at the Captain, his expression changing to one of shock. He gazed over at the companions, then turned back toward Captain Gelpas. The noble opened his mouth to speak, but no words came out.

"Would you look at that," Donnie said with clear enjoyment, "he's actually speechless. Never thought I'd see the day."

Aksel stifled a laugh. The other companions reacted similarly. The corners of Captain Gelpas's mouth upturned slightly, but somehow he managed to keep a straight face. "Now I'm sure you are used to giving orders in Dunwynn," Gelpas said firmly, "but this is Ravenford, Sir Fafnar. Here everyone answers to Baron Gryswold, and I am his right hand. So if you would kindly move yourself and your horse out of the way?"

Fafnar, still recovering from his initial shock, turned red in the face. He was obviously not used to being talked to that way. "Well..." he finally managed, "I... still don't believe it." The obstinate noble opened his mouth to say more, then stopped himself. He let out a heavy sigh, then replied with his usual smugness, "Very well. After all, what is one to expect from such a backwater town? One could not anticipate the proper forms of propriety to be followed here."

Captain Gelpas's face now reddened. He placed his hands on his hips and glared at the Dunwynn noble. "Are you questioning the Baron's choice of guests?"

Fafnar's reply was deliberately measured. "No, no, I wouldn't dream of questioning the choices of the Barony of Ravenford. By all means, let these ruffians pass and join us inside the keep." He paused a moment then added, "All but *that* monstrosity." He pointed directly at The Boulder. "That is a weapon of war and has no place among the lords and ladies inside. I refuse to let such a thing anywhere near the Duke."

Gelpas threw up his hands in exasperation. "*Sir* Fafnar..."

"It's okay, Captain," Aksel interrupted him.

Gelpas halted in midsentence. He turned to look at the little cleric. He was still red in the face, but his anger was tempered by his surprise. "Are you sure, Cleric Aksel?"

Aksel retained his composure. "Indeed. We were planning on having The Boulder guard the gate anyway."

"And I will have guards around it to make sure it stays there," Fafnar added self-righteously.

"They would be better served patrolling the perimeter," Aksel pointed out to the stubborn noble, "but you can waste your men however you want."

"Do not propose to tell me what to do with my men, knave," Fafnar shot back with indignation.

"*Gentlemen!*" Gelpas roared. All eyes fell on the Captain. Gelpas, now having everyone's attention, continued in a more civilized tone. "The *Baron* is waiting. We have no more time for debate." He fixed Sir Fafnar with a hard stare. The noble regarded him coolly from his saddle but otherwise remained silent. "Now then, if you will please follow me." It was more of a statement than a request.

Aksel nodded to the Captain. He took a moment or two to communicate with The Boulder, mentally commanding it to stand guard. Aksel then slid down off The Boulder to the ground below. At the same time, Fafnar waved his troops over. He ordered four of his men to dismount and take up positions around the stone creature. Aksel shook his head in disgust. *What a waste of manpower.*

"Like that will make any difference," Elladan commented.

Captain Gelpas watched the proceedings with his arms folded. When the Dunwynn troops were done, he addressed Sir Fafnar, his contempt for the noble thinly veiled. "May we proceed now?"

"By all means," the Sir Fafnar responded loftily.

Gelpas took a deep breath, then spun around, striding briskly toward the gate. He waved for the others to follow. The companions quickly fell in behind him. Sir Fafnar spun his horse around and trotted beside them. As they passed under the gate portcullis, he whispered under his breath.

"Don't think this is over."

"You can bet it isn't," Lloyd replied, glaring hotly at the pompous noble.

When they entered the castle grounds, a Dunwynn soldier came trotting over to Sir Fafnar. Gelpas halted, as did the rest. The soldier beckoned to Fafnar, who in turn bent down toward him. The Dunwynn soldier whispered something into the noble's ear. Sir Fafnar's expression became anxious. He sat up and quickly dismounted, handing his reigns over to the soldier. Fafnar spun toward Captain Gelpas.

"If you will excuse me Captain, I must report to the Duke," he said in a self-important tone.

"By all means," Gelpas responded.

The noble nodded curtly, then spun around, striding off in a hurry in the direction the soldier had come.

"I thought he would never leave," Donnie said when he was out of earshot. His observation was met with a round of chuckles. Even Gelpas smiled. The Captain then led them across the courtyard. Preparations for the evening's events were well underway. Off to their left, a large stage had been set up against the wall of the keep. A tall scaffolding rose above the platform, a dark backdrop currently hanging from it. A few rows of long benches were lined up in front of the stage. On the other side of the courtyard were the gardens. A few well-dressed individuals roamed around there.

Most likely some early guests, Aksel surmised.

A number of long tables stood at the entrance to the keep. They were arranged perpendicular to the castle except for the head table. That one ran parallel to the structure. Aksel addressed the Captain. "It looks like things are proceeding as planned."

"Yes, we do seem to be on schedule," Gelpas responded proudly. His voice dropped, and his expression grew serious. "All except for the final security plans."

"Not to worry," Elladan assured him. "We mapped out a strategy this morning."

Gelpas nodded. "Well, the Baron is eager to hear your thoughts."

"Then let's not keep him waiting any longer than he already has," Aksel agreed.

The group hurried up the stairs and filed into the keep proper.

An hour later, the company exited the keep. The meeting with the Baron had gone well. Gryswold approved of their plans and arranged the seating accordingly. With Maltar gone, Glo would sit at the main table with the Baron and Baroness. Lloyd would be seated there as well, next to the Lady Andrella. The young man was extremely honored, thanking the Baron profusely.

Gryswold had grinned at him broadly. "We Penwick men need to stick together."

Aksel noted that both Sir Fafnir and the Duke of Dunwynn were also seated at the head table. He had drawn both Lloyd and Glo aside, cautioning them to keep conversation with the nobles to a minimum. Glo nodded his understanding. Lloyd's response had been a bit more disconcerting.

"Don't worry. As far as Fafnar is concerned, from now on my swords will do all the talking."

They had also introduced Donatello to the Baron and Baroness.

Gracelynn graciously responded, "Any friend of the Heroes may be considered a friend of ours."

Donnie briefly derailed things with a side conversation about painting portraits. Luckily, Aksel steered the conversation back on track. They arranged for Donnie to sit at the table next to the Baron's, along with Elladan. The bard's seat was reserved for when the show ended.

Seth, Aksel, and Martan would be stationed on the grounds, watching for signs of the Serpent Cult. Gryswold gave Seth leave to access the upper floors of the keep and roam the rooftops. He also supplied them with the key to Maltar's old tower. It had been locked up for some time now—ever since he had left the keep in favor of his home across town. Gryswold had held onto that key all this time, although he alluded to the fact that Maltar had a second key, which Aksel found interesting. Once the party was over, he thought they should explore the tower thoroughly. There may be some clue inside as to the whereabouts of the missing mage.

With the security plans finished, they took their leave of Gryswold and Gracelynn. The Baron confided that they needed to meet with some dignitaries from Dunwynn and Penwick. He did not seem thrilled by the prospect of the former. Now the companions stood out in the courtyard once again. They quickly moved off the stairs and out of the way of the servants who were hustling in and out of the keep, still preparing for tonight's festivities. Aksel addressed the group.

"Well, we all know our assignments. There are still a couple of hours until the party begins..."

"Ves!" a voice interrupted him. It was Martan.

Aksel noted the archer staring across the courtyard. Following his gaze, he saw a young woman over by the gardens. She had long, golden blonde hair and wore a flowing bronze gown. She was holding the arm of a tall, white-haired gentleman garbed in long brown robes. Skipping around them enthusiastically was a little blonde girl in a pale blue gown.

"And Maya," Glo said with a trace of amusement. "I was beginning to wonder if we were ever going to see them again."

"Me, too," Martan said, sounding entranced.

Elladan clasped the archer on the shoulder. "Pull yourself together there, friend. We've got work to do."

Martan responded with a wan smile. "Oh, right. I guess I'll go set up on the top of the tower." The archer took one last look over at Ves. She was smiling and laughing with the old gentlemen. Martan bowed his head for a moment, then took off in the direction of Maltar's tower.

"Friends of yours?" Donnie asked. He was staring with keen interest in the direction of the two girls.

"It's a long story, best saved for another time," Aksel replied.

Glo squared his shoulders. "Well I'm going to go talk with them." Before anyone could object, he strode away toward the three figures.

Elladan gazed over at the stage. "And I need to prepare for my act. Lloyd, care to join me?"

"Sure," Lloyd replied. His tone was distant, his mind apparently somewhere else. Aksel assumed he was still thinking about their run-ins with the pompous Sir Fafnar.

"Mind if I tag along?" Donnie asked.

"Sure, I'll put you to work," Elladan said with a half-smile.

"I live to serve." Donnie bowed with a flourish.

The trio moved off, leaving Aksel and Seth alone in front of the keep. Seth appeared impatient, fidgeting from one foot to the other. "I think I will go do some scouting around. I saw some new wagons in the performers' camp on our way up."

"Go ahead," Aksel told him. It was just as well. Seth was not one to sit idly by anyways.

Seth headed out across the courtyard, toward the gate. "See you in a bit," he cried back over his shoulder.

Aksel, alone now, sat down at the base of the stairs. He reviewed all that had happened the last few days. The morning's events in particular played through his mind. He kept coming back to their encounter with the Dunwynn riders and the way they'd blanched when he said he was Maltar. An amusing idea suddenly came to him. Aksel laughed aloud at the thought. It would require a spell, and a prop or two. It would not be perfect, but if he could pull it off, it just might catch their enemies off-guard. Aksel stood up, a satisfied smile on his lips. He walked briskly through the busy courtyard toward the tower. *This is going to be very interesting.*

29
GLOWING EYES IN THE DARK
They looked like eyes—two large, glowing eyes in the inky blackness

Seth passed through the gate and out of the keep. The road was lined with approximately twenty flamboyantly-dressed men and woman. Beside them were carts filled with props and the like. The entertainer at the front of the line stood with his hands up in the air as a castle guard patted him down. A second guard rifled through the handcart beside him. A thin smile spread across Seth's lips. It appeared that the Baron wasn't taking any chances. Seth veered away from the road and strode down the hill toward the campground. He had made a point of exploring the camp yesterday and counted close to forty entertainers with nearly as many tents and wagons. On their way up to the keep earlier, he had spotted a few new coaches parked on the opposite side of the camp, away from the road. That might have been coincidence, or it might have been purposeful. Either way, Seth was going to check them out.

Seth continued downhill until he entered the camp. It was still quite busy in here, a number of performers rushing about, gathering their things for tonight's performance. He slowly weaved his way through the wagons and tents, until he was almost to the other side of the campground. Seth snuck up behind an empty tent, then cautiously peered around the corner. The new set of wagons stood just beyond. No one appeared to be milling about. Seth counted eight new wagons in total. They were all fully enclosed, like small houses on wheels. Each was quite tall, though they varied in size and color. Some were brown, while others were green, and still others were yellow with green trim. He estimated the smallest wagon to be about eight feet by twenty. The largest was probably ten feet by twenty-five.

That one would need at least four horses to pull it. Each wagon had a door in front, shuttered windows on the sides, and a hatch on top. All the shutters were pulled closed. In front of each wagon was a ladder leading up to the front door. They were on hinges and could be folded up and out of the way. Seth was familiar with these types of wagons. In fact, there were already two or three in the main campsite. An entire set like this typically belonged to either a circus or a tribe of gypsies, but there were no markings on the sides of the wagons. *Definitely not a circus then. No gypsies wandering around, either.*

Seth had a funny feeling about this. There should be at least some people moving about, especially with the party beginning in just a few hours. Something was definitely not right here. He wanted a closer look. He grabbed his cloak and whispered the word, *"Invisibilitate."* He could still see himself quite clearly, but knew that to the rest of the world he was invisible. The halfling crept silently into the new camp area. He stole around between the enclosed wagons, looking for a marking or some sign of life. He found nothing—not a single clue as to where these newcomers were from. The wagons themselves were all locked tight, not that that would have stopped him. He could have easily picked the locks, but a door seemingly opening by itself would certainly appear suspicious. With no other options, Seth continued to skulk around between wagons.

A sudden movement made him freeze in his tracks. He slowly turned his head. The wagon next to him rocked slightly. It was as if something large had fallen inside. There were no noises accompanying the movement, though.

Strange. There should have been some noise, at least.

Seth waited silently until the rocking died down. He paused a bit longer after that, but there were no further movements. *I need a look inside that wagon.*

Like all the rest, the shutters were closed tight. The door was still out of the question. That left the hatch. It was his best bet. If he was careful, whoever was inside might not see it open. Seth briefly glanced over his shoulder, but the camp around him remained vacant. He gingerly moved forward to the side of the wagon and carefully scaled it, taking great pains to make no noise. He finally reached the roof and hauled himself up. Seth silently padded across the roof to the hatch in the center of the coach.

Locked. Of course.

It took him less than a minute to pick it. Seth slid the hatch open a crack, taking great care not to make any sound. He knelt down and peered inside. Through the slit, he could see nothing but black. Even with his keen eyesight, he couldn't make out any details within the cabin. He continued to stare, waiting for his eyes to adjust to the dark.

Abruptly, two glowing shapes appeared in the inky darkness. They started out as slits, then gradually grew into thin, oval-shaped orbs. Seth held his breath, his eyes transfixed on those twin orbs. He watched curiously as they slowly spun to the left, then the right. They finally settled back to where they started. The orbs began to change shape once again. They grew more and more oval. On top of that, a dark slit appeared in the center of each one. Now they looked like eyes—two large, glowing eyes in the inky blackness. They were definitely not human though. They were more cat, or—*snake like!* A chill went up Seth's spine. If this was indeed a snake, the thing was huge! He watched in fascination as the eyes grew larger.

Whatever this thing is, it's rising up toward the ceiling!

Seth forced himself into action. He rolled away from the hatch and launched himself off the top of the wagon. He noiselessly tumbled to the ground below. Seth stayed there for a moment and took in his surroundings. There was still no sign of movement, nor sound to be heard—only distant noises from the other side of the camp. He had seen enough. He now knew how the Serpent Cult had made it into town. It was time to warn the others.

Seth stood up and snuck toward the inhabited part of the camp. He had gone no more than thirty feet when he heard a noise behind him. He glanced back over his shoulder. The hatch slid open on the top of the wagon from which he had just come. Nothing came out of the hatch, but then he heard a voice yell something in a strange tongue. The hatch slid back into place with a *bang*. Seth began to move again, faster this time. The sooner he was away from this area, the better.

Donatello sat in the first row in front of the stage. He leaned back leisurely and took in the sights as Elladan and the tall warrior, Lloyd, rehearsed for tonight's show. The duo stood in one corner of the stage, while the rest of the wide platform was populated with other acts. There was another singer, a magician, and a pair of acrobats, all warming up. Many more performers lined the benches around him. All were colorfully dressed, eagerly awaiting their turn up on stage. Donnie hadn't seen anything like it this side of the annual fair in Lukescros. The Baron and Baroness were going all out for their daughter's coming-of-age party.

As he lounged there, a sultry form strode by. Donnie sat up, his interest immediately piqued. The woman was tall, her long, shapely legs and the gentle curve of her hips quite apparent in the form-fitting white leather pants and forest green leather boots she wore. A tight white shirt and forest green vest accentuated her slender shoulders and tapered waist. All this was capped with long, luxurious, light brown tresses, highlighted with golden strands that shone in the late day sun. The luscious locks fell down her shoulders, reaching nearly to the small of her back. This woman exuded confidence. She moved with a practiced grace as she strode toward the stage. As she turned to climb up the stairs, Donnie got a look at her face. She was just as beautiful as he imagined. Her face was heart-shaped, with sparkling blue eyes, an elegantly tapered nose, and high cheekbones.

She would look superb on canvas.

Donnie watched with keen interest as she strode across the stage. She finally stopped in front of Elladan. She then threw her arms around the bard's neck and kissed him soundly. A wry smile crossed Donnie's lips. He should have known. The most beautiful woman he had seen thus far in Ravenford, and she was already involved with the bard. The brown-haired beauty produced a lute and the two entertainers began to sing a duet. It was difficult to hear with all the noise on stage, but from the little he caught, he was duly impressed. Lloyd put down his drums and jumped off stage, striding over to the bench where Donnie sat. He plopped himself down next to the elven artist.

"Who's that?" Donnie asked nodding toward Elladan's companion.

"Oh, that's Shalla," Lloyd replied genially. "She and Elladan are good friends."

"No doubt," Donnie remarked, not taking his eyes off the pair.

"They're doing a duet in tonight's show," Lloyd continued.

Donnie nodded. "I figured as much. I've seen Elladan perform before, you know—back in Lukescros, at the fair last year."

Lloyd glanced at him, a wistful expression on his face. "I've been to the fair there. Not last year though. How did he do?"

"He barely lost to Cassilla Nightbird," Donnie told him.

"*The* Cassilla Nightbird?" Lloyd asked, his eyes widening.

"The one and only." Donnie gave him a knowing smile. Cassilla Nightbird was the most famous songstress in Thac—possibly in the world.

"I didn't take you for a music lover," he confided in Lloyd.

The tall youth laughed. "I'm not, exactly. An old friend of mine is a singer. In fact, she's on tour with Cassilla right now."

Donnie raised an eyebrow. *That's impressive.* He was about to ask more about this friend of Lloyd's when they were interrupted. Someone behind them was crying out the young man's name. Donnie spun around.

A slender young woman in a gorgeous, emerald green gown strode towards them. She was quite lovely. She had an oval face with a tiny nose, pert lips, and a delicate chin. Her electric blue eyes stood out against her cream-colored skin. Her youthful features were framed by well-coiffed tresses of strawberry blonde hair. Parted down the middle, they flowed around her face then were pulled back where they fell past her shoulders. Elegant pearl earrings dangled from her ears. A matching pearl necklace fell across her amble bodice. She was quite obviously nobility. He and Lloyd rose from their seats as she reached them.

"There you are, Lloyd!" the young woman declared. "I've been looking all over for you. There are some people I would like you to meet."

Donnie doffed his hat and bowed low. "And who is this ravishing young lady?"

Lloyd sounded somewhat embarrassed. "Oh, this is the Lady Andrella. Andrella, this is Donatello. He is a good friend of Elladan's."

Donatello did a double take. "*The* Lady Andrella? The one for whom tonight's party is being held?" He was completely taken off guard by her abrupt appearance here.

"Guilty as charged," Andrella replied with an impish smile. She gave him a courtly curtsey then added, "It's a pleasure to meet you."

"Oh, no, your Ladyship, the pleasure is all mine," Donnie said with an extravagant wave of his hand, smoothly recovering from his momentary lapse.

She smiled brightly at Donnie, then spoke in a polite voice. "If you will please excuse us." She brushed past him and grabbed Lloyd's hand, dragging the young man off with her, back toward the keep.

"More and more interesting," Donnie murmured. This was quite a group he had fallen in with—Elladan by himself seemed to be well on his way to fame and fortune, but these folks were taking things to a whole new level. From what he had just seen, the Lady Andrella, the proverbial heir to the Duchy of Dunwynn, the largest city on the east coast of Thac, was smitten with the young Lloyd. Assuming that nothing came between the two, he just might very well be associating with the next Duke of Dunwynn.

Well then, Donatello, it looks like your luck is finally turning around.

He sat back down to watch Elladan and Shalla rehearse. His mind was a million miles away though, visions of being the court-appointed artist for the City of Dunwynn dancing through his head.

Elladan was still rehearsing with Shalla when the screams rang out. He spun around and saw the other performers fleeing off the stage. A sudden breeze kicked up all around them.

"Up there!" someone cried.

Elladan peered upward and saw the source of the mayhem. A dragon hung above the stage, about 50 feet in the air! Its great wings beat slowly, kicking up the wind around them, as it descended toward the stage. It had reddish-brown scales, speckled here and there with turquoise-colored spots. That was a copper dragon.

"I don't know what all the fuss is about," Shalla said from behind him. She was shading her eyes with one hand as she stared up in the sky. "It's only a metallic dragon, after all."

A short laugh escaped Elladan's lips. "Not everyone is knowledgeable about dragons."

She shook her head. "More's the pity—this one's a beautiful shade of copper."

"I couldn't agree more," a voice added from off to one side. They turned to see Donnie climb up on stage. "Too bad we can't explain that to all these panicky folks." He nodded towards the crowd behind him. "Folks are running like mad and screaming for the castle guards. This might get ugly fast."

Elladan gazed around the courtyard. The crowd of performers cowered behind the rear benches, and some had already broken into a run. Farther back, castle guards charged across the field toward the stage. *Donnie is right; this could get ugly.* While copper dragons were friendly, any dragon that was attacked would not hesitate to fight back. Many innocent folks might die.

Elladan turned to Shalla. "Go and see if you can calm those folks down. We'll handle the dragon."

"Right." Shalla ran to the end of the stage and leapt off. She took out her lute as she strode toward the crowd and played a soothing tune. "Everybody quiet down," she sang in a dulcet tone.

The copper dragon had touched down in the middle of the stage. Elladan whispered to Donnie. "I think I know of this dragon. Follow my lead."

He strode across the stage toward the dragon when movement out in the courtyard caught his eye. The castle guards had reached the benches and were forming a line in front of the stage. *Oh, great. That's the last thing we need.* Elladan stopped in his tracks. *First things first. The dragon would wait. It was not the aggressor here.*

Then Shalla was there, talking calmly with one of the guards. It was Francis! *Thank the gods.* Elladan knew this guard would be reasonable. He saw Shalla point up toward him. Francis' eyes flickered his way and the guard sighed with obvious relief. He waved up toward Elladan and cried, "You sure you've got this?"

"Not a problem," Elladan answered, flashing the guard a half-smile.

"Very well." Francis turned around and held up his hands, forcing the other guards to stand back.

Elladan gave Shalla a quick smile and mouthed the words *Thank you*. She winked back at him.

"That's quite a woman you've got there," Donnie said.

Elladan nodded. "She certainly is."

Elladan swung back around to face the dragon. The creature sat comfortably on its hind legs in the center of the stage, its wings folded in close to its body. Its sinuous neck protruded forward, and its turquoise eyes were regarding him curiously from behind the long snout. Overall, it was not large by dragon standards, perhaps fifteen feet tall where it sat. Elladan got the impression that the dragon understood everything that had been said around it. Yet dragons were a very proper race. They appreciated being spoken to in their own language. Luckily, Elladan had an ear for sounds, and picked up languages quite easily. One of those languages just happened to be Draconic.

"*Hail, friend,*" he said to the dragon in its own language. "*Might you be Calipherous?*"

"*Indeed I am,*" the dragon replied in its native tongue. The words rumbled from its large throat in a deep baritone. "*It's very kind of you to speak to me in my own language.*"

"*Courtesy is what separates us civilized folk from the others,*" Donnie said in perfect Draconic. Elladan cast a glance at the other elf, his eyebrow arched. Donnie merely smiled and winked back at him. Elladan shook his head. The slight elf never ceased to amaze him.

"*Indeed, that is true,*" Calipherous said in his deep reverberating voice. "*It is a paramount virtue which is lost on many, including those of my own race.*"

Elladan let out a deep sigh. "*The same can be said about many of the races. Some are still very young and immature, the humans perhaps more than not; although there are some shining examples—we have befriended a few as of late.*"

"*That is heartwarming to know,*" Calipherous rumbled. "*Long have we dragons watched the other races. The humans have the most promise, but still seem the quickest to aggression.*"

"I think that is more out of fear than anything else," Donnie responded. *"In fact, your presence here right now is upsetting some of these folks."*

Nicely done, Donnie! Elladan thought.

"I do not mean to intrude," Calipherous replied, lifting its large head to scan the grounds around them. *"However, I am still in search of my charges. Do you know of them?"*

"We were told by our friends that you were searching for them," Elladan answered. *"They are the ones you encountered yesterday. The elven wizard, the halfling, and the tall human in red."*

"Ah, yes," Calipherous responded in a ponderous rumble. *"They were indeed a courteous group. They saved my life actually. I believe I owe them a debt."*

This was going far better than Elladan hoped. Calipherous felt indebted to his friends. He could use that as leverage. *"Well then, we are their close companions. I think that they would appreciate it if you could come back tomorrow instead. There is a party going on tonight, and, as you can see, you being here is upsetting some of the townsfolk and partygoers."*

The copper dragon lifted its head once more to survey the courtyard. It peered back down at Elladan, then replied in its deep rumbling voice. *"Very well. I will honor your request and return on the morrow. Good day to you, kind elves."*

With that, the dragon unfolded its large wings. It beat them a few times and lifted off into the air. Elladan and Donnie both stood their ground, despite being buffeted by the quick-moving air. The dragon continued to rise upward until it was fifty feet off the ground. With three great beats of its wings, it launched itself off toward the east. Within seconds, it had passed over the courtyard, the castle gardens, and shot out over the bay.

Elladan watched the dragon depart with clear admiration. It was a magnificent creature, even if it were a bit small. Abruptly, clapping and cheering broke out around him. He tore his eyes away from the receding form and gazed down from the stage. A crowd of guards, performers, and servants had gathered around them. They were applauding their saviors. Shalla was at the forefront, a wide grin on her face. Elladan exchanged a quick glance with Donnie. Nodding to each other briefly, the duo stepped forward to the edge of the stage.

Together they reached down to the songstress. A brief laugh escaped Shalla's lips. She then reached up and grasped their hands. The duo hauled her up on stage and then the three of them stood back. They grasped shoulders, Shalla in the middle, and then as one, bowed for their audience. The crowd went wild! A chant of "Heroes, Heroes!" quickly went up through the throng.

Francis came forward to the edge of the stage. "Thank you all. We were certain we were going to have to fight that creature."

"Men," Shalla whispered under her breath. "Why is fighting always the answer?"

Elladan suppressed a laugh, instead smiling at the well-meaning guard. "I'm glad we could help."

"Well then, best we all get back to our preparations for this evening," Frances replied. He spun around and led the guards away.

The rest of the crowd dispersed, and performers once again took the stage. Elladan, Shalla, and Donnie climbed down and out of the way. They'd all had enough rehearsing for the day. The threesome stopped in front of the first row of benches. There they turned to watch the other performers practice. They stood there in silence until Shalla spoke up. "I have to agree with the guard. That was rather valiant of you both."

Elladan gave her a half-smile. "That was nothing. You should've seen the time Donnie faced down an irate noble, his three sons, and a whole platoon of city guards!"

"I seem to remember you providing a helping hand in there," Donnie replied with glint in his eye.

Shalla's eyes flickered from one to the other, her hands going to her hips. "Why do I suspect there was a woman involved in all of that?"

Donnie did not miss a beat. "Is there a better reason to do anything than for the love of a woman?"

Shalla gazed sharply at the slight elf, then a smirk crossed her lips. She laughed softly, then turned to Elladan. "Oh, I am definitely in trouble, aren't I? This one is as much of a charmer as you!"

30
TURNING THE TABLES

I appreciate your concern, my friend, but these devils are threatening my daughter!

G lolindir heard the screams from across the courtyard. He saw the dragon landing on the stage, the hysterical crowd, and the castle guards spurring into action. Recognizing the impending recipe for disaster, he immediately took off across the courtyard. He had only run a short distance when he pulled up short. Elladan had interposed himself between the dragon and the crowd. The bard and his friends had things well in hand. With the dragon gone and the crowd dispersed, Glo approached the trio. Elladan and Donnie were bantering and laughing while Shalla stood there with her hands on her hips. She did not appear angry, though, instead smirking and laughing at the duo.

"Are these two giving you trouble?" Glo called lightheartedly to her.

Shalla returned his gaze, grinned and winked. "Nothing I can't handle, but thanks for asking." She reached out and smacked Elladan on the arm. "At least one of you elves is a gentleman." Her tone was serious, but her eyes danced with amusement.

Elladan gave her a smoldering stare. "Have I not been a gentleman with you?"

"It is not me that I'm worried about, you silver-tongued fox. It's all these other women I'm suddenly hearing about!" she declared with feigned anger.

"Do not malign my friend for his love of women," Donnie said, rather overdramatically. "You are the most wondrous creatures in all the world. How could we not love you?"

Shalla appeared to be caught off-guard by the remark, her cheeks flushing slightly. She quickly recovered, though, stepping back and fanning her face with her hand. When she replied, her tone was melodramatic. "Oh, my! Now I have two silver-tongued foxes to deal with!" Shalla turned to Glo and winked, continuing to feign distress. "Perhaps you are right, Glolindir. These two might indeed be too much for one poor defenseless female like myself. Perhaps you could distract them while I run for the hills?"

Glo watched with amusement as the lady bard began to run from them. She moved her limbs in exaggerated slow motion. Not to be outdone, Elladan fell on one knee. "Please do not run away, fair Shalla! I promise to change my errant ways if only you'll stay."

Shalla spun around in mid-step to see the elven bard on one knee. "Oh, Elladan!" she cried, her hand going to her forehead. She was nearly in front of Glo. Abruptly she fake-swooned backwards. He instinctively reached out and tried to catch her, nearly dropping her altogether. As it was, he barely caught the damsel, falling on his own butt in his attempt to save her. Glo found himself sprawled on the ground, with Shalla laying on top of him. The lady bard laughed hysterically. Elladan and Donnie stood over them, wide grins on their faces. Shalla sat up first, then Glo followed. Without warning, she spun around and threw her arms around his neck.

"Thank you for saving me, good sir!" She leaned into him and kissed him on the cheek. Glo felt the blood rush to his face.

He heard Donnie snicker. "Don't look now, Elladan, but I think she's fallen for Glo."

That comment elicited groans from both Glo and Shalla. Elladan, however, rolled with it. He raised the back of his hand to his forehead and cried, "Alas, I have lost her."

Shalla spun back around to look at Elladan. She then broke down into uncontrollable fits of laughter. Elladan and Donnie both joined in. Glo shook his head. These three were incorrigible. Their laughter was contagious, though, and he found himself chuckling along. "You three missed your calling. You should have been actors."

Shalla turned around and gazed at him with a fond expression, placing a gentle hand on his face. "Ah, but we are actors, my dear— every time we go out on stage."

"It's true—every time I give a performance," Elladan agreed. "We wouldn't survive long in this business without stage presence."

Glo gazed from Elladan to Donnie and back to Shalla. "Well, I see no shortage of that here."

"You are a dear." Shalla leaned forward and kissed him one more time, then got up and brushed herself off.

Glo also picked himself up off the ground. All this banter had distracted him. It had been fun—a much-needed break in the tensions of this day. Now, though, they needed to get back down to business. "So what happened with Calipherous?"

Elladan's answer was rather nonchalant. "Not all that much really. Shalla kept the crowd calm and the guards at bay..."

"...while we explained to him that he was scaring the locals," Donnie finished for him.

"And then we asked him to return tomorrow," Elladan ended the story.

"Nicely played, gentlemen." Glo nodded to the threesome. "For a moment there, I was afraid there was going to be a battle."

"So did we," Elladan admitted. His expression suddenly changed to one of curiosity. "What about you? What happened with Ves and Maya?"

Glo sighed. "Exactly what you would expect. As soon as they saw Calipherous, they pulled another disappearing act."

"Come again?" Donnie's gaze shifted from Glo to Elladan.

Glo hesitated in his response. Nice as he seemed, he did not know Donnie all that well. He felt it best to steer clear from an in-depth discussion about the three sisters. He cast a quick warning glance at Elladan, then answered. "The first time we saw Calipherous was back on the Endurance. The girls were afraid of the dragon and went into hiding."

Donnie's hand went to his chin. "Hmm, any chance they could be the charges the dragon was looking for?"

Glo was duly impressed. This Donatello was smarter than he let on. He would have to be more careful what he said in front of him from now on, or at least until he knew him better. "That's a distinct possibility."

Elladan smoothly redirected the conversation. "What did happen before Calipherous showed up?"

Glo gratefully turned his attention to the bard. "It was rather strange actually. Ves and Maya were quite friendly at first. They seemed genuinely glad to see me. However, when I began to question them, Ves became rather elusive. I could not get a straight answer out of her."

"Well, she is a woman after all," Elladan said with a devilish grin. That elicited another smack on the arm from Shalla.

"Who was the man she was with?" Donnie asked while watching the couple's playful antics. "He looked like a Druid..."

Glo ignored the tussling bard and bardess. "Indeed, as a matter of fact, he is the town Druid, Almax. I got the impression that he and Ves already knew each other."

Truthfully, Glo thought that there was more going on here than met the eye. The sisters and this Almax knew something they refused to share with anyone else. Perhaps it had to do with the sisters' true form.

Elladan's tussle with Shalla finally ended. "She never told you why they didn't show up until now?"

"No, she did not," Glo admitted glumly. He still felt the sting of the sisters' lack of trust in them. "However, I did find out that they are here as Almax's guests. It seems that the Druid is in high standing in the Baron's court."

Donnie's eyebrow arched upward. "That's interesting. Not everyone has great love for the Druids. This Baron Gryswold seems to be a tolerant fellow."

Elladan opened his mouth as if to reply, but never got the chance. Without warning, Seth appeared in their midst. He was red in the face and gasping for air. "Guys!" he croaked, "we've... got... trouble..." He bent over, still breathing heavily as he attempted to catch his breath.

Glo felt a wave of apprehension wash over him. It took a lot to rattle the halfling. Whatever had happened, it was extremely serious.

"I just...saw... a snake..." Seth continued, his breathing still somewhat ragged.

"What kind of snake?" Elladan asked with clear apprehension.

"Big snake..." Seth said holding his arms as wide as he could.

"How big?" Donnie asked, his eyes widening in disbelief.

"*Really* big," Seth replied, finally having caught his breath.

Glo and the others listened intently as Seth related his encounter at the campsite. When he was finished, they were all silent. It finally made sense. That was how the Serpent Cult got into the town unseen. "Very clever, hiding amongst the performers, and it brings their pet snakes to our doorstep."

Donnie put the obvious question out there. "So do we gather the troops and attack these wagons?"

Elladan shook his head. "No, that would only tip our hand."

Seth nodded. "If we do that, they might see us coming. Some of them could get away."

"What are you going to do?" Shalla appeared pensive, glancing from Elladan to Seth.

Elladan turned to her and spoke in a reassuring tone. "We let them come to us, that way we can be sure to get all of them in one place..."

"...where we can eradicate the entire group," Glo finished for him.

A sly grin crossed Donnie's features. "Sounds dangerous. I like it!"

Shalla stared at them as if they were all crazy. Glo tried to explain further in order to allay her concern. "Not all that dangerous. We know where they are coming from, and we know what their objective is—and, thanks to Seth, they don't know that we know. So instead of them surprising us, we will surprise them."

Shalla did not appear completely convinced. "I just hope you know what you are doing. It still sounds extremely dangerous to me."

"But I live..." Donnie began.

Shalla cut him off. "So help me, if you say something stupid like *I live for danger*, I'm going to hit you!"

"But... I do," Donatello replied, with a hurt expression.

Glo did his best to suppress a smile. "Anyway, we should warn the others."

Donnie told them how Andrella had commandeered Lloyd. Glo

offered to get him and inform the Baron while he was there. Seth would head for the tower to tell Martan what they had discovered. That just left Aksel. No one had seen the little cleric since they all split up. Donnie offered to go look for him. Elladan and Shalla would park themselves in front of the keep in case he showed up back there. They all agreed to rendezvous with the bards when they were done. The companions split up and went their separate ways, each with an errand vital for their defense against the attack that was sure to come.

Glo entered the keep in search of Lloyd. He found the young man in the throne room with Gryswold, Andrella, and three knights in armor. The knights wore red tabards with a heraldic similar to Lloyd's. Gryswold motioned for Glo to join them. He introduced him to the knights: Sir Brennon, Sir Duncan, and Sir Calric, all from the City of Penwick. Glo had interrupted a discussion concerning the latest news from Lloyd's home town—a subject that all five were deeply engrossed in. It took some patience, but after a while Glo was able to pull the Baron aside.

"What is it?" Gryswold whispered anxiously.

"We have some news concerning security, your Lordship. We thought that you should hear it."

The Baron nodded, his expression grim. He turned to the Penwick knights. "My apologies, gentlemen, but something has come up that demands my immediate attention."

Sir Brennon, the senior of the Penwick knights, asked, "Is it something we can help with?"

Gryswold responded kindly. "No, that's quite alright, but I will need to borrow young Lloyd here." He turned to Andrella. "Would you be a dear and entertain our guests until we return?"

Andrella arched a delicate eyebrow but said nothing. She curtsied and responded elegantly, "Why, of course, Father."

"Thank you." He gave her a thin smile. Gryswold turned to Glo and Lloyd, and motioned for them to follow. "Gentlemen."

Gryswold stopped to send a guard to find Captain Gelpas. He then led Lloyd and Glo into one of the side meeting rooms. Once they were there, Glo told them what Seth had found. He ended up repeating himself when Gelpas joined them shortly thereafter. Glo finished with their recommendations on handling the situation. Gryswold sat silently for a long while. He drummed his fingers on the table loudly, his face a grim mask as he considered all that had been told to him. Finally, he sat forward.

"I agree with your plan. I don't want any of these monsters getting away this time. Let's set the trap and pull them all in."

"The guards will be ready, your Lordship," Gelpas declared.

Gryswold peered gratefully at the Captain then shook his head. "Thank you, Gelpas, but no. I don't want anyone inadvertently tipping our hand. Master Seth went to great trouble to give us this advantage. I want to keep it that way. This stays between you, me, and the heroes."

"Are you sure, your Lordship?" Gelpas asked. His tone was respectful, but he was obviously apprehensive about the dangerous plan they were hatching.

"Yes, Gelpas," Gryswold answered grimly. His hard expression softened somewhat as he stared at the faithful Captain. He reached out and placed a hand on the man's shoulder. "I appreciate your concern, my friend, but these devils are threatening my daughter!" Gryswold turned away and began to pace. "I will not have any of them get away to just try again later." The Baron spun back around. His face was red with anger and he slammed his one fist into his other hand. "I want them all dealt with in one swift blow!"

"I understand, your Lordship. It shall be as you say," Gelpas saluted the Baron.

Gryswold saluted him in return. His anger faded and he suddenly looked very tired. He sat back down in his chair and took a deep breath. At that moment, he appeared less lordly and more the aging family man.

Lloyd had been quiet until then. Now he stepped forward and knelt in front of the Baron. "Your Lordship, I swear to you, I will give my life if need be to protect you and your family. No one will hurt Andrella while I live and breathe!"

A smile spread across Gryswold's haggard face. He reached out and laid a hand on the young man's shoulder. "I know you would, young Lloyd. You are a Stealle through and through. Your father would be proud."

"Thank you, your Lordship." Lloyd stood up and stepped back next to the others.

"Thank you, my friends," Gryswold smiled at all of them, though he still appeared quite weary. "Go now. Do what must be done."

Lloyd and Glo both bowed and left the Baron with Gelpas. Back in the throne room, they found Andrella still conversing with the knights from Penwick. As they exited the side room, her eyes flickered toward them questioningly. Lloyd stopped briefly to talk with them. "I am truly sorry, but something extremely urgent has come up. I would very much like to continue our talk later, if possible."

Sir Brennon appeared concerned. "Is there anything we can help you with, lad?"

Lloyd's expression was grave, but thankful. "Thank you, but no, it is a task that the Baron assigned to my companions and me. We must handle it ourselves. But I truly appreciate the offer."

The three knights all nodded their understanding. "Well then, good luck with whatever it is," Sir Duncan added. "And remember, Penwick folks stick together. If you're ever in need, we'll have your back."

Lloyd gave them an appreciative nod. "Thank you. That is comforting to know."

Andrella's eyes shifted from Lloyd to Glo, an eyebrow raised as she studied the duo. Yet the young woman continued to play the consummate diplomat in front of her guests. She did not question them any further. Glo and Lloyd left the throne room and walked down the castle hallways side by side. He heard the young man murmur under his breath, "No one will hurt Andrella. No one!"

"No, Lloyd, we won't let them," Glo agreed. He reached out and placed a hand on his friend's broad shoulder. Lloyd peered at him and nodded, a grim smile on his lips. The two of them hastened down the hall and out into the courtyard.

Aksel was in Maltar's tower when Seth found him. He had rum-

maged through the mage's things, looking for the props he needed for tonight. Strangely enough, there were still a lot of Maltar's
belongings here, even though the wizard had abandoned the tower
years ago. Seth briefly told him what he had found. It was a stroke of
luck that he had stumbled onto the Serpent Cult. It was even better
that he had done so without them knowing. Aksel was concerned at
first with the idea of letting the cultists come to them. After careful
consideration, he found himself agreeing with the plan. If the Baron
also approved, then they would indeed lay a trap for the Serpent Cult
from which there would be no escape.

Seth and Aksel found Martan on the top of the tower. The archer knelt by one of the parapets, gazing out over the front of the
keep. Seth related his story once more to the archer. Meanwhile, Aksel gazed out over the hilltop. The entire entertainers' campground
could be seen from here. The myriad of tents and wagons stretched
almost across the entire hillside. Aksel could barely make out the
wagons farthest from the road. Only their tops were visible from
here. There was no way of telling if anyone was moving around
down there.

"Keep an eye out," Seth told Martan. The halfling handed the
archer a small oblong object. "If you see any movement at all, throw
one of these off the top of the tower into the courtyard below."

"What is it?" Martan asked. He inspected the object in his hand.

"It's a smoke bomb," Seth replied. "When it hits the ground, it
will break open and let out a cloud of white smoke. It should be
visible clear across the yard." The archer nodded, looking quite impressed.

The duo left Martan at the top of the tower and headed back
down to meet the others. They joined them in front of the keep, ar-
riving the same time as Lloyd and Glo. All the companions were now
gathered around, sans Martan. Glo spoke to the group, his expression even more intense than usual.

"Gryswold agrees with our plan. It's all up to us now."

Lloyd's expression was also quite grim. In fact, all the companions appeared quite serious.

"That settles it then. We lay a trap," Aksel declared. "The only question is how they intend to get inside the castle. That snake Seth described is not exactly small enough to sneak through the grass."

"No, it was not exactly your garden variety of snake," Seth agreed, a slight smirk on his lips.

Glo gave a firm nod. "At this point, I think that all we can do is watch and wait. We all keep our eyes peeled for anything out of the ordinary. We know it's coming, and we know from where."

Seth's smirk grew wider. "That just leaves when and how."

Aksel rubbed his chin vigorously. That was the puzzling part, although the how had him more concerned than the when. "Well, there's no time left to figure that out. The party will begin in less than an hour. Guests will soon be filtering in." He glanced over toward the front gate. Captain Gelpas and Lieutenant Relkin were already standing out there in full dress uniform. "I suggest we all get into position. I'll head over to the front gate now. The Boulder will be ready when we need him."

"And I'll head straight to the rooftops," Seth added, dangling a large brass key in front of him.

"Raven's already in flight around the castle grounds," Glo reported, with that faraway look in his eye.

"And we will stick close to the Avernos family," Lloyd declared, nodding at Glo and Donnie.

Aksel smiled grimly. It would take a small army to get by those three. Ironically, that might just be what they would be facing. "Okay then, let's get on with the show."

"Hey, that's my line," Elladan said in mock protest.

31
BIRTHDAY GALA
Thier voices blended in exquisite harmony

I t was dusk outside, the eastern horizon now completely dark. Stars began to appear in the blackening sky. Over to the west, the last vestige of the sun's rays peeked over the castle walls. Guards and servants went about lighting the courtyard. Torches lit up the castle walls, except for the stage area. The front of the keep, dining area, and stage were all illuminated by fancy lanterns seated atop tall stands. The show would soon begin. Gryswold and Gracelynn sat in the audience, front and center. Glo had the distinct honor of sitting at Gryswold's left. On Glo's other side was seated Qualtan, the town abbot and head cleric. The Lady Andrella sat to her mother's right, with Lloyd to the right of her.

Elladan waited patiently on stage for the rest of the audience to be seated. He was wrapped in his cloak, hiding his sparkling outfit from the crowd. As the final guests were led to their seats, Elladan disappeared from view. Glo peered around the platform. His keen eyes spotted the bard peeking through the dark backdrop at the back of the stage. Once the last guest was seated, Glo nodded to Elladan. Elladan nodded back. Glo stood up and signaled Lloyd. The young man rose from his seat and walked to the base of the stage. He picked up his drum and began a soft, steady, rhythmic beat. Glo exchanged glances with Elladan once more, and they both began to cast spells. The lanterns around the stage dimmed. A cloud of fog appeared in the center of the stage. It grew thicker and thicker, billowing out across the platform. It continued to expand until it spilled over the sides. Murmurs rippled through the audience as the scene unfolded.

Abruptly, four balls of light appeared inside the fog. They illuminated the cloud, revealing a dark silhouette in the very center. A musical chord was struck, and then the figure moved forward. As the figure stepped out of the fog, the music grew louder. Sparklers erupted across the front of the stage. "Oohs" and "aahs" could be heard throughout the audience. There was a brief glimpse of a white-clad shape, then the stage went pitch black. The drumbeats stopped altogether, and silence overtook the makeshift theater. As the seconds crept by, the audience began buzzing with anticipation. The tension mounted as they sat there in the inky darkness. The lanterns flared back to life and the entire stage lit up.

Elladan stood in the very center, dressed in full regalia, garbed from head to toe in white leather with gold-studded sequins and white tassels hanging from his sleeves. A musical chord was struck, and the bard lunged to the right. He pointed his fingers as if he was holding a blade. He looked like a magnificent swordsman. The crowd ate it up, cheering and clapping. Another chord and Elladan reversed his pose. This time he lunged to the left, exposing the back of his costume to the audience. Across the length of his back, sequins outlined the shape of a gold dragon. The torch light sparkled brilliantly off the golden spangles. It was positively mesmerizing. The crowd clapped and cheered even louder. Glo heard a familiar voice cry over the din.

"Ooh, Ves! Look at that. It's beautiful." He turned his head and saw Maya standing on the bench a few seats down. Sitting next to her was Ves and the Druid Almax.

"Maya, get down!" Ves chastised the young girl. She sounded quite embarrassed by her little sister's behavior.

Anything further was drowned out as the crowd applauded the bard's dramatic entrance. Elladan waited until the clapping died down, then a lute magically appeared in his hand. The elven bard quickly broke out into a fast-paced tune designed to get the crowd up and on their feet. Before long, folks were dancing in the aisle while Elladan himself glided across the stage. His motions were a cross between dancing and swordplay, his movements a combination of grace and flair. It was not your typical bardic performance. Most bards just stood onstage and sang, but Elladan was a showman. The crowd had never seen anything like it. They were captivated.

At a lull in the song, Glo heard Maya's voice once more. "I want to dance and sing like that, Ves. Do you think he'd teach me?"

"I'm sure he has more important things to do," Ves replied in a disapproving tone.

When Elladan finished, the entire crowd rose to its feet. The applause was deafening. During the ovation, Glo scanned the crowd. He observed that not everyone had risen—a group of individuals in the first and second rows was still seated. Predictably, they were all dressed in powder blue. Glo recognized a particular sour face among them. It was Fafnar. Over the applause, he caught a few remarks from the Dunwynn contingent—words such as "vulgar" and "crass." He then heard Fafnar's voice, a bit louder than the others.

"What do you expect from a bunch of country bumpkins?"

Glo's eyes shifted to Gryswold and Gracelynn. The Baron's face momentarily clouded over, but it quickly disappeared. The Baroness showed no sign of having heard the comment. The Lady Andrella, however, turned her head in the direction of the foppish knight. She immediately spun back toward the stage and clapped even louder crying, "Bravo, Bravo!"

Glo could not help but smile at the young lady's reaction. The cheering and clapping started to die down. Up on stage, Elladan waved to the crowd. He flashed the audience one of his best smiles. "Thank you. Thank you."

The exquisite form of the lady bard Shalla appeared on the stage. She sauntered over toward Elladan and stood by his side. The crowd quieted down in anticipation. Elladan nodded to her then addressed the audience. "This one's for all the ladies."

Elladan began a heart-wrenching ballad. It was in stark contrast to the energy of the previous number. His superb voice warbled through the lower ranges until he reached the chorus. Shalla then joined in with him. Their voices blended in a perfect harmony. The song was so poignant and heartfelt that some of the ladies were indeed weeping. Glo himself was moved by the melody. When Elladan and Shalla finished, the entire audience sat in silence. Then, as one, they rose to their feet and gave the duo another standing ovation.

The Dunwynn retinue remained seated still. This time Glo overheard snippets such as *too flowery* and *sickly sweet*. Strangely enough, Fafnar was silent. Glo stole a glance at the Dunwynn Lieutenant. *Was that a tear in his eye?* The noble abruptly covered his face with a handkerchief.

Back on stage, Elladan turned to his partner. "How about a round of applause for the lovely Miss Shalla Vesperanna!"

The audience clapped ardently for the lady bard. Shalla curtsied gracefully and then pointed toward Elladan. "Ladies and Gentlemen, the incomparable Elladan Narmolanya!"

The crowd went wild. Now it was Elladan's turn to bow. When the noise finally died down, he announced, "That is it for us."

The audience responded almost as one. "Awwwww..."

Elladan flashed a bright smile. "But don't worry, there is plenty of entertainment to follow, and the lovely Miss Shalla and I will be back at the end of the show!"

The crowd cheered once more. When the applause died down, Elladan introduced the next act. He and Shalla then exited the stage. Things had gone remarkably well thus far. All the guests had arrived. Each entertainer had been checked at the gate. The guards had been warned to look for telltale serpent tattoos. Every cultist they had encountered so far had one. Therefore, it was a safe bet that no Serpent Cult member had made it into the keep. Further, Aksel and The Boulder watched the gate. Martan stood vigil from atop the tower. Seth roamed the rooftops. Finally, Raven circled high above the keep. There was nothing more they could do for now. They just needed to stay alert.

The entertainment went on for almost two hours. Elladan continued to emcee the show. He talked with the audience while the stage was set, then introduced each act. Jugglers juggled. Acrobats tumbled. Dancers danced. Clowns made the audience laugh. Magicians did magic. Other bards sang. Except for the entertainment, all was quiet. There was no sign of Serpent Cult activity.

Glo grew apprehensive. *Just what were they waiting for?*

When the last performer was done, Elladan and Shalla took the stage once more. The crowd cheered at the return of the duo. Elladan's voice boomed over the audience. "Thank you, my friends. This is a little number we cooked up to keep you entertained while you are escorted to your tables. Servants will be coming around to guide you, so please wait for them. Meanwhile, we hope you enjoy the finale!"

The two bards launched into a fast-paced duet. They twirled around each other as they sang, just as the first time Glo saw them on stage. The bard and bardess took turns with their individual vocals. When they reached the chorus, their voices blended in exquisite harmony. The duo continued to flirt with each other as they sang and danced. The chemistry between them was electrifying. The audience ate it up.

As the first chorus finished, servants began escorting the guests to their tables. Gryswold and Gracelynn were seated first. Glo remained by their side. The rest of the head table was filled next. The others seated there included Andrella, Lloyd, Sir Fafnar, the Druid Almax, Ves, Maya, Abbot Qualtan, and Sir Brennon. Directly across from Gryswold, next to Sir Fafnar, sat a middle-aged gentleman. He was dressed in a blue doublet decorated with extreme finery. The gentleman was tall and thin, with dark hair, a pencil thin mustache and a goatee. From his heraldic, Glo could only assume this was the Duke of Dunwynn. The pair was turned sideways, facing the stage. They continued to watch the performance, whispering back and forth to each other. The Duke maintained a neutral expression. Fafnar, on the other hand, wore that same smug look he had when they first met him.

Up on the stage, Elladan and Shalla brought some of the other entertainers up to join them. The stage filled up as the last number expanded into an encore for the entire troop of performers. As the mega finale went on, the other tables filled up. Donnie was seated next. Along with him was Haltan the merchant, Sir Duncan, Sir Calric, and two knights Glo had never seen before. The first was a stark-featured man. He had black hair, a neatly groomed beard, and a thin mustache. The second was a statuesque woman with a striking head of fiery orange hair, bobbed short at the shoulders. Both wore bright white tabards adorned with a single pale red flower over a shining suit of silvery chain mail.

Glo leaned over and whispered to Gryswold. "Who are those two?" He nodded his head toward the new knights.

Gryswold whispered back, "That's the Dame Alana and Sir Craven. They are Knights of the Rose."

Of course, the famous Knights of the Rose! Glo should have recognized their symbol. He had come across the name many times in his studies. They were a holy order dedicated to Cormar, the God of the Winds. A force for good, they had been around for centuries. The Knights of the Rose had even participated in the battle against the Thrall Lords some hundred and fifty years prior. Their ancestral home was the Wind Tower. It was a huge, three-hundred-foot tall tower surrounded by a small town of the same name. Glo vividly remembered passing the tall structure on the caravan ride to the east coast. That was the same fateful trip where he, Seth, and Aksel first met Lloyd. Glo noted that both the Dame Alana and Sir Craven had swords strapped to their sides. That bode well. If it came down to a fight, which he suspected it would, two Knights of the Rose would be handy allies.

Things moved along now. Dinner would soon be served. Once that was over, there would be a few speeches and then a birthday cake for Andrella. The festivities would wind down after that. If the Serpent Cult was going to make a move, it would have to be soon. Yet it remained a mystery as to how they intended to get inside the castle. Glo silently wondered if the others had seen anything as of yet.

At that same moment, high above the party, Seth climbed around the roof of the keep. From this vantage point, he had a good view of the courtyard below. He could also see well down the hillside. The performers' campsite appeared quiet from here. There was no sign of movement amongst the tents and wagons. The town of Ravenford stretched beyond the base of the hill, all the way to the bay. Its streetlights and houses twinkling like jewels in the night. It made Seth think back to that evening when they first laid eyes on the town. Though it had only been a couple of weeks, it felt like ages ago.

Seth had been roaming the rooftops for almost two hours. The keep was huge, with multiple levels, dormers, and countless chimneys. It was a lot of area to cover. He started by making a sweep of the perimeter. It was just before sunset, so he had gotten a good look at the surrounding countryside. The hillside behind and to either side of the keep was rather steep. It was climbable, but not easily so, and there were guards patrolling the parapets. The only easy access to the castle was the route up the hill from town. Any attack from that direction would require a confrontation with The Boulder. Seth was convinced that the attack would not come as a direct assault. Somehow, the Serpent Cult intended to sneak their way into the castle. He was just not sure how.

Seth continued to scale the rooftops, searching for anything out of place. It was like a maze up here. There were dozens of corners to hide in. He took it upon himself to check each and every one. He had just finished another circuit. He rounded a dormer near the front of the keep when he suddenly froze. Ahead of him on the rooftop sat a lone figure!

Seth stayed absolutely still. He observed the figure for a good half minute, but couldn't make out any details. There was not much light up here, and the form was wrapped in a dark cloak. Even with his keen eyesight, he could tell nothing other than the figure was rather short. It was certainly no giant snake under that hood. The figure remained seated, either unaware of his presence, or not threatened by it. Whoever it was, they appeared engrossed with the proceedings below. Seth carefully scanned the nearby rooftop. There was no one else in sight. Certain that they were alone, he moved forward, stealthily inching his way toward the solitary form. Virtually silent, he approached the figure from an angle outside its field of vision. It neither moved nor made any indication that it knew he was there. Still, he had the strangest feeling it was aware of his presence. As he got closer, the figure shifted slightly. Seth caught a brief glimpse of light colored hair peeking out from underneath the hood. Seth stopped in his tracks. He stood straight up and shook his head. *I should have known.*

The solitary figure was none other than Ruka! Where there were two Greymantle sisters, the third would not be very far behind. Seth nonchalantly strode to where she was sitting and unceremoniously plopped himself down on the rooftop next to her. Ruka did not appear startled at all. She sat there unmoving, staring at the party below. Seth said nothing, merely sitting in silence next to the wayward Greymantle sister. After a few minutes, Ruka finally spoke. She did not remove her hood or turn to look at him.

"You would think they would have better things to do than dress up in such frilly clothing and sit around all night."

"Not my thing, either," Seth agreed.

Down below, almost all the guests had moved to the tables. The performers were all on stage, led by Elladan and Shalla in a sort of mega finale. Ruka's arms were wrapped around her knees. She began to rock back and forth.

"The singing wasn't bad, though, but the other acts were just silly. And the thought of having to sit around a table and make small talk? What a waste."

Seth's mouth twisted into a half-smirk. "Why do you think I'm up here?"

Ruka turned to look at him. She regarded him silently then smirked back at him. "You are surprisingly sensible—for a halfling that is."

"I could say the same about you," Seth responded, unperturbed by the offhanded compliment. "You show an amazing amount of common sense for a *human*."

Ruka stared at him intently. It appeared for a moment as if she was going to say something more, but she turned back to watch the party below.

Seth eyed her carefully. *Strange.*

Martan sat atop the tower overlooking the keep. He had an excellent view of the hillside below. He could also see the proceedings inside the courtyard. The archer's thoughts were elsewhere at the moment though. *Why hadn't Ves met us at Maltar's? And what was she doing with that older man? Why was she ignoring us?* Who was he kidding? *Why was she ignoring him?*

He had been lost in contemplation when a sudden movement startled him. A small black form landed on the parapet next to him. He nearly jumped out of his skin! He quickly realized it was Raven. Martan's keen eyes had spotted the bird flying overhead in the night sky. She had been making a circuit around the castle grounds all evening. Why had she suddenly picked now to land next to him? Maybe the wizard was checking up on him?

Martan shook his head. *I'm just being paranoid.*

These heroes were nothing like the Black Adders. They'd been nothing but kind to him, especially Elladan. Even Seth, the most cynical of them all, had helped to save his life. He owed them a great debt. He had a job to do, and he was not about to let them down. It was no use pining over Ves like some schoolboy. She would do what she wanted. She was a beautiful lady and he was just a common archer.

Get over it, he told himself harshly.

Martan turned his gaze toward the campsite down the hill. He peered specifically at the wagons at the far end. That was where Seth had his encounter earlier. He could see no movement there now. In fact, the entire campsite appeared deserted. That only made sense. Every performer was inside the castle at the moment. The archer continued his vigil, scanning the surrounding grounds.

Wait. That's strange.

Martan noticed sections of grass that appeared sunken in. He did not remember seeing that before. He leaned out over the parapets searching the grounds with his keen eyes. Martan now saw that the sunken sections were almost in a straight line—in fact, there were multiple lines. Furthermore, the lines stretched from the campsite all the way to the keep.

That's not normal!

Martan spun around. He considered dropping the smoke bomb Seth had given him, but what if he was wrong? He didn't want to panic everyone only to find out it was for nothing. As he wrestled with himself, he noted Raven still sitting there on the parapet. The bird was gazing directly at him. Martan stared back at the creature for a few moments. *Maybe if he talked to it...*

Martan felt foolish, but it appeared to understand the elf. He pointed at the sunken sections of ground below. "Do you see that? Can you get a closer look?"

Raven hopped forward and craned its neck toward where he was pointing. After a few seconds, it turned its tiny head toward him and cawed loudly. It then spread its wings and soared away toward the disturbed ground below. Martan's mouth dropped open. *That is one smart bird.*

32
POMP AND CIRCUMSTANCE

I am sure she would be taught how to be both rude and snobbish with equal aplomb

Back down in the courtyard, the grand finale came to a close. The singers all blended in one last harmonic chorus. The acrobats and dancers tumbled and twirled in unison. The rest of the performers lined up behind the others and swayed back and forth to the music. The magicians cast one last set of light and smoke effects, even setting off some pyrotechnics. The combined result was stunning! The audience, now at their respective tables, rose as one. They gave the entertainers a standing ovation. On stage, Elladan, Shalla, and the other performers grabbed hands. They all proceeded to bow in a line. The applause continued for a while. The entertainers graciously bowed once more. Finally, the clapping died down and everyone resumed his or her seats. Back at the head table, Andrella gushed on about the show. Her eyes were wide and her cheeks flushed as she went on about the performers, sets, and costumes.

"That was spectacular! So many different acts, the costumes, the sets, the dancing, the music. It was *so* exciting! And that Elladan and Shalla, they were marvelous! I don't think I've ever seen two bards dance like that."

"See, I told you, Ves!" a familiar small voice cried. Lloyd turned his head and saw it was Maya who had spoken.

"Hush, Maya," Ves scolded. "Don't speak out of turn."

"No, no," Andrella spun to face them. "It's quite alright, really. That was truly something special."

She spun back to Lloyd. "And they make such a cute couple, don't they?"

"Ummm... I guess," Lloyd replied absently. His mind was elsewhere at the moment. An attack was imminent. He could almost feel it. He abruptly noticed Fafnar across the table whispering into the ear of an older nobleman. Lloyd had been so preoccupied that he hadn't really paid attention to the man before. Now he took a good long look. The nobleman was tall and thin with black hair, a thin mustache, and a goatee, all showing faint traces of grey. Dressed in a fancy blue outfit, there was a heraldic plastered across the front of his doublet. Lloyd nearly blanched. This was no mere noble he sat across from—it was the Duke of Dunwynn himself!

The Duke suddenly turned to meet his gaze. Lloyd was momentarily startled, but quickly recovered his composure. He nodded politely to the infamous noble. The Duke, however, did not respond. He merely stared back at him for a short time, then turned away. Lloyd was a bit put off. He supposed it was to be expected though. From everything he had heard, the Duke was an arrogant man. He was always touting the superiority of Dunwynn. He seemed to think it was his sovereign right to spread Dunwynn's rule to his neighboring cities and towns. This expansionist policy did not sit well with the rest of the east coast, especially not with Penwick. In fact, in the last decade or so, a number of minor skirmishes had broken out between Dunwynn and Penwick ships. Eventually, an accord was reached. It banned either city's vessels from crossing an imaginary line at Colossus Point, the promontory at the southern end of Merchant's Bay. This entire time, Sir Fafnar had been whispering into the Duke's ear. Finally, the Dunwynn noble sat back. The Duke turned his attention toward the Baron. He cleared his throat. Everyone at the head table turned to look at him.

"Ahem... Baron Gryswold, I am not familiar with this young fellow sitting next to Lady Andrella."

Gryswold fixed an eye on the Duke. "Oh, my apologies, Kelvick. This is the young noble Lloyd Stealle of the House of Stealle, one of the paramount families in Penwick. His father is an old friend and the Admiral of the Penwick Navy. His mother, another old friend, is the High Wizard of that fair city."

"Really? That is rather fine lineage," the Duke responded, gazing briefly at Lloyd. He nodded almost imperceptibly to him. Lloyd nodded back. The Duke turned back to the Baron.

"I must confess that I am surprised. I did not realize that there were very many families of nobility left in Penwick—excepting, of course, for your own Avernos clan."

Gryswold was obviously irritated by the Duke's thinly veiled dig at Penwick nobility. "I assure you, Kelvick, there are numerous families of fine upbringing still in Penwick. "

The Duke's reply was rather smug. "Oh, I stand corrected then, but nobility and refinement are not exactly the same thing. This little performance of yours, while novel, was not exactly the kind of culture that someone of Andrella's stature would be exposed to in Dunwynn. Of that I can assure you."

Lloyd's jaw nearly dropped. Gryswold's face turned positively scarlet. He opened his mouth to speak, but before he could utter a word, another voice rang out across the table.

"No, based on our experience with your nobles, I am sure she would be taught how to be both rude and snobbish with equal aplomb."

That was Glo! His scathing words caught Lloyd by surprise. The only other time he had heard him talk that way was during their first run in with Sir Fafnar.

Gryswold coughed violently, raising a hand to cover his mouth. From where he sat, Lloyd could clearly see the Baron trying to suppress his laughter. The Duke regarded Glo disdainfully. When he finally spoke, his tone was filled with contempt.

"And who is this *elf* who speaks to me so insolently?" The word elf was said as if it were a disease.

Gryswold finally managed to contain himself. "Ahem, *this* is the Wizard Glolindir. He is Maltar's apprentice. As my good friend could not be here this evening, I asked the mage to stand in for him."

"And you couldn't find someone other than an *elf?*" the Duke practically sneered.

"Some would think it an honor to have an elven wizard in their midst," Glo responded mildly. "I guess it is too much to expect someone so caught up in appearances and propriety to recognize talent—even when it is right in front of their face."

Lloyd's eyes went wide. He had always heard that elves thought themselves superior. He had never seen a hint of that from Glo, Elladan, or Donnie. Not until their run-ins with Dunwynners had Glo shown this side of himself. It was as if the arrogance in humans caused the elves to react haughty in response.

The Duke stiffened. He regarded Glo for a few moments before responding. "What I recognize when it comes to elves is arrogance and a tendency to look down on all the other races."

Lloyd thought for sure Glo would lose his temper at that. The elven wizard, however, surprised them all. He sat back in his seat and laughed.

The Duke seemed taken aback by his reaction. "Did I say something amusing?"

Glo continued laughing. "Yes, actually. I was just thinking about how my father used to say the same thing, except from his viewpoint it was about the other races. He would go on and on about how they were only concerned about themselves. How the elves could be damned for all they cared."

Glo sat forward in his seat and stared intently at the Duke. "My experience up until now has been the exact opposite. But after meeting you Dunwynn folk, I can see why he thinks that way."

Glo must have struck a nerve. The Duke of Dunwynn appeared shocked. His mouth literally hung open as he gaped at the elven wizard. The look quickly faded. His face reddened with anger. He began to reply.

"Why you insolent..."

Before he could utter another word, the Baroness Gracelynn interrupted him. "*Gentlemen*! This is supposed to be a celebration for Andrella's birthday! Can we please put aside our differences for this one evening?"

Glo turned to her and bowed his head. "I certainly can, your Ladyship."

The Duke, caught in mid-sentence, took a few moments to collect himself. He continued to glare at Glo. The anger finally drained from his face, and he turned his gaze toward his sister. "Yes, yes," he responded deferentially, "we wouldn't want to do anything that would mar Andrella's birthday." He turned to glare at Glo. "We will save this discussion for another time, *elf.*"

Lloyd did his best to hide a smile. He actually wanted to cheer for Glo. These Dunwynn "nobles" were an arrogant lot, and it was nice to see someone stand up to them. His eyes flickered around the table. Nearly everyone had thin smiles on their lips or were covering their mouths. All except for Glo and the Duke, who glared at each other unflinchingly, and Sir Fafnar, who wore an even more sour expression than usual. Abruptly, Glo started in his seat. He bolted upright, his eyes going out of focus.

"Are you alright..." Gracelynn began.

Glo ignored her, turning his head from side to side, scanning the courtyard intently. Lloyd immediately realized what was going on. Glo must have felt something from his familiar. Lloyd pushed back his own chair and emulated Glo. As far as he could see, though, everything appeared normal.

"Whatever is that elf doing?" the Duke complained.

Lloyd paid him little heed.

"They're here!" Glo cried.

Gryswold now rose to his feet as well and joined them in scanning the grounds.

"Who's here?" the Duke asked even louder. He spun around in his seat and looked behind him. "Whatever is the elf babbling about?"

"Where?" Gryswold asked, ignoring the Duke as well.

Glo pointed in front of them. "Toward the gate! They're underground!"

Lloyd started. *Underground? Of course! That's why we can't see them.*

"Got it!" he yelled, spurring into action. He dashed around the other guests to the end of the table. Rounding the corner, he broke into a run toward the castle gate. "Protect Andrella!" he cried back over his shoulder.

Behind him he heard the Duke's plaintive cry. "Protect her from what?

33
PARTY CRASHERS
You shall all bow down before us and worship our Serpent God

L loyd Stealle rushed across the castle grounds, intent on heading off the enemy. As he ran, he caught a glimpse of someone beside him. It was Donatello speeding along, his rapier drawn and ready. Donnie nodded grimly to him. Lloyd nodded back. The duo continued their sprint toward the castle gate. As they raced along, Lloyd brought his will to bear and his weapons flamed to life.

"Nice trick there," Donnie said. "Can you teach it to me sometime?"

Lloyd opened his mouth to reply but he never got the chance. The ground began to shake all around them. The duo skidded to a halt. The trembling grew worse. Suddenly the earth blew open directly in front of them. Large chunks of dirt and grass went flying in all directions. There was now a large hole in the ground a dozen yards from where they stood. The quaking did not stop though. Off to their right, the earth split open once more. More chunks of dirt and grass went flying through the air. Over to their left, another hole blew open, then another. The eruptions continued all around them until they were surrounded on three sides by large holes in the ground. Finally, the trembling stopped. Lloyd and Donnie stood side by side in defensive positions, scanning the broken earth around them. Something began to rise out of the first hole. It was large, mottled green, and scaly. A pair of huge yellow glowing eyes followed. They fixed themselves coldly on Lloyd and Donnie.

"Well that certainly doesn't look friendly," Donnie tried to jest. His voice cracked nervously on the last word.

The daunting sight repeated itself all around them. They watched in horrific fascination as seven massive reptilian heads slowly rose out of the ground. Multiple pairs of yellow glowing eyes fixed themselves on the motionless duo.

"I think it brought its friends," Donnie quipped, his voice still betraying his nerves.

The heads were covered with mottled green-scaled skin. Long snouts with huge gaping jaws protruded outward. The open maws exposed long dripping fangs and forked tongues that darted in and out. The huge heads continued to rise out of the ground. These were followed by massive serpent-like bodies. Each trunk was as thick as a large man. Those yellow eyes remained fixed on the duo until they reached a height two heads above Lloyd himself—all except for the rearmost. That creature rose another two heads higher than its brethren. It towered over the others. Its enormous head must have been a good yard across, easily wide enough to swallow a man whole. Astride three of the serpents, including the huge one, sat a dark-robed figure.

"I believe we have found them," Donnie joked once more.

Hearing his voice, the two closest serpents' began to hiss. The sound was positively malevolent.

"Then again, maybe they found us..." he trailed off.

Lloyd and Donnie fell into fighting stances, waiting for the imminent attack, yet, it did not come. The serpents and their riders held their ground. It was as if they were waiting for something. Lloyd took advantage of the momentary respite. He surveyed his opponents closely. There was no doubt that the large serpents were deadly. Those jaws could most likely snap off a limb and those fangs were each the size of a sword. They could easily skewer a man. Further, they were probably poisonous. It was a terrifying sight, but Lloyd refused to let it scare him. He was prepared to give up his life in defense of Gryswold, Gracelynn, and most of all, Andrella. His mind remained icy calm as he continued to scan the enemies around him.

He was not fooled by the serpents' large size. He assumed that they were fast. It would be difficult to get in close enough to strike them. Worst case, he could use a spiritblade technique to get behind one of them. That would be it, though. If he used it more than once, it would drain him too much. He would be useless after that. Then he noticed something. There was a rhythmic swaying to the large torso as the serpents held themselves aloft. If he could catch them at the right moment, he might be able to get in a strike or two before they could bring those tremendous jaws to bear. He started to whisper to Donnie when he was interrupted. The dark-robed figure on the largest snake stood up in his saddle. He threw back his hood.

It's Voltark!

It was just as they suspected. The dark mage was alive. The assassins had indeed stolen his body in order to revive him. As Voltark began to speak, Lloyd whispered under his breath. "Donnie, notice the way they're swaying back and forth."

Meanwhile Voltark had begun his ultimatum. "We are the Serpent Cult. You shall all bow down before us and worship our Serpent God, or you shall die here tonight!"

Lloyd ignored him, keeping one eye on the huge serpents and the other on Donnie. Finally, the slight elf whispered back. "Yeah, I see it. If we time our attacks just right..."

"There you are, you poor excuse for a black mage!" a familiar voice cried out from behind them.

Lloyd glanced over his shoulder. Glo stood on top of the head table. The rest of the guests had drawn back to the steps of the keep. *Good old Glo.* His friend was drawing Voltark's attention away and making himself a target. Lloyd also caught a brief glimpse of some other figures rushing their way. They were still a ways back, and he only saw them for a moment. He definitely saw that two of them were wearing red tabards. His heart swelled with pride. He would be fighting beside Penwick knights, some of the noblest men in the land.

Meanwhile, Voltark had recognized the elven wizard. "Ah, if it isn't Glolindir," the dark mage sneered. "Come to convert, perhaps?"

Lloyd swung back to face Donnie. They nodded to each other then slowly began to circle away in opposite directions.

"Actually, I was planning on killing you again," Glo shot back.

Lloyd smiled despite the desperateness of the situation. *Good, Glo, keep him talking.* If he could just buy them a little more time, they might just have a chance after all.

"We shall see who kills whom," the dark mage bragged. "The odds seem in my favor this time." He spread his hands toward the giant serpents all around him.

Lloyd cast a side-long glance at Donnie. The slight elf, rapier in hand, nodded back. They were in position. As Lloyd prepared to strike, music wafted its way over the field. He recognized the tune immediately. It was Elladan playing his song of inspiration. This time, however, the song was deeper, richer, as if coming from two instruments instead of one. Lloyd did not look but could only assume that Shalla had joined in to accompany the bard.

Voltark turned toward the stage. "Ah, and, of course, Elladan. Playing a dirge for your friends no doubt? You might as well. You'll all soon be dead!" The dark mage laughed maniacally at his own joke.

Lloyd paid him little heed. He was intently watching the huge serpent in front of him. He carefully timed the rhythmic motions of the creature.

There!

Lloyd swiftly launched himself forward. He covered the few yards between himself and the creature before it could react. As the huge head swung down to catch him, he slipped under it and slashed with his burning blade. The black metal of his sword sank deep into the serpent's exposed underbelly, effortlessly slicing through the exposed skin. Dark blood spurted from the sizzling wound as the creature rocked back violently. Its head went flying up into the air, leaving it wide open for a second attack.

Lloyd had been prepared to dodge out of the way but instead took advantage of the situation. He spun around and sliced deep again into the wounded creature with the same dark blade. He caught the beast in almost the same exact place, practically slicing its huge torso in half. Lloyd jumped back. He watched the huge serpent wobble wildly as its split torso hung in the air. Then it collapsed in a heap. Dark blood spilled out, along with its insides, onto the ground.

Loud cheers rose up from behind him, but he was too busy watching the other serpents to acknowledge it. They were far from out of the woods just yet. Glo took the opportunity to needle Voltark once more. "I guess your snakes are not quite as tough as you thought!"

It worked. Enraged, Voltark screamed at the top of his lungs. "Attack! Kill them. Kill them all!"

Lloyd braced himself as all the large serpents moved forward. Suddenly, the earth shook around them. The serpents paused in their tracks, swinging their heads around from side to side, searching for the source of the sudden earthquake.

Lloyd's lips parted into a grim smile. He knew what it was this time. He peered toward the castle gate just in time to see The Boulder come marching through. A contingent of castle guards ran close behind the stone golem. Lloyd did a double take. Sitting on one of The Boulder's shoulder was *Maltar?* At least it looked like Maltar. It was the same purple robe the wizard had been wearing the last time they had seen him.

Maltar cried out, "Voltark, you hack! Prepare to meet your maker—again!"

It even sounded like Maltar. Voltark swiveled around on his huge mount. He seemed startled at the sight of the infamous wizard, but recovered quickly. Voltark cried out to the other two dark robed figures. "You handle the elf. I'll take care of the old fool!" The dark mage spurred his giant serpent toward the gate to intercept the golem and its rider.

Lloyd grinned. If "Maltar" could just keep Voltark busy, they might get out of this alive after all. The young warrior prepared himself for an assault on the nearest serpent. It had been distracted by The Boulder and was just swinging back now to face him. Just then, Lloyd heard a cry to his right.

"Woah!"

That sounds like Donnie!

Lloyd glanced over just in time to see the elf tumble out of the way of a large serpent. For a moment it looked like he was going to be sandwiched between two serpents, but the one serpent slithered by him, its two glowing eyes solidly fixed on Lloyd.

Lloyd back-stepped and repositioned himself. He now had two serpents bearing down on him. Lloyd prepared for the fight of his life. He might not survive, but neither would he back down. Only one thought ran through his mind.

Protect Andrella.

Glo stood on top of the table, watching the battle unfold in front of him. Lloyd had already slain one of the giant snakes. Now he and Donnie were doing their best to hold the rest of the serpents at bay. Help was only a few scant yards away. Captain Gelpas, two of the Penwick Knights, and the Knights of the Rose were racing to their aid. At the same time, Voltark whirled his giant serpent around to meet The Boulder. Glo watched in amazement as the two behemoths approached each other. That had to be Aksel astride the Boulder, but his disguise was near perfect. Perfect enough, anyway, so that Voltark believed he was facing the actual Maltar. That would keep him busy while Glo dealt with the other dark mages.

Those two had maneuvered their mounts outside the battle. They were now both taking aim at him. Luckily, they were not very skilled. Their motions were slow, and Glo was able to easily read them. He cast a quick counter spell before they were even finished. Luckily, there was no one near him. All the other guests were huddled against the stairs of the keep. Gryswold had ushered them there once Kelvick and Fafnar stopped their complaining. The two Dunwynn nobles had raised a huge stink, scoffing at the claims that they were under attack, until of course, the giant serpents had burst into view.

Now Glo stood alone as the dark mages released their spells. Fist-sized balls of fire erupted from their hands. Twin flaming spheres shot across the courtyard toward him. Glo smiled grimly as the fireballs rocketed his way. He reminded himself that this is what he wanted. Better him than someone else. At least he had a chance of survival. As the balls of fire closed in on him, time seemed to slow down. He noted every detail vividly. The fireballs were only a few feet away when they expanded in size. They blotted out his view.

Glo brought his arms up to shield his face. He was just in time. The twin spheres exploded. The blasts nearly knocked him off his feet. The entire world disappeared. Flames completely enveloped him. Had he not guessed right, he would have been incinerated in an instant. The fire absorption spell he had cast saved his life. Still, it did not cancel all the effects of the blazing flames. The light was blinding, even through his closed eyelids. The heat was fierce. It crawled over his bare skin and through his clothes. The roar of the fire rang in his ears, drowning out all other sound.

It felt like an eternity being caught in the center of those flames. In reality, though, it was only a few seconds. The magical fire finally winked out. Glo dropped his arms, blinking as his eyesight readjusted to normal. The table below him and everything on it was either charred or melted from the extreme heat of the two fireballs. Suddenly he heard screams behind him. Glo whirled around and saw that despite his best efforts, some of the guests had been hit by errant flames.

Dragon dung! He had urged them to seek refuge in the keep, but these nobles were stubborn. They were mesmerized by the battle and seemed intent on watching the whole blasted thing. Thank the gods for Ves and Gracelynn. The two women immediately spurred into action, healing those who had been injured. He was just about to spin back around when a sudden movement caught his eye. A figure in blue sat up in the grass between him and the others. He immediately recognized the man. It was Sir Fafnar!

What in the devil is he doing there?

Whatever it was, Fafnar was extremely lucky. He was just out the range of those balls of fire. Glo opened his mouth to yell at the noble when Fafnar cried out, "Nooo!"

The noble scrambled to his feet and rushed toward him—yet his eyes were not fixed on Glo, but instead on the grass between them. That's when Glo saw it—something red on the ground a few yards from his feet. He felt the blood drain from his face. It was a body, burnt nearly beyond recognition. All that was left was a few tatters of red tabard that clung to melted armor.

Sir Calric! What was the knight doing close to him? Had he not warned them he was making himself a target? Now the knight was dead, burnt to a crisp. As the horror of it sunk in, something suddenly snapped inside of him. From somewhere deep down, a flood of anger and rage came boiling to the surface. Without thinking, Glo whirled around and pointed a finger at one of the dark mages. He spoke two deadly words, "*Pessulum Electrica.*"

In response, a spark appeared at the tip of his finger. It hung there for a fleeting moment, then a bolt of lightning erupted from that spark. It arced across the battlefield in the blink of an eye. The bolt passed through one of the front line serpents and then lanced through the unprepared mage and his serpentine mount. The thunderclap was deafening. It reverberated off the walls of the keep in a resounding echo. The attack was over in under a second, but the results were devastating.

Glo watched with grim satisfaction as smaller arcs of electricity still danced around the evil mage. Both serpents shuddered violently, their bodies sizzling in pain. Then the dark mage swayed in his saddle. He fell off his mount, hitting the ground six feet below. The black-robed figure remained there, unmoving. The two serpents, still alive, were rocked by the bolt. Their torsos jerked around randomly from the large amount of current that had passed through them. Glo, however, was far from done. No sooner had the first bolt hit its mark when he turned toward the second mage.

"Donnie, look out!" he cried as he called forth the magic a second time. His fellow elf didn't even look. Instead, he dodged nimbly out of the way as another bolt of lightning leapt from Glo's hand. The bolt shot across the field, spearing the serpent Donnie had been fighting. It passed through the creature, catching the second mage and his serpentine mount.

Another deafening thunderclap rocked the keep. The bodies of the two serpents and the evil mage sizzled from the intense electrical force. When it was over, the second mage fell to the ground, unmoving like his comrade. Satisfied that vengeance had been meted, the elven wizard shifted his focus. Unfortunately, he was a moment too late.

Voltark now hovered high over the battlefield. The dark mage had just sent another fist-sized ball of fire rocketing across the courtyard, directly at him. Glo had no time to cast another spell of protection. If he leapt out of the way, he might just be able to dodge the blast, but then the folks behind him would take the brunt of the attack. Glo made up his mind in that split second. He stood his ground, covering his face as the fireball reached him. It expanded in size and exploded right in front of him!

At first it was just like before, blinding light, intense heat, a roaring sound, but no sense of burning. Then he began to feel it. His skin started to tingle. The tingling turned into pins and needles and then finally a burning sensation. The pain grew until it became excruciating! Mercifully, it stopped after only a few seconds. Glo felt himself slump down onto what was left of the table below. Then he fell backwards. Before he hit the ground, two strong arms grabbed hold of him. He felt himself gently laid on the ground. Glo peered up and saw the angelic face of Ves hovering over him.

"Thank you," he croaked, his throat almost too dry to speak.

"Don't talk," she told him firmly.

His body was numb. He felt somewhat detached as he watched her run her hands over it.

"That was a very brave thing you just did there," she said, "taking that last attack to protect the others."

"You know... how much I like... fire," he whispered.

She smiled down at him. "Yes. Perhaps a bit too much."

Blue light erupted from her fingertips and enveloped his body. He felt nothing at first. Gradually, feeling started to return to his body. She whispered to him softly as the healing energies coursed through him. "I am so sorry. I should have gone with my first instincts about you."

"That's okay," he managed, his voice starting to sound normal again.

"No, it is not," she declared firmly. "When we were told what Maltar was like, we decided to distance ourselves from you." She peered down at him fondly. "We should have known better. What you have done here today proves the kind of people you are."

Glo attempted a smile. "We only just... found out ourselves... about Maltar."

Ves nodding her understanding. "When this is over, you and I shall have a serious talk. Now lie still and let me finish healing your wounds."

She smiled one last time. Her expression then grew serious as she poured divine energy into the elven wizard.

34
MAGE FALL

See how easily your wizard falls?

Donnie had dodged out of the way of a second serpent. That put him right in front of the serpent he had been originally fighting. He had tumbled yet again to avoid its gaping jaws. As he sprang up once more, he saw a blinding flash. It was immediately accompanied by a huge thunderclap. He caught a momentary glimpse of the serpent behind this one surrounded by electrical sparks. The creature shuddered in place. Then he had to again tumble away to avoid being chomped.

This is getting ridiculous. He had speared this giant garden snake a few times now. There were gaping holes in its torso that bled profusely. Still the creature refused to die. He was finally positioned for another attack when he heard a shout from behind him.

"Donnie, look out!"

Without hesitation, he tumbled out of the way. A split second later, he was quite glad he did. A brilliant bolt arced across the field and passed through the serpent he had just been fighting. The creature stopped in its tracks and began to shudder and sizzle. That must have been the elven wizard, Glo.

Nice shot, Donnie smiled appreciatively. Now was his chance. While the serpent was still recovering, he sprung forward. He planted a boot on the snake's back and swung up onto its neck. Then with both hands, he lifted his rapier high into the air. He shoved down on it with all his might through the skull of the vile serpent. His sword sank deep into the creature's head. The beast shuddered all over, its body recoiling violently. Donnie hung on with both hands as the giant snake writhed below him. Then, all at once, it stopped. The serpent hung suspended for a moment then fell forward to the ground unmoving. Donnie sat there and took a deep breath.

"Phew!" *Thank the gods that was over.* The battle, however, was still going on around him. To his right, he spied two knights that had joined the fray, engaging yet another serpent.

Wait. Were his eyes deceiving him or was one of those knights a woman? A very attractive woman. He was just thinking he might join that fight when he heard a loud grunt from behind him. Whirling around, he saw the large warrior, Lloyd, on the ground. A serpent closed in on him and would surely catch him in those huge jaws before he could recover. Leaping off the corpse, Donnie shot forward. He cried out as loud as he could, "Hey, ugly, why don't you pick on someone your own size!"

The creature, originally intent on Lloyd, stopped. It swung around to face him. Donnie came to a quick halt. He now had the serpent's undivided attention.

Lucky me, Donnie thought as he began to circle around it. Beyond the giant serpent, he spied Lloyd already up on one knee. Instead of standing, however, the warrior stayed in that position. It was if he was praying. The large serpent suddenly lunged at him. Donnie leaped backwards out of the way. Suddenly, the creature stopped. Its jaw went slack and its eyes rolled back in its head. Then the serpent collapsed to the ground. Standing directly behind it was Lloyd!

But how? A second ago, the young warrior had been kneeling on the ground a half dozen yards away. How had he gotten behind it so fast? Donnie hadn't a clue, but that didn't matter right now. Lloyd had gutted the beast and now it was dead.

"Thanks!" Donnie saluted the warrior.

"No, thank you!" Lloyd grinned and saluted him back.

Donnie heard a cry from behind him. It was a decidedly feminine cry. Whirling about, he saw the comely redheaded warrior on the ground. Her fellow knight inserted himself between her and their serpent adversary, brandishing his sword in front of him. Without another thought, Donnie launched himself forward.

"That's no way to treat a lady!" he yelled as he charged across the field.

As Donnie ran off to help the fallen knight, Lloyd surveyed the battlefield. Sir Brennon and Sir Duncan were teamed up on one serpent. The two knights had flanked the creature. They were alternating attacks on the beast, keeping it off balance. The serpent was beginning to waver from multiple wounds in its hide. He had no doubt they would soon take it down. Behind him, Captain Gelpas, Francis, Relkin, and a fourth guard were fighting another serpent. It looked like a tough battle, but they, too, were using the strategy of alternating attacks. It appeared they had things well in hand.

Over by the gate, The Boulder and the giant serpent were trading blows. The stone golem swung at the huge snake with both fists. The creature rocked visibly with each impact. The large serpent immediately retaliated, slamming its entire body into The Boulder. The force of the blow knocked the stone golem back a few steps. Pieces of rubble chipped off the stone golem's already fractured torso and fell to the ground below. It was a titanic struggle, but it looked like the serpent was taking the worst of it. He saw "Maltar" standing off to one side. Voltark, however, was nowhere to be seen. Then he heard the mage's voice. It came from directly above him. Lloyd glanced upward. The evil mage hovered fifty feet in the air over the battlefield. He cried out in a booming voice, "You cannot defeat us! See how easily your wizard falls?"

Lloyd started. *Our wizard falls?* His eyes shifted toward the tables. Glo was nowhere to be seen.

Voltark was still bragging. "The imposter and your golem will go next. Your warriors are nothing, mere blades of grass to be mowed beneath our feet. Can you not see? The Serpent Cult is the future. Embrace our cause now... or die!"

Voltark must have taken down Glo. He would do the same to the others as well unless someone took care of him first. Lloyd glanced up at the dark mage once more. Voltark had gone silent, staring down at the field below. He weaved his hands in an intricate pattern, preparing to cast a spell. Lloyd followed the dark mage's gaze. He was staring at Sir Brennan and Sir Duncan!

Lloyd's blood went icy cold. *No more! This ends now!*

He grabbed his cape and spoke a single word. *"Fugere."*

The young warrior launched into the air, rocketing upwards. Above him, Voltark was just about to release his spell. Lloyd tried to close in faster, but found he couldn't. He had reached his maximum speed. He was not going to reach Voltark in time!

He opened his mouth to scream at the mage. The sound died on his lips. A beam of brilliant white light lanced up from the ground. It caught Voltark square in the back. A split second later, two arrows embedded themselves in the mage's side. In almost the same heartbeat, a bolt of lightning arced across the sky. It slammed into Voltark, causing him to shudder. The evil mage's spell was disrupted. He floated off balance in mid-air, reeling from the effects of the multiple attacks. As he attempted to right himself, Voltark screamed. "You'll pay for that!"

Not if I can help it, Lloyd thought grimly. He rose swiftly, both hands grasped tightly around his black blade. Too late, the dark mage spied him. The hatred written across his face quickly changed to a look of terror.

"Nooooo!" he wailed fearfully. He tried to back pedal in mid-air as Lloyd came within reach.

Lloyd did not hesitate. He lashed out fiercely with his jet-black sword. The young warrior put all his strength into one great swing. The black blade arced through the air, catching the evil mage in the side. The blade did not stop. It passed right through the villain, cleaving him neatly in half! Voltark's hewn body seemed to hang in air for a moment, then the two halves fell away to the ground below.

Wild cheers filled the courtyard. Lloyd hovered in midair, his dark blade still clutched in one hand. He glanced over toward the keep. The crowd of guests were all staring up at him, pumping their fists and cheering for joy. He quickly spied Gryswold and Gracelynn. The Baron's fist was in the air, and he was cheering loudly. The Lady Gracelynn, a bit more reserved, wore a satisfied smile.

Lloyd continued to scan the crowd till his eyes fell on Andrella. The young lady waved up at him with both hands, a wide grin spread across her face. Lloyd breathed a sigh of relief. They were all safe. Andrella was safe. He continued to hover there, turning his gaze toward the battlefield below. He was just in time to see Sir Brennan and Sir Duncan finish the serpent they had been battling.

Seconds later, the lady knight wielded the final blow on the serpent in front of her. Donnie and her companion knight were close at hand. Gelpas and the castle guards had their serpent on the ground. They were hacking away mercilessly at it. Lastly, The Boulder had grasped hold of the huge serpent. Its thick stone arms slowly separated. The Boulder was attempting to rip the creature in half! Lloyd watched on in awe. The large serpent's body could not stand the strain. There was a great rending sound as the huge creature literally split in two. The stone golem dropped what was left of the gigantic snake to the ground at its feet.

The battle was over. They had won.

More cheers went up across the courtyard as Lloyd descended to the ground below. Donnie, Gelpas, the knights, and the guards all gathered around. They grasped each other and cried out in victory. Without warning, Lloyd was almost bowled over. A small blonde figure jumped into his arms.

"You were magnificent!" Andrella cried breathlessly.

She wrapped her arms around his neck and leaned into him. The young lady then kissed him full on the lips. Lloyd was taken completely off-guard. At first he was uncertain how to react. Andrella, unperturbed, continued to kiss him ardently. Lloyd completely lost himself. He lifted her into the air and kissed her back wholeheartedly. More cheers went up all around them.

He vaguely heard some intermingled words such as "Alright!" and "That's our boy!" and "It's about time!"

He was too preoccupied to notice who said what. Finally, he felt a hand on his shoulder. A familiar voice spoke.

"I would like to thank you and your friends, young Lord Stealle..."

Lloyd reluctantly opened his eyes. He put Andrella down, but he did not let go of her. Still holding her gently in his arms, he turned to see Gryswold standing next to them. The Baron smiled broadly at the couple.

"...but I can see that my daughter has already shown you our appreciation."

Lloyd grinned sheepishly. "It was my honor to defend you and your family, your Lordship." A sharp pain suddenly went through his side, making him wince.

Andrella grabbed onto him tightly, fear in her voice. "Lloyd, you're hurt!"

Lloyd reached down and placed a hand over his ribs. He winced again. They were most likely broken. It must have happened when the serpent slammed into him. Lloyd quickly straightened up, attempting a smile.

"It's nothing," he told her, trying to shut off the pain with his mind. He was exhausted from the battle, though, and it was difficult to do so.

"Here, let me see that," the Lady Gracelynn stepped forward. She briefly examined his side. "You've got a couple of cracked ribs. We'll have that fixed up in no time. Andrella, escort our young hero inside."

"Please, ladies, there's no need to make a fuss," Lloyd said uncomfortably.

"Trust me, lad," Gryswold advised him. "Never argue with a woman, especially when she is taking care of you."

"Truer words were never spoken," added a familiar voice.

Turning, Lloyd saw Elladan standing there. Shalla and Donnie were at his side. They all watched him with broad grins. Standing next to the trio was Aksel. The little cleric was still in Maltar's robes, but his face looked like his own once again.

"I would listen to Lady Gracelynn if I were you," Aksel counseled him. "She's quite an accomplished healer."

Lloyd opened his mouth to reply, then stopped himself. They were determined to take care of him, no matter what he said. A brief vision of his sister flashed through his mind. When she declared he needed healing, there was no stopping her. He realized this was one battle he was not going to win. "Alright."

"Now come with me," Andrella said in a no-nonsense tone. She left her one arm around his waist, then took his other arm and put it over her shoulder. The young lady proceeded to walk him back toward the keep. The others all accompanied them. Only Gelpas stayed behind with the castle guards. There was still a mess to clean up in the courtyard. The guests cheered as they walked to the keep. A chant of "Heroes" sprang up amongst the crowd.

Everyone Lloyd saw appeared elated, until he spied the Duke and Sir Fafnar. Both men wore sour expressions. They were clearly dissatisfied for some reason. Lloyd did not have the faintest notion why. After all, hadn't they stopped the Serpent Cult attack? Wasn't everyone safe?

Lloyd shook his head. He had better things to do than worry about the irritating nobles. He found it strange that there was still no sign of Glo. Despite Voltark's claims to the contrary, the elven wizard had helped them in the end. Aksel had caught Voltark with that beam of light. It was obviously Martan that had pegged the mage with those arrows, but it had to be Glo who hit him with that bolt of lightning. So where on earth could the wizard be? And where was Seth, for that matter?

Lloyd's eyes swept the courtyard once more. Aksel, Elladan, Donnie, and Shalla all trailed behind them as Andrella dragged him toward the keep. He even spied Martan running across the courtyard toward them. However, the little halfling was nowhere to be seen. As Andrella led him up the steps, Lloyd hoped his two missing friends were alright.

HERE ENDS BOOK TWO OF
THE HEROES OF RAVENFORD
THE STORY CONTINUES IN BOOK THREE
DARK MONOLITH

About the Author

F.P. Spirit has always loved fantasy. From the moment he received his very first copy of Lord of the Rings back in high school, he was hooked. Today, somewhere between work and family, F. P. manages to write sword and sorcery fantasy fiction.

His novels, Ruins on Stone Hill, Serpent Cult and Dark Monolith, are the first three books in the series Heroes of Ravenford. The series chronicles the adventures of a band of young heroes in the dangerous world of Thac.

You can learn more about F.P. Spirit by visiting his website at:
Fpspirit.com

Connect with and follow F.P. Spirit on Facebook (HeroesOfRavenford) and Twitter (@FP_Spirit)

Made in the USA
Middletown, DE
08 March 2018